Your Love Is King

Book 2 in the Royal Pains series

By

Bridget Midway

Dedication

To the patient readers who wanted to know about Prince Robert, I sincerely hope this story satisfies your curiosity. I am thankful you have embarked on this journey with me. Please enjoy Book Two of the Royal Pains series.

Stay sexy,

BridgeT

Acknowledgments

To Niki Browning, who created an awesome book cover for me and was patient with me in this book publishing process, thank you so much. You are far too talented to be making covers for the likes of me, but I'm forever grateful.

To Kathryn Lively. Thank you for being the great editor you are to edit this book in a pinch. You have no idea how much I appreciate your help.

To the hiccups and misfortunes that have happened in my life, I am happy for each and every one of them. They forced me out of my comfort zone to do something I didn't think I could do. It's high time for me to take more control of my writing life. The things that have happened to me have opened my eyes to that reality.

As always, thank you to The Jimmy. I know the last couple of months before this book released have been difficult. Thank you for always giving me space, always checking on me, and always being supportive. You are my best friend. I love you more than you can ever know.

Chapter One

Prince Robert shouldn't have been nervous. Although his older brother, Lucian, had always been unpredictable and a certified handful, he seemed to excel at on-air interviews, even ones done live like this one. At least this time Lucian did the interview without nursing a hangover. Robert hoped Lucian came to this important event sober.

Even with Helene Nix, Lucian's beautiful fiancée, by his side, Robert doubted his impulsive brother could be serious about anything, including announcing his engagement and upcoming marriage to the Baldington's Palace's former public relations head. Robert hoped Lucian read the talking points their new public relations director had given him and Helene, and that the duo stuck to the script.

Robert shifted from side to side behind the camera crew as he watched the couple pay attention to the respected yet stodgy Lesilitho local journalist getting the official statement.

Don't say anything stupid. Don't say anything stupid.

Robert hoped his thoughts didn't materialize into anything audible. He had to cross his arms over his chest when he noticed Helene crossing her legs. He winced. Robert thought that with her being a former employee that she would have known that Baldington Palace women crossed their legs at the ankles. Then again, how could he fault her when his own brother appeared on camera without a tie for this official announcement. The defiant act had Robert wondering if Lucian would do anything else reckless during this live interview.

"Prince Lucian, you have made two huge announcements recently." The journalist sniffed and it sounded like a pig snort.

Robert covered his mouth to prevent the audible gasp from escaping. Lucian did not. He chuckled before he answered. Classy.

"Yes, well, I rather enjoy ripping the Band-Aid off quickly." Lucian smiled.

When he reached out and held Helene's hand, Robert removed his hand and audibly huffed. Royal couples should not show outward affection like that in public. The interviewer briefly turned his head toward Robert, but quickly returned his attention to Lucian and Helene.

"When I'm sure about something, it's difficult for me to change my mind. Even though we aren't a ruling monarchy like in other countries, say in Africa, we do honor our legacy." Lucian cut a gaze to Robert as though acknowledging that he remembered the vital facts to cover in the interview. "I knew very early that I would not be appropriate in the role to take over for my father. My brother is more suitable as the next in line to be king." Lucian nodded in Robert's direction before he glanced over at Helene. "I also knew my heart and soul belong to this woman. She understands me like no other. I would be completely and utterly lost and inadequate without her. I'm very lucky to have her love me, the real me."

When Lucian exhaled so did Robert. Robert felt Lucian's sincerity as he regarded the woman they had known for most of their lives, ever since her parents moved there to work for Robert's family. Now she would be a part of their family. Knowing that made Robert smile.

He never had a sister. African American or not, Robert didn't see Helene or her parents as anything but kind and loving people and, most importantly, family. He still couldn't believe that his brother saw more than that in her. As children, Robert, Lucian and Helene all played together despite both Lucian and Helene being a few years older than him. Robert loved Helene, but not in the way where he imagined her naked or wanted her for his sexual pleasure.

Truth be told, it had been a long time since he envisioned himself with a woman for more than just the hedonistic play he liked to indulge in from time to time like at that club in Chicago, Illinois.

It would be a long time before Robert would make a return trip back to the States. He had to be careful playing now. Robert had a bit more freedom in the military when he would go to dungeons in other countries to prevent from getting caught. He had to satisfy his urges through online video chatting and attending expensive, membership-only clubs. At one time, he attempted to dominate a friend of Helene's over the phone.

With Helene's parents working at Baldington, they had limited time to leave for vacations, including with their one and only daughter. They allowed her to bring friends there for extended sleepovers. One of her friends caught Robert's attention from her very first trip there, not exactly for the best reasons.

Philippa Powell seemed to be the opposite of Helene, and it had nothing to do with her dark skin tone. Whereas Helene could be reserved, Philippa made an impression whenever she entered the room, which annoyed Robert. Her loud laughter could have been heard back in the United States where she lived.

She started coming to the palace at the age of fourteen, the same age as Robert at the time. Each summer she stayed in their home, Robert would have thought she would have changed her attitude, learned their ways and customs. She hadn't.

Then one night during the summer right before she had planned on attending college and before Robert went into the military, Philippa, Lucian, and Helene decided to go skinny dipping. Knowing better and fearing the worst, Robert opted to sit out this inappropriate behavior. The more he watched Philippa splashing in the water, the more Robert's annoyance grew. Then she emerged and a different feeling took over.

Philippa managed to cover her slick body with her discarded clothing. In the moonlight, Robert couldn't see her body clearly, only her silhouette, the outline of her breasts and the roundness of her ass.

She skipped over to him sitting on a rock nearby. "You're not coming in?"

Robert shook his head. "Lucian has already had his ass caught on camera. I don't need to show mine. You never know who's watching." He peered around the area, looking for lights or a glittery flash from a camera.

Philippa snickered. "Paranoid much?"

"Realistic. Besides, someone must be the lookout. Someone has to be the protector."

Before Philippa could come back with another one of her sassy retorts, Robert heard the hum of a car engine before he caught the headlights in the distance.

He emitted a high-pitched whistle, one that he knew Lucian would understand. He saw Lucian putting his arms around Helene to still her in the water. Robert wrapped his arm around Philippa and pulled her down below the log he had been sitting on while he watched the action.

He placed his index finger to his lips in front of Philippa to signal for her to be quiet. He braced himself, prepared to hear another one of her loud responses. She said nothing. When he regarded her, he found her staring at him almost in wonder.

When the car went by them, he held her arm to help her back up to the log. "Are you all right? No scratches or anything?"

Philippa waited a beat before she finally answered. "No. I mean,

I'm fine." She looked out in the water where Lucian and Helene continued to splash around now that the threat had disappeared.

"You do look out for us." Philippa wiped her face with her shirt.

"Not everyone can be wild. For those who are, there needs to be a person to keep them grounded. There's always a designated driver. There's always a straight man. There's always—"

"The person tying someone else down." Philippa winked. "So to speak."

Her comment had increased the temperature of the blood pumping in his body, a strange reaction to her light-hearted comment. "What would you know about being tied down?"

She snickered. "Nothing. It was just a joke."

"I like your sense of…humor." He had almost said *curiosity*. She had his piqued.

"Is there a reason we didn't talk more while you were here?" Robert faced her, and it hit him that she sat completely naked.

The thought must have entered her mind as well. Before she answered, she slipped her shirt over her head and shimmied into her cutoff denim shorts. Philippa stuffed her bra and panties into her pocket. It took all of Robert's willpower not to stare at her breasts covered by her thin T-shirt.

"I tried talking to you. You were always so *busy*." When she said busy, she complemented the word with air quotes.

"Perhaps I'll have some free time while away for training. I won't know anyone."

"But you're a prince. Everyone knows you."

Robert hated that. People knew of him, but they had no idea what he wanted. They also knew him from what the media had dubbed him: Queen Killer or Prince Rob, which he hated worse than Queen Killer.

"I don't have friends enlisted." Robert looked out at the pond when Lucian and Helene's splashing became louder. "Do you do video chats?"

Philippa shrugged. "Sometimes. With my grandma." She framed her face with her hands. "She said she likes to see my face."

"I would, too."

Philippa dropped her hands.

"May I get your phone number?"

"Why?"

Her reaction surprised and impressed him. Most young women eagerly gave Robert and Lucian what they wanted. Philippa showed she wouldn't be that easy.

"I would like to call you, make sure you're doing well at your educational institution." He held his hand out to her. "May I have your phone?"

She hesitated before finally pulling out her phone. She didn't hand it to him. She asked for his number and called it like she needed to hear it ring, verify that he shared a legitimate number. Smart woman.

Robert had waited until Philippa had gotten back home to make his first and only call. With one call, he had pushed himself out of his comfort zone and realized what he wanted to do.

What started off as harmless flirting and teasing quickly turned to a session where he had Philippa naked and writhing. By the end, she had run. He never heard from her again. No more trips to Baldington. Helene rarely talked about her. Robert hadn't meant to frighten her, particularly now that he had awakened a new need inside of him.

Despite Philippa's ghosting treatment, the experience didn't ease Robert's need to feel a woman's flesh or wield a toy to make her cry and succumb to him. He would have to hold onto that feeling until –

damn – what? He couldn't continue. He would have to walk away from it. He shifted in his spot again for a different reason.

"I love her." Lucian broke another royal rule by kissing Helene on camera before they married.

Protocol dictated that Prince Lucian and Helene would kiss for the first time in front of their adoring royal subjects on the balcony at Baldingon Palace after the wedding ceremony. Robert would need to have a talk with his brother after this interview. As the next in line to the throne now since Lucian abdicated his spot, Robert had a duty to bring honor and dignity back to their royal family. Going back to the standard rules would be good for all. Lucian could do whatever he wanted behind closed doors…just like Robert.

Lucian kissed the back of Helene's hand and held it to his chest. Outwardly, Robert wanted to be incensed. Inwardly, though, his heart drummed by his brother's public display of affection.

Lucian slipped his free hand into his jacket pocket. Robert noticed that Helene gasped and shifted a little. Robert chalked the reaction up to being overwhelmed by the kisses. As someone who lived in the palace for years and worked directly for the family for five years, she had to know the gravity of what her future royal husband had done.

Robert had never seen Helene looking unflappable, and the bulk of her job involved explaining Lucian's bad behavior, like missing speaking engagements and antics caught on camera phones. Her breathless expression had to come from love. Robert had never seen that between a couple except for Helene's parents, who also worked there in the palace.

Robert's mother, the queen, had died shortly after he had been born. King Clive, his father, hadn't found another relationship since then. Lucian bedded any and every woman he encountered, until

Helene. Robert surprised himself when he found himself drawn to the BDSM lifestyle.

Hell. No surprise. He wanted control. He got it as a Dom.

"What's next for you two?" the journalist asked.

"Wedding plans, of course." Helene's voice sounded shaky at first, but eventually smoothed out to her normal tone.

"Yes, we will get a wedding planner to organize all of it. Hopefully, our nuptials will happen sooner rather than later." Lucian interlaced his fingers with Helene's and rested them on his leg. "And we'll be involved in Prince Robert's official announcement as the next in line. It should be a grand and stately affair, as well it should. He'll be great in the role."

For as inappropriate at times that Lucian could be, he proved with statements like that that he had a heart and soul. Robert took a deep breath, allowing his chest to fill with pride. He hoped his father felt the same way.

At the end of the interview, Robert had the staff walk the journalist and the film crew out of the palace while he addressed Lucian and Helene. "Good job."

Lucian waited a beat after staring at Helene before he addressed his brother. "Glad you approved, although we could have done without your audible disdain for me loving on my fiancée."

Robert glanced at the woman who he felt comfortable enough to call his friend. "You know the protocol about—"

Lucian cut him off. "No, *you* do. That's why I gladly gave up my right to be next in line for you. You are King Protocol."

Helene chuckled. "Stop teasing him." She tugged on Lucian's hand before turning to Robert. "Despite our disregard for the rules, I hope that you're happy for us."

"Of course. It's the reason I've arranged for Edith to start planning the wedding." Robert pulled Helene into a hug. He only broke from it when she yelped and jumped back.

Robert stared at her before regarding his brother when she wagged her finger at him.

"Um, that wasn't because of the news about Edith. I do love her, but…" Helene trailed off before she looked at Lucian, who gave her a knowing nod.

"I had a different idea for who I wanted to help plan our special day." She ran her hand up her arm.

Robert already felt the short hairs on the back of his neck standing on ends. He didn't like changes to his plan. "Edith is very capable. She has worked with your mother to plan multiple parties for the palace in the past."

"Yes, like Father's last birthday party. You remember what a raging event that was, right?" Lucian smirked before he mocked a yawn. "Father is a king and a man of a certain age. A calm, subdued affair is what he wanted. Helene and I are young, and we want—"

Helene placed her hand on Lucian's chest. "We want to be respectful of the Baldington Palace institution, of course." She offered a comforting and reassuring smile. "We want to be able to add our own spin to our ceremony."

"And what does that look like to you two? A beach wedding? Something with a DJ?" Robert volleyed his attention back and forth between the two of them.

"Don't be ridiculous." Lucian shook his head. "We want strippers and have DJ Khaled to officiate."

Robert started to open his mouth when he noticed Lucian and Helene laughing. "Haa, haa. You two are so funny."

"What's funny is the idea that you think you can govern what we do." Lucian wrapped his arm around Helene's shoulders while slipping his hand in his side jacket pocket.

Like King Clive's little dog, Helene released another squeak that bordered on sounding like a bark. She covered her mouth and pushed away from Lucian.

"Will you gentlemen please excuse me? I need to change."
Helene started to leave when Lucian held her hand and pulled her back to him.

"Are you sure you want to change now? We could be asked to pose for pictures, and there could be…other things." Lucian raised his eyebrows.

Helene leaned forward. "It's the *other things* that concern me." She screwed up her lips like she tried not to laugh.

Lucian gave her a quick kiss and broke from it to trail his lips to her ear. Robert could only imagine what he must have been whispering to her. He didn't have to guess what caused his future sister-in-law to jump and twitch at odd intervals. Robert saw Lucian reaching into his jacket pocket again and within seconds, Helene's body jerked.

Robert attempted to hide his displeasure of his brother's brazen antics by turning his back on the duo.

"I'll see you all later for lunch." Helene pulled away from Lucian, but he held onto her hand.

"Dinner. I'll bring something for an intimate lunch for us." He punctuated his statement with a wink.

Helene smiled. "See you at home. Love you."

As soon as Robert heard the door close behind her and heard the chauffeured car pull away, he tore into Lucian. "Really?"

Lucian shrugged. "What?"

Robert pulled at Lucian's jacket and reached into the same pocket Lucian had been slipping his hand into throughout the interview.

From it, he removed a small, black remote that had an on-and-off switch along with a speed setting.

The device had to go to something salacious like some sort of vibrating toy, probably inserted in Helene's vagina. No wonder the woman twitched and yelped at odd intervals.

Robert should have been relieved that he couldn't hear the vibration during the televised interview. That didn't stop the flames from swirling around his head and neck.

"An hour. Just one damn hour. You couldn't hold off BDSM play for the interview?" Robert got in Lucian's face and kept his voice low.

"No, we couldn't. Just because we're getting married and I happen to have some royal blood running through my veins doesn't mean we've lost our sense of fun." Lucian moved in closer to Robert. "Tell me, baby brother. When the urge hits you to play, are you able to wait?" Lucian cocked his mouth to the side as he anticipated his answer.

"Yes. And with this new responsibility, I plan on stopping all my, um, ties—"

Lucian interrupted him. "Pun intended."

Robert continued. "And association with the lifestyle."

Lucian blinked and crossed his arms over his chest. "Really? You think you can just switch off your need to play just like that?" He snapped his fingers.

Robert nodded. "Of course. We're humans. We grow out of things. I no longer play cops and robbers like I did when I was a young boy. I don't need to succumb to my hedonistic needs." He rubbed his hand across the back of his neck, now suddenly hot from this conversation.

Lucian held up two fingers. "There are a couple of things wrong with your assessment. One, if you consider being a Dom as something childish or a phase, then you're not a true Dominant. Weren't you the one who told me months ago that I needed to take the Lifestyle seriously? Now you're willing to walk away from it that easily like it meant nothing to you, like the play you did was nothing more than a phase?"

Robert shrugged. "People change. I've changed. Now with this new responsibility, I can no longer do what I used to. I have a legion of citizens and a palace full of employees who will be looking at me as the symbol of Baldington. I can't disgrace myself or our family name."

Robert meant every word. Shortly after Lucian dropped the news about him wanting to relinquish his rightful place in the royal line, Robert has thought about nothing but how he could successfully incorporate his BDSM side into his new life and responsibility. Bottom line, he didn't see a way to do that successfully. He assumed Lucian saw it the same way, which forced him to make the decision he did.

"What is your other point?" Robert needed to know what Lucian thought of him. If Lucian had these ideas running through his head, others might as well.

Lucian exhaled before he spoke. "You're ashamed of being a Dom."

Despite being brothers, Robert didn't think he and Lucian had a lot in common. Although they both had brown hair, Robert kept his style conservatively with a part on the side while Lucian kept his hair a bit too long for Robert's liking. Both shared the same hazel eye color, only Lucian's looked like he aimed to seduce.

Robert did have an inch or two over his older brother, and he felt, because he worked out more and consistently than Lucian, that he had a better body than Lucian. Even with their differences, Robert couldn't believe they shared the same desire for this extreme lifestyle. Robert really wanted something for himself.

"I'm not ashamed of what I've done." Robert glanced around their immediate area to see if anyone could hear their conversation. "That doesn't mean that I need to continue doing what I've done, especially when it comes time to find an appropriate partner to be by my side and eventually marry."

Lucian chuckled. "My hope for you is that she's into it. What will you do then? If it's true love and not some arranged marriage situation that I believe you'll do because, well, you're you, what will you do? Turn your back on love?"

"I will be able to tell if a woman is into it or not before things get serious."

Lucian nodded. "Like you could with Helene?"

Damn. Robert hadn't seen that coming.

"I feel sorry for the woman you'll end up with who will only get a façade of the real you." Lucian shook his head. "Are you even dating anyone now?"

Robert shook his head. "No. But Princess Elena is single, and she—"

"Elena? From Morocco? That stuck-up blonde with the frozen face? Jesus, she's stiffer than you." Lucian let out a loud belly laugh. "You think she's going to let you tie her down or spank her? She doesn't even look like she would even enjoy sex."

Robert held up his hand. "Keep your voice down." He scanned the area again. "I told you that I'm not going to do that anymore."

"Good. If you tried it with her, I think she would have you arrested for assault and she'll have reign over two kingdoms." Lucian held up two fingers.

Robert shook his head. "No. Not going to happen. She's a lovely woman. We're both in our mid-twenties. We would be a great symbol for the people of Lesilitho." If he repeated that enough in his head, he would start to believe it.

Lucian stared at Robert for a moment before pointing at him. "You know what you need?"

"Oh, I can hardly wait to hear this from you." Robert stood solid with his feet shoulders' width apart. "Go ahead. What do you, of all people, think I need?"

Lucian's sneaky smile slithered over his face. "A challenge. You need a woman, or a man, I'm not judging, who will buck you at every turn. You need someone you can convince." He put his hand to his chest. "I'm not the one. If you get someone who will simply submit, you'll get bored." He stared at Robert for a moment. "Yes, that's exactly what you need and should have. Maybe you should go to Sluvakistan to that club where I—"

"Thank you for your concern about my love life, but I'll be fine." Robert could maintain control even outside of the Lifestyle.

"Baby brother, when the right woman approaches you and you see you can't do without her and she without you, and you're both into that kink, you'll do whatever you can to make the two of you happy. Trust me."

Robert glared at Lucian. "I have more self-control than you."

Lucian snickered. "Of course. You're great at everything." He took the remote from Robert's hand and hid it back in his pocket. "Because you can dominate submissives and slaves in a controlled environment doesn't mean you have dominion over everything." He poked Robert in his chest. "And in regard to my nuptials to Helene, you will not control any part of that."

"I have every right to call the shots regarding your wedding."

Robert stiffened his back. "As future king—"

"God damn you." Lucian gritted his jaw. "Had I known you were going to be an absolute prick about this, I would have kept my line to the throne." He got in Robert's face. "I gave up that honor because I want to live my life the way I want." He glanced around the room. "You want this. You want all the ritualistic bullshit that comes with being in this place. I don't."

"So what? Am I supposed to thank you for you being an irresponsible shit?" Robert crossed his arms over his chest.

Lucian grabbed Robert's lapel of his jacket and pulled him forward. "Watch yourself. Don't think I can't beat your ass again like when we were children."

Robert felt his eye twitch. "I'd like to see you try."

A palace assistant knocked briefly on the door before rushing into the room. "Excuse me." She nodded before addressing both men. "It seems the palace grounds no longer have Internet service. We have the technical department looking into it."

Lucian released Robert and beamed. "There you go, Prince Robert. There's your cause. Make sure you get the 'net back up so the wonderful citizens of Lesilitho can know what Father ate for breakfast." He turned to the young woman. "Prince Robert will address this concern for you." Then he turned to Robert. "I'll be busy planning my wedding."

"Congratulations, sir." She smiled sweetly and bowed her head again.

"Thank you. I've waited my whole life for someone like her." He shook his head. "I'm not going to mess this up like this." He ruffled his fingers in Robert's hair.

Robert managed to push his childish brother back. "Must you always be disruptive?"

"I thought you had a bug in your hair. I was mistaken."

The young woman giggled while covering her mouth.

Lucian strolled away. "See you at dinner." Behind the assistant's back, Lucian made an obscene gesture indicating he would be pleasuring his fiancée orally before exiting to his private car to go back to his home on the property.

"Is there anything else you need?"

The young woman stood in the way Robert had directed the staff to stand whenever they regarded anyone in the royal family, with feet together, toes pointed straight, chin up with their hands by their sides. Perfect. The modest heels worked well with her skirt that hit below her knees. She remained buttoned up to her neck.

"Yes, did I hear that Princess Elena will be in town soon?" With Lucian getting married, Robert felt the need to follow suit. Even though his brother chose to marry someone with no royal lineage didn't mean Robert had to do the same.

"Yes, sir. In a week I believe."

"Verify that information. Then see if she's available for dinner during her visit." Robert hadn't spent a lot of time with her, but she seemed pleasant enough.

She kept her blonde hair styled very conservatively, which matched her wardrobe. They would make a proper couple. As far as his BDSM desires, he would have to suppress that side. He could get the intoxicating feeling of hearing a woman moan after a command out of his system long before he courted Elena.

Robert offered a congenial smile to the assistant before excusing her. He wouldn't call himself a vain man, but for once he wanted a mirror to check to see what Lucian had done to his hair. He smoothed his hand over his head and immediately felt his hair poking up and in several different directions.

"Damn bastard."

Once he had time alone, he strolled around the space, taking in the silence. The quiet reminded him of the way Philippa had stopped talking to him.

Robert had other pressing items to consume his time. He had to reconcile in his head that Lucian would be out of the house and able to ruin the reputation of the family even more. Pinning his hopes on Helene to keep him straight wouldn't be an option since it looked like she liked pushing boundaries as much as Lucian.

Whether Lucian liked it or not, Robert would have to babysit the two of them while preparing for his new role as next in line to the throne and upping his speaking engagements. No wonder he didn't have time for a full-on relationship. With his family, he had already planned to have his hands full. As long as Robert could convince Lucian and Helene to go along with his plan, it would make their lives much easier.

The news about some outside person planning Lucian and Helene's wedding sounded ridiculous. Damn, Robert had meant to press Lucian and Helene about the identity of the person they wanted to plan their nuptials. After the tension Lucian had caused when his playful spanking of a Sluvakistan resident nearly caused a riot, he couldn't be trusted in making sound decisions. Lucian redeemed himself by arranging the shipment deal with the States that brought jobs to thousands. Robert wished his brother could be that mature and responsible all the time and not when he had to do the right thing.

A slamming door and stomping footfalls outside of the room caught Robert's attention.

"Excuse me!"

Robert heard raised voices coming from outside of the sitting room that accelerated his heart. Even though he knew their security detail wouldn't fail him, he planted his feet on the floor and prepared for a potential fight that he would not flee from if confronted. What came through the door surprised him on several levels.

"I'm supposed to be here." A woman with dark brown skin, a crown of curly hair on her head, and wide brown eyes stormed into the room in her tall, black leather riding boots and tight sprayed-on looking jeans. Her battle-ready stance had Robert mirroring her, planting himself in the middle of the room to show dominance and unbuttoning his jacket to prepare for a potential confrontation.

Then his heart pounded hard.

She stopped when she saw Robert while the assistant who Robert had previously dismissed trailed behind her. "Oh. Hi." She extended her hand. "It's good to see you again, Prince Robert. If you don't remember me, I'm Philly Powell." She said her name like he hadn't seen her naked body before and had heard her climax. "I'm here to plan Helene's wedding."

Fuck. The woman he had played with online and thought he would only see at Helene's wedding now showed up to complicate his life further by being the person Lucian and Helene had hired to plan their wedding. No matter how good Philippa Powell looked in person, and no matter how much her lilac and vanilla scent swayed him, he couldn't allow her to be involved in the wedding other than being a guest. She would have to go.

Chapter Two

Philippa "Philly" Powell had agonized over her decision to come back to Lesilitho. She loved hearing from her old childhood friend on this job. She knew it would mean interacting with the man who had made her come without touching her, and the man who made her question her life, mainly the idea of who controlled it.

From the first visit, Philly didn't find Prince Robert charming, funny, or even cute. He used to be the one who made sure they all returned to the palace on time, sometimes earlier, when they had gone out during her visits with Helene. She questioned her decision about sharing her phone number with him. Then she quickly figured out why she should have trusted her instincts, but not for the reasons she thought. What happened during that call caused Philly to doubt a lot about herself.

"Are you going to leave me hanging?" Philly left her hand in the air for him to accept it.

"I apologize, sir. She—"

"She has a name." Philly cut the woman off before she could say something offensive. "My name is Philly Powell."

The young woman with a tight chignon resting at the back of her head cleared her throat before she continued. "Ms. Powell rushed through the front door. She came here in a royal car, but no one seems to know why or who she is."

Still carrying a scowl on his chiseled face, Robert approached her. He accepted her hand.

Philly found her breathing accelerated while her shoulders relaxed once he touched her. She hated that she fell for this simple gesture.

His grip clued her in that he carried measured strength, different from how she saw him years ago. He held her hand tight but not so tight to hurt her, but just enough for her to know who ran things. His grasp made her recall their one phone conversation where he drummed his fingers on his desk when he spoke to her.

He glanced at the attendant. "I know Ms. Powell. She's a friend of Helene. She's been to Baldington before." He didn't smile or even offer a pleasant demeanor. He looked pissed at her presence.

Fine. Two could play that game.

Philly shook his hand. "Nice to see you." To compensate for his lack of joy, she smiled even wider. She had always been told she had a winning smile that could sway any adversary. "You're looking well. It's been, what, five or six years since—"

Prince Robert pulled back his hand. "Will you excuse us for a moment?" Prince Robert briefly spoke to the woman who had followed Philly into this grand estate before returning his full attention to her.

"Yes, sir." She bowed her head and strolled out as fast as she had come into the room.

When he seemed satisfied that she had given him the privacy he needed, he spoke. "Thank you for making the trip back to our small country." He clasped his hands behind himself.

Philly blinked, not expecting this cordial response considering the fact it looked like he wanted to rip her head off only moments ago. "Why are you talking to me like you don't know me?"

Robert's eyebrows knitted together. "Are you kidding me?"

That hard, steely exterior came crumbling down after her question.

"What?" She shrugged.

"You drop off the face of the earth without warning, and then show up here like everything is normal between us?" He spoke between gritted teeth and kept his voice low.

For such a good-looking man, he came off as uptight, which didn't match the man who had convinced her to get naked during their only video chat. Thinking about that had her knees trembling.

Philly always associated hazel eyes with being sparkly and gorgeous. His looked dim and dour. The light in him must have been doused a long time ago, maybe after she stopped talking to him.

In heels, she could top six feet. Prince Robert had a few inches over her. She couldn't tell what his body looked like since he didn't swim with the rest of them that night and he never undressed during that call, but he definitely filled out his meticulously tailored dark blue suit very well.

Her heart started pounding hard. Philly always liked a man in a suit. She wondered if he did the cowlick in his hair on purpose. Did he want to show her that he didn't have to be so put together all the time?

"Are you still hung up on that call?" Philly snickered and tried acting like that one interaction meant nothing to her. "That was years ago. Let's get past that." She kept her stare in his eyes to drive home her point.

Prince Robert leaned in close to her. "You didn't like what we did?"

Her smile faded. "It was okay. But it was only one time, and it wasn't like the two of us were dating."

He started to stroll around her. He shook his head. "Interesting. What a great little actress you are." From behind her, he whispered in her ear. "Tell me. Are you lying now or did you fake that orgasm from years ago?"

His warm breath swept over her ear and cheek. Philly had to

wrap her arms around her body to prevent herself from shaking.

Philly turned around to watch him circle her like a shark.

"Just because I came doesn't mean that I was satisfied." She waited until he got in front of her. "Just think of it as like a one-night stand but over the phone." Philly took a deep breath. "I started my own business. I plan weddings and other large events. I told Helene. She offered me the job of planning her wedding, one of the biggest ones out there."

"Fortunately, we have someone capable of handling the wedding arrangements for my brother and his fiancée." He clasped his hands behind his back as he spoke to her. "Your services will not be needed."

Wait. Had he just fired her?

Philly had to take some serious deep breaths before she spoke to him. She wanted to yell at this pompous asshole who must have thought he had the right to tell her what to do still. He didn't, and she would let him know that.

"You can't do that." She shook her head. "You are not—" She lowered her voice. "—the lord and master over me. This is not a game."

"What we did wasn't a game, either." Robert glared at her. "I am not accustomed to being dismissed without reason." He took a step back. "Putting my personal feelings aside, you are more than welcome to come to the wedding."

"Oh, how gracious." She hoped her sarcastic tone resonated with him.

"But you will not be planning this wedding."

"Seems like you are taking this personal."

Stop staring at his full lips. Stop imagining sucking on his lower lip.

Philly cleared her throat. "I'm afraid I'm not going to leave here until the people who hired me dismiss me formally. That would be Helene and Lucian." She gripped her purse strap while cocking her hip to the side.

He glared at her for a moment. "That's *Prince* Lucian."

"Are you serious? We have all skinny dipped before. Oh, wait. Lucian, Helene, and I did. You watched. You always watched." She stepped up to him with her arms folded. "Lucian is not as, um, rigid as you."

His eyes transformed to slivers. "You have no idea how hard I can be."

No one could scare Philly with a stare down. Not her asshole ex-boyfriend. Not her past teachers, who told her she wouldn't amount to anything. Not even the bankers who had refused to loan her the money for her to start this wedding planning business. She certainly wouldn't get intimidated by a handsome prince in a suit, no matter how he had made her body sing. So, why did her knees buckle and her heart drum even harder?

From where he stood, he smelled like money. He carried a scent of old leather-bound books and fresh spring water. She also noticed his hair.

"Look, I'm not here to cause any problems. I'm just here to do a job for my friend." Philly did her best to catch this fly with her honey. "I thought maybe I could catch up with you, too, while I was here."

"I'm the exact same man I was before with one exception. You're not the only one who can walk away from the Lifestyle."

Philly blinked. "Oh, so you don't do what you did to me when—"

He widened his stance in front of her and put his finger to his lower lip like he wanted to study her features. "Do you understand the job you want to do? You're not planning a party for just anyone. This is the first-born son of King Clive."

"I know." Philly nodded. "When did you stop, um—"

"There is a way a royal wedding has to be done." He crossed his arms over his chest and sank into his stance.

Since he didn't want to talk about them, Philly had to change directions and continue on this train of conversation Prince Robert wanted them to take. "I'm a fast learner. Tell me what needs to be done and I can do it. But you know that." Her teachers didn't think she had it in her to learn like her classmates. She proved them wrong.

Prince Robert held up his hand and ticked off each finger as he spoke. "We will have dignitaries and other royal families and celebrities here. Do you think you can handle an audience like that?"

Philly nodded. "I can, but do you really think people will come in three months?"

His eyes widened. "What's happening in three months?"

"The wedding, of course. Helene and Lucian said they want to get married before the year is up. And, of course, I—" She stopped. "Hold on. I have to do this." She reached up and smoothed down his errant strand.

Prince Robert didn't move. The way he looked at her, she felt like he saw her soul, like she stood before him naked and bare like after that swim or during that one call. After making sure to put his hair back into place, including keeping his side part clean, she lowered her hand.

"Thank you. You don't have to attend to me." His tone softened a bit.

"I know." Her body didn't, though. She still felt the need to make sure he looked presentable.

"This discussion is not over." He stormed out of the room.

"Where are you going?" She followed him outside.

"Going to see my brother." He called for a car like he would a taxi in New York. "I can't believe the two of them. This plan is insane."

"I'm coming with you. They're the ones I'm supposed to meet with anyway. They said they would be here." Philly ran into Prince Robert's back when he stopped mid-trek to the long, sleek black car that pulled up in front of the building.

He turned around to her. "Excuse me. I don't need you to come with me while I have a conversation with my family."

Even running into him accidentally allowed Philly to experience his hard body. Damn, he felt good. She had to focus. Think about the work. The work and her life had both been the reasons she had stopped talking to him.

When the driver got out and opened the back door, Philly shimmied her body between Prince Robert and the car to block him from going inside. "Excuse *me*. If I'm going to be fired from a job, I want to hear it from the people who hired me, face to face." She ducked into the backseat and slid over to the far side.

The inside of the car appeared as dark as the outside. The black roof liner matched the black suede seat cover and the black carpet. That new-car smell hit her immediately. She took a deep breath, enjoying the scent.

The car shifted a bit as Prince Robert stepped inside. He continued to keep a safe distance from her in the car. He sat on the opposite side from her and kept his attention forward.

Because too much silence made her skin crawl, Philly spoke first. "For what it's worth, it's nice being back in Lesilitho."

Robert remained silent as he kept his stare ahead.

"You look—"

He finally glared at her.

"Good." She nodded.

He stared ahead again. "Since you stopped accepting my calls and you didn't visit Helene here, I don't know what happened with you. What degree did you get when you graduated college?"

Suddenly, the inside of the car felt overwhelmingly hot. She avoided answering the question to continue talking about his appearance. "The older you get, the more you and Lucian look alike. I've seen pictures of him on magazine covers."

He returned his attention to her.

"You two have the same eyes. His are a bit playful."

He looked away again.

"I don't know if you remember me telling you about my three older brothers. It's safe to say that I didn't date much in high school." Philly laughed.

He didn't. She watched his jaw twitch like he gritted his teeth.

As much as Philly hated silence, she despised dishonesty. She would get the truth out of him. "I see you have a problem with me planning this wedding, and it has to be beyond the other thing." She didn't want to say much in front of the driver. "Why is that?"

Prince Robert didn't answer.

She would poke the bear. "Is it because I'm a woman?"

He shook his head but still didn't look at her. "No. The person who I want to plan this wedding is a woman. She's also from Lesilitho. She understands our customs and ways. She understands the right processes. She completes all her tasks. With her, I don't have to wonder if she's going to bail on me."

Ouch. That hurt. Philly did deserve that for how she stopped talking to him.

"Does it bother you that I'm American?" She now wondered

what the other woman he wanted to plan the wedding looked like.

Damnit. She had no right to be territorial or jealous. *She* left *him*.

"No. I have no problem with where you're from or your gender." He waved his hand dismissively at her.

Time to really get this party started.

"Maybe you have a problem with me because I'm black. Is that it?"

The glare he gave her transformed the backseat area into an instant igloo. "That is a disgusting question and assumption. I have absolutely no problem with race. I understand there is racial tension where you're from, which is deplorable." He pointed down. "Don't bring that mindset here to our country."

Time to put the poking stick away. "I'm sorry." Good to see this reserved man have some bite and backbone about something other than not hiring her for a job she had already secured. In that moment, she saw the man who could convince her to do things she had never done before for anyone. "I don't understand what the big deal is. I thought the family was cool with them hiring me. We've been talking over the past week."

He snickered. "Of course."

"I have a feeling they want to do things their way. My job is to give them their vision."

At her statement, Prince Robert turned to her. "My job is to protect the legacy of my family and maintain the dignity of our station."

"Wow." Philly slumped back in her seat. "That's a tall order for just one man."

He looked ahead and shifted in his seat like he wanted to prepare to jump before the car even stopped. "It would be, but I'm sure my brother understands the gravity of this ceremony and will see things my way."

The car pulled into a cobblestone driveway that had a guard at the gate. The driver and guard spoke for a bit.

"When you are sent home, please do not take it personally." Prince Robert put his hand to his chest to show some sincerity. "As a matter of fact, I would like to give you a tour of our country."

"Country? Not the city?" Philly sat up taller.

"It's small enough that we could tour it in a day." He smiled and it seemed genuine.

"I've seen most of the city, remember? The four of us would do a lot of traveling back then." A lot of those memories she would cherish, particularly the ones where Prince Robert acted like a prince and looked out for her, like when he offered her his jacket when the nights got too chilly.

"You can see the country during the light of day." Again, his voice softened as though a good memory filled him, too.

"Would you still offer me the tour if I stayed on and do the job?" Philly had no plans of going home with no pay and her tail tucked between her cheeks.

He didn't answer her. When the car still sat at the guard shack, Prince Robert leaned forward to speak to the driver.

"Why aren't we moving?" He pointed toward the road that must have led up to a house. "Go on to Lucian's house."

The driver adjusted his driving cap on his head. "It appears that Prince Lucian asked for no visitors until dinner time. Would you like to leave a message for him?"

"This is ridiculous." Prince Robert pushed the door open and stormed up the driveway.

"Holy shit." Philly chased after him.

Thank goodness she wore comfortable boots. She had struggled to get them off through the TSA security check at the airport, but they looked so good with her skinny jeans.

As she trailed up the driveway behind Prince Robert, the back of his jacket flapped up, exposing his perfectly rounded ass. She didn't know what the people of Lesilitho did for fun and exercise, but he certainly didn't miss out on the exercise.

Although she tended to go for stubborn jerks, he didn't fit the bill as her type. His race had nothing to do with it. She liked someone with a bit more thug tendencies. Then again, each boyfriend with that trait had broken her heart in the worst way.

When Prince Robert arrived at the door, he didn't bother knocking. He grabbed the handle and opened the door. With a guard at the gate, no reason to lock doors around here.

"Are you sure you should be here?" Philly followed close behind him until she ran into his back when he stopped abruptly.

Philly peered around him and saw what halted him in his tracks. She saw a very naked Lucian fucking her childhood friend from behind over a chair while Helene wore a black blindfold over her eyes, and had a handcuff dangled from her wrist. Philly peered down to the floor and spotted a pair of black lace panties that had a silver egg dangling from a wire in the panty seat. Clothes littered the cute cottage that now became a sex den.

"Fuck!" Lucian's eyes went wide as he glared at Prince Robert and Philly.

"Yes, Master Lucian! Don't stop." Helene leaned her head back and smiled, obviously oblivious to the intrusion to her privacy.

"We should go." Philly tugged on the back of Prince Robert's jacket to get him out of the house while keeping her voice down to a whisper.

"I'm sorry." Prince Robert stumbled backward and left the

volume of his voice the same as when he had tried to politely fire her.

"What? What was that?" Helene removed the blindfold in time to see the front door close as soon as Philly and Prince Robert ducked out of the house.

The closed door didn't prevent Philly from hearing Helene screaming.

Prince Robert linked his fingers together and rested them on top of his head as he strolled away from the front of the house like he needed to collect his thoughts. Philly thought she heard him cursing under his breath.

To break the tension, she spoke. "I guess it's okay to just call you Robert instead of Prince Robert, huh?"

Robert didn't look at her. He kept staring down the long driveway they had stormed up like they prepared to go to battle.

"Good news." Philly smiled but her insides had turned to molten lava to match the embarrassed heat permeating through her cheeks.

He turned around to look at Philly.

"Now that they've seen me barge in on them, I'm sure I'll get fired now."

Chapter Three

Why couldn't the driver and guard just say that Robert's brother and Helene needed time alone to have sex? Knowing Lucian, he would have told the guard specifically what he had planned. Lucian had no filter. That attitude kind of reminded him of Philippa.

From what Robert remembered of her, Philippa could be loud, stubborn, and opinionated. For that reason, maybe she had done him a favor by stopping their strange virtual relationship. No way could a woman like this be appropriate to arrange Lucian's wedding. That said, having Philippa see his brother and future sister-in-law going at it like animals, Robert knew employing Edith would be the best decision. Edith would be able to get his unruly brother on track. Philippa would encourage Lucian's mocking behavior.

"May I ask you a question?" Philippa filled the silence hovering between them.

"You may ask anything. I am under no obligation to answer." Robert dealt with a lot that day. He didn't need an interrogation right now.

She snickered. "Of course. It's your world."

That comment got the hairs on the rest of his body to stand up. "You had options. You walked away." He held his hands up. "I didn't stop you. I didn't come after you."

"I know."

The somber tone in her voice made her come off as defeated. Did she want him to go after her? No. Philippa didn't come off as a woman who didn't speak her mind. She would have told him what she wanted, which made her a great submissive.

He couldn't think about her that way. Not anymore, not until she returned home, and he could forget about her again. Who was he kidding? He hadn't forgotten about Philippa and the lasting impression she'd made on him.

"You had a question, Philippa." Robert lowered his hands and put them to his hips.

"Did I hear Helene call him *Master Lucian*?" Philippa nodded her head toward Lucian's home.

Robert stopped moving to acknowledge her. So, she had heard Helene call his brother his scene name, and that made him feel like he truly had intruded on them. Robert also had a twinge of jealousy that he had not only found the love of his life, but he also managed to incorporate BDSM into their relationship. Robert couldn't achieve that.

When Robert didn't immediately answer, Philippa strolled up to him and stood directly in front of him. "And why was she in handcuffs? What was that thing on the floor?"

Robert hadn't even noticed the handcuffs. He only noticed his naked brother and did his best not to even look at Helene other than her blindfold.

Enough about them, Robert had a woman before him asking questions that, if answered correctly, would either get her to run back to America or get her curious. If she became interested, what would that look like? Could they continue where they left off but in physical way this time?

No. He can't think about that. Robert had his eyes on the prize. The light at the end of his tunnel contained a king title, a potential princess, and a normal, quiet, respectable life. He couldn't be that irresponsible eighteen-year old again.

Despite not wanting Philippa to work on Lucian's wedding, he couldn't deny her beauty. Never could. Her wide, brown eyes had him transfixed into his spot. Robert normally didn't go for women with closely cropped hair, but Philippa's brought out the beauty of her delicate face. She had full lips that covered a stunning set of bright, white, straight teeth. Even without trying, she looked regal. Too bad she went by a nickname that didn't sound like anyone in a royal family. Her real name did.

Beyond her face, he couldn't ignore her body. The form-fitting black turtleneck she wore accentuated her rounded breasts. He had to thank God for her sprayed-on jeans and the knee-high boots that made her legs look a million miles long.

Robert stopped doing an assessment of her body to think about her inquiries. "I did hear Helene call my brother *Master Lucian*." He lowered his hands to his hips. "I didn't notice anything else." He took a deep breath.

"I didn't think Helene would…" Philippa trailed off as she kept her gaze to the ground. "And Lucian. I knew he could be kinky, but…" Again, she drifted off in her comment. "Did he copy you or did you copy him?" She chewed on her lower lip. "Did you tell him about us?"

Robert shook his head. "Of course not. I swore." He looked back at the house. "Did you tell Helene or anyone else?" His heart raced a little as he thought about his secret becoming public.

"Hell no." She cocked her head like she couldn't believe he had even asked her that question. "Not really a shining moment for me."

Robert realized that her embarrassment about their play relationship bothered him more than the idea of her being bored with him.

Philippa opened her mouth to answer at the same time the front door of Lucian's house flew open. Lucian, now in the pants he wore during the interview and nothing else, slammed the door behind himself and stomped over to Robert.

"What the fuck, man." Lucian got in Robert's face. "You're not some little kid anymore. You can't keep barging into my personal space like you have the full damn right. You don't. Stay the fuck away from me and Helene when we're at home."

"Watch the language." Robert glanced at Philippa. "A woman is present."

Lucian turned to Philippa. "Jesus. I didn't even notice you. Philly, how are you?" He pulled her into an easy hug.

Philly embraced him hard. "I'm good. It's great to see you again. I mean, uh—"

"I get it. It's great to see you, too. Not necessarily under these circumstances." Lucian took a step back from her after kissing both cheeks. As though a switch had been engaged in Lucian's head, he became the charming and cordial, even smiled at her. "Helene will be so happy to see you. I wished we could have met under more appropriate circumstances. But I'm glad you made it here safely."

"Her visit is the reason why I came over here. She said she came here to be your wedding planner." Robert attempted to be just as genial. He couldn't muster the emotion. "I told you—"

Lucian held up his hand. "Let me stop you right there." He looked at Philippa.

"With what just happened in there, I don't blame you if you wanted to cut me loose and go with this other person Robert said he had arranged to do your wedding planning." Philippa looked Lucian in his eyes. "But I'm not going to quit."

"Good. I mean, it's not like you haven't seen me naked before." Lucian laughed until he noticed Robert. "The skinny dipping. Oh, you didn't do it with us. I forgot." He nodded. "I want you to do my wedding." He glared at Robert. "In two months."

"Two? What happened to three? Are you crazy?" Robert ran his fingers through his hair. "Rumors will go flying that you're getting married so fast because she's pregnant." He had been pacing when his statement made him stop. "She's not pregnant, is she?"

"Maybe I'll announce that at the wedding so I can see that surprised look on your face." Lucian pointed to Philippa. "She stays. Welcome aboard." He nodded to her.

"You're not firing me?" She put her hand to her chest.

"Of course not. You're our friend. Besides, after something like this, the rest of your job should be a cakewalk." He headed back to his house and opened the door. He spoke to Robert while standing in the doorway. At the same time, Robert's car rolled up the circular driveway, stopping a few feet away from them to give them a little bit of privacy. "I've already phoned the guard and told him that the next time you come up here uninvited that he has my full permission to shoot you on sight."

Philippa chuckled, thinking Lucian had made a joke. Too bad Robert's brother didn't break a smile.

Lucian directed his attention to Philippa. "As we mentioned in our last call, you can stay in Moonwalk Manor up the road."

Robert stomped toward Lucian. "That's *my* house. You have no right to promise that space to anyone else. I have personal items in the house." Thankfully, Robert kept the doors locked to the places he wanted to keep hidden. Even with that, he didn't want anyone close to his collection. "You can't—"

"It's your home once you get married. Right now, it's unoccupied. Besides, you still live in Baldington, and it was Father's idea for her to stay there. No reason to put her up in a hotel." Lucian stepped back into the house but held the door open. "Your luggage should be there for you already."

Great. Robert's father knew about this woman's involvement and her visit and no one bothered to bring him in on the news. Dinner tonight would be interesting.

"She could stay in your old room in Baldington." Robert didn't want Philippa in the place that meant more than his future home. He hadn't even gotten to spend the night there, although he had already made plans in his head on how he would use his special toys. He wanted to get one good play session out the way before he started his official duties.

"I don't think any self-respecting woman should stay in Lucifer's Den. Isn't that what everyone called it?"

Robert wanted to curse and scrap with his half-naked brother right there and then. He had to remain composed. Lucian had an uncanny way of pushing Robert's buttons.

"Where is Moonwalk Manor?" Philippa peered around the area.

Lucian pointed in the direction toward the palace. "It's about a mile that way. The two of you passed it on your way here. Dinner is at seven." Lucian glanced at his watch. "Helene and I will pick you up on the way. That will give you some time to get cleaned up and relax. I'm sure you're experiencing a bit of jetlag. Does that plan sound good?"

Philippa nodded. "Perfect, actually. Thank you. And please thank and apologize to Helene for me. I didn't mean to interrupt anything."

Lucian put his hand up to her. "Not a problem for you. You didn't know." He glowered at Robert. Then he slammed the door.

Robert grumbled as he headed back to the car. The driver held the door open. Before stepping inside, he waited for Philippa.

"Thank you." She stepped inside and occupied her place far from him.

After Robert got in the car, he kept his attention on the scenery outside. Robert's plans crumbled right before his eyes with this one intrusion. He glanced at Philippa and returned his attention to the landscape going by them as the driver took them to his future home.

"So good to see Lucian again."

Philippa's voice became light, almost soothing like she wanted to talk him down from a ledge.

"Except for falling in love, he really hasn't changed that much." Robert recalled their conversation before Lucian emerged from the house. He needed some answers to satisfy his curiosity.

The car approached an unmanned security gate. After swiping a badge and entering a code, the gate opened.

"This is your home?" Philippa sat up like she wanted to view it through the windshield.

"Yes, well, it will be." Robert shifted in his seat. "The home is mine after I marry."

"Oh, so you're single."

The driver cleared his throat as he approached the front of the modest three-bedroom, two-story, stone-covered home. Robert spotted another vehicle there at the home. The Baldington staff had dropped off Philippa's luggage. Two women stood outside the front door with their hands clasped in front of them. The driver stopped the car and got out to open the door for them.

"I am unmarried right now." Robert got out. The gentlemanly side of him extended his hand to Philippa this time.

After a beat, she accepted his hand to have him assist her out of the car. "Thank you."

"Certainly." Robert faced the driver. "I'll show her around the home. Please wait here for me."

The driver bowed his head. "Yes, sir."

As Robert and Philippa walked up the cobblestone walkway to

the front door, the women beamed.

"Sir, as Prince Lucian requested, we have placed Ms. Powell's luggage in the home. Would you like for us to unpack them for you?" The woman directed her second statement to Philippa.

"Oh, wow." Philippa peered back to Robert. "Um, no. I can do that. Thank you."

Both women nodded their heads simultaneously before Robert formally dismissed them.

Robert opened the front door for Philippa. "Welcome to Moonwalk Manor." He honestly thought he would be saying that to a woman who would be his wife, not a woman he played with through a computer screen.

Philippa looked around before she faced him. "Why does this look so familiar?"

Philly knew that Helene and Lucian had planned to put her up someplace. She never expected to have a whole house to herself. This massive home couldn't all be for her.

"What looks familiar to you?" Robert worried his brows a bit as he regarded her.

When he didn't fly off the handle over every little thing, he could be quite charming and handsome. The suit. It had to be the suit. He didn't wear them back when they hung out as a group.

"I don't know. The wood floors." Philly gazed around the room. "The curtains. There's something about this place that seems familiar."

Robert cocked a smile at the side of his mouth. "Let me show you around." He raised his hands in the air. "Living room."

"I can see that." She nodded as she peered around. "Very nice."

Lots of heavy wood furnishings decorated the space. Large,

elaborate paintings of various landscapes hung from each wall. Philly approached one to admire it closer.

"Don't touch any of the paintings. They're hundreds of years old. The oils in your hands will affect them." Robert held his hand up like a hostage negotiator trying to convince her to do the right thing.

Philly did an exaggerated finger snap. "And here I was going to smear my hands all over them as soon as you left."

"Cute."

She agreed about that assessment for him. Damn, she must be jet lagged if she thought that about him.

"Follow me." He walked over an Oriental rug runner to a room behind the living room. "Kitchen."

The space extended further back than Philly had expected. A large wooden island sat in the middle with copper pots hanging over it. An expansive, white farmhouse sink sat under a portrait window that faced a lush, green backyard with colorful flowers all over the place.

"If I remember correctly, you enjoyed cooking."

"Still do. I'm surprised you remembered that." Philly stood at the sink and stared at the scene. "Whoa."

"Over here is the—"

"Wait. Just wait." Philly continued taking in the serene landscape until she felt a body standing next to her. No way would she break her attention from this. "I would be here every day to look at that or sit out there." She wrapped her arms around her body. "How beautiful. I could be so creative out there."

"Creative, how?"

At Robert's question, she finally gave him her attention. "I still paint." She glanced back at him. "You probably don't remember that."

His eyes widened. "Really? Did you share that information with me?"

"I'm sure I did." She shrugged. "Or maybe with you, I didn't."

"What does that mean?" He moved in closer to her.

"Never mind. I guess we didn't have that kind of relationship." She snickered.

"Sounds like your painting is important to you. You're still doing it after all these years? You must be really good." Robert sounded interested. Maybe he wanted to get her off her game to convince her to go back home.

"Nothing special. I won't be shown in any gallery or anything."

"Not all art needs to be acknowledged or rewarded. I happen to like when a person is creative just to free her soul. Is that what it does for you, Philippa?"

To hear her name on his very proper tongue sounded both titillating and odd. "Sure. It's something I've done for as long as I can remember. I can express myself." She took a deep breath. When she realized how much of herself she had exposed to this man, she sobered to the situation. "You want to show me the rest of the house? I'm suddenly tired."

Robert nodded. "Sure. But first…" He peered in cabinets and the refrigerator. "Good. Looks like they stocked it with fresh food for you. It stays empty otherwise."

He showed off the library, a den, and a bathroom before taking her upstairs. "The end of the hall will be your bedroom." Robert opened the door and allowed Philly to step inside.

Heavy curtains covered the windows and cloaked the room in darkness.

"Let's get some light in here." He went to one set of curtains and pushed them open.

With a bit of light, Philly noticed the dated yet classy decorations. She felt like she had stepped into a nice bed and breakfast in some quaint, little country town. Now that she thought about it, she really had.

Robert turned on a lamp that sat on top of a nightstand. "When you close the curtains, you won't be in complete darkness."

"This is all royal property. Why have curtains at all?" Philly would have nothing covering the windows and allow the outside to infuse in the home.

"Privacy is valued around here. You'll learn very quickly that your personal space will be invaded." Robert stepped over to a set of double doors. "The bathroom and walk-in closet."

Philly peered into the room and found a huge bathroom that had a separate bathtub and standalone shower, along with a double sink. Beyond the bathroom, she saw another doorway. She stepped inside and opened it and found a closet that looked bigger than her current bedroom in her Virginia condo. She also found her luggage. The staff had set them in the closet but didn't open them.

"Please make yourself at home." Robert walked toward the bedroom door. "There's a landline phone there on the nightstand. In the drawer is a list of important numbers."

"Including yours?" Philly opened the drawer and found the typed list that included Baldington Palace security, numbers to the various properties there, their car service, and even a number to their public relations department. She did not see a number for Robert.

"You don't still have my number from when—"

"No." She shook her head.

Robert dropped his gaze for a moment like her answer disappointed him. "If you need me, you can call the main palace number or the security office. They know how to reach me." Robert rested his fists on his hips.

"Of course." Philly had almost forgotten she stood in the presence of royalty. He certainly didn't forget.

She couldn't blame him for wanting separation from her. She cut him out like a tumor that would have destroyed her. This must have been his way to protect himself.

"On the back are the gate codes if you need to leave the property. Call the car service and they can take you anywhere." He walked out of the room with Philly close behind him.

"What about these rooms?" Before Robert could answer, Philly tried the doorknob. She found the first door locked.

"Don't go into these rooms." Robert pointed to each door. "These are locked for a reason. The open spaces I've shown you are where you can go."

She blinked. "Okay. You've gotten my curiosity up. What's behind the doors? A special cousin no one talks about? Is it a dead body? Do you have the family jewels in there?" Even though he told her he had the other door locked as well, she tried that knob just in case. She found resistance.

"There's nothing for you in either rooms. You have plenty of room in the rest of the house." Robert descended the stairs.

"The other rooms aren't bedrooms? If it is, I could stay in that room instead." Philly's heart started to race.

She hated this part of herself. She feared nothing except being alone.

"Why would you want to stay in a considerably smaller room when you have access to the master bedroom?" Robert stopped midway down the stairs to regard her.

"You could stay here, too. I know you aren't married, but there's no rule saying you can't room here with a guest, right?"

Your Love Is King   Bridget Midway

Chapter Four

Robert had to study Philippa for a moment to see if she wanted to trick him with her offer for him to stay in the same house with her. She had pushed him away.

"It would be a mistake to stay here with you." He started to leave when her one-word inquiry halted him.

"Why?"

He pointed to one of the locked doors. "You know why the inside of this house looks so familiar? Behind this door is the room where I had my phone conversation with you."

Philippa glanced at the door before bringing her attention back to him. "That can't be. The room you filmed in had toys and things all over the place."

"Exactly. It's the reason I keep the door locked. If you aren't interested in that type of relationship, you may not be comfortable with a man who shared that experience with you."

His logic seemed to get through to her as she took a step back from him and crossed her arms over her chest like she needed to make a barrier.

Robert almost wished she had fought a bit more for him to stay. Maybe her enthusiasm about playing would spark his interest again.

No. He had to be done with it all.

"What are you going to do with the stuff in there?" She nodded toward the closed door.

"Burn it. Trash it. I won't need it." He smoothed his hand down his shirt. "Besides, with all the planning you're doing, you would probably be more comfortable without someone being under your foot. However, if you would like the extra company—"

Philippa's eyes widened.

He continued. "—I can have Edith stay with you."

Philippa's beautiful face scrunched up into a ball. "Who?"

"Edith is the person I wanted to plan my brother's wedding. She lives in town. I would still like her assistance in the planning process. Perhaps she can stay with you in—"

"No thank you." Philly went down the stairs past Robert. "I'm good."

"Good with the planning or good with staying here by yourself?" He followed her to the front door.

She crossed her arms and headed to the front door. "Both." She opened the door, which looked like it signaled the driver to spring into action.

He got out of the driver's side and went over to the passenger side back door, ready to open it for Robert. Robert had more to say.

"Earlier, we started a conversation that we didn't finish." He stood in the doorway and very close to her. "You asked about what you heard and saw in Lucian's place when we entered."

"You mean when you barged in." Philippa snickered.

"Don't avoid the topic." Robert needed her to be direct. "You heard Helene call my brother *Master Lucian*, right?"

She nodded. "Yes, and?"

Robert heard the driver close the passenger side door, but Robert didn't look in that direction. He kept his full attention and focus on Philippa.

"What do you think about that and about the handcuffs?" He had to hear her perspective.

She shrugged. "To each their own, I suppose."

"But something like that is not for you anymore. You wouldn't be interested in engaging in that kind of relationship again?" His heart drummed and he wanted it to slow down because he could hear the beats in his head. He wanted to hear every word she uttered.

"You're trashing your past. I can move past mine. If I couldn't, I wouldn't have accepted this job and come back here knowing I would see you again." She moved back and forth in her spot. "Why are you asking me this? Why would you care?"

Robert had to think fast and hit her with honesty. Philippa could spot a liar from a mile away. "As an employee of Baldington Palace, we ask and expect that what you see and hear on our grounds will remain confidential. If you haven't already, you'll need to sign a confidentiality agreement confirming you will not run to a tabloid about what you experience here."

She shook her head. "I haven't before, right? I have no problem with signing that contract if it means I can work and get paid." She extended her hand. "Deal?"

Robert dropped his gaze to look at her hand before he accepted it. The warmth of her hand didn't surprise him as much as her strength. He shook it slowly before pulling her close to him. "See you at dinner."

He released her and strolled to the car. After getting inside, he peered at the door to see if Philippa would still be there to see him off. She had already closed the door. Because he had barged into Lucian's place, he suspected she had the door locked in every way she could.

The driver went down the long driveway back to the main road that went to Baldington Palace. Robert gazed out of the window back at the house. He had to blink when he clearly saw Philippa in the bedroom window removing her turtleneck, exposing her breasts in a black lacy bra before she disappeared off to the side, probably to go to the bathroom.

She had proved his point about needing curtains. Had she done that on purpose? He had felt nothing but contempt from her when she had dismissed him and the odd relationship they had created.

Nothing seemed to impress her except for when people did things for her, like the offer to unpack her luggage. Robert thought he would have chipped away at her armor by asking her about her feelings on BDSM play. As embarrassing as walking in on his brother and future sister-in-law in the middle of sex had been, it had given Robert the perfect opening to ask Philippa her thoughts on it. He wouldn't have known how to broach the topic otherwise.

Seeing her again conjured memories of their past. After getting back to Baldington, Robert hurried to his private quarters and dismissed his personal butler and room attendants. He normally didn't do what he had planned, but he needed to get his lustful thoughts of Philippa out of his head.

The more he thought of her, the more his cock throbbed until he had a hard-on that could drill through the stone at Moonwalk Manor. Robert stripped out of his clothes after making sure to lock his doors. He turned on the wall-mounted TV and turned the volume up to a rugby match that had a lot of crowd cheers, enough that the noise would drown out what he planned to do.

Robert sat naked on the bed and retrieved his tablet. When he tried connecting to his email, he got a message reminding him that the Internet services there had not been repaired yet.

"Damn." He could still do what he wanted by thinking about Philippa and her lips and her legs and her breasts.

No. He had something better. Not as great as the real thing, but very close.

Robert got his laptop and went to a file in his hard drive. If Philippa knew that he had saved their video chat, she would jump down his throat and destroy his computer and, if she wanted, his reputation. After this, he would delete the file…maybe.

Robert reclined on his back in his bed on top of the covers and placed the laptop next to him. He started the video at the same time he held his shaft.

The opening scene showed Philippa sitting sweetly in front of the camera. "I had a wonderful time in Lesilitho this summer." Even without makeup, she looked flawless. "Thank you and your family for letting me stay there."

"You're welcome." Even now, Robert remembered how his cock throbbed while he talked to her. "Are you in your dorm room?"

She shook her head. "I'm home alone. I leave for school this weekend." She shrugged. "Parents are on a cruise. The one brother who still lives at home and my oldest brother are in Seattle visiting relatives. My other brother is out with his girlfriend. He won't be back tonight. My brothers will be back to see me off to school." She sighed, which heaved her chest up into the camera's lens. "Just little ol' me. Why? Do you have something in mind?"

Robert had liked her baiting him. "As a matter of fact, I do. I need you to take off all your clothes."

Philippa had laughed at his demand, but he found nothing humorous about it. "You're kidding, right?"

"No." Robert had kept his answers short. Before she could keep questioning him, he explained himself. "I would like for us both to try something new. It'll be safe because I'm in a place away from the palace, and you're alone. I promise that what we do, I will not tell anyone else. Will you do the same?"

Philippa had looked around. "What is it do you want to try?"

"Dominating you virtually." He drummed his fingers on the desk where he sat. Then he picked up his phone. "Look at these." He pointed the phone to the various toys he had hanging in a room at the empty home that he would get when he married.

"What is all that? Are you in a dungeon or something?"

"It's a dungeon I've created. There's a side of myself I want to explore. I trust you. I want you to see if it's a lifestyle you might like as well." Robert's hands now got as sweaty as they were when they had had their conversation. "What do you say? Are you ready to try something different with me?"

He realized now what a grand leap of faith he had made in a woman he had only seen a handful of times at his home. He did trust her. It helped that he had been attracted to her as well, enough to ask for her phone number, and even more so to believe she wouldn't reveal this side of himself.

"One minute." Philippa darted away.

Robert almost wondered if she had second thoughts. Moments later, Philippa sauntered in front of the camera, naked save a pair of black stilettos that had straps going up her legs like rope.

Robert placed his hand on his bare chest as he watched the video. He listened to himself give her directions.

"Nice."

Philippa nodded. "I had to make sure all the doors were locked just in case." She didn't cover her body, not that she needed to be modest. "I've never done anything like this before." She giggled. "I can mark this off my bucket list."

Robert sat up taller. "I want you to speak only when spoken to. When you respond, you will address me as *Sir*. Is that understood?"

Philippa regarded him for a moment before she put her hands to her hips. "I don't know if I like that."

"I will make this experience worth it."

She sighed. "Yes, Sir." She had a bitterness to her tone.

"Good. I want you to kneel with her hands on your thighs."

She got down on her knees and placed her hands on her thighs as instructed. A small image of Robert licking his lips appeared in the corner of the video.

"She is a beauty," he mumbled to himself.

Here Philippa showed her full self to him. She had longer hair that she kept still in curls that went down to her shoulders. Her full breasts heaved up and down with each of her heavy breaths. Her dark skin resembled velvet. Robert wanted to kiss every inch of her.

Robert shook his head. Love and feelings had nothing to do with where Robert wanted to go with as his next level in their country. Even as a figurehead, he could be an appropriate king. Right now, though, he would do something very inappropriate. The difference between him and Lucian had to do with their levels of discretion. Robert would do acts like this behind closed doors.

"If this is something you like to keep doing, I would want you to say a statement to me each time," Video Robert said to her. "Repeat after me. It is day one of my submission. I am learning to be yours."

Philippa had swallowed hard. "I don't know. Do you know how long it took me to decide on a college? I'm still undecided on my major." When he didn't speak, she did. "It is day one of my submission. I am learning to be yours." She leaned her head back and looked conflicted. "Christ."

"This is supposed to be fun for both of us." He didn't like her looking so bothered.

Philippa nodded and smiled.

Robert found he missed that genuine smile, not the one she had flashed him earlier when she talked about securing the wedding planning job. Shortly after this conversation, Philippa stopped talking to him. The longer he looked at her in the video, the more he saw her smile fading. Maybe at this point she knew she had planned on stopping their clandestine relationship before it could really get going.

Robert didn't want to think about their failed virtual relationship now. He had a need he had to satisfy. He stroked his cock slowly at first, making sure to pulse the tip.

A bit of pre-cum oozed from the opening, signaling what would be happening the longer he watched the recording.

"You look very beautiful." Robert remembered telling her that when they chatted.

"You look very handsome." She beamed.

The video version of Robert took a deep breath and sat up taller. "Have you been good this week?"

She smiled. "Yes. Would you like to hear about my activities?"

"Of course." Robert remembered that he smiled.

"I volunteered to feed homeless people in Virginia Beach." She rubbed hands back and forth over her thighs like she anticipated something happening. "I picked up an extra shift at work and a customer left me a hundred-dollar tip. I thought it was a mistake and offered to give it back to him. He refused to take it." She licked her lips. "I killed at my public speaking meeting."

"I always said you could convince an Eskimo to buy ice cubes."

Philippa laughed. Robert wondered if he could get her to smile and laugh again.

"Do you want to know what I wore?" Her breathing increased.

"Of course."

"I wore jeans, a white T-shirt, and sneakers at the volunteer event. I had on a denim skirt and a blue blouse at the coffee shop job. And I wore a sweater dress during my debate." Sweat formed on her forehead.

It matched the sweat that sprang up on his head now as he increased his speed. His body trembled as he watched her, knowing what would be happening shortly.

"All your outfits sounded appropriate except for one thing." Robert held up a finger.

"Yes, Sir?" Philippa cocked her head to the side, but the look in her eyes told him that she knew what he would mention.

"Were you wearing any undergarments for any of these outfits?"

She shook her head slowly. "No, Sir."

"Why is that?"

Robert stroked himself faster. He felt his cock throbbing under his hand.

"I'm not a fan of undergarments."

"I remember that from the midnight swim." Both Video Robert and the real one made that statement at the same time. "Show me."

Without questioning what he meant, Philippa spread her knees apart over her carpeted floor while keeping her hands on her thighs. With her legs apart, he admired her shaved pussy. The outside lips glistened, showing off her excitement.

"Are you wet?"

Philippa nodded and balled her hands into fists. "This is so strange. I have never even sent a guy I was dating a sexy picture of me, and here I am doing a video chat with you naked. But I feel so sexy."

Back then, Robert had agreed. Then she cut him off without a word.

"I'd like to see you touch yourself."

The statement ignited fast action from Philippa. She used one hand to grip her breast that filled her palm. Her hard nipple poked out between her fingers. She used her other hand to delve in between her legs.

Robert barely heard the introduction of her fingers inside of her pussy thanks to the cheering crowds on his TV. Good thing that sound remained embedded in his memory.

Philippa drove into herself hard and fast, her motions matching Robert's now. He imagined that he would love to touch her, smell her essence, taste her, fuck her. Not make love to her, although he wanted that as well. Robert wanted to step out of the norm, get her against a wall, and pound into her until they both went limp.

Why the hell hadn't he approached her when she last visited? Philippa seemed willing.

"Mmm, Robert." She collapsed onto her side and continued pleasuring herself. "So close."

He watched her body shake.

"Don't come. Not yet." Real Robert felt his sac tighten.

"What? I can't do that." She gazed up at the camera. "Please?"

"No." He shook his head. "Not yet. You must learn to control yourself and obey me."

Philippa kept her eyes squeezed shut while it looked like she both tried slowing down her rhythmic motions and speeding up as though her body demanded more. "Can't."

"Don't do it." Even as Robert in the recording made the directive, he couldn't slow himself down or prevent himself from coming.

"Remembering your face." Philippa increased her thrusting. "Your eyes. Want to see you. Why can't I—" She stopped talking while her body became overcome with tremors and she released a long, low wail.

As though he had given the directive to himself, Robert reached down to cup his balls at the same time he pumped his shaft and projected his milky cum over his stomach and chest.

Philippa slowed her movements until she finally stopped. She had just enough strength to peer into the camera and smile. "Oh my God. I've never…"

"You disobeyed me. I told you not to come." If only Robert could have followed his own orders. He peered down at his body at the ejaculate sprayed over his stomach and chest.

She remained on the floor on her side. "I couldn't help it."

"You will have to be punished." Before he doled out her penalty, Robert had made another request from her. "What do you taste like?"

Philippa removed her fingers from her vagina and pushed herself up to her knees. "I don't know why I did this." She shook her head. "I shouldn't have done this."

Robert wanted to taste every bit of her. Then and now. "It's okay. I'll keep this a secret. We can keep doing this and establish a real relationship."

Philippa shook her head. "No. I can't. We shouldn't have done this. *I* shouldn't have done this." She reached for her phone and disconnected the call.

Robert remembered attempting to contact her several times after that event. Each time, she did not answer his calls or text messages. Maybe Philippa had done him a favor by stopping all conversations. By doing that, he had managed to forget about the possibility of having a long-term BDSM relationship. Then she came back.

What the hell was he thinking? He didn't need to consider her at all as someone he could play with potentially, not when he had designs on wooing someone else, a person appropriate for him to be involved with and could potentially make a future. Damn if Philippa didn't look enticing. Legs, ass, breasts, and those lips. Through those lips came smart-ass remarks. He didn't need her there. Baldington didn't need her services.

Lucian couldn't be swayed as far as releasing Philippa from this job. Helene would want her friend there. Robert would have to convince his father to go with Edith and get rid of Philippa.

Now he needed to figure out a plan to get Miss Philippa Powell out of Lesilitho.

Chapter Five

Philly had taken a nice, long, hot shower, hoping beyond hope the scalding water would give her some focus and wash away any lingering doubts and feelings down the drain. Since high school, Philly had made it a point to never let anyone shake her confidence. She knew coming back to Lesilitho for this job would challenge her. She underestimated her feelings for Robert. She also didn't factor how he would react to seeing her again.

If he had it his way, she would be out of a job and headed back to Virginia. Too bad she didn't have anything there for her. Philly had quit her steady day job as the event planner for the Cavalier Hotel at the Oceanfront to take on this job, which she hoped would catapult her career as a wedding/event planner into the stratosphere.

If Robert had any say so in her career trajectory, she would be headed back to Virginia with nothing but a cool story and an unfortunate view of her friend in a compromising position.

Philly slipped on a pair of black leggings and threw on a T-shirt without a bra. The more she thought about her day, the more she didn't want to see Robert again. He stirred up feelings in her that she thought she had erased after she made the hard decision to stop communicating with him.

If she attended the dinner tonight, she would keep looking at Robert and remembering the things she had done for him in the interest of kink and fun. At some point, the play stopped being fun for her and started to become more. Too bad it didn't for him.

No, she would find something to eat and crash early. She knew of one easy way to knock herself out. Philly opened the nightstand drawer to retrieve her trusty vibrator. Had the women who had brought her luggage in the house had unpacked her belongings, they would have encountered her pink, slender, life-like toy that had managed to get her through many sexual droughts.

Philly had expected to experience another long bout of it while being stationed in this foreign country. She didn't have a problem with cutting the wedding date down a month. The less time she would be in Lesilitho, the faster she could get back home to a potential new career hopefully. She didn't have a man waiting for her to return. Philly hung her hat on this one job catapulting her new business venture so that she wouldn't worry about dating.

She gazed down at her toy. "Another Saturday night together again."

Philly threw the toy on the bed and made her way back to the bathroom. She wrapped a silk scarf around her head to protect her hair and to get ready to sleep immediately once she came...*if* she came.

Lately, Philly struggled to achieve an orgasm. First, she blamed her bodily change on her last relationship. She couldn't even make herself happy on her own no matter how hard she tried, and she did try...a lot.

Funny. When she and Robert had played over the computer and he had asked her to pleasure herself in front of him, she had no problem and she came against his wishes. Maybe the trick to getting her back to her old self involved her imagining Robert and defying him again. He did look good in his suit. She fell for his eyes again. When she looked at his hands, she thought about them caressing her body, from her neck down to her toes.

Philly padded back to the bedroom, ready to give her sex drive another spin when she heard a knock at the door.

"What the hell?" Philly slipped on a pair of slippers she had packed and padded down the stairs. She noticed right away the lack of a peephole in the door. "Damn." She huffed. "Who is it?" She raised her voice to be heard through the heavy wooden door.

"Philly, it's me. Helene."

Philly beamed as she unlocked the door and swung it open, prepared to greet her friend. Helene stood on the other side, clothed and happy while she stood next to her fiancé.

Philly barely noticed him as she threw her arms around the woman she hadn't seen in a couple of years. "Helene. So good to finally see you in person." She held onto her friend for dear life, not wanting to let her go. Then she heard a clearing throat.

Philly gave Helene one last squeeze before she gazed to the side and noticed Lucian, also now clothed in simple shirt and suede black jacket that paired well with his jeans.

"Good to see you again." He held his arms open.

Philly embraced him, too. "Come on in." She went back into the house. "Would you like something to drink? I saw one of those cute little coffee maker machines in the kitchen that can make coffee, tea, hot chocolate and even hot apple cider." She stopped talking when she noticed their confused expressions. "What?"

"Why aren't you dressed for dinner? Looks like you're about to head to bed." Helene held Lucian's hand.

Philly peered down at herself like she didn't know she had plans to stay in for the night. "Yes, I changed my mind about dinner. It's been a long day with traveling and everything. I want to take the night to decompress and get some sleep. I'm sorry. I should have called you to tell you not to bother to come get me."

Lucian nodded. "I understand. It's been a long journey here. I'm sure you're exhausted. I hope you have no plans of backing out of arranging our wedding." He released Helene's hand to wrap his arm around her waist. "Helene has said nothing but great things about you and your work. Since you stopped coming to the palace, I haven't heard what you're up to now. What other weddings have you done before? Anyone I know?"

Philly glanced at her friend before looking at Lucian. "I'm afraid Helene has bragged about me a little too much. I've done some wedding planning at the hotel I worked at in Virginia Beach, but you would be my biggest client." She swallowed before she continued. "And my first."

She had expected Lucian's eyes to bug out of his head at her confession.

Instead, he smiled and even laughed a little. "Damn, I wish you were coming to dinner now. I wanted to see Robert's expression when you admitted that to him. Now I can't wait until you do our wedding."

"You're not nervous?" Philly rubbed her hand up her arm over the long-sleeved shirt.

"Nervous? Why? You could have a circus in the background and an Elvis impersonator marrying us, and I wouldn't care. All I care about is that at the end of the day, I walk away with this beauty on my arm. And if you can manage to piss Robert off while doing it, I would be doubly thrilled."

Helene gave a playful smack again Lucian's midsection. "Stop teasing your brother." She stared at her friend. "Philly is good, and she works hard. She'll do a great job." Then she turned to Lucian again. "Would you mind giving us a couple of minutes?"

"Sure." He kissed her temple. "I'll wait for you out in the car." He regarded Philly. "I believe we have an appointment with you tomorrow to go over our wedding plans, right?"

Philly nodded. "Right after breakfast."

"No sleeping in for us." He gave Helene a playful swat on her backside before exiting the house.

When the door closed, Helene started a new conversation. "I'm sorry I exaggerated your skills a little with Lucian."

"Why did you do that?" Philly didn't need anyone trying to make her out to be something she could never be. She didn't mind working hard without the lies or pretenses.

"I wanted to reassure him that you were the best one for the job." Helene held Philly's hands. "I still believe that. I remember being able to come home and stay with my cousins and we would hang out all the time. We had no money, no car, and no game, but you always managed for us to have a good time whatever we did. That's why I believe in you. You can make whatever we want to do work."

Philly needed to hear that boost of confidence. "Thank you."

"And don't worry about Robert. His bark is definitely worse than his bite." Helene shook her head. "I get it. He wants to honor Baldington Palace and the institution created before us. That doesn't mean Lucian and I want to thumb our noses up at tradition. We want to do what we want." Helene started to turn to leave when Philly held her arm to stop her.

"Speaking of doing what you want, earlier today—"

Helene rolled her eyes. "If you could forget that you saw me screwing my brains out, I would be forever grateful."

"Too late." Philly snickered. "I have a question about what I heard. Did you call Lucian your master?"

Helene held onto the door handle and without a pause said, "Yes."

Philly stared at the woman she had been calling her friend for years. "You don't worry about someone finding out and releasing that information to the public?"

Helene shook her head. "We're both grown and what we do is our business. Everything we do, we agree upon." She released the door to move in closer to her friend. "To be honest, it's the best sex I have ever had in my life, and my best relationship." She smiled. "Going into the BDSM lifestyle with Lucian wasn't easy. I'm not going to lie. I struggled with finding out about his desires and then struggling to come to grips with the fact that I wanted to do that, too. He's made it so easy to love it and him. And BDSM is a godsend to our relationship."

Philly huffed. "You're going to have to explain that one. I don't get it."

"Our communication has improved so much. We were already both so honest. The Lifestyle makes you put all your feelings out there. There are no pretenses or judgments. He accepts me for me, and I do the same for him. And did I mention that the sex is out of this world? He knows what turns me on and how to get me to come harder than I ever had with anyone in my life." Her face became somber. "The Lifestyle isn't for everyone. But it works for me and Lucian."

As though he had heard her, the door opened and he stepped through again. "Honey, we need to go. I think the paparazzi are out and about." He nodded his head back toward the street.

Helene rolled her eyes. "I hate them. They won't leave us alone." She hugged Philly again. "We can talk more later. Maybe lunch tomorrow."

"That would be great." Philly smiled.

"Yes, you two catch up while you can. The two of us will be visiting several countries soon. Nigeria, New Zealand, Spain." Lucian reached out for Helene's hand.

"That's right. We've been invited by dignitaries to visit before our nuptials. Should be fun." She held Lucian's hand.

"The things we'll do on the plane and in all those countries. Cannot wait." He glanced at Philly. "See you in the morning."

The two left and she locked the door behind them. Philly didn't need to look out the front window to see their car drive away. She heard the tires over the cobblestone driveway.

Philly turned off the lights downstairs before retiring to the bedroom. As she walked by the two bedroom doors Robert had told her to stay out of, her curiosity spiked. She wanted to see the toys she had seen during their chat.

The old Philly would have picked the lock and seen the toys herself. Her heart raced with the idea of smelling the leather and seeing the various implements designed to push her body to its limits.

As she reentered the bedroom, Philly thought about Helene's words. The same friend she knew back in the day who didn't like to get dirty and cried for hours when she had gotten a splinter in her finger now liked her sex kinky. Philly didn't see that coming. The idea of having amazing sex intrigued her. She stared at the vibrator on her temporary bed.

"I'll stay content with my trusty battery-operated pal before I get down with having my ass beat for fun."

She reached for the pink faux phallus when something out the window caught her attention. Did she just see a flashlight on the property? Who the hell was there?

* * * * *

After taking a shower, Robert got dressed in jeans and half-boots with a pullover blue sweater. He arrived at the dining room for his family's dinner. He had to admit that his father's tradition – and insistence – that the family all sit down to dinner warmed Robert's heart. Even Lucian made it a point to make it to dinner with Helene in tow.

Robert couldn't allow the dinner to happen without giving a formal apology to Helene. He approached her and noticed immediately that she didn't make eye contact with him.

"Hey." He leaned forward and gave her a standard kiss on her cheek. In a lowered voice, he said, "I apologize for coming into your home like that earlier today. It was uncalled for and an invasion of your privacy. Please forgive me."

"I love you." Helene smiled. "But if you do that again, I fully support Lucian's directive to have you shot." She patted his shoulder before taking her place at the table.

Robert released a breath he had been holding until Lucian came up next to him and put his arm around his shoulders. "The king of bad decisions."

"Isn't that you?" Robert would only take so much ribbing about this one instance.

"For once, I'm the good one. I'm behaving. You are the one we worry about." He slapped Robert on the back before sitting next to Helene.

"Me? I'm fine. Never better. As a matter of fact—" He stopped after taking inventory of the guests. "Where's Philippa?"

"Who?" Clive placed a napkin over his lap as he regarded his youngest son.

"The woman Helene and Lucian invited to plan their wedding." Robert pointed to the duo.

"Oh my goodness." Ginny, Helene's mother, put her hand to her chest as she took a place at the table on the opposite side from her daughter. "Philly is here?"

"Really?" Quincy, Helene's father, smiled so wide it split his head in two. "I haven't seen her since you two were in college."

"She's here." Helene nodded. "When Lucian and I went to pick her up for dinner, she said she was too tired to make it."

Robert let out an audible grunt. "Unacceptable. How is she to learn about our traditions without interacting with the family?"

"Son, you need to give her a break. She's traveled a long way. I'm sure she's tired." Clive held up his hand to Robert to calm him down.

"I would be calm if your other son didn't drop a major bombshell and—"

"Robert," Lucian said between gritted teeth.

"Lucian wants to get married in a couple of months."

There. Robert had said it and put the attention back on the couple. He wanted to see what his father and Helene's family would say about that. This would be the ammunition Robert would need to get his father on his side as far as getting rid of Philly and keeping Edith.

"Thanksgiving wedding?" Clive picked up his wine glass.

Lucian nodded. "Close. Just right after it."

"Almost your mother and my anniversary."

Lucian held Helene's hand and smiled at her as he spoke. "That's kind of what we were going for."

Shit. Lucian, the charmer, struck again.

The wait staff served up the salad first. While they did, Robert unleashed his argument in a calm manner. He had already lost face when his father sided with Lucian on the change of his wedding date.

"Father, with Lucian stepping aside as the next in line for the throne, the perception may be that he wants to distance himself from the royal family." Robert placed a cloth napkin across his lap.

"Here you go." Lucian huffed. "Are you being serious right

now?"

Robert nodded. "Deadly. Chatter already started on social media about him linking with an American company."

"One that brought a lot of jobs and industry here, I might add." Helene stuck up for her man, which gained her a sweet peck on her cheek.

"And Lucian's marrying someone—" Robert stopped when he noticed the stares from Helene's parents. "—who is not from Lesilitho. If our Internet service wasn't down right now, I could show you the comments."

"Excuse my language, but I could give a damn about what people say about me." Lucian stabbed a red cherry tomato on his plate. "No one makes me happy but Helene. End of story. And if your next statement is that Philly shouldn't be the one to plan our wedding, you are going to lose that battle, too."

Robert looked at his father. "We need to show a united front to the people. They need to see our loyalty to our country. Edith has planned events for us for years."

Robert heard a grunt, but it didn't come from Lucian or even Helene. He snapped his attention to across the table to Ginny.

"Mrs. Nix?" Robert felt his eyebrows furrow.

"I like Edith. She's a dear, sweet woman. Has stories for days about this palace and the people who have come and gone here." Ginny shook some pepper over her salad while keeping her gaze down to her food.

"But?" Clive probed.

She sighed before lifting her head. "She's not very progressive or forward thinking. She doesn't understand social media. She still insists on serving entrees that were popular in the seventies and eighties." She looked over at Lucian and Helene and smiled. "I know you two don't want that."

Lucian shook his head. "No, ma'am. See, Father, Mrs. Nix gets it."

Robert felt himself losing this battle. "Fine. So, she's a little too traditional. The most important thing is that she understands our traditions. That will be important when the ceremony is televised and streamed for all to—"

"Televised?" Helene dropped her fork on her plate. "When did we agree to that?"

"All royal events are televised." Robert volleyed his attention back to his father. "Your wedding to Mother was televised, right?" He remembered watching the video of it as a child. His mother looked so elegant and regal.

Clive nodded. "Yes, it was. But it was a different time." He brought his attention to the happy, yet concerned, couple. "It looks like they didn't intend for their wedding to be made into a spectacle. This should be a happy occasion for all." The silver in Clive's hair looked like it glittered under the lights in the dining room. "Lucian, Helene, has Philly planned large events like this kind before?"

Lucian glanced at Helene and gave her a slight nod that Robert noticed. He wondered what that meant between the two of them.

"Yes, she's planned weddings and events before." Helene sat up taller.

Clive shrugged. "If you two are willing to vouch for her, I don't understand the issue of hiring her for their event."

Robert dropped his utensils. "Father, you have to—"

Clive held up his hand. "A compromise would be to have both Philly and Edith plan and orchestrate the wedding. I'll make sure Edith doesn't insist on a fruit cake for your wedding cake."

The statement prompted a ripple of laughter at the table from everyone but Robert.

"Make sure Philly signs the confidentiality contract before she starts any work. The royal budget can't take another hit if Lucian slips and shows off his royal jewels." Clive took a sip of his red wine.

"Too late." Lucian uttered the statement under his breath but loud enough for Robert to catch it.

"Also, if Lucian and Helene do not want their wedding shown live, then we should—"

"No. You can't agree to that one." Robert shook his head so hard, his neck hurt. "You have those to princes in England televising everything they do. We're just as good as them if not better."

"Robert, I'm not competing with anyone." Lucian drew his eyebrows together. "You're getting a little manic about all this. Shouldn't you be worried about your own ceremony instead of focusing so much time and attention on what I'm doing?"

"My event is all planned out." Robert held up his hand and ticked off the important items. "I have my suit. So does Father. The royal orchestra is practicing daily. We'll do a rehearsal a week before. And the royal printers have already printed the programs." He leaned over close to his father. "By the way, Edith planned all that."

"Great. A snooze fest. Glad my part in it is small." Lucian finished off his salad.

"Robert, this will be their one and only wedding. Don't make this an unpleasant experience for all." Clive adjusted his glasses on his prominent nose and offered his trademark smile.

"Fine. I will ask for this. If she screws up even once, she's out."

"Once? Hell, even baseball players get three times at bat." Quincy shook his head.

"That is true." Helene took a sip of water. "Seems awfully unfair. What do you have against my friend?"

Robert sighed. "Nothing. She's a lovely person." Especially out of clothing, he could have added.

"She is. You should get to know her, especially since she'll be here for the next couple of months." Helene pushed her plate away, which signaled a staff member to collect it and others at the table.

If Helene knew how much Robert really knew Philippa, she would be shocked. Not only had he seen Philippa naked, he had seen her orgasm face, a sight burned in his memory. Too bad he wouldn't be seeing that again.

"I would have gotten to know her had she bothered to join us for dinner." Robert wiped his mouth. "Okay, three strikes and she's out. Can we all agree to that?"

"As long as the same rule applies to Able Edith." Lucian snickered.

"Of course." Robert placed his hands on the table. "But I'm sure she'll be just fine."

"Good. Then it's settled." Clive smiled wider.

"With the exception of televising the wedding. We still need to—" Robert noticed a couple of security team members rushing toward the back of the house. He pushed back from the table. "Excuse me. Don't wait to start dinner without me."

"But you won't know the traditions unless you're here."

Lucian joke didn't land with Robert.

Robert grabbed one of the guard's arm and spun him around. "What's going on?"

"Excuse me, sir. We got an alarm at M.M."

When Robert furrowed his eyebrows, the young man continued.

"I apologize for the acronym. Moonwalk Manor. An intruder alarm was tripped."

Robert sighed. "There is someone staying at the house right

now."

The man nodded. "We know. An outside alarm tripped while the guest was in the house. Someone is on the property."

Robert didn't ask for any further explanation. He bolted from the house and took off in one of the security cars to the house where the woman, who had managed to recapture his attention in a matter of minutes, stayed.

Chapter Six

Philly knew she had seen movement outside. The hell she would survive beating every mean girls' asses throughout school and fighting off the quarterback on the football team when he got too handsy to be taken out by some idiot in a foreign country.

As soon as her friend and Lucian left, Philly had planned on being with her battery-operated tool. Then she caught sight of a flashlight darting around the property.

No one in the family, including that very thorough Robert, mentioned anyone else being at the estate. Whoever roamed the backyard would soon find out that they messed with the wrong woman.

Philly reached into her purse and pulled out a white canister of dog-repellent spray. Her oldest brother had given it to her when he grabbed an extra can from work as a mail carrier. If spraying the contents in her attacker's eyes gave her time to escape a bad situation, she would use it. Tonight, she would be breaking this in and breaking someone down.

She doused the lights in the bedroom as though she had planned on turning in for the evening. She crept to the front door. She remembered seeing large rocks in the flowerbed next to the door. The plan would be to disable the intruder with the spray and then knock him or her out cold with the rock. Then she would call for security.

"Okay, asshole, get ready." Philly held the door handle, counted herself down from five, and swung the door open when she got to *one.*

Closer than she had expected, she saw a dark figure approaching the door. Adrenaline fueled her as she held up the canister and sprayed the contents. She didn't expect to see one dark figure ducking and another coming behind and getting a face full of the spray.

Since the first person ducked, Philly had to go to Plan B. She grabbed a rock that filled her hand with jagged pieces cutting into her palm and cocked it back, ready to throw it.

"Hold it!"

Philly saw two large hands come up while the person behind him screamed and writhed in pain. When the hands lowered, she saw Robert.

"What are you doing here?" She kept the rock up and ready to throw just in case this prince had something else in mind.

"The security team got a report of an intruder here. Did you leave the property?" Robert held up his hands at chest level.

"No. After Helene and Lucian left, I saw a light like a flashlight around the house. Someone was here." She finally lowered the rock, mainly because her shoulder had become sore.

"And you were going to take whoever it was down with Mace and a rock?" Robert lowered his hands.

Philly peered behind him. "Took down one of your guards."

Robert glanced behind him. Another security guard attended to the man, who continued cursing as he rubbed his eyes.

"Yes, and what if the person had a gun? You could have been hurt or worse." He ran his hand over his hair.

"I could have, but I would have gone down swinging. I'm not a princess who needs saving." She looked back at the injured guard again. "Do you want to bring him in? Maybe run some cool water over his eyes?"

"They're going to take him to the medical staff at the palace. The rest of the team will check out the property." Robert took a step closer to her. "Are you all right?"

She gazed into his eyes and saw sincere worry fill them. "I'm fine." She wrapped her arms around her body to stave off the chill in the autumn air. "I'll feel better when I know there is no one around the house."

"Understood. I'll check the rest of the home." Robert started to step inside when Philly stood in his path.

She started to tell him she didn't need him or his services. Couldn't he see that she had done a damn good job of protecting herself? As she stood there, she understood that she didn't own the house. Quite frankly, she couldn't even go in all the rooms.

Philly released a long, exasperated sigh before she stepped aside. Robert said nothing as he checked all the windows downstairs first, tugging on each one and ensuring the locks had been fully engaged.

Once he completed the sweep downstairs, he put his hand on the bannister before going upstairs. He peered back at Philly. "Have you eaten dinner yet?"

"No. I'll probably have some cereal or something." She didn't really feel that hungry except for one thing.

Damn. Since when did traveling make her this horny? Who was she kidding? The flight had nothing to do with her increased libido. Seeing Robert again brought back some scintillating memories. She wouldn't let him know that.

"I don't recall seeing cereal in the kitchen." He nodded his head towards the room. "We were about to sit down to dinner at the palace. You can join us there."

Philly glanced down at her staying-in-for-the-night look. Although she had taken a shower, she really didn't feel like getting dressed again to sit with a stuffy group, well, except for Helene and Lucian. As soon as she got her friend alone, she would have to delve deeper about her proclivities.

"Thanks for the offer, but I'm in no mood to get dressed again. It's been a long day." This conversation made it even longer.

Although she appreciated him being thorough, she wanted Robert out of the house already.

"Put on a pot of boiling water and heat up some pasta. It's time for us to have a frank discussion. It's better to do that over dinner." Without getting confirmation from her that she would agree, Robert headed up the stairs.

"I told you. I don't want—"

A knock sounded on the front door as Philly screamed up the stairs at Robert.

"What?" Her nerves had already been pulled banjo tight. She didn't need anything else ruining her evening.

"Excuse me, ma'am. We've done a full check of the outside." The security guard removed his black cap and tucked it under his arm as he addressed her from the porch. "We found no one and nothing suspicious. On palace orders, we'll stage a couple of guards at the gate entrance. If you need us, ring us. Do you have our number?"

Philly nodded. "Yes. I programmed it all in my phone. Thank you."

"Would you like for us to check out the inside as well?" Still, he didn't come into the house.

She shook her head. "Robert is doing that now."

"*Prince* Robert?" The lilt in his voice sounded like he doubted her story.

She nodded. "He's upstairs." At that moment, a door closed, which confirmed her story.

As though he didn't believe her, the guard craned his head in the house and peered up, even waiting when she heard heavy footfalls coming down the stairs. When Robert appeared, the guard blinked, bowed his head, and disappeared.

Robert stood in the area between the stairs, the living room area, and the kitchen. "All clear upstairs. All the windows are locked." He glanced in the kitchen. "Did you put on the pasta? I'm starving." He rested his hand on his stomach.

Philly snickered. "I appreciate you coming over with your security team." She stopped and thought about her statement. "You're a prince. Royalty. Why did you come with the team? You could have let them handle this."

He held up one finger. "One minute, please." Robert stepped outside of the house. Philly approached the door to lock it behind him when Robert came back through again and closed it behind him. "I dismissed the car."

"You what?" She moved passed him to go to the front window.

Ignoring her inquiries about coming with the security team and letting his driver go, he continued. "I don't even know if there is pasta in the house." He rubbed his chin. "Did you check the cupboards after I left earlier?"

She huffed and walked by him. "What's your deal? You don't trust your team?" Philly entered the kitchen and opened three cabinets before locating boxes of various pastas.

"I trust them." He sat in one of the barstools at the kitchen island as she retrieved a pot. "Without checking behind them, I know that if the staff provided pasta they should also have some sort of sauce."

Philly had to laugh.

"Did I say something amusing?" Robert rested his elbows on the island.

"Amateurs would use the jar stuff." She opened the refrigerator door and grabbed tomatoes and green bell peppers. Then she located onions from a wooden box on the counter. "It's easier and tastier to make your own sauce."

She filled a large pot with water and started the gas burner. "Why did you let your driver go? I thought you weren't going to spend the night here." She kept her back to him while she prepared their meal.

"I'm sure he's hungry, too. I didn't want him waiting on me while we talked."

Philly went into autopilot as she prepared a simple meal. Whenever she cooked, she could turn off her mind from obsessing about the details of this job and concentrated on something she enjoyed, something she excelled at without question. She likened the feeling to the time she played with Robert. He commanded her so well that she had to listen to him, with some exceptions. At times, she had to respond to her body's needs.

By the time she finished preparing the meal, Philly realized that Robert had remained quiet the entire time. She turned to him with two plates full of food in her hands.

"Looks good." He nodded as she placed a plate in front of him.

"I don't know how you did it." She sat across from him. "I wasn't going to cook anything at all. Here I prepared a full dinner." She twirled some spaghetti around the tines of a fork before she took a bite.

"You did what made you happy. No explanation needed." Robert took a bite of his meal.

Philly watched him. As he chewed, he looked like he gave an approving head nod. She suppressed a smile and took a sip of red wine.

"Something does need explaining, though." He wiped his hands.

"What's that?" She held onto her wine glass.

"Philly."

"Yes?"

"No, your nickname. You don't go by Philippa?" He picked up his fork and took another bite. "You should go by your real name. It sounds better."

"Only you and my mother agree on that." She shook her head. "I was named after my father, and even he calls me Philly. With three boys, my parents thought they were going to have a fourth. Surprise." She raised her hands to illustrate her parents' surprise reaction. "For as long as I can remember, everyone has called me Philly for short."

"People should call you Philippa."

"And it's a good thing the world doesn't revolve around you." She took a healthy bite of her spaghetti with homemade sauce and growled her approval.

"If it did, the only way I would call you Philly if it was a scene name with the understanding that I meant the version spelled F-I-L-L-Y. I wouldn't want you broken, though, like a horse." He gave her a salacious stare. "Definitely trainable."

She swallowed and had to take a drink of her water before she spoke. "I don't know how to take that. Most women would be offended by the idea of getting trained by a man."

He pointed his fork at her. "But not you because you understand what I mean."

She shook her head. "I don't." She dropped her gaze back down to her plate. "I don't know if I want to understand."

For not feeling like cooking, the meal turned out great. She would have to rely on this starchy, heavy dinner to help her sleep. Trying to prove her worth to Robert drained her of her energy to do much more than eat.

"My family and I had a discussion about you before I came over here." Robert kept his stare on her.

"No wonder my ears were burning." When she noticed his confused, puppy-dog expression complete with a cocked head, she clarified her statement. "It's a saying in America. If you say your ears are burning, it means someone is talking about you out of earshot."

"Interesting." He nodded.

"What was discussed?"

"My father agreed to let you stay on to help plan the wedding." Robert didn't seem happy about that decision.

"Great. I have my clients' blessing and now the blessing of the king. What an honor." She did mean that. "Kind of wished I could have made it over to dinner to meet him."

"You'll see him in the morning for breakfast." Robert hovered his fork over his meal. "You are joining us for breakfast, right?"

Philly nodded. "Of course. Nine—"

"Eight."

"I mean eight o'clock. My meeting with Helene and Lucian is at nine." Philly finished off her meal and hoped this would be the end of their conversation.

"You will be working with Edith."

Philly's heartbeat slowed a little. She wouldn't have to split her earnings, but the fact that she would have assistance on this very important job stung her a little. "Not a problem. I think that's a great idea. Have someone from your country to represent Lucian working along with someone from America to represent Helene. Seems fair." She hoped her statement and smile swayed his thoughts.

His scowl showed it didn't. "The other thing we discussed was the fact that if you make three mistakes, you will be dismissed of your duties." He took another bite of his dinner. "Same applies to Edith. This event is too important to have any errors."

"I get that. I won't do anything to embarrass the couple or the family." She stood and took her plate to the sink.

"You don't have to wash those. Someone will be by in the morning to attend to them and any laundry you may have."

Philly faced the sink, keeping her back to him. "Just like unpacking my luggage." She peered over her shoulder. "Do any of you do real work, get your hands dirty?" She snickered.

"I did come over here when I thought your life was in danger." He rested his hands on the counter.

Philly stared down at her hands in the sink. "I don't mind cleaning up after myself. Hard work won't kill me."

She started washing the items she used to make dinner. After rinsing off the pot, she looked for a dish towel to dry it. When Philly didn't see it on one side, she checked the other and found Robert standing next to her with the towel in his hand.

Philly extended her hand to accept the towel when he surprised her by taking the pot from her hand and drying it. She didn't question his actions. She continued washing each dish and utensil while Robert remained on drying duty.

"You said you wanted to talk." Philly glanced at him. "Now is a great time considering my free time will be cut short."

"Back when we used to hang out, you, me, Lucian, and Helene, why did you agree to our arrangement?" While keeping his attention on her, Robert put away the utensils he dried.

"It was all so weird. I had never done anything like that before, especially not for a man I wasn't dating at the time." She shook her head.

"Why me then?"

She looked down and snickered. Then she held up two fingers. "Two reasons. You seemed safe."

Robert groaned.

"No. I don't mean in a bad way like you were boring." She handed him the last dish to dry. "I mean I knew I could trust you. I knew no matter what I said to you or whatever we would try, you wouldn't say anything to anyone. I thought you had a lot of integrity." She chuckled a little. "And maybe I thought you were a little cute."

He laughed. "Really?" He held up his hand and put his index finger and thumb a sliver apart. "Just a little?"

She reached up and spread his two digits just a hair apart. "Just a little."

"And the other reason?"

This confession would hurt, but she had to do it. "As a joke."

Robert looked as confused as when she had to explain the burning-ears saying.

"I thought it was funny and a little prudish of you when you didn't come swimming with us." She shrugged. "I even wondered if you were still a virgin."

"Really? I was eighteen at the time just like you. You thought I hadn't had sex before?" He braced his hands on the counter behind him.

"Actually, I didn't think you had seen a woman's naked body before." She watched him cock his head as he regarded her.

"If you found me attractive and you felt safe with me, why did you stop? If I'm remembering correctly, I thought you were having a great time."

She knew he would ask this. He had every right. Philly wouldn't sugarcoat the answer. "Everything we did got in my head. I wondered why I wanted to try this. I thought about what you must think about me. Then I beat myself up for wanting this for myself. Was I a deviant? Did I lack self-respect?"

"You feeling that way is my fault. As your Dominant, I should have—"

Philly held up her hand. "Please don't. I don't need the rules of what it is that you do."

"Because you're scared to try it again?" His voice lowered.

Her knees shook for some reason. "Because I don't need it." She needed to tell her body that.

"Are you sure about that?" He leaned back against the counter as he regarded her.

"As sure as I know you don't want it either." She peered out of the kitchen to the stairwell. "You have a whole room full of your past that you want to remain hidden. You're no different than me. You just have a lot more to hide."

"I have a different life and a different responsibility." He crossed his arms over his chest.

Damn. Even in a simple sweater and jeans, Robert still looked good.

"You managed to hide yourself behind your family and your royal history to shut yourself off from people. I'm surprised you asked me about my name." She adopted the same stance he did. "The last thing I ever want for myself is to be someone's dirty little secret."

"Keeping what we did confidential was agreed upon by both of us, not just me." Robert remained still.

Philly's shoulders relaxed. "But you managed to take over. You seemed so together for being my age. Back then and now, you are very definitive on what you want, which I'm sure makes you great at things you do on your fetish side."

"But it wasn't enough."

She shook her head. "I was missing that personal connection. Doing things on my own became stale."

Robert peered up in the direction of the bedroom where she would be staying. "Doesn't say much for your plans for this evening, does it?"

Silence hung between them for a moment while she digested their long, overdue conversation.

"Looks like I didn't die after all." He hung the towel on the oven door handle.

"You didn't have to do that. I know it's not the type of thing you all do." She dried her hands and headed toward the front door to give him the hint that he should leave.

"You don't really know me." He followed her to the front door.

Philly started to open her mouth to say the same thing when he stopped her.

"I know. I don't really know you, either. Not the real you, although I think I got close." He walked into the living room and sat in an oversized chair while Philly occupied the couch across from him.

"So now what?" Philly curled her legs up on the couch, which grabbed Robert's attention.

"Now you need to tell me what it is that you want." He leaned forward as though what she would admit would be life changing.

"I want to do this job, get more clients, and live comfortably on my own without anyone's help." To prove her point, she kept her stare on his eyes without wavering.

Robert nodded. "That's great. What about on your personal side?"

"You first. I feel like I'm revealing a lot about myself." She snickered. "It's just like the call. I'm all exposed and you're protected."

He held his hands up. "I have my responsibilities here. Our

traditions dictate that, now, as the next in line to being king, I should marry another royal."

"Oh." Philly ran her hand over the plush arm of the couch. The soft fabric tickled her palm. "Lucian didn't choose a princess to marry."

Robert snickered. "I'm sure you can tell that Lucian marches to a different beat than the rest of the family."

"So do you. You can't call yourself a typical royal with what you like to do." She pointed up toward the room.

"Liked. Past tense." Robert shook his head. "Old me."

"You wouldn't want to do it again?" Philly didn't know why she even broached the question, but the idea of him abandoning the wild, unexpected side of him had her wondering if her departure had anything to do with his decision. "How did you get started in, um—"

"BDSM. Let's be adult about this and put a label on what it is we're talking about here." He pushed his sleeves up his arms as much as he could, like this conversation made him warm.

Philly started to feel a rise in her temperature for a different reason. "Fine. How did you get started in BDSM?"

"It wasn't from my brother, if you're curious about that. I wanted control of my life." He peered down for a moment before he continued talking. "Shortly after I was born, my mother passed away suddenly. Because the press only knew that the last time my mother was in the hospital was to have me, they linked her sudden death because of complications from having me." He shook his head. "Far from the truth, according to my father, but I took that in. The unkind press and a few online trolls dubbed me as *Queen Killer*."

Philly gasped and covered her mouth. People could be so cruel, especially to a child. "How terrible."

"When I got older, the press dubbed me as Prince Rob, meaning I robbed the people of their queen. My father kept me sheltered from that kind of news as much as he could. But it stuck with me." He wiped his hands over his thighs. "I thought if I could have some control, I would feel better and I could make others feel good." He peered at her. "Did you feel good during our conversation years ago?"

She opened her mouth to answer and found herself tongue-tied for the first time. Philly took a deep breath. "It felt sexy to expose myself like that to you. I can't do something like that again. I was a reckless eighteen-year old." She pointed at him. "So were you. You could have had a room full of boys looking at me, and I could have run to the press and exposed you."

"But I didn't, and I knew you wouldn't." He rested his elbows on his knees as he leaned forward. "I agree with you on one thing. We did a lot of things wrong back then. But we're older now. Wiser." He scanned her from head to toe. "Single. We could—"

"I am exhausted." She stood. "I think it's time for you to go. Call your royal Uber or whatever your car service is called. I'll see you in the morning."

"We aren't done talking." Robert remained seated.

"I'm done. I don't need to hear anything else you have to say." She shook her head.

"I have a proposition for you."

She chuckled. "I've heard this before. Last time I was naked and masturbating in front of you. I'm not doing anything like that again."

"Please sit." He pointed to the couch where she sat before.

"Please call your driver and go. I'm really tired and I—"

"Sit. Now." He gave her that same stare that had her locking doors in her parents' house and stripping out of her clothes.

She grumbled. "This is ridiculous." Then she sat down. "Call your driver and I'll listen."

Robert removed his phone from his pocket and punched a couple of keys on the screen before he returned the device to its original resting place. "Done. He should be here in fifteen minutes."

"What are you proposing?" Philly wouldn't agree to anything. She barely liked the idea that she had been placed on some three strikes, probationary period with the family. At least one mistake wouldn't get her ejected.

"You need to have a better understanding of Lesilitho and our culture. I can help you with that."

Philly's stomach fluttered a little thinking about Robert being her private teacher. "Really?"

"Yes. I can have a tutor come over each day to give you our history." Robert gave her a polite smile like his offer had pleased her.

The fluttering stopped. "A tutor? Of course. Here I thought maybe *you* would show me how much you know about your country to give me the tour."

"I have my own ceremony coming up to prepare for." Robert stood. "By the way, if someone else comes over, you may want to clean up a bit. I mean in the bedroom."

Philly thought about what he must have meant, but then it hit her. "I didn't expect anyone to go in the bedroom, but I'm not ashamed of having a vibrator and being able to take care of my own needs. You should know that already."

She watched Robert blinking at her statement.

"Did you think I would be embarrassed? I'm a grown woman. Everyone does it." Her eyes widened and she put her hand to her chest. "Oh, God. Do you have some literal handmaiden to take care of you?" Philly peered down.

Holy shit. Did she see a distinct outline of his cock through his jeans? If so, he definitely had a reason to carry the swagger he had. She had to get him out of the house. Now.

"I distinctly recall how you handled yourself." Robert moved in closer to her. "I don't remember you using a toy though." He held one of her hands and brought it up to his face. "Just your hands." He kissed the back of it. "Tell me. What would you have imagined while you used your toy?"

This first touch from Robert made her head feel light. The strength of his hand contrasted with its softness. She wanted him to touch her all over. How would his hand feel on her bare flesh?

Damn it. Why did her mind go there with him?

She shook her head. "Don't do this." She attempted to pull her hand away from him.

"Do what?" Robert tightened his grip.

"You. Me." She waved her free hand between the two of them. "Continuing the joke."

"The joke was only on your end. I was serious with my actions and intent." He moved in closer to her. "I've learned a lot over the years. I have another proposal for you."

Philly pulled her hand out of his grip. "What? You want me to go to some BDSM club and get trained by someone else just like I have to learn about your country from some stranger? No thanks."

"No. Let's pick up where we left off, but this time in person." Robert sounded so sure about this unorthodox plan.

Chapter Seven

"Are you crazy?" Philly darted to the door to make sure Robert left the house.

"I said the most rational idea here." He caught up with her and stood between her and the door as though preventing her from opening it. "Listen. Back then when you and I played, I had no idea what to do or how to be."

"And now you're all evolved?" She glared at him, hoping at some point he would get the message that doing something physical would be a mistake. A good mistake. A sexy one. Nonetheless, a mistake overall.

"Better. I'm trained." When Philly started to turn away, he held onto her shoulders. "Look, one of the main basics of a good BDSM relationship is that there's trust. You said even back then when you didn't know what to call what we did, you trusted me, right?"

She sighed hard. "Sure, but I also used to believe in Santa Claus and the Easter Bunny."

"I'm real. You can still trust me because you know what's at stake."

She regarded him for a moment while she let his words sink into her thoughts. "How do you know you can trust me?"

Robert released her. "After all these years, you haven't said anything to anyone about what we did. You have a business you want to start and grow. Outing your client isn't the best way to do that. Plus, tomorrow, our staff will have you sign a non-disclosure agreement. What we do here will be a part of that agreement." She started to open her mouth to contest what he said, when he concluded his thought. "What we do will not be documented in the paperwork, but implied that everything you see and experience while on palace grounds will not be shared with anyone else."

She took a step back. "Why? You just said that you are going to trash all that stuff in the room. Now all the sudden you have a need to use the toys and you want to use them on me?"

He nodded. "I realized as we talked, there are aspects of the lifestyle that can benefit us both."

"How?" She couldn't wait to hear this.

"You have put a lot on your plate." He held up his hand and ticked off items on each finger. "Starting a new business from nothing, doing this on your own, trying to put on a high-profile event."

"Don't forget the part where I'll have my work scrutinized by a micromanaging egomaniac." Philly cocked her head.

Robert's back stiffened. "The point is, you're going to have a lot on your shoulders and will have to make a lot of decisions. At the end of the day, I can take all those pressures off you. I'll dominate you, make all the decisions for you, make you feel something other than stressed. All you have to do is exactly what you do now, which is to be blunt and brutally honest. That's something we didn't have at the end of our phone conversation."

"What do you mean by that?" She felt heat rising to her chest and her face.

"Something in what I did to you triggered you somehow. You should have shared that with me. We can talk about that more before we play so I can keep you safe." In a move that surprised Philly, Robert reached forward and brushed his thumb over her cheek.

Philly remained still, melting under his touch as he brought his hand down and brushed his thumb over her bottom lip.

She snapped out of feeling and backed away from him. "You said that this arrangement will be beneficial to both of us. What do you get out of it?"

Robert pulled his hand back. "Control. I can feel like what I do can make someone feel good."

"You can do that through sex." Philly sauntered around him to get to the door. "Is that what all this is about? You caught sight of my vibrator and think I'm some easy lay?"

He shook his head. "No. BDSM is sensual and it can be sexy, and you might achieve an orgasm through play, if I allow it. But what I'm asking is to play with your body, push you to your physical limits to show you that you can withstand anything."

"I know that." She grabbed the door handle. "You think I need you to show me how strong and tough I am?"

Robert got in close to her. "I know you're tough. I know you're strong. I know you have opinions. I also know that you deserve a break."

This arrangement sounded too good to be true…for him. Philly still couldn't wrap her mind around the fact that she would be bowing down to a man who already thought he walked on water. Then he made that confession about what he thought of himself after his mother passed. She couldn't imagine carrying a burden like that for over twenty years. No wonder the man became a control freak.

Speaking of which, Robert has wanted her to leave since she got there. This tactic might be a ploy to expose her and get her out of there faster. Philly couldn't be foolish about her decisions.

"I appreciate the offer, as unusual as it is. However, I'm going to have to pass." She started to open the door, but he placed a hand on top of hers to stop her.

"Let me understand you. As a joke, you tried to make me uncomfortable with the idea of your nudity or maybe you thought I would be giddy that a beautiful woman gave me her number."

Philly blinked. "You think I'm beautiful?"

Robert didn't answer her. "And when I take control of the conversation and pushed you out of your comfort zone so that you did something that made you feel good, according to you, you don't want to take advantage of that?"

"Because I fear that the one who will be taken advantage of if I accept this arrangement is me." She didn't bother to turn her head when she heard the crunch of the tires of the car picking up Robert sound outside the door. "If I say yes to this, what's going to stop you from running to your father and saying, 'See. I told you she's not right for the job'?"

"Because then I would have to admit what I offered to you, and I'm not going to do that." He waved his hand between the two of them. "Whatever it is that we do will be our business. I wouldn't blackmail you or hold it against you. The three-strikes stipulation would only apply to the wedding planning. I'll come up with other punishments for the other deal, that's if you accept it."

A knock sounded on the door that broke up the crackling electric tension sizzling between them. The intrusion allowed Philly to finally open the door.

The same driver who had dropped off Robert stood on the front step. "Are you ready, sir?"

"Give me one moment, please." Robert closed the door on him as the driver headed back to the car. "I will allow you some time to think about this offer." He raised his hands in the air to show a peaceful gesture. "No strings attached. Except in a BDSM sense, we will not be committed to each other. I will keep what we do as a secret, and I would expect you to do the same."

"And no sex will be involved?" Philly had to be sure on Robert's expectations even though she had no plans on accepting the offer.

"No sex." He held out his hand. "Shake on it?"

Philly dropped her gaze at that large hand that could either send her body over the pleasure stratosphere or make her crumble in pain and regret. "Like I said, I'll think about this and let you know, although I don't see me getting involved in something like this with someone like you."

Robert lowered his hand. "And what is that supposed to mean?"

"I have had my heart broken by guys I used to date, but at least I knew what to expect from them. With you, I have no idea what you have up your sleeves, and I hate feeling used." She opened the door just enough that the cool, crisp autumn air flowed through the crack.

"I wouldn't use you. If anything, we would be using each other." He approached her. "The other difference is that we would be setting the rules so that no one would get emotionally hurt." He held her elbow. "I'll give you a week to make a decision. See you at breakfast."

Robert gave Philly a kiss on her cheek. When he moved over to her other cheek, he stopped midway, leaving his lips just above hers. Robert lowered his head and brought his lips closer to hers.

Beyond her power, Philly craned her head up and accepted him. The initial contact, their first kiss ever, buckled her knees until she had to grip his hand to keep steady.

Robert's firm lips vibrated against hers when he moaned. He slipped his free hand behind her back and pulled her forward, pressing her body against his. His solid frame felt good against her body. The kiss both made sense and had her questioning her actions. Despite being very vulnerable and exposing her full self to him, this kiss seemed more intimate than anything she had ever done with him or any other man.

Robert continued holding Philly's hand as he raised it and pressed it against the wall above her head. Philly slid her hand down his chest to below his belt. She heard him moan when she rubbed her hand up his impressive length. He already felt hard as soon as she touched him. The more she rubbed her hand up and down his shaft, the harder he became.

In an unexpected move, Robert turned her around so that she faced the wall. He pressed himself against her ass, sliding the length of him between her cheeks. The feeling alone had her pushing herself back against him.

Philly couldn't take much more of this. "I've always wanted to feel your touch." To illustrate her point, she reached back for his free hand and brought to the front of her body and placed it under her shirt. "Please touch me."

He nibbled the side of her neck before inching his hand up her stomach to cup her naked breast. Philly gasped at the connection.

"No bra. I like that." He massaged her tit first before twirling her nipple with his thumb. "Should I check to see if you're wearing panties?"

God, she wanted him to do just that and more. "Your driver."

"He can wait." Robert kicked the door to make sure it had been closed all the way. Then he moved his hand to her other breast to massage it.

"This feels so good." She continued rubbing herself against him. "Are you sure you can't spend the night?"

"I'm sure if I did, neither of us would get any sleep." He moved his hand down to below her hip bone but right above her slit. To encourage him to move down lower, she curved her hips upward.

"Robert." Her legs buckled. "Is this happening?"

In a teasing manner, he moved his hand back and forth over

millimeters, never getting too close to her pleasure zone. "This is real and long overdue. You smell so good and feel amazing. The real you is much better than watching you on video."

"You mean during our chat?" She put her hand on top of his that he had so close to her pussy.

She felt his head move up and down like he nodded.
"Masturbating to a recording of you earlier today didn't give me the real you. Maybe we should try being intimate if you don't want to do the BDS—"

Philly's body went cold as she pushed him back, which broke the hold he had on her wrist against the wall. "What?"

Robert's heavy-lidded gaze changed to something of a surprise. "What's wrong? I thought you wanted—"

"You kept a recording of me?"

To his credit, he didn't stop looking in her eyes. "I did. But I've never shown anyone else. I missed you, and—"

"You're a liar. You swore to me that you would never record me. Now I find out that you did and continued to keep it." She adjusted her clothing. "I'm not giving you three strikes. I'm done. Delete that recording and stay away from me." She opened her door. "You can take your offer and shove it. I knew you only wanted to do it because you wanted sex."

"I'm not going to apologize for desiring you, but sex was not my intent." Robert leaned forward like he wanted to kiss her other cheek like he should have done before.

"Oh, no." Philly moved away from him and opened the door wider. "You talk a good game about BDSM and how it has nothing to do with sex, and here you..." She stopped herself from replaying what she had enjoyed only moments before. If he had kept on going, she would have had him take her right there. "Have a good night."

"I'll see you in the morning." He walked out.

Philly closed and locked the door behind him. Royal or not, Philly encounter the same type of men no matter where she went. Robert crossed the line. It didn't matter the reason why he kept the video. She hoped he enjoyed it. If she could help it, she wouldn't be seeing him again.

Take that, Prince Robert.

Chapter Eight

Robert had had a hard night, in more ways than one. He had never encountered a woman like Philippa, one who spoke her mind freely and had no shame in her body or her sexuality.

That body. Even in what he assumed had constituted her sleep attire, he found her alluring. While cooking dinner for them last night, Philippa had reached up for something above, which lifted the back hem of her shirt and showed off her ample backside. Perfection.

When Philippa seemed unphased at Robert's discovery of her vibrator laying across the bed – his bed – he remembered how much his heart raced. Then when she looked him in the eyes and admitted she enjoyed masturbating, he felt his cock throb. Between her look and attitude and that amazing kiss, Robert had had a full erection and wanted to stroke himself to get relief by the time he had gotten to his car.

Who the hell was this Philippa Powell and how could he get her to trust him?

Robert barely got any sleep, and now in the morning, he paced in the dining room, awaiting his family and Philippa for breakfast. He blinked in a good way when he saw a very drowsy-looking Lucian schlep through the door, thankfully without Helene.

Robert stormed to his brother and grabbed his arm to pull him to a spot in the room away from the doorway where other attendees might overhear their conversation.

"Good morning to you, too." Lucian shrugged out of Robert's grip when they got by the window. "What gives with this rough treatment?" He leaned in closer. "You know I'm the one that likes to give."

"Who's Philippa?" Robert wasted no time in getting to the bottom of this mystery.

Lucian shrugged. "Have no idea. Is this someone who claims I've been with her or something?"

Robert shook his head. He growled, "Philly."

"Oh, that's her real name?" Lucian laughed. "I thought her parents had a sense of humor, like the Beckhams naming their child Brooklyn because that's where he was conceived." He started to walk away from Robert. "Are you having a stroke or something? You know her. She's been to this place several times before. Why are you acting weird?"

Robert pulled Lucian back and lowered his voice. "Did you bring her here to fuck with me?"

Lucian craned his head back. "Look. I know you like order and structure and you have this weird obsession with trying to plan our day, but believe me, we didn't hire her because we thought you would be pissed about it." He chuckled. "That is a nice consolation prize, though."

Robert shook his head. "No. You had said something to me about finding someone I could train who wouldn't be easy and who would—"

Lucian held up his hand and his expression went serious. "Wait. You think we brought Philly here for you to play with her?"

Robert glanced at the doorway to make sure no one had shown up, least of all Philippa. "Did you?"

His brother snorted. "You have got to be out of your fucking mind. Helene and I wouldn't have set up a friend like that. I've seen you play. You're a little intense. I think that's the real reason you've never really collared anyone."

Robert titled his head. "And why is that?"

"No one wants to be collared by you. You have the technique down, but you shut down all your emotions. A sub might as well use a vibrator to get off if she wanted to get pleasure from something mechanical."

At that statement, Robert gripped Lucian's arm again, but this time, held onto him with all his might. "Why did you say that?"

"What? What is going on with you this morning? You look both exhausted and excited at the same time." Lucian stared at his baby brother. "What happened to you last night when you ran out after the salad course?"

Robert exhaled before recounting the events of last night. "I noticed the security team scrambling last night during dinner. I asked them what was going on. There was a perimeter alarm at Moonwalk Manor where Philippa is staying."

"Jesus, man, just call her Philly like the rest of us. Do you have to be so proper when it comes to her?" Lucian attempted to peel away Robert's grip.

Robert sunk in harder and continued with his story. "I went with them."

"Why? That's security's job. What if the intruder had a gun?" This time Lucian managed to remove Robert's hand in order to cross his arms over his chest. "As the next in line to the throne, you have to be a bit more careful than that."

Robert hadn't considered that he had put his own life at risk, or the ramifications of his actions now. "I wasn't thinking about that."

"Obviously."

"I was concerned about our guest. I checked out her house." He cleared his throat. "I went upstairs to the main bedroom. She had a…" He peered around again.

"Come on, man. Say it. What? A dead body? A gun?" A

salacious expression crossed Lucian's face. "Another woman?"

Robert shook his head. "A vibrator."

Lucian laughed. "What? Are you twelve? So, she likes to diddle with her cookie. You don't rub one out every once in a while?"

"Yes, but I'm a guy, and—"

"You don't think women masturbate?" Lucian strolled over to a tray with pots of hot tea and coffee. He opted for coffee and poured himself a cup before the wait staff could arrive to do that job.

"No, I know they do." Truth be told, he enjoyed watching a woman pleasure herself in front of him. "When I mentioned something to her about maybe hiding her toys, she practically laughed in my face. She was unashamed about everything."

Lucian took a sip of his black coffee as he regarded his brother. "Don't you love American women?" He winked. "Honestly, I think you're making a big deal out of nothing. She was in the privacy of, well, your home, settling in for the night and doing something adult. Hearing about this makes me glad we hired her. She's open, uninhibited, and free. She's comfortable with herself and pulls no punches. You should be comforted by the fact that if you question her about anything, she'll be bluntly honest with you."

Lucian had a point, which ruffled Robert's feathers a bit. He hated when his brother made sense.

"You and Helene didn't bring her here to discipline her and distract me from your wedding?" Robert could honestly say in the short while Philippa had been there, she had distracted him.

This time Lucian got close to Robert and lowered his voice. "I'll tell you what you told me when Helene, Ginny, and I went to the States when everything was going down with the other country. Don't. Fuck. With. Her. I like her. I want her to do a great job for our wedding. It's important to Helene, which means it's important to me.

If you fuck with her and scare her off, I will never forgive you, and I hope to God that she runs to the press and tells the world that you're a Dom."

"That's a fucked-up thing to say." Robert crossed his arms over his chest.

"You would think that it would be fucked up if everyone knew you like BDSM. And you would deserve for your cover to be blown if you approach her about BDSM play and she bolts because of it. Leave her alone. Find your fun somewhere else." Lucian put his hand on Robert's shoulder. "It's a shame, though. The first woman who has got you interested in play is the one woman you can't touch."

At that moment, Philippa strolled through the door looking oddly elegant for breakfast at eight o'clock in the morning. She wore a simple, blue, long-sleeve dress with high heels that matched her dark skin tone, making her legs look a mile long despite being hidden under a dress that went down just below her knees.

She kept her makeup simple except the top of her cheekbones looked sun-kissed the way it shimmered, and a nude lip color covered her full lips. Her eyes, though, got him every time he looked her way. So big and expressive.

"Good morning, Lucian." She approached him and gave him a hug, a feat considering Lucian still had a coffee cup in his hand.

He managed it by only hugging her with one arm and keeping the other one far from her to keep from spilling on her.

Philippa turned to Robert and presented him with a simple but professional smile. She held up her hand to him. "Prince Robert."

He accepted her hand and his thoughts immediately went to visions of imagining her gripping her breast in one hand while delving in and out of her pussy with that pink vibrator he saw with her other. "Good morning, Philippa." He watched her shiver when he mentioned her given name.

"Whenever I hear my name like that, I think that I'm in trouble." She continued shaking his hand.

"You might be." At least, Robert knew he had problems ahead with her. "And I thought we had established that you can call me Robert."

She pulled her hand back. "I wasn't sure. I felt like some things had changed between us." She turned to the table and sat down in a chair at the end, but not at the head of the table.

Robert cleared his throat, which snagged her attention.

"What?" She removed the napkin from beside the plate and placed it over her lap.

"There's an order. Father sits at the head of the table. His sons flank him. Lucian sits there." Robert pointed to the chair opposite from her. "Therefore, you are in my seat."

Instead of springing to her feet to give up the spot, she smiled. She said nothing as she crossed her legs and stared at him.

Robert glared at her. In a play setting, this bratty move would garner her a swift spanking. Before he could admonish her, Clive walked in with Helene by his side.

"A new guest at the table." Clive looked at Philippa and smiled. "Are you Helene's friend, the one who's supposed to be helping to plan the wedding?"

Philippa stood. "I am. We have met before several years ago. Call me Philly." She extended her hand.

"Call me Clive." He shook her hand. "You do look familiar."

"I only came here a few summers, and I hung out with Helene and her family." Philippa looked over at Helene.

"Father. Philippa is an employee of Baldington." Robert gripped the back of the chair next to the seat he should have occupied. He struggled not to notice Philippa's rounded ass under that dress that sculpted her body. "Protocol dictates that she should call you King Clive."

"In public." He cut his eyes at his son. "In the sanctity of my own home, we can drop the pretenses and be civil."

"Practically family." Helene embraced Philippa and gave her a kiss on the cheek before taking her place next to Lucian. "She knows all my secrets."

"Almost all of them." Philippa winked at her friend before sitting back down in the same spot.

Flames ignited Robert's body as he watched this force of nature take over the structure he had grown to appreciate.

Clive volleyed his attention between her and Robert. "A new order. I like this. It allows me to get to know other people better who come to the house." He looked squarely at Robert. "Son, take a seat."

Robert did so next to Philippa. As he draped the napkin over his lap, he leaned over to her and whispered, "Strike one."

Let the games begin.

* * * * *

Great. Philly thought if she dressed the part and came to breakfast ready to get to work that Prince Pompous would have nothing to complain about regarding her involvement with the planning of the wedding. Plus, after seeing him last night in his jeans and being so protective and that damn kiss, she had a lot of inspiration to play with herself, not to exhaust herself, but to truly pleasure herself as she thought of Robert and his big hands. Then he talked.

Must he always be so arrogant and demanding? Why did she allow that kiss and more? She shifted in her chair when she thought about Robert's hand on her breast and where he had his other hand. As she straightened out the napkin draped across her lap, she purposely pressed against that same spot. Then she glanced to the side at Robert and caught him looking at her. The same fluttery feeling in her belly from last night returned.

"Philly, please tell me about yourself. What's your background?" Clive stopped eating his meal to listen to her.

She liked that trait. Philly sobered to the situation and plastered a smile on her face. "I was born and raised in Virginia Beach."

"Oh, that sounds nice. That is our sister city." Clive glanced at Lucian. "Must be nice to go to the beach whenever you want." He took a sip of his tea.

Philly shook her head. "Virginia Beach is a big place. Not all of us live by the water. I lived in the city, not that close to the beach at all. But I enjoyed where I grew up. I was the only girl with three brothers, and I was the youngest. I tried so hard to hang out with them. Sometimes they would let me tag along, especially when they realized how fast I was. When we played football in the neighborhood, I was always picked to run with the ball. No one could catch me."

Clive chuckled. "An athlete. Makes you competitive. I like that. And where did you attend college?"

"I did a year at Oxford with Helene before I left it and worked full-time at the Cavalier." When Philly noticed the silence at the table, she looked over at Clive.

"You didn't earn your degree?" He wrinkled his forehead.

She shook her head. "No. I had to put my own self through school. By the time it was time for me to go, my parents ran out of money to help me after they put my brothers through school. I got a grant for my first year. After that, it was on me, and I didn't have the funds. I had always planned on going back, but I work too many hours to make the time."

"Interesting. Helene has her degree. I assumed that her friends would be like her." Clive picked up his fork to resume eating.

"Helene is special. I certainly could have gotten a student loan, but I didn't want to be in debt for the rest of my life. I'll eventually get back to school. But the great thing about me not finishing is that I have a ton of work experience that I can use for this assignment." Philly smiled at her friend who sat across the table from her and winked.

Quincy appeared at the entryway into the dining room. "A guest has arrived. Edith Throckmorton is here."

With a name like Edith Throckmorton, Philly knew this woman had to be the female version of Robert. She matched that assumption apart from her age. The elderly woman with white hair wore a black skirt that brushed the tops of her feet that were outfitted with black, heavy-looking orthopedic shoes. A black cardigan covered the crisp, white shirt she wore. She carried her coat in the crook of her arm.

"Good morning." Even Edith's voice came off as haughty. "I apologize for being late."

"Mrs. Throckmorton, you were scheduled to be here at nine. You're fifteen minutes early." Robert placed his napkin on the table and stood.

"That's late in my book. I normally like to arrive thirty minutes before any appointment." She focused her dark eyes on Philly. "I don't think we've had the pleasure."

Philly stood and smoothed her hands down her dress. "I'm Philly Powell. If you are the Edith I've been hearing about, you and I will be working together to arrange Helene and Lucian's wedding."

The gasped Edith emitted echoed off the walls.

Oh, no. Not another one who didn't want Philly to be there.

"Work with someone? I hadn't been told that I would have a partner. Has my performance in the past been unsatisfactory?" Edith put her hand to her chest, which got Quincy and Robert to assist her to a chair at the table.

"Your work has been exemplary." Lucian smiled. "Helene and I wanted both our sides represented in our wedding. The best way to do that would be to pair you with someone from the States."

Philly poured a glass of water and placed it in front of Edith. "I do look forward to collaborating with you, Edith."

"Call me Mrs. Throckmorton." She cut her eyes at her as she lifted the glass of water and took a sip.

Philly hid her balled hands behind her back and refused to smile at Edith's request. "I want to make sure this wedding is what Lucian and Helene want. I've already talked to them about their vision." She turned around to look at Robert. Was he looking at her ass before he looked up? "Robert has arranged for me to sit with a tutor to learn more about Lesilitho and the culture here."

The same young woman who walked Philly into the palace when she had arrived stood at the entryway of the dining room. "A professor from our local university is here."

Damn. Robert had been serious about getting that tutor. Philly cursed under her breath and hoped Robert hadn't heard her.

"He's early. Edith and Philippa are supposed to meet with Lucian and Helene after breakfast." Robert threw his napkin on the table.

The attendant clutched her tablet to her chest. "He's fine waiting an hour for his appointment. He needs time to set up. I believe there's a PowerPoint presentation involved."

"I guess that's my cue. I'm going to go freshen up a bit before I start if that's okay." Philly pushed her chair under the table.

Robert looked beyond Philly to address the palace employee. "Please have him go to the library."

"Helen and Lucian, I just need five minutes. Please." Before anything else could be said, Philly rushed out of the room to…where? After all the times she had been there and places she had gone in the house, she didn't know where to go to now.

Now she felt her life had turned to shambles. She controlled nothing, not even her own thoughts. Professors, library, lessons. Philly felt like she had been transported back to school again.

"Hey, hey. Wait up."

The sound of her friend's voice behind her got Philly to stop in her tracks. Helene raced up to her and held Philly's shoulders.

"What's going on with you? You seem upset." Helene rubbed her thumbs over Philly's shoulders.

"I am. I'm pissed." If Helene hadn't been holding Philly's shoulders, she would have been pacing the floor.

"Why?"

Philly jutted her thumb over her shoulder. "First of all, did you hear that woman in there? 'Call me Mrs. Throckmorton.' I'll call her an ambulance if she thinks I'm going to be her little helper. And Clive seemed so disgusted I didn't finish college."

Helene shook her head. "He's more liberal thinking than you think. I think it surprised him because he knows me and my family and he expects everyone I know to be just like me." She put her hand to Philly's cheek. "But like you said about me, you are also special. You are going to do great things, and I don't mean with just my wedding either."

"I want to do the best job, and not because it's you. This could launch my business. I mean, you know my struggles." Philly wouldn't be admitting any of that to Clive and his family, especially

Robert. "Here I thought I was done with school and the teachers who thought I wouldn't amount to anything. Now I have to go through that again to, what? Prove myself? And to who? Robert?" She snickered.

"Robert has his own way about him, but he means well." Helene held Philly's hands.

Philly couldn't hold back her emotions or her words. "Robert and I kissed last night."

Helene peered behind herself as though checking to see if anyone else could hear their conversation. "You did?"

Philly nodded. "After dinner when he was headed back here. He kissed me on my cheek to say goodbye and it happened."

"Did you like it?"

All at once, Philly's body went hot all over. "He is a good kisser." She would leave his skilled hands out of the conversation. "But as you can see this morning, none of that matters. He still wants me gone."

Helene blinked. "You didn't kiss him to secure this job, right?"

Philly puffed air between her lips. "Of course not. I would do a lot of things for work, but I'm not a trick. I think it was some old-school crush rearing its head for the moment." She waved her hand in the air. "I think we both got it out of our systems. Now I can get to work."

Even with one strike now against her. Who knew Robert would have been so bent out of shape over a damn chair? Made her wonder what he would be like as a Dom and what his punishments would be like. Philly shivered.

"You're not going to say what else happened last night?" Helene worried her brows as she regarded her friend.

To make her point clear, Philly shook her head. "No. It's done.

He's got his own agenda and I have mine."

"I understand. I know how focused you can get when you're into a job. Wouldn't be good to start anything if you can't give yourself fully into it, and I don't see you as someone who would string anyone along." Helene smiled. "If anything, you now know that Robert finds you appealing on some level and is not completely against you." Helene patted Philly's shoulder. "Even if he did, this is Lucian's and my wedding. Whenever you're ready, we can meet with you and Edith on the details, okay?"

Philly nodded. Helene had made some great points, but Philly knew better. She knew that Robert saw their wedding as a reflection of him and their country. After his confession about the video, she knew she couldn't trust him.

Philly exhaled. "If I get fired from this job—"

"You won't."

"If I do, I'll still show up to the wedding. But as soon as you say, 'I do' and the wedding cake is cut, I'm out of here. I thought it would be so neat to be in a new place and be around royalty. You and Lucian are the only things making this experience tolerable." Philly wouldn't quit, and she damn sure wouldn't cry about this. That didn't mean she had to enjoy it.

After only being there a couple of days, she couldn't imagine what the next couple of months would hold in store for her.

Philly looked down the hallway and saw Lucian with Edith. The older woman had her arm wrapped around his, and he led her to another room.

"We'll be in Father's office waiting for you two." Lucian winked at Helene.

"Let me get my purse and tablet. I'll see you there." Philly gave a quick hug to her friend before going back to the coat closet where she saw Helene's father put her jacket and purse. She retrieved her belongings and turned around to find Robert behind her.

With her head held high, she threw her purse strap over her shoulder and started to walk by him. Robert stood in her path to stop her. When she did, he took a measured step to the side and sidled up next to her.

He crouched down slightly to get down by her ear. "I didn't mean to make you uncomfortable with the kiss last night."

She swallowed. "And your hands?"

"Let me be clear. I'm apologizing if my actions caused you distress. Did it?" He lowered his voice and the sound rumbled through here body.

Philly shook her head. "No."

"Good. Because I liked the kiss and definitely liked what I touched." He released a long sigh. "One strike and one week. Hope you make your decision before time is up." He started to walk away.

"I have. I told you. I don't want to—"

"Excuse me." Edith's harsh tone cut through the room. "We have royalty waiting."

Did the woman not see that Philly stood there with a royal herself? Bitch.

Instead of finishing her conversation with Robert, Philly went to the office where Edith had herself situated at the head of a small table in Clive's office. King Arthur had it right. Round tables made everyone equal. To level the playing field, Philly sat at the other end, which must have impressed Helene. Her friend gave her a wink and a thumbs up sign out of sight of Edith the Enforcer.

The meeting went as expected with the discussions centered on the font sizes on announcements, place settings, and even the menu. Edith decided she would take care of the guest list, while Philly asserted herself in the menu and entertainment department. Philly knew she would work well with Ginny to get a great menu together where Ginny could relax at her daughter's wedding without worrying about her kitchen staff. Philly had been around Helene and Lucian enough to know their taste in music.

"I think we have the major items down." Edith closed her flowered spiral notebook and put her pen into her multi-pocketed white purse.

"I still have questions that need to be answered." Philly faced the couple. "Are there any special songs or musicians you want at the wedding or reception?"

Edith gasped. "My child, we have the royal orchestra."

Philly cut her eyes at her. "Unless your name is either Philip or Mary Powell, I am not your child. Call me Philly, Philippa, or Ms. Powell. Don't think because I'm old enough to be your granddaughter that it gives you the right to speak to me like I'm not worthy."

Edith pursed her lips while her face turned several shades of red.

"Have a drink of water." Philly pointed to a crystal pitcher of water on a tray with matching glasses. "As I was saying, musicians or songs."

Helene looked at Lucian and shared a sweet smile. "Actually, we do. Two classic songs that we would like played and sung by this group we found on YouTube."

"Is this a joke?" Edith put her hand to her chest.

Lucian looked at his watch. "Mrs. Throckmorton, it's about time for this appointment to end." He stood. "Let me get your coat and walk you to the door."

Edith volleyed her gaze between Lucian and the two other women. "I certainly will go and speak to King Clive about this."

"Wonderful. If he's accepting appointments now, you may be able to catch him. Make sure you see Quincy, his personal butler and Helene's father, to make that appointment." Lucian beamed as he walked the mature woman out of the room.

Philly released her breath. "That woman is not going to be happy until she sees me gone and you walking down the aisle in a very modest dress."

Helene shook her head. "She'll be disappointed on both fronts."

"So, what are the songs?" Philly prepared to type the names out on her tablet.

"The first is 'Baby, Obey Me.' It was originally sung by Dean Martin."

Philly chuckled. "A little on-the-nose, don't you think?"

Helene laughed. "That song was my pick for us. The other song is 'I Only Have Eyes For You' by The Flamingos."

"Wow. Yes, both songs are classics." Philly typed in both names.

"And there is this group out of Virginia Beach actually who sing contemporary songs in a classic way." Helene shared the name of the group. "If you can get them to do it, Lucian and I would love it."

"Sure. I'll have to do some research and see if we can get them here. If they're as good as you say they are, I'll have to make sure they sign an NDA before the wedding." Philly thought that it may be better to go back home to ask this group face-to-face rather than do it by email or conference call. The separation may do her some good.

Philly heard Helene's breath catch a little. Philly turned and saw Robert standing behind them. Guess privacy didn't exist there either.

"Your lesson is starting." Robert's low voice still sounded assertive.

Philly took a deep breath before she shoved her tablet in her purse. "Fine. Show me to the library." She wouldn't go down without a fight.

"Not that lesson." Robert did the unexpected and took her hand.

He led her to the front door where they walked by a very angry older man with wiry salt-and-pepper hair.

"I cancelled university classes to be here, and now I'm being dismissed? Why?"

Philly overheard the man yelling to Quincy at the top of his lungs. "What's going on?"

Robert brought her to a long, slick, black vehicle where a driver held open the back door for her. "Instead of getting a lesson from a historian, why not hear it from royalty?"

Philly put her hand on the car door as she stared at him.

"I'm going to teach you about Lesilitho. We're going to explore my country. I'll show you what's important to our family." He smiled, and it seemed genuine. "See. I do listen."

"But what about Edith and the lesson?" Philly pointed toward the palace.

"They'll be fine. And we can stop off at Moonwalk if you would like to change into something more comfortable and get your phone to take pictures or notes." He peered at the inside of the car. "Your chariot awaits."

Chapter Nine

Robert hated to admit any of his shortcomings. When he overheard Philippa telling Helene that her attempts to get him to like her had all failed, he really felt like an asshole.

After stopping off at Moonwalk, Philippa darted inside and changed into short boots, jeans, an oversized sweater along with a jacket. She shared that she planned on using her tablet to take pictures at different locations.

"Slow down." Robert tapped on the partition glass to alert the driver. Then he pointed to a row of tan-colored buildings with orange-tiled roofs and cathedral-like peaks on the corners. "Over five hundred years ago, this building was the original Baldington Palace."

Philippa stared at it through the tinted backseat window. "Really? Doesn't seem that regal at all."

"It wasn't. Not really. King Rufus, who would have been my great, great, great grandfather, commissioned to have the current Baldington Palace built. Now this structure here is used as a museum." Robert leaned in behind Philippa to get a better glimpse of the place.

"It's holding up great for being over five hundred years old." She turned her head too quickly and her face ended up directly in front of his.

Robert couldn't move. At his proximity, he felt her warm breath over his lips. It would have taken nothing for him to lean forward and kiss her again. Had he done that, he would have done more than feel her up.

Shit. He needed to stop thinking like that. He now struggled with what hat to wear: wedding organizer, Dominant, or lover.

"Sorry. Didn't know you were so close." She settled back into her seat.

"I was going to see if there was anything I needed to point out to you, like any special landmarks." He peered around the grounds where a few people milled around.

"We can get out and look." As soon as Philippa reached for the door handle, Robert placed his hand on top of hers.

"No."

"Why?"

He instructed the driver to keep going before he answered. "It wouldn't be safe. I don't have my full security detail with me."

She smiled.

"Why are you smiling like that?"

"I know that even without your guards, you would still protect me. I can't believe you came out with them to make sure I was okay. You didn't have to do that, and you did. Thank you." She nodded.

Robert's heart started to pound. "I didn't do anything any other man wouldn't have done in the same situation."

Philippa shook her head. "No. I can tell. You're different. You're a protector. You look out for your family. You look out for your country. You looked out for me, and you don't even like me."

"That's not true. I never said I didn't like you. I didn't like the idea of anyone else outside of our country planning this important wedding. I would have treated another person in your spot the same way." He needed her to understand his position and that his feelings had nothing to do with her.

"You're saying you do like me?" She cocked her head as she stared at him.

"I think I've shown that." Despite the intended hard posturing she presented, Robert found her adorable. "I think you're determined. I can tell you're stubborn. And you're passionate." He meant the last compliment to be about her work ethic.

From the way she softened her look and settled back into the car seat, he figured that she must have been thinking about the same thing that ran through his head now: That vibrator. Her tits. Her full lips. Suddenly the inside of the car felt stuffy. He tugged on the collar of his sweater.

"We've been doing a lot of driving around. Don't you want to stop and stretch your legs a little?" Philippa glanced at her phone. "It's past lunch time. I'm starving."

"We're a couple of hours away from Baldington." Robert wanted to show her all of Lesilitho, which meant taking her to the borders of other countries.

"Hours? How about we stop somewhere, and I go in to pick up something for us? No one knows who I am. I won't get hassled." She fished through her purse for her wallet.

"Absolutely not. I will not have a guest of mine fetching food for me." Robert gazed out of the side window at the places lining the road. Then he peered out the back window to see if they had been followed. "This place here. Stop here. We'll all go inside."

The driver pulled the car to the front. "I'll wait for you two here."

"No. We all go. I'm sure you're hungry, too, and you've been driving us all day." Robert adjusted in his seat to get ready to exit the car.

Truth be told, he did want to walk around for a little bit. Being so close to Philippa without being able to touch her started to wear on his nerves.

Inviting the driver wouldn't help him get closer to her, but he didn't want to appear like a total tyrant…not yet.

No. For once, Lucian had been right about one thing. If Philippa planned on working for Robert's family, he couldn't cross the line with her. In his head, Robert decided the line not to cross would be the sex one. He could dominate her regularly and be able to walk away. He'd done it before with play bottoms at other clubs.

The restaurant they stopped at had no inside dining space, but plenty of picnic tables around. The driver got out first and opened the back door on Robert's side. Robert moved over to the open door, and then he put his hand out to Philippa.

She waited before accepting it and sliding out of the car with him. Robert gave some directions to his driver before placing his hand at the small of Philippa's back to guide her to a table that didn't face the roadway as much.

"What did you tell him?" She sat down with her back to the road.

Robert sat across from her, facing the road and the driver at the order window. "I asked him to get some dishes that this country is known for. I'm assuming you are not a vegetarian. I noticed you ate some meat during breakfast."

"You watched me?" A sly smile creeped over her face.

"You were sitting between me and my father. Of course, I noticed." Although he liked Philippa's flirting game, he wouldn't fall so easily.

"Speaking of this morning, you told me I already had one strike. Is that true?" She reached into her purse and pulled a small bottle with a clear gel inside.

"Yes. You knew the rule and still broke it." Robert wouldn't waver on his stance.

She poured some of the gel into her hand and placed the bottle in front of him. When he hesitated to pick it up, she explained the contents. "It's hand sanitizer. Just thought you would want to use it before eating."

He smiled and put a bit of the vanilla-scented liquid in his hand. "Thank you." As he rubbed it in, he made an assessment. "You said I'm a protector. If that's the case, you're a nurturer. You want to make sure everyone is happy."

"That's from my years in the catering and hospitality industry." She started to put the bottle back in her purse and stopped when she must have remembered the third person in their party. She did retrieve her phone and looked somewhat relieved when she noticed something on it.

"I don't think smoothing down a person's hair is a requirement in event planning." He tapped his fingertips on the tabletop. "But appreciated."

"Give me one second." Philippa typed something on her phone before putting it back in her purse.

The driver dropped off three bottles of water before he returned to the service window again.

"Thank you for taking me out to see your country." Philippa gazed around the area, which did not look as noteworthy as other parts of his country. "I imagine you must have missed out on doing other things than just babysitting me."

"I did, but this is important, too." Robert saw two men stand in line to order and it made him keep his head down a bit more to hide his identity.

"Why is your brother's wedding so important to you?"

He gazed up. "His wedding will put a spotlight on our little country. If it's done right, we'll get more recognition, which means more interests, which can lead to more business association. Yes, we are royal and we're more of a figurehead family than a ruling one. But our presence is important to our country. This wedding can finally put us on the map. And now that I'll be a successor, people will be looking at me if the wedding is a success or failure."

"Oh, wow. I never thought about the domino effect." She shook her head.

"Yes, and the other result of me being next in line now is the number of interested women, and some men, who want to be by my side. It's crazy. I go from the invisible little brother to an eligible bachelor in a matter of seconds." Robert hated the extra attention.

As the younger brother with no real immediate stake to the throne, he could do as he wished, which included playing in exclusive clubs while keeping his identity a secret. Now everyone wanted a piece of him.

The driver brought two trays full of food. Although Robert loved Ginny's cooking, he couldn't get enough of Lesilitho's traditional dishes. Before diving in, he noticed the look on Philippa's face, like she wanted to figure out a puzzle.

"I don't recognize anything on this tray." She stared at all the food.

Robert pointed to on dish in a white-and-red container. "That is pickled cabbage, onions, and carrots. It's delicious. You should try it."

Philippa picked up a white plastic fork and let it hover over the food.

He pointed to another dish. "That over here is smothered fries. That's a beef gravy with mushroom." He spotted something else the driver bought that Robert truly loved. "Ah, my favorite." He picked up a fried, golden-colored disc. "This is fried cheese." He held it up to Philippa's mouth. "Open."

She sniffed it first, gazed at him, before she finally opened her mouth and took a bite. After a few chews, she smiled. "That is really good. Better than fried mozzarella sticks." She snagged the rest of the treat from his hand and devoured it.

"If you liked that, you'll enjoy the sausage."

She nearly choked on the water she had been sipping. "What?"

Robert pointed to a white paper plate that had three bacon-wrapped sausage links on it. He cut into one and, like the cheese, held it up to her mouth. "Try it."

Without hesitation this time, Philippa took a bite. "Wow. Sweet and savory."

He wanted to comment that her description matched her completely. The trio ate the dishes and talked about each one…until Robert heard a camera flash. He gazed up and saw a man and woman taking pictures of them eating.

"Let's get to the car." He got to his feet and held Philippa's hand as they headed to the vehicle.

The driver kept right up with them. He held the door open as they ducked into the back seat. Then he jumped into the driver's seat and pulled off quickly.

"Oh, wow. Does that happen a lot?" Philippa looked through the back window at the paparazzi.

"Only when I'm off palace grounds. Quite frankly, I'm surprised we were able to get through a full meal before they swarmed in." Robert opened the partition window. "Take Ms. Powell back to Moonwalk. We'll drop her off first before I go back to Baldington."

"Yes, sir."

Robert closed the partition and cloaked it so that the driver couldn't see or hear them. "It'll be a long drive back home. Get comfortable."

"You don't want to talk? I'm curious to know more about you." Her yawn said otherwise. "What happened with your last relationship?"

Robert couldn't look at Philippa. "That's a conversation for another time."

"Oh." She raised her phone in the air. "I was going to Google it, but Internet connection around the palace is terrible."

"Yes, the technical staff is working on it."

"What do you like to do for fun?"

Robert let the question linger longer than he should have. Philippa had been honest about the vibrator and just about everything she had been asked. Had they been alone, he would have told her about his love of rope play.

"I like playing tour guide." He smiled.

"Okay. I'll take that." Philippa leaned against the window. "Your country is beautiful."

"Thank you."

"Seeing everything gave me ideas for the wedding." Her speech sounded slurred, but Robert had assumed he had heard her the altered speech pattern because of the ride, hearing the gravelly road under the vehicle's tires and roar of the wind outside of the windows.

He blinked. "Ideas? Like what?"

Like that, Philippa had already fallen asleep. Yes, it would be a long ride home.

* * * * *

Philly felt the gentle rocking as she slept. When she felt the movement stop, she woke from her slumber only to find that she had curled up next to Robert and had her head on his chest and her hand on his muscled thigh.

"Holy crap. I'm so sorry." She jerked back from him.

Robert laughed a little. "No apologies necessary. You were

tired." He cleared his throat as the driver parked in front of Moonwalk Manor. "It felt good to have you against me…in a good way this time."

She looked out the side window. "Wow. We're already here." Philly stretched her arms over her head. "Want to come inside?" As though she needed to clarify, she immediately said, "For coffee or tea. Plus, we could talk more."

"I actually would like that." Like at the place they ate, when the door opened, Robert got out and then helped Philly by holding her hand.

"Thank you." She strolled up to the door.

"You can go back to Baldington. I'll ring if I need a car to take me back." Robert stood in the doorway.

"Are you spending the night here, sir?" The driver stood at the bottom of the steps.

"Like I said, I'll ring if I need the car. Good night." The sternness in his voice that he had used on Philly now returned.

"Yes, sir. Have a good evening." He bowed and went back to the car at the same time Robert closed and locked the door.

Philippa kept her back to the kitchen as she slowly crept backward to it. "It's a little chilly. Want some coffee?"

Robert did crave something rich and dark, but coffee wouldn't satisfy that need. "Sure. I'll put on a fire."

"Really? I would have thought you had people to do that." Philippa retrieved two mugs and selected two pods to make coffee.

"I do. As I have mentioned to you before, I am not feeble or incapable."

To prove his point, he loaded logs into the fireplace, made sure to open the damper, and started a fire by the time she came into the den area with two white mugs of coffee. Or was that hot chocolate? Robert smelled a distinct aroma of chocolate when she approached him.

"I should throw this in your face." She sneered as she handed him the mug. "I can't believe you kept the recording." She set her drink down before she took a seat by the fire. Then she removed her boots and curled her legs under her.

"I apologize for going back on my word. It's certainly not my shining moment as I pride myself on my integrity." He took a sip. The bitterness of the pitch-black liquid matched Philippa's steely demeanor. Definitely not chocolate. "If it means anything to you, when I got back to my room, I deleted the video."

"Even out of your recycle bin?" She glared at him.

Robert tried hard not to smile. "Yes."

"Immediately?"

He took another sip of his coffee. "No."

She groaned. "What? You had some pressing royal event you had to do?"

"No. I wanted to watch it again." Robert kept a tight hold of his mug, allowing the heat to warm his hand. "After kissing you and touching you, I found myself wanting more."

This time Philippa took a drink.

"I knew that if there was going to be any way to convince you to submit to me while you're here, I had to regain your trust. Deleting that video was the first step." He took another drink and set the mug down. "Thank you for the coffee."

"You're welcome."

"Not my favorite blend." He stared at her. "If you start training, you will learn what I like, how I like it, and how I like to be served." He relaxed back in the chair, not even flinching when he felt his phone vibrating in his pocket.

"And what is it that you like? To drink I mean." She removed her bulky sweater revealing a tank top with skinny straps underneath.

The way her nipples protruded against the white fabric, he knew she didn't wear a bra. Suddenly, Robert's temperature rose, and it had nothing to do with his proximity to the fireplace.

"Tea, of course. Call it a European thing. No sugar or cream." He wagged his finger slowly. Then his phone vibrated again.

As he watched Philippa licked her lips and lean forward, no way would he break his attention from her to see who disturbed him.

"And how do you like it served?" Her voice dipped into a soothing octave.

"To properly serve me, you need to be naked except for approved footwear."

"Approved meaning, what?" She put her elbow on her knee and rested her chin on the heel of her hand.

"High heels. Not too high. Just enough that it pumps up a woman's ass, like what you wore for our phone conversation." He shifted in his chair, causing the wood and leather seat to creak.

"The person would bring the cup to you and that's it?" She shrugged.

He shook his head slowly. "Of course not. You would walk in after I have taken my seat. You will walk slowly. You want my full attention." He put his hands side by side with his palms up like a platter. "You will have the mug in your hands like this." He pointed to the floor in front of himself. "You will kneel."

"And look down?"

"Of course not." He leaned forward. "You would serve me. I expect you to always look me in the eyes and remember who you serve."

She brought her legs down and crossed them. "Is that all?"

Robert cocked his lips to the side in a half smile, amused by the fact that she wanted to know more. She hadn't called him disgusting or demanded that he leave. "No. You would wait in your kneeling position until I have taken my first sip and establish that the beverage is satisfactory. If it is not, you will do it all over again until I am satisfied."

He noticed Philippa's breathing increased. "And you're so sure the person who will serve you will be me? In your description, you kept referring to me."

"Because you kept asking questions. When you ask questions about it, it stops being a mere curiosity and starts being a lesson." He patted his hands over his thighs. "Come to me."

Philippa paused before she stood. She took two steps towards him before she stopped. Robert cocked his head as he watched her. Had she changed her mind about all of this? Would she be asking him to leave?

Then she pulled her shirt from the waistband of her jeans and then over her head, exposing her naked breasts. She unfastened her jeans and shimmied out of them as well. Now in her panties and thick, wooly socks, she took another step toward him before she eventually slipped her panties down her legs.

She padded over to him and stood naked before him before she dropped down to her knees. Then she put her hands up in front of him, wordlessly requesting him to place the mug on her hands.

Robert picked up the ceramic cup and placed it on her hands. He noticed her hands shaking a little.

"Steady. Don't want you spilling this on your body." He swept his thumb down the side of her face.

"This was a lot easier than I thought." She smiled before she got a faraway look in her eyes.

He had to get her out of her head. "Are you saying you want to take this step?" He leaned close to her. "You can do this. *We* can do this." He accepted the mug from her hands and took a sip. "Last part." He placed the coffee on the small table next to him, leaned forward and gave her a quick peck on the lips. "You're smart. You're beautiful. You're assertive. I want you to want to do this."

She held his hand that rested on his lap. "Why me?"

"Why not you?"

Philippa took a deep breath before she made a confession. "I lied to your father earlier."

Robert almost pulled his hand back from her but waited. He had to hear her out first.

"I struggled all throughout school. I was always behind the other kids as far as schoolwork. My parents talked to my teachers. They all dismissed me as playing too much because I excelled at athletics. Luckily, my parents didn't believe that. They took me to the guidance counselor, who suggested I enrolled in a trade school." She snickered but must have noticed Robert's expression. "That's a school to learn blue-collar work like welding or plumbing." She shrugged. "No one thought I was smart. As a result, the boys in school thought dumb girls were easy. They preyed on me hard, so much so that I had to knee our school's quarterback in his nuts when he tried to jump on me in the girl's bathroom."

Robert squeezed Philippa's hand to show her support. He wished he could have been with her in high school to look out for her.

"It wasn't until I was a senior in high school that I found out I have dyslexia." She smiled. "I was kind of relieved to put a name on why things looked different in my head. I got with a tutor who helped me with some tricks to help me grasp concepts. I worked really,

really hard and managed to get into a great university." She dropped her gaze. "That first year was tough, and the professors made it clear that they would not be giving me additional help." She brought her gaze back up to Robert. "My parents could afford putting me through school. I dropped out because I felt overwhelmed. Since then, I have worked hard at everything I've done." This time she squeezed his hand. "I decided to start my own business because I believe in myself. I know I can make something of myself. I'm not asking for a handout. I just need a chance."

Robert moved his knees apart and scooted to the edge of his seat to get closer to her. "I didn't know about your issues."

"I told Helene when we attended school together for one year when she was a senior and I was a freshman. She helped me as much as she could. But once she left, I couldn't do it."

He held her shoulders. "Yes, you could have. I know that." He pointed to her, putting the tip of his finger to her chest. "You can do anything you put your mind to doing." He made her sit up taller. "You are one of the toughest women I know. That makes for a great submissive."

She laughed. "Isn't that an oxymoron?"

He shook his head. "When you say yes to this, I'll teach you the difference between the myths and the facts."

The buzzing from his phone vibrated in his pocket again. Robert cursed as he reached for it.

"What is it?" Philippa sat back and watched him.

"Someone keeps calling and sending me text messages." Robert looked at the calls and saw they came from the palace's new public relations director.

He went straight to his text messages and saw screenshot after screen shot of announcements about Lucian and Helene's wedding that came from Philippa's account.

"Shit!" He bolted to his feet, swung his leg over her head and move away from her.

"What's wrong?" She stood but didn't cover her body.

In another time, he would have admired her naked form and done more. His full concentration went to this monstrous mistake.

Robert flipped his phone around to her. "Did you post to your social media that you were planning the wedding and announced the wedding date?"

"Yes. Was that wrong?"

His eyes went wide. "Yes! Baldington posts the official announcements. We hadn't shared with the media yet about the date or who we have planning it." He shoved his phone in his pocket.

"I'm sorry. I did it when we were at that restaurant because I finally got Internet service." She dove through her clothes. "I can remove the post and retract my statement."

"Forget it. You can't unring a bell." He messaged his driver to pick him up along the road. No way would he wait in this home with Philippa.

"Where are you going?" She held her clothes in front of her body.

"Back to Baldington. If you were my submissive, I would have you over my knee after making you write a hundred times, 'I misbehaved and I should be punished.'" He got to the door and held up two fingers in front of her. "Strike two." Then he held up one finger. "One more and you're out of the planning party. You have a good night."

Chapter Ten

Philly fucked up and did it big. She had to stop thinking that she worked for some small corporation. She had to recognize that she worked for a royal family with a large staff and exacting standards. Her well-meaning social media post caused Robert to retreat from her faster than that poor boy she had rejected back in high school.

Since the night Robert had found out her mistake, she hadn't seen him in a week. His absence bothered her more than she thought. Philly resorted to sketching the landscape around the house when she didn't keep herself busy with the wedding planning.

She kept up with meetings, which had Edith giving her an Arctic-level cold shoulder, barely acknowledging her existence in the room when they did meet. Word of Philly's error traveled fast. She wouldn't let that deter her. Her mind did go back to a comment Robert had made to her before he stormed away from her. He wanted her to write a phrase one hundred times.

Philly snorted. "I'm not in elementary school anymore."

She tapped her pencil over her sketchbook page. Absentmindedly, she wrote the sentence to see it in print. *I misbehaved and I should be punished.*

Her heart drummed after she wrote the sentence. She chalked up the reaction to anger. No. That emotion didn't really describe how she felt. She had done something wrong. Philly got that same embarrassed heat in her cheeks and chest again. The guilt forced her to write the sentence again.

Philly continued writing, her hand moving on its own without her thinking about the act. By the time she realized she had been punishing herself, she had written the line fifty times. She flipped the pages back to see her work. At this point, Philly wanted to see if she could complete this punishment. What would Robert think if he were to see that she had taken on his unintended penance?

Her nipples hardened and sweat formed on her forehead. To get her mind off her unorthodox reaction, Philly put pencil to paper and continued with her discipline until she reached one hundred.

Philly leaned back, flipping the pages of her book and admiring her work. Luckily, Robert would never see this to know she listened to him and completed this challenge, his penalty. Then again, maybe she should show him this. Maybe that would take away one of her strikes.

Philly took her sketchbook and tablet to see Helene. Just because Robert didn't want to see her didn't mean that she still didn't have a job to do.

"Don't worry about your mistake." Helene smiled to reassure Philly. "I made plenty when I first started working here. You live and learn. I do feel sorry for you, though."

That statement brought up the hairs on Philly's arms. Did Helene know that Philly had ruined her chances with Robert?

"You've officially attached your name to us and our event. You are now a part of the media feeding frenzy." Helene patted Philly's hand. "If I were you, I would lay low and keep the guards at Moonwalk happy. Paparazzi will be coming after you to get the scoop on the wedding."

"Can I confirm that you are going to walk down the aisle in Daisy Dukes as long as you can fit your baby bump in the shorts?" Philly attempted some humor to her mistake.

Helene laughed. "I think a story like that would be hilarious, but I'm not sure if Robert would be a fan."

Hearing his name sent a strange tickle through her body. "Have you seen him recently?"

"Earlier today. He looked good. Happy." Helene headed to the door. "Guess it was just a harmless kiss you two shared the other night."

The smile melted from Philly's face. "What do you mean?"

"He's going out with Princess Elena from Morocco tonight."

"Oh." Philly had to hide her disappointment, a feat considering how easily she wore her emotions on her face. "I didn't know he was seeing someone."

If Robert had serious romantic plans on someone else, why did he try to convince her to submit to him? Why had he touched her the way he did when they kissed? She had gotten naked and presented him his coffee. Philly wouldn't have done that for anyone.

"Robert is on this kick to find an appropriate partner." Helene did air quotes when she mentioned *appropriate partner*. "He's really into being a royal prince." She stood. "I hope he doesn't sacrifice love to accomplish his goals." Helene opened the door. "And don't worry about the nickname the media has now dubbed you."

Philly felt her forehead crease. Since getting to Lesilitho, connecting to the Internet had been spotty if not nonexistent. She couldn't keep up with current events because Robert hadn't outfitted the home with a TV. Who does that in this day and age?

"What nickname?" Philly held the door while Helene stood on the front porch area.

Helene sighed before saying the name. "Silly Philly." She dropped her gaze for a moment. "They're saying you're too new, too inexperienced, too American for the job."

"Damn." If Helene saw that then she knew Robert had as well.

Helene put her hand on Philly's shoulder. "Don't worry. The media used to call me Hell on Wheels because I kept my mouth closed on all of Lucian's antics. Don't let it bother you." She turned to go to her awaiting car and stopped. "Are you going to join us for dinner tonight? The town is hosting a sort of celebratory dinner for me and Lucian on our upcoming nuptials."

Philly leaned on the door as she regarded her friend. "You think it's a good idea for me to be there and confirm that I am a part of the wedding process?"

Helene shrugged. "The cat is out of the bag. Might as well let the pussy run free."

Philly laughed. "Yes. I'm definitely going to do that."

"It's a black-tie dinner." Helene looked at her watch. "Come to Baldington in about two hours. We can get ready together. You can use my hair and makeup team. Of course, you can wear anything in my closet if you want."

Philly drew her friend in for a hug. "Thank you for believing in me. I won't let you down."

Helene patted her back. "You better not. What was that? Strike one?"

Philly pulled back from her. "Two." She huffed. "I sat in Robert's chair at the dinner table that first time."

Helene groaned. "He's such a child. Even if you have a million strikes, you're staying on. I'll fight for you."

That sounded good, but Philly had a feeling that Robert had his father's ear more than Helene or maybe even Lucian.

After Helene left, Philly made sure to lock the door. What she had planned, she didn't want to be surprised by an unexpected visitor. She saw how Robert felt entitled enough to barge into places where he shouldn't. His future home would be no exception.

Philly hurried up the steps to the bedroom where she slept and she went to the attached bathroom. She searched through her makeup bag, pushing past the streaks of dark brown and black eyeshadow stains on the white inside lining.

"Ah, ha!" At the bottom of the bag, Philly picked up a long, black bobby pin.

She hadn't done what she had planned on doing in years, but she needed this. Philly rushed to the locked door where Robert said he housed his secret stash. After dropping to her knees, she peeled off the smooth ends of the pin and used the hair accessory in the lock, twisting and turning it until she heard the telltale click of the internal tumbler.

"You still got it, girl." Philly smiled as she rose to her feet, took a deep breath, and opened the door.

As soon as she did, she wished she had saved that deep breath for inside the room to breathe in all the scents of leather. Robert hadn't lied. He had the walls all lined with different spanking implements. Floggers, paddles, whips, chains, rulers and yardsticks. Philly padded in the room and ran her fingers over the stringy leather falls of the floggers that he had lined up to her eye level. The straps tickled her fingers in a delicate way that she knew the toy wouldn't be used to inflict that type of sensation.

Then she went to the center of the room where he had a leather-covered sawhorse. Philly rested her hand on the top and brushed it back and forth, imagining who Robert may have had in there and who got to experience this piece.

She crawled on top of it like she would a real horse, and pressed her chest against the bar, making sure to position it between her breasts. She closed her eyes and imagined being naked. What would Robert want her to do?

He would be commanding, instructing her on her every move. The idea of that made her exhale. Her shoulders relaxed, although her heart continued to pound out of control.

Christ, what was wrong with her? What did she find so exciting, yet comforting, about this lifestyle? Or did she react that way because of Robert?

Philly opened her eyes and climbed down from the piece before she went to the large wooden X across the room. She crept to it and faced it for a moment before turning her back and positioning herself against it with her hands in the air. Her fingers brushed the fur-lined cuffs that dangled from the tops of the cross. She easily slipped one hand inside one closed cuff to see how it would feel.

Instantly, she wanted the cuff on tighter. Philly leaned into the post and rubbed the side of her face against her extended arm. As good as this felt, she knew she needed more. It didn't look like she would be getting her fill – or fix – from Robert.

Philly pulled her hand from the cuff and headed for the door. She would leave it unlocked to check out the items Robert amassed a little closely later. Since she had already broached one room, no reason not to peek in the other.

Philly crouched down and managed to picked the lock on the second bedroom door faster than the first one. As soon as she got it unlocked, she turned the knob and swung the door open wide. To her surprise, she found the room devoid of anything. No furniture. No toys. No ancient paintings on the wall. Nothing.

Why had Robert even bothered to keep the room locked if he had nothing inside? Philly thought she would have found even more BDSM toys inside, maybe even a bound slave, waiting to get word from Robert to eat or sleep or speak.

The emptiness of the room, though, had Philly's heart pounding harder than the first room. The emptiness allowed her to think too much about what Robert could do in the room. Maybe he had his playthings sit alone in this room in the dark with their thoughts and nothing else.

Philly reached around to the other side of the knob, turned the lock and slammed it shut. She wouldn't be asking Robert about this room. Like the place contained radioactive materials, she backed away from it.

No reason for Philly to think about the possibilities of either room. Right now, she had to prepare for a fancy dinner, one that required probably something better than the one or two nice dresses that she had brought specifically to wear to the wedding and reception.

Hours later, after getting primped and preened by Helene's stylist team, Philly arrived at a historical building that the city had transformed into an elegant meeting space for just Helene and Lucian. That didn't stop Philly from thinking about Robert's dinner out with some princess. He had his life to live and so did she.

As they walked up to the building with paparazzi lining the red carpet, Philly pulled Helene to the side. "Are you sure I'm dressed okay?" She didn't want another demerit due to her appearance at a public event.

"You look fabulous." Helene patted Philly's hand.

Helene had gorgeous gowns in her dressing room, but the black, sleek dress with a slit that went up almost to her hip bone pulled her attention too many times for her to ignore. The strapless gown fit her like a glove.

Helene leaned in closer to Philly. "Lucian bought that dress for me to wear to one of our special outings, but it definitely works for you."

Great. Philly wore a dress that Lucian had meant to be part of a BDSM scene. Would Robert hate that? Probably. Or maybe he would find her just as enticing.

The thought of that had her walking differently with her head held high and a bit more sway in her step that caused the slit in her dress to open. Philly didn't know if the way she walked or that she came in with Lucian and Helene that got her some notice.

A young man sidled up to her with his hand extended. "We have not met. Gustav Melovich, but my friends call me Gus."

Philly's intuition meter immediately signaled to her not to trust this man. She shook his hand. "Nice to meet you. Philly Powell."

He pulled his hand back and clapped. "The infamous Silly Philly."

Now she didn't mind it if people called her by her birth name. "Philly will do." She started to walk away from him and join her friends.

"I work at a local television station and I run a column in the Lesilitho newspaper. I would love to get a story from you." He followed her into the dining room area.

"Sounds great. You can submit all formal requests to the Baldington Palace public relations department."

"And thank you for confirming that you do, indeed, work for the palace."

She stopped, turned to him and smirked. "I was in the car with Helene and Prince Lucian. Not a lot of detective work to do there."

He chuckled. "You're funny. Are you this funny when you work with Edith Throckmorton?"

Philly had had enough of this persistent fellow. Now she wished she had her own security detail like her friends. "I'm going to find my seat. I suggest you do the same."

"I will. But you know, we don't have to talk about those two." He pointed to Lucian and Helene. "You're in with the family. Any interesting stories about King Clive or Prince Robert? How's he been since Lucian gave up his spot to go to him?"

Philly could have said Robert seemed wound tight, but he had always been high-strung. Since their first meeting, he liked maintaining control. The thought of his controlling nature and that kiss had her knees buckling.

She needed to get herself together. She took way too long to answer the question. "Prince Robert is just fine." Philly turned away from him.

"Thank you, Ms. Powell."

She glanced back to see him bowing to her.

"Hope you have a wonderful evening." He winked before departing.

Philly stood next to Lucian.

He leaned down to her. "Are you all right?"

She nodded. "Just talking with the local media." She nodded over to Gus.

"Ah, the human equivalent of a leech. Stay far from him. He can take a simple answer and twist it into something scandalous. I did more shit based on his articles and reports than I ever did in real life."

Philly laughed.

Lucian smiled as he pointed at her. "That's the spirit. You're laughing." He wagged his finger at her. "You're doing way better than Robert is doing tonight." He faked a yawn. "Robert is with the human equivalent of a sloth. You, on the other hand, will have a great evening with us tonight."

Philly smiled even wider, not because her friends wanted to make sure she had a great time, but the idea that Robert would be bored. She hoped she invaded his thoughts in the best way, both as a wedding planner and as someone he could play with in a scene.

Without talking to him in a week, she didn't know.

* * * * *

Damn if Robert didn't think about Philippa during this dinner with Elena at Baldington, particularly after what he saw. Philippa met with Helene at the palace to go over wedding details. Robert had made it his mission not to see Philippa after her latest stunt of revealing wedding details, particularly her involvement. When both had taken a break, he walked by the office where they had been working. After noticing a notebook, Robert decided to peek to see Philippa's plans, see if she really wanted his brother to have a beach wedding. What he saw shocked him.

First, Robert admired her sketches. Even in pencil, Philippa managed to capture the dimensions of a simple flower. She had talent. As he flipped pages to look at her work, he encountered a page with one sentence written over and over again. *I misbehaved and I should be punished.* The more pages he turned, the more he saw it until he got to the end, one hundred.

Jesus. Something he said in jest, she had taken to heart. Philippa did the punishment. His skin prickled and his gut tightened. When he heard the women returning, he walked away without encountering them. That didn't stop Philippa from taking Helene to Moonwalk Manor for more privacy. She must have seen him.

At that point, he wouldn't have known what to say. For now, he would have to concentrate on this date, this bland, boring, painful date.

Robert thought about taking Elena out to a restaurant, but with Lucian and Helene's special dinner, he wanted to make sure the focus remained on them.

If Robert didn't initiate the conversation, he and Elena didn't speak, much different than Philippa, who seemed to not like the silence. Elena kept her stare on her food although her posture remained erect and stiff. As far as table manners, she did everything in a textbook manner. She knew which utensil to use and when. She waited for Robert to signal the staff to collect their plates and drop off their next course. When she did speak, she kept her answers short and direct, nothing like Philippa, who could extract a conversation out of thin air and keep it going, therefore keep him interested.

Why the hell was he with Elena? Oh, yes. Her princess title. If Robert married her, he would keep the legacy going of marrying another royal like his father had.

"Are you enjoying your dessert?" Robert wiped his mouth after taking a bite of Ginny's delectable sweet potato pie masquerading as a posh tartlet.

He enjoyed Ginny twisting her American treats into something appropriate for a royal family. Plus, her food all tasted delicious.

"No." Elena placed her fork across her plate to signal that the one bite of crust that she ate gave her the information she needed to tell if she would want more.

"No? You didn't find it to your liking?" He took another bite while waiting for her answer.

Elena shook her head this time to punctuate her point. "Seemed too sweet and full of fat and grease."

Robert shrugged. He enjoyed the dish and continued. When he did, he noticed that Elena picked up her fork again and attempted to eat more.

"Don't feel obligated to finish it if you don't like it." He started to turn to signal the staff to remove their plates.

As much as he had tried, he felt nothing for Elena. He hated to admit that Lucian could be right about anything, particularly about trying to marry someone because of a tradition.

Robert had to admit that Elena looked beautiful. Her pale skin appeared smooth and clear except for her pink cheeks. Her brown eyes did not hold the same mystique and sexiness like Philippa's. Her slight frame had him wondering if she could hold herself up in a stiff breeze. Watching her try to down the dessert that she didn't like to make him happy turned his stomach.

He held up his hand. "Please stop. If you are still hungry, we can provide you something else you may like."

She smiled, showing off a glaring set of straight, white teeth that had him questioning if Elena had veneers covering them. "I want to like what you like."

Oh, hell. Robert thought that coming from a royal family herself, she would be above trying to please him by doing everything he liked. Time for this date to end.

"Elena, thank you for a wonderful evening." He placed his napkin on the table. "I hate to cut this short, but with my ceremony coming up, I'll need the time to prepare." That sounded like a legitimate way to kill this evening.

She placed her fork on her plate again and looked relieved to do so. "Certainly. I understand. Thank you for this date." She looked beyond him. "May I freshen up before I leave?"

Robert stood. "Of course. I'll show you to the powder room."

Elena held up her hand. "I remember where it is from the last dinner here thrown by the king. Thank you." She walked primly way, taking short steps like she held an anal plug in her tiny ass.

Imagining that almost had Robert laughing. He remained standing and retrieved his phone from his pocket. He noticed he had a text message from someone in the palace's social media team.

With the Internet service back up and running, they monitored all activities about the palace and the royal family. He had to blink a few times when a staff member sent a post on a gossip site that said the American wedding planner, Silly Philly, gushed over Prince Robert and called him *fine*.

Robert wanted to be angry with the comment, but his heart beat too hard and too loud in his head to let the anger surface. Philippa called him *fine*? No, she wouldn't have done that. Not after he had warned her against making statements to the press, and not after the cold shoulder he had been giving her over the past week. Avoiding her didn't stop him from recalling her naked body and seeing her kneeling before him.

Damn it. Robert didn't want to confront her again tonight, but it looked like he would have to do it. This would be her third strike. He could get her off the property and maybe then he would stop fantasizing about her. All relationships took work. Perhaps he needed to not dismiss Elena so easily and buckle down to make this union work.

Elena returned to the room, and Robert slipped the phone back into his pocket.

"Thank you for a lovely evening." He shook her hand. Robert would have kissed her cheek, but he didn't want to go that far with her, a different reaction from Philippa.

He walked her to the door and made sure to see her go off in her chauffeured vehicle before he cleared it with his security team for him to drive himself over to Moonwalk Manor.

When he pulled up to the security gate, the guards shared that Philippa had arrived home herself. Good. Robert wouldn't have to wait.

He drove up to the home and approached the door. He started to go inside when he remembered what happened when he had done the same thing to Lucian and Helene. Against his character, Robert rang the bell and then knocked on the door.

He couldn't hear anything through the thick door for a few seconds.

"Who is it?" Philippa's voice sounded strong but concerned.

"It's Robert." He heard nothing until finally he heard the lock tumblers engage and the door opening.

The snapshot of the social media post had showed Philippa in her gown. The small picture didn't do the in-person view justice. Her succulent thigh showed through the high slit, and the strapless bodice framed her breasts beautifully, making them look high and rounded.

"What are you doing here?" She held onto the door, not willing to give him an easy passage into her temporary digs.

No, Philippa and Elena shared nothing in common. Elena would have let Robert in without question, not out of desire, but obligation.

"We need to talk." Robert stood in his spot, not accustomed to having to get permission to enter his own property.

"Sounds serious." She took a step back and opened the door wider, her way of ushering him in the home.

Robert walked inside and went to the den area. Like last time, he started a fire, mainly because the chill in the room had gotten to him. When he turned to Philippa, he noticed she rubbed her hand up her bare arm.

"Have a seat." He pointed to a chair across from him where he sat. When he noticed she didn't sit down, he sat up taller.

"What is going on? You haven't talked to me in a week after I posted about the wedding. Now you're here and acting all serious…after your date." Philippa crossed her arms over her chest.

Robert blinked. "You knew I had a date tonight?"

"Helene told me when she invited me to their dinner." She cocked her hip. "Hope you had a great time."

"Doesn't seem like that's your true feeling. Are you jealous?"

Philippa chuckled. "Are you kidding? What do I have to be jealous of?" Yet she dropped her gaze to the floor, an easy tell that she wanted a secret part of herself to remain buried deep.

He scanned her up and down. "This is what you wore to represent the royal family at a serious event?"

"I borrowed it from Helene. But you didn't come here to criticize my wardrobe or talk about your hot date, right?"

"You are right about that. And my date was not hot." He wanted to add that it lacked excitement, but he wouldn't give her that satisfaction. Robert gripped the arms of the chair. "Did you tell a local reporter that you found me attractive?"

Philippa blinked. "No. If it's the guy I'm thinking of, he kept trying to get me to say something about the family. I didn't bite. Then he asked about you and how you were taking the news about being a future king. All I said was that you were just fine. If he posted that I said something other than that, he twisted my words."

Robert remained quiet as he thought about the question posed to Philippa. He wished he could say that he had settled into the role. He hadn't. Each day, he welcomed the upcoming responsibility, but yet he felt no one respected him.

"You mocked me at the dining room table when you refused to move from my seat." He stiffened his back. "You prematurely announced your involvement in my brother's wedding." Robert removed his phone from his pocket and held it up to her. "Now you have embarrassed me in public with your comment as well as misrepresented yourself as an associate of the royal family."

Philippa almost looked pensive as he ticked down each of her recent infractions. "Wow. Sounds like I have been doing everything wrong in your eyes, like I'm a bad girl or something."

Robert swallowed hard at her statement. It didn't help that he struggled to keep his gaze from dropping to that succulent thigh showing through her dress.

He needed to put some distance between her and him or he would be making a huge mistake. "I'm afraid that the only decision to make here is—"

"Wait." Philippa held up her hand. "Hold that thought." She left the room for about a minute before returning, still in the same dress and heels but with her hands behind her back this time.

Robert thought she left the room to change into a different outfit, maybe something easy to travel in if she had planned on leaving right away. He could have the family jet prepared for her.

"I've been doing a lot of thinking since coming back to Lesilitho." A serious expression covered her face. "Seeing you again has made me question a lot of things, beyond the sensual aspect. You're tough on me."

He started to open his mouth, but she barreled through her speech

"I don't mind you being rough." She shifted in her spot. "I actually like it. I like rules and structure and parameters." She took a step forward. "You're going to say that you came here to let me go." She shook her head. "I'll be damned if I give up this job that easily. My infractions should be based on the work I do for the wedding. Sitting in the wrong seat at the table should not have gone against me, but I understand it. You set a rule and I ignored it. So, now I would like to propose something." She stood in front of Robert and pulled her hand from behind her back where she had hidden a leather paddle, one of *his* leather paddles. "You train me and it'll help me plan the wedding. But tonight, you can discipline me." She put her hands on the coffee table in front of him so that her ass stuck out, primed and ready for him. "Spank me."

Chapter Eleven

Philly hadn't planned on presenting this option to Robert. The time seemed right.

"No."

She looked over at Robert from her hunched over position. "Excuse me?"

He shook his head. "No, no, no." Robert held the paddle in his hand. "How the hell did you get this?"

"I picked the lock." She planted her feet apart like she needed to brace for the spanking. "I was curious. I wasn't disappointed. I love the smell of leather and wood. One day, I stripped down and laid on the sawhorse until I fell asleep." She glanced at the paddle in his hand. "I sleep with that paddle each night. I hold it like a teddy bear." The more she spoke, the freer she became. "I'm ready for this."

"Did you go in the other room?"

She swallowed hard. "Yes. I kept it locked."

He snickered. "The room with nothing in it is the one you kept locked?" He paced next to her. "You violated my privacy." Robert stopped moving to stand next to her.

With him being so close while holding the paddle, her nerves got to her. Philly shifted a little like she needed to rethink her plan. She had no Plan B in this. She wanted to organize this wedding to boost her career, and she wanted Robert to make her submit to him. She would no longer settle.

"Forgive me for breaking into your—"

"No. There is no forgiveness. I asked that you do one thing, and you went against my wishes. I can't trust you." He kept his voice low and steady.

Philly heard the anger seething below his controlled demeanor. "Actions have consequences." Her sweaty palms stuck to the wooden tabletop. "I'm prepared to accept my punishment."

"You are not because that's not how the lifestyle work. Without a discussion, I wouldn't discipline you, particularly not with this paddle. That would be irresponsible." His voice softened but still sounded assertive. "Are you making this offer because you're trying to keep your job?"

Philly glared at him. "No. I am the right person for this job. I listen to what they want."

"Just not me, right?" Robert placed the paddle on the table in front of her hands, nearly touching the tips of her fingers.

The shaking returned. Philly took a deep breath to control it. "I promise I will listen. I want to learn."

"And if you were to lose this job, you would still want this? You want to submit to me?" He got down to her ear. "You want me to dominate you? Say it. I need to hear you say it."

Philly didn't verbally answer. While bent over, she reached behind herself and pulled up her dress to expose her ass. "I want you to dominate me. I want to submit to you. Give me rules. Give me structure. I need it." She looked him in the eyes. "I want to serve you." She smiled. "It is day two of my submission. I'm learning to be yours. Sir."

"No. No!" He retreated to the doorway but didn't walk through it. "This is all wrong. I shouldn't have let you stay here. I shouldn't have kept those items in that room. I can't have those two sides meeting. Not here."

Philly listened to him speak out loud as though no one stood in the room with him and could hear him. She remained still, almost afraid that if she moved, particularly toward him, that he would bolt.

"I do believe things happen for a reason." She peered back at him. "What we did years ago we did as kids. We were both playing a serious game. I'm not here as a child anymore. I'm a woman. You're a man." Her gaze dropped down his body to the distinctive bulge in his pants.

Good. He did want her.

"I need more in my life than to merely be. I need to feel something. That might be the reason that I'm here now." She shook her head slowly. "I don't believe in coincidences. I believe in what I see and feel. I'm ready." She looked ahead again.

Robert didn't speak. He strolled behind her, evident from the heat of his body permeating her flesh over her ass and the backs of her thighs.

"Nice thong." He touched her back. "There are a million reasons we shouldn't do this, you know that, right?"

"Give me a few." She readied herself to give answers.

"You work for my family. Therefore, you work for me."

"True. During the day, I work for Helene and Lucian. If you want me to partner with Edith, I will. But at night and afterhours, I have my own time." She arched her back up when it started to ache from being in her position. She heard Robert groan from her movement. Sweat formed over her back. "I know you're worried about if this side of you got out, if what we do became public. If I was going to expose what you do, I would have done that years ago." She swayed back and forth, knowing Robert watched her every move.

He grunted a little. "There's a problem."

Philly stopped moving. "What is it?"

"What if I don't want to simply play with you?" He slid his hand down her ass cheek, letting the tips of his fingers coast the seat of her panties.

She shivered. "You want more?"

"I want you. I always have. You know this." His answer came tinged with a bit of anger and maybe regret. "You ran."

"I'm here." She couldn't allow him to dwell in the past. If only she could give that advice to herself. "We're adults now."

Robert waited a beat before he spoke again. "We can't let anyone know, not even Helene."

Philly hoped he couldn't see her shoulders relaxing after he made his statement. "I agree. This would be just for us." She straightened her legs, which hiked up her ass even more. She heard Robert swallowing hard.

"What am I thinking? We can't do this. We can't go into a relationship."

"We don't have to. We can make this fun. Temporary. You're not committed to anyone yet, right?"

He paused before he answered. "Not yet."

She exhaled. "I'm definitely single. Going on our instincts seems to work for us."

"I will not discipline you in the way you want."

Her heart sank. She stood and turned to him. "Why?"

"I didn't tell you that you could move, did I?"

Philly's heart started racing again. She resumed her previous position. "No, Sir."

"If you are serious about doing this, I need to get to know you better." He placed his hand on her lower back.

She had to part her lips slightly to take in the oxygen she needed to keep standing and her drumming heart pumping. Then she felt him sliding her dress down over her ass, covering her again.

This time when she stood up straight, she felt liquid metal coursing through her veins. If Robert didn't want to play, then she didn't have to obey.

"After all these years, you're saying you don't know me?" She crossed her arms over her chest as she squared off against him.

He shook his head. "I know the jokes you find funny and what foods you like and that you're strong-willed." He moved in closer to her. "I don't know your triggers, meaning I don't know if spanking you will bring out a negative response."

Philly snickered. "It's discipline. Shouldn't I respond negatively to that?"

Robert looked like he wanted to hide a smile. "It depends, which is why I want to get to know you better."

"I guess that means we're not playing tonight, right? Isn't that what you call it?" She moved in closer to him so that she felt his warm breath over her face.

Robert shook his head.

"Is your date over?" Philly glanced at the doorway to the room as though Robert's dinner companion could be standing on the other side.

"You think I would have left her at the palace to come here?" He dragged his finger down the side of her face.

"Was there another reason for you to stop your date and rush all the way over here?"

Robert didn't speak. He cupped her cheek and drew her face closer as he lowered his head. When he pressed his lips against hers, Philly melted against him. This felt amazing, felt right. She held his arms at the same time he slipped his tongue into her mouth.

Who knew this crowned prince could be this hot? Not so uptight after all.

Robert broke from the kiss, but he continued holding her face. "Shouldn't do this."

Damn. He can't be having second thoughts. "It's okay." She put her hands on his chest. "I want you. We can make this what we want."

He regarded her for a moment. "I don't have any protection on me."

She smiled. "I'm always prepared." She held his hand. "Upstairs."

Philly didn't have to say any more than that before Robert tightened his grip on her hand and rushed to the staircase. Before ascending, he planted another soul-stirring kiss her, one that contained more passion than she had ever felt from him or anyone else she had ever kissed before.

Robert tugged on the top of her dress.

When she heard a small rip, she pulled back from him. "Don't tear it. I borrowed this from Helene."

"I'll buy her another damn dress." With both hands, he split the dress apart, breaking her zipper.

He let the garment fall to the floor, leaving her in only her thong and her heels. Now Philly couldn't wait to get to the bedroom. From how Robert reacted, he must have felt the same way.

Robert removed his jacket and let it fall on top of her shredded borrowed gown that probably cost more than her first car. She started to climb the stairs, but he stopped her. Before she could question him and see if he doubted their obvious next steps, he kissed her again before dragging his lips over her cheek and down her neck.

Goosebumps covered her flesh. "Please." Her body ached for him, not just a touch or for her vibrator. Him. Philly wanted to feel Robert the way she imagined he would feel the night she masturbated for him on camera.

Robert lowered his head to her collar bone, nipping it with his teeth until he got down to her breasts. He cupped one in his large hand and massaged it while he held the other and licked her nipple.

"Yes." Philly raked her fingers through his hair before gripping his silky strands.

He twirled the tip of his tongue around her hard nipple. Each pass caused her body to jerk. Why the hell had she worn heels with a clasp on the sides? She wanted to kick off her shoes and pull down her thong to get to this man.

Robert licked over to her other breast and gave it the same treatment. He sucked her nipple until she wanted to scream and cry at once.

"Bedroom. You need to be out of your clothes." She eased her hands down to the collar of his shirt.

He gave her one last suck before taking her hand and going up the stairs. At the top, he glanced at the secret room that she managed to breach before he brought her to the bedroom.

"Philippa."

Finally, she liked hearing her real name, so much so that she loosened his tie and pulled it from his collar, letting it fall to the floor. Then she worked on his shirt.

Robert hooked his fingers into the sides of her thong. Now she liked being in her heels. The additional height allowed him to pull down her underwear just below her cheeks.

Philly pulled his shirt down his arms. "Whoa."

"What?" He glanced down at himself and looked around the room.

"I can't believe you were hiding all that when we went swimming." She swept her fingertips up his muscular arms to the muscled planes of his chest.

"I can't believe you look exactly the same from when I first met you." He gave her a quick kiss. "You're beautiful." He gave her a sexy but nearly sinister glare. "It's going to be a shame what I'll do to you when it comes time to play."

Robert took a step back before crouching down to untie his shoes. He toed out of them before unfastening his pants and dropping them. As he stepped out of them and removed his socks, Philly undid the clasps on the sides of her shoes to remove them before shimmying out of her thong.

As she stared at his body and his long, thick cock sitting up hard with a slight curve, he stared at her. At the same time, she said, "Damn," when he did.

Philly opened a drawer to the nightstand next to the bed. She had brought the protection in case she had met someone in Lesilitho to help her pass the time. She never expected her experience would be with Robert, Prince Robert of Lesilitho.

She placed a string of condoms on top of the stand.

"You are prepared, aren't you?" Robert stepped up to the side of the bed.

Philly stared at the bead of pre-cum at the top of his red, mushroom tip. She reached for him. She wrapped her fingers around his shaft and immediately felt him throbbing in her hand. Hard, strong.

She eased to sit on the edge of the bed to accept him in her mouth. Robert had other plans.

"No." He held her shoulders. "If you put me in your mouth, this will be long over before it begins." He dragged his thumb over her bottom lip. "You have no idea how long I have fantasized about your mouth and the things it could do to me."

Philly smiled at the idea that he had fantasized about her. Then again, he did admit to jerking off to a five-year old video of her. She immediately remembered her own recent issue. She hadn't been able to make herself climax in a long time. Because of that block, she hadn't been with anyone sexually because she didn't know if she would disappoint her partner or herself.

Shit. What if she couldn't achieve an orgasm with Robert?

"Robert, I need to tell you something." Philly released him and moved back on the bed.

He didn't touch the condoms. He climbed in the bed with her. "What is it? Is this your first time?" He chuckled as he slipped down by her legs and spread them apart.

"What are you doing?" She reclined back but kept her head up to watch him.

Robert didn't speak. He held her nether lips apart and took a slow, deliberate and satisfying drag of his tongue from the opening of her vagina to her sensitive clitoris. The feeling had her jackknifing off the bed. Her legs shook as he continued licking her.

Philly knew Robert had to have some aristocratic training like horseback riding or even fencing. The man needed to add Prince of Cunnilingus to his title. He flicked his tongue over her clitoris, and the sensation tightened her stomach.

"Fuck. Close. Close." She curved her hips up to match the motion of his mouth.

Robert sucked on her hardened nub, which had her body shaking. Philly could do this. Her body hadn't fully betrayed her yet. She hung on the edge, savoring the intense feeling and hating not being able to cross it. She fisted the delicate bed covering under her body.

Get out of your fucking head, girl. Give in. Give in.

When she found herself not being able to come, she reached over to the string of condoms and opened one. "Please. Please. Inside."

Maybe feeling Robert's cock in her aching pussy would be the difference. She wouldn't be fucking a stranger. She would be with a friend, one who had managed to watch her come before. She could do this with him. She wanted Robert.

Robert seemed like he had ignored her pleas as he continued pleasuring her with his mouth. Then he got up on his knees and accepted the condom from her hand. She watched him roll it on himself before he nestled his body in between her legs.

He held himself before positioning the tip at her opening. As soon as he eased inside, she arched her back and clawed his shoulders.

Robert pressed his lips against hers, and she tasted her salty essence. He pulled back far enough that Philly thought he would pull out completely before he eased back into her.

"Wet." He nodded before reconnecting his stare to hers. "The best." He increased his tempo. "Best." He kissed her again.

"Better than the fantasy?" Philly attempted to smile but she remained fixated on whether she could actually come.

Don't think about it and just do it.

Before Robert verbally answered, he planted a kiss on her. "Absolutely." He pulled back again, ever so slowly, before thrusting in deep. "We should have done this years ago."

He increased the speed of his thrusts before he pressed his chest against hers. The pressure of his hulking form felt like a relief. Philly wrapped her legs around him to keep him cemented in his spot. She wanted him to keep her restricted even more, make sure she didn't move except for her hips that she managed to undulate under him to match his thrusts.

Robert eased his hand up the side of her body to her tit, which he grabbed with such force that she gasped in a good way. He used his thumb to circle her nipple.

The feeling forced Philly to break from the kiss to turn her head to the side. Damn, this man knew how to play her body.

Robert released her breast to bring his hand to her chin. He turned her head to make her look at him. He didn't speak as he stared in her eyes, but Philly wanted to tell him to move his hand down to her neck and hold it, squeeze it.

She had never had that desire before Robert. To test him, she held his wrist and tried bringing his hand down to her neck.

Robert took her cue as something else and managed to capture her hand to press it above her head against the bed.

Yes! That fluttery feeling returned to her midsection. She pressed her hardened nipples against him again as she wrapped her other arm around his shoulders.

Philly felt herself getting close to a real orgasm. "Yes. Robert, yes." She had never been one of those weepy chicks, but if he could get her there, she would bawl her eyes out without shame.

Before the celebration could happen, Robert turned over onto his back, carrying her with him so that now, Philly rode him.

She blinked at the new position while he held her hips.

"God, you look good up there." Robert raised his hips.

Damn, if that didn't feel good. Philly's body took over and she gyrated on top of him, moving her hips back and forth. Maybe if she listened to her body, she could do this.

In the new position, Robert impaled her with his cock. Philly moved faster and faster. She couldn't get enough of his body and the way he gripped her.

She leaned down to press her chest against his again. As she had hoped, he wrapped his arms around her and held her. Again, she felt a stirring in her stomach. Her pussy constricted, something Robert must have felt.

"Jesus." He bolted up while still holding her and positioned his legs over the side of the bed. "Come on, Philippa. Do it. Do it."

She heard him speaking between gritted teeth. Philly squeezed her eyes shut and prayed in her head to let the orgasm that had been within her reach to come through.

Robert stood and carried Philly to a nearby wall to give her the fucking she never thought she would get from this proper royal. Sweat dripped from his forehead as he pounded her.

The aggressive position had her toes curling. Inside, Philly wanted to scream. One side of her wanted to have that orgasm that Robert worked so hard to extract from her. The other side wanted to scream out of frustration. What the fuck was her problem?

"I'm – I'm –" Robert shook his head and buried it on the side of Philly's neck.

"Yes, do it." Philly held the back of his head and stroked it.

Robert grunted as he made three more hard pumps inside her before he stopped moving. He panted hard as he held her up.

Unfortunately, Philly's heart continued racing. As much as she loved feeling Robert inside her, she wanted to pull away from him. Maybe if she had some alone time, she could get herself there. All wouldn't be lost. Of course, she had been trying to please herself for a while and lost that battle each time. No matter what, Philly refused to fake it.

Robert kissed the side of her neck up to her lips where he gave her the sweetest of pecks after a hard session. Then he looked her in the eyes. "Yes, we do need to talk."

Chapter Twelve

Robert's dream had come true the moment Philippa brought down his paddle and she lifted her dress to present herself to him. Although he had been angered at the idea that she had broken into the room, he got hard hearing her talk about sleeping with his paddle and lying naked on the sawhorse. Sex topped his wish list. Then something happened, or rather, nothing happened on Philippa's end.

Robert went from a date with a woman who was willing to do anything for him to one who required a lot of work. He had too much going on in his life to take on this challenge. As soon as he looked into her eyes, his protective nature kicked in and he wanted to continue holding Philippa.

"Are you going to put me down or are we going to stay against the wall like this?" Philippa attempted to smile but she dropped her gaze to the floor as soon as her smile slipped down her face.

"We're going to shower." He slid out of her and carried her to the bathroom where he finally disposed of his condom.

"I guess you should shower before you go." She went over to a window and peeked through the curtain. "Please don't tell me you've had a driver out there waiting for you this entire time."

Robert started the shower and placed his hand in the streaming water. "No. I drove myself here." When the water reached a temperature he liked, he held his hand out to Philippa. "Come."

"If only." Her mumbled statement managed to be audible over the rushing water.

Robert led her in the glass enclosure and closed the door. As she stood with her back to him, he put his hands on her hips and turned her around so that he could look her in the eyes. He knew Philippa could take this type of honest conversation.

"Now I understand why you wanted to talk."

She dropped her gaze to his chest.

He quickly put his hand to her chin to raise her head. "You didn't come."

She shrugged. "I don't know what's wrong with me."

"I know I made a joke about it, but are you really a virgin?"

"Shit. No." Philippa shrugged away from him and turned to the streaming water. "I dated after you. Guys back home." She nodded. "They were tough. Questionable."

"What does that mean? Questionable?"

"My family and friends wondered why I dated a couple of them." She moved her hand up her arm under the stream of water. "One of them didn't have a job, but he looked good and thought the world of me…until he got a friend of mine pregnant. The other was pursuing his master's degree. Smart guy who loved himself. He could only get off if he stared at himself in a mirror while we did it. With both, I couldn't come. And I wouldn't fake it. It's not you. It's me."

"Now it sounds like you're breaking up with me and we haven't even gotten started yet." He tried laughing to lighten the mood.

Philippa didn't look to be in a jovial mood.

"When did this start? Did you fake it when we talked on the—"

She didn't allow him to finish his question. "No. That was the last really good orgasm that I had. Since then, I can't get there." She put her hand to her stomach. "I can feel it building like it's going to happen, and then nothing. It's like I see the bridge and I can't cross. I see the light at the end of the tunnel, and I can't reach it. It's frustrating as hell, and I wish it didn't happen, not with you." She continued her shower. "I thought with you it would be different. I hoped with you it would be."

Robert wrapped his arms around her and held her close. He had other plans. He wanted to continue this conversation. "Thank you."

Even through the rushing shower stream, he heard her snickering. "Why are you thanking me? I just told you that I didn't get off when we had sex."

"I know. But you tried telling me beforehand. You owned up to it afterward. And, most importantly, you didn't try faking it." He kissed her shoulder. "I think if I had had sex with some other women who are only impressed by being with a royal, they would have lied and faked their reactions with me."

She rubbed soap up and down her arms and legs. "You're a prince. A true-to-life prince. You could have any woman you want and have better sex."

"The sex was wonderful. We have to figure out how to get you to the big O."

"We?" She craned her head around.

After connecting his gaze to hers, he nodded. "We made a deal about you being my submissive while you're here. We can add this to our arrangement."

"You truly are a protector and a good friend. Or maybe you're just horny." She turned in his arms. "I'm a mess. You've tried getting rid of me from this job since I got here. Am I worth the hassle?"

The longer he stared into her eyes, the more he knew the answer. "Yes."

She screwed up her lips. "I'm not."

Philippa took the fastest shower he had ever seen anyone take, and he had once seen Lucian sneak in from an all-night party, shower, change into a pressed suit, and arrive at a royal dinner in less than ten minutes.

"There is no we. You were right. We shouldn't have had sex. I'll never learn." Philippa cursed under her breath.

"What's that supposed to mea—"

Philippa opened the shower door. "You should go back home after you shower." She stepped out and grabbed a towel to wrap around her body.

Before Robert could object, she closed the shower door.

Oh, no. Robert thought he had kept his Dom side dormant while with Philippa. She had awakened the beast in him with her actions. He grabbed the door and stopped himself. He couldn't believe it, but he actually heard Lucian in his head telling him advice Robert had given him before. Robert needed to maintain control and not let her bratty reactions prompt him to action. He would finish his shower and return to the bedroom with a plan.

After cleansing himself, Robert shouldn't have been surprised to see Philippa wearing a multi-colored headscarf, a long-sleeved T-shirt, and having the bed covers up to her neck. The physical barrier she tried to create would be easier to penetrate than the mental block she had that shut him down at every turn. Her reaction had him wondering why she had a fascination with the Lifestyle.

He left the bath towel on the sink and padded naked into the bedroom. "Training starts now." He stood at the foot of the bed and watched her.

"Aren't you leaving?" She pointed to the doorway.

"It would be easy for me to do that, but I'm tired of easy. I suspect you are, too."

Philippa shook her head. "There's where you're wrong. I'm looking for easy. I've had to fight for respect, for work, for a chance."

He held up his hand. "Stop talking." When she cocked her head like she had more to tell him, he continued. "During the day, you will work on planning the wedding. You will work with Mrs. Throckmorton."

Philippa sighed and it turned into a groan.

"When appropriate, you will attend royal events." He cleared his throat. "Including the ceremony to officially name me heir to the throne."

Philippa's mouth hung open. "As your date?"

He planted his feet shoulder-width apart to be more grounded. "As my special guest."

Her shoulders slipped down like what he said disappointed her.

"When it is time for us to play, I will give you a secret code word or phrase or maybe a signal."

Philippa drew her knees up to her chest and wrapped her arms around them. "Like what?"

Robert hadn't planned that part yet. He didn't know how to answer her. Would he do something like tug on his ear to get her attention? Maybe he could say something like *fire* or tap on his leg.

He glanced to the side and caught his reflection in the mirror beside the bathroom door. As he stared at his reflection, a smile crept across his face.

Robert turned back to Philippa. "I'll ask you, 'How's my hair?' That will be my code that it's playtime."

She looked like she fought against smiling, but she eventually gave in to the emotion. "I like that." She pushed the covers off her body and continued holding her knees against her chest. "Now what?"

Robert went to the other side of the bed and got under the covers. "Tell me about your childhood."

"Wow. Not sexy at all." She slipped down under the blankets and laid on her side with her back to him.

He put his hand to her shoulder and turned her onto her back. "We've established that during play you will call me *Sir*. Before we play, you know what line to say to me." He tapped the center of her forehead. "I could do some mindfuck. Or there's verbal humiliation."

She shook her head. "I wouldn't like that."

Inside, Robert sighed in relief. He didn't like doing verbal humiliation scenes, even if the woman wanted it. "Good. I like when you tell me what you like and don't like. This helps." With her on her back, he placed his hand on her chest.

"What are you doing?" She placed her hand on top of his like she wanted to remove it.

"Feeling your heartbeat. I'll know if you're lying or not when you answer." That excuse sounded plausible, and he would use the touch to feel if her heart raced with certain answers. Bottom line, Robert wanted to touch her.

"I don't lie."

"Except to my father at breakfast that one time. Why did you lie then?"

Philippa took a deep breath. "I didn't make up that story about my parents because I wanted to appear better than what I am or anything. Growing up the way I did made me feel like I had been raised by wolves. I don't know if my brothers felt the same way. My parents relied on my older brothers to take care of me, and they did. They looked out for me, taught me how to fight, how to play football."

"American version."

Philippa smiled. "Yes. My parents thought they were doing us a favor by giving us very little direction in life. I would ask when I should come home from a date and they would say that they trusted me to make the right decisions. We prepared our own meals."

"No wonder you're a great cook." He patted her chest.

"Thank you. They even gave us money for us to buy our own school clothes. If you ask them, they were making us independent."

"I'm asking you." Robert eased his body closer to her. "How did all that independence make you feel?"

"Tough, like I could handle anything and anyone." She snickered. "I always tell myself, if the person can't cook me and eat me, I have nothing to fear." She remained quiet for a moment after her knee-jerk answer. After a beat, she said, "Other times I felt scared, like walking a tightrope without a net underneath." She brushed her fingers over his arm. "I break into the one bedroom with all your scary toys and I got excited. I open the door to the empty room and that place scared me to death. The emptiness scared me."

Robert brushed his thumb over her skin. He felt her heart drumming a solid rhythm. "I can help you."

At that statement, Philippa grabbed his hand and shoved it from her body. "I don't need help or anyone to save me. I'm fine." She turned back over onto her side. "Besides, you've been given everything. What would you know about overcoming anything? You were born into royalty. Despite being the second-born son, you're going to be the next king. You have women lining up to do whatever you want. There's nothing you can show me about feeling—"

"Vulnerable?"

She remained silent before she turned off the light on her side. "Goodnight."

* * * * *

Philly didn't know how she managed to sleep at all. After what should have been amazing sex that ended with her being angry and feeling even more isolated, she lashed out at Robert for simply being there and being himself.

She didn't think of herself as a runner, but she needed to put some distance between herself and the handsome prince. The heavy curtains that normally remained tied back from the windows now covered them. That must have been Robert's doing.

Philly reached for her cell phone next to the bed to check the time. Nine in the morning. Damn, she would have been late had this been a weekday. With it being Sunday, she could sleep in more.

After taking a deep breath, she peeked behind her to see if Robert remained sleeping. After the terse way she ended their night, she would be surprised if he stayed. The empty bed confirmed her assumption. Guess he didn't want to deal with the hassle after all.

She threw the covers from her body and went to the bathroom first to relieve herself and brush her teeth. As she looked in the mirror, she caught the view of the oversized shower stall behind her. She and Robert could have done so many things in there after their slightly unsuccessful triste. Well, her unfulfilling night. Robert did manage to get his rocks off, but not without some guilt and regret. She saw that clearly in his eyes once he figured out Philly's issue.

No matter. She came here for a job, not to be psychoanalyzed or judged or even fucked despite packing a pharmacy-level supply of condoms.

Philly padded downstairs and felt a warmth hit her at the bottom step. Did that fire that Robert started last night continued through the night? She approached the kitchen and opened the cabinet above the coffeemaker.

"It's about time."

The voice scared Philly enough that she screamed and dropped the coffee pod to the floor. Robert sat in the same chair he had sat in

last night when he started to fire her as the wedding organizer. He
wore his pants but nothing else. No shirt. No socks. No shoes.

"You're still here." She approached the family room area. "I
thought you—"

She stopped talking when she spotted something shocking or
rather someone. Christ, two strangers. A brunette nude woman stood
behind Robert. A black mask covered her eyes as she stood stock
still. In the corner sat an older man with a shaved head and a graying
beard.

Philly dropped her gaze to Robert.

"Good morning." He smiled. "How's my hair?"

Philly's heart started racing with that simple line for a couple of
reasons. "Messy, like you had a rough night." She glared at the
woman. "And even worse morning." She pointed to her. "Who's she
and what is she doing here?" She started to say, "In my house," but
the home didn't belong to her. The longer Philly stood in the room,
the more she felt like she didn't know what the hell to think.

She assumed the man had to be a part of Robert's security detail.
He remained silent as he watched the three of them.

Robert pointed to the same chair Philly sat in last night after
dinner. "Have a seat."

Philly cocked her hip. "I'd rather stand."

A darkness clouded Robert's face. "I will not repeat myself. If I
do, then—"

"Then what?" Philly jutted her chin out at him. It didn't help that
she caught the woman behind him gasping when Philly dared to defy
him.

Robert stood. Even in his pants, his body still impressed her. "Let
me give you a lesson in BDSM and obedience." He reached down
into a wicker basket by the chair he had occupied and pulled out

something that looked like a leather duster. It had straps of black leather dripping from a long, leather-covered handle. "As a submissive, or even a slave, you have power." He leaned over to the woman and whispered something in her ear.

The intimate if not brief conversation raised the hairs on the back of Philly's neck and twisted her gut. How dare he bring in a woman to fuck in front of her just because Philly couldn't come. She balled her hands into fists and started to storm out when she watched the woman hold onto the arm of the chair and bend over, wordlessly and full of trust.

"I can play with your body or your mind. I can make it easy or intense." He placed his hand on the woman's back.

Philly watched her jump and grip the chair arm tighter before her body settled.

"If the play gets to be too much, she has a safe word she can utter." Robert let his arm dangle to his side as he swung the implement back and forth.

"If she says the word, you'll stop?" Philly's knees knocked together as she anticipated what would happen next.

Robert nodded as he reared his hand back.

"What's the word?"

He didn't respond to Philly. He let the heavy-looking leather straps connect to the woman's bare back. The thudding sound echoed throughout the room.

"One, Master." The woman's voice sounded soft yet stern, a stark contrast to the action.

She wanted this? Why did she call Robert *Master* and not *Sir* like Philly had?

Robert hit her with the whip-like toy again and again, over her back, on her ass cheeks, one after the other. Philly watched the woman shaking. Her pale skin started turning pink and then red with streaks.

"What's her word?" Philly shifted uncomfortably in her spot.

She couldn't take her stare off the woman, this stranger that she wanted to kick out of the house only moments before. Now she wanted to take her in her arms and hold her. Robert hadn't done that to Philly. She could tell he wanted to put her through this same treatment, this punishment.

Robert continued the beating until Philly heard the woman saying, "Yellow."

He put the implement in the basket before he placed his hand on her back. At that point, Philly felt she could exhale. This barbaric treatment had ended.

She watched Robert leaning down and whispering in her ear again. Philly hoped for his sake the man whispered his apologies to her. She didn't know this woman, but she didn't think she deserved this discipline.

The woman nodded and gripped the arm of the chair tight again, which constricted Philly's gut. Robert reached into that evil basket again, and this time pulled out a paddle, her paddle, the one Philly had gotten from the secret room, the one she laid with when she went to bed.

Robert glanced at Philly. "Sit."

Philly wanted to oblige him this time. Her legs wouldn't move. She even pounded on her thighs to prompt her to sit her ass down before she got this beating. She couldn't.

Like he did with the other toy, he reached back with the paddle and smacked her ass cheek with it.

The woman grunted. "Thank you, Master." She curled her toes into the rug.

"Sit down, My Filly." Robert did it again and again. Sweat glistened off his perfect body.

As much as Philly wanted to look away, she couldn't. Her attention remained transfixed to the scene. The longer he worked on her, the more Philly thought she had caused Robert to snap like this. She never imagined he could be this sadistic.

He paddled her using the long board for what seemed like hours. The brunette took it. Her knees buckled a couple of times. When they did, Robert slowed the action. When the blindfolded woman straightened herself up again, the torture started over.

Philly managed to make her way over to the woman on wobbly legs and drop down to the floor in front of her. Without being told, she managed to pry the stranger's fingers from the chair to hold them.

From where she sat, Philly felt the woman's panting breath over her face. Her clammy hands trembled so much that Philly tightened her grip.

Robert inflicted another pounding hit to her backside. That got Philly's attention. She glared at him. Robert returned her stare, unapologetically as though daring her challenge him.

Philly kept looking at him until she felt something odd. The woman she had been attempting to console had placed the tip of Philly's index finger in her mouth. Like a pacifier, she sucked on it gently, emitting moans in between. When Robert paddled her again, she changed her motions to lick the tip of her finger.

Philly couldn't help but bring her attention to the finger nestled in this stranger's mouth. The woman taking the punishment that Philly knew had been meant for her licked the tip like she wanted to lave Philly's clitoris. The gentle motion had Philly imagining Robert between her thighs and making the same motion. Her stomach tightened and her clit throbbed. Robert spanked her again, and the woman cried out, breaking her connection from Philly's hand.

"Yellow." Philly nodded. "I heard her say it."

The woman shook her head.

"Don't talk for her." Robert continued paddling her. "And don't you ever lie to me."

Philly wanted to treat him like she had done to that quarterback. Instincts took over and she charged him. "Stop it. Please stop hurting her." She tried pushing him.

Even though her might couldn't move him from his spot, Robert did stop punishing her.

The woman turned her head. "Did I do something wrong?"

Philly got by her face and started to remove her mask.

"No!" Robert dropped the paddle and held Philly's hands. "What is going on with you? I thought you wanted to see what I'm like as a Dom. I arranged for her to come here so you could see this."

Philly shook her head. "I want you." She looked back into the kitchen. "I want to do the tea ceremony. I want to try new things with you." She pulled her hands from his. "I can't do this." She stood in the doorway between the den and the kitchen. "You and your new friends need to leave. Now."

Chapter Thirteen

Robert had never been asked to leave a home, particularly one that he technically owned, and not by someone who identified as a submissive. At least, Philippa thought she wanted to be a submissive.

After Philippa had fallen asleep, Robert decided to give her a surprise. He contacted a local dungeon master, known for his discretion, and the same man who had trained Robert, to see if he had a willing play bottom he could use as a demonstration.

Robert had expected that with seeing this scene, maybe Philippa would be open to having him play with her. Maybe then, she would relax and be able to achieve and orgasm. Far from it. If anything, Philippa seemed totally closed down and she wanted him far from her.

Philippa seemed to be open to the being his submissive. She looked happy when he came up with their phrase meaning he wanted to play. She appeared comfortable with her body, disrobing without much argument or coaxing. She even slept with his paddle. She checked every box. Why did this scene upset her?

"Master, should I—"

Robert turned to the woman still in the blindfold. At least she followed directions. "Your Master will perform your aftercare."

With that statement, the woman got down on her knees and bowed her head as though she had been trained to be in that position at the mention of aftercare.

Robert turned to the man who had trained him. Master Jude rose from the chair and sauntered to his slave.

With his hand on top of her head, he looked at Robert and said, "She's not ready."

Robert didn't want to hear that. He wanted Philippa to want this type of dominance. He had been trained in so many forms of impact play that he could do any of them in his sleep. What would it mean for him to have her refuse what he knew best?

"Take all the time you need." Robert nodded down to the slave. Master Jude nodded.

Philippa had already retreated upstairs. Robert took the stairs by two to the bedroom, picking up the clothes he had discarded the night before along the way. He had expected to find Philippa in bed with the covers over her head. Instead he found her pacing back and forth. As soon as he hit the doorway, she glared at him.

"Why are you still here?" She didn't stop moving.

"Last I checked, this is still my home." The Dominant side of him came out when it probably shouldn't have.

Philippa had been shocked by what she saw. He needed to do a little mental aftercare on her right now.

"Fine." She headed to the closet. "I'll go. I had planned on staying at a hotel anyway."

Robert blocked her from entering. "Wait. Please have a seat."

"Are you going to whip me like you did that woman down there?" Philippa pointed toward the door. "And who the hell is she anyway? How did she get here? Did you have sex with her?"

"No." Robert answered that question immediately. He pointed to the chair next to the bed. "Please have a seat."

Philippa huffed before sitting down. "This had better be good."

Robert slipped his shirt on first. "I thought about you. While you slept, I thought you would want to see me discipline a woman so you can understand my style." He buttoned his shirt before tucking it in his pants.

"You looked like you really hurt her." Philippa looked past him.

"Do we need to call an ambulance?"

Robert shook his head as he sat down on the bed. "Her Master brought her here. He was sitting in the room. He's doing aftercare on her now."

As soon as he said that, he heard what sounded like the front door opening and closing. He guessed the two of them did their business and left.

"If BDSM is about that, I don't want any parts of it." Philippa shook her head.

Robert knew better. She had all the key ingredients of being a great submissive. He started to make an argument for himself when the front doorbell chimed.

"Fuck." Robert didn't mean for the curse to become audible. He had told the cleaning staff not to come over that day.

"Did your friends come back?" She stood to go back downstairs.

"Doubt it." Robert felt comfortable ignoring the intruder until he heard the bell ring again but this time accompanied by three solid knocks.

"You've got to be kidding me." He slipped on his shoes and socks. After putting on his jacket, he shoved his tie in the pocket.

"Who do you think it is?" She started to go downstairs, but Robert beat her to the door.

Robert sighed. "Whoever is at the door is not going to leave. I'll answer it. You stay here." He meant that in more ways than one.

He trotted downstairs. With the wooden door still closed, he screamed through it to the person on the other side. "Who is it?"

"Robert?"

Robert immediately recognized the voice. He opened the door. "Lucian? What the hell are you doing here?"

"I should be asking you the same question." Lucian started to push his way inside, but Robert put the weight of his body and all his strength behind the door to keep him out. "What are you doing? Why can't I come in?"

"What is it that you want with Philippa?" Robert had to thank God that he had gotten dressed before this unexpected visitor showed. "We're working on wedding planning."

"That's why I'm here. She wanted to check out a musical act for us. I have the family jet ready for her to leave."

"Leave? To go where?"

Why hadn't Philippa said anything to him about this trip?

"Virginia Beach. She was going to check them out and make them an offer to perform at our wedding. If she leaves tonight, she can make one of their shows by tomorrow, which will be good for you."

Robert blinked. "Good for me? How?"

"You've made it obvious that you don't want her here. She'll be out of your hair for your big ceremony. You won't be your normal, uptight self, thinking she'll do something to embarrass you." Lucian rolled his eyes.

Robert didn't think of Philippa as an embarrassment, not now. After the breakthrough that they had, he certainly didn't want her to leave. Not without him.

Lucian pushed on the door again. "Will you let me in now so I can talk to her? There's a schedule to keep."

Robert pushed back. "No."

Lucian took a couple of steps back on the porch. "No? No to what?"

"No, you can't come in. No, she's not going to Virginia Beach. No to this whole plan." He shook his head.

"You don't control her. If anything, I—"

Robert had to cut off his brother from what he started to talk about controlling Philippa. "I invited her to my ceremony. I want her to be there."

Lucian's eyes widened. "Really? Why the change of heart? Realized you were being a royal prick?"

Robert shrugged. "Something like that. She can't go. However, after the dinner, we can go to the States and see this musical act together."

"We? You mean Philly, Edith and you?" Lucian pointed to Robert.

"Edith would not be on board with something like this."

"Which sounds like that would make you happy." Lucian scratched his head. "I don't get this sudden change of heart in you."

"Guess you can say I'm trying to be more open minded. Isn't that what you said I should start doing?"

Lucian nodded. "Yeah. Guess better late than never." He craned his head to look in the house. "I still find it suspicious that you won't let me inside. You didn't kill her and you're cleaning up the crime scene now, right?"

"You're such a fucking child." Robert felt himself rolling his eyes.

"And you're still so easy to get." Lucian reached through the open door and ruffled Robert's hair before turning away. "Tell Philly I said hello. See you later." He raised his hand in the air to wave goodbye before getting into his chauffeured ride.

Robert closed and locked the door before returning to the bedroom. He found Philippa in front of the bedroom window, peering out at the scene.

"Lucian was at the door to tell you that he arranged for the family jet to take you back to Virginia Beach to see some musical act for the wedding." He leaned down. "We need to talk."

Philippa shook her head. "No, we don't. I'm here for work. You managed to distract me. That can't happen again."

Damn, that should have been Robert's line.

"I still want you to come to my ceremony." He wouldn't take no for an answer on this.

"I'll be there…for Helene and Lucian." She headed to the bedroom door. "Anything we had or thought we could have is gone. And you should be, too."

Too tired to fight, Robert strolled to the bedroom door to leave. He stopped in front of her. "I have really great instincts as far as the lifestyle and people." He pointed to her. "I know you, Philippa. I know you better than you think you know yourself. We could both benefit from this."

"I see no joy or benefit of having you whip me."

"Flog."

"What?"

Robert stopped in the middle of the stairs. "I used a flogger on that play bottom, not a whip." He regarded her for a moment. "No. You're not an impact-play type of submissive. But I can find your sweet spot. It's there." He trotted down the stairs to the front door.

Philippa kept up with him.

He opened the door and turned to her. "I'll see you at the ceremony. Afterward, we are going to check out the schedule for this musical group and see when we can go."

Philippa cocked her head and looked at him with suspicion in her eyes. "You want to come with me to Virginia Beach?"

He nodded. "I insist on it."

"And you'll respect my decision on what I do for the wedding?"

"I do respect your decision. That doesn't prevent me from being honest. If there's something I don't like, I will voice my opinion."

She nodded. "Fair. That doesn't mean I'll listen."

"I'll go back to the palace and pack. You do the same." He kissed her temple.

"Yes." She exhaled. "Is there anything you want me to pack?"

"I like that you're referring to me for these decisions. I think you do want to play." He rested his hands on her hips. "What is the weather like in Virginia this time of year?"

This time, she laughed. "It's Virginia. As the saying goes, if you don't like the weather, wait five minutes." She wriggled out of his hold. "Um, it's autumn, so layering items would be best. Sweaters with some short-sleeve shirts."

He nodded. "I want you to pack skirts and dresses."

She snickered. "Chauvinist much? Modern, American women do wear pants, you know?"

"I know." He leaned forward so he had his head by her ear. "I also know I need easy access to your pussy. Unless you don't want to play."

She furrowed her eyebrows. "I told you. I can't do what you did to that other woman."

Robert shook his head. "You wouldn't have to. I'll figure out another way."

She leaned against the closed door. "Dresses and skirts, but no panties. Anything else?"

"You know the kinds of tea I like and how I want it prepared. Make sure to bring it. I will create an agenda for you. I expect you to follow it to the letter."

"If I don't?"

Robert gripped her hair at the top of her head and pulled her head to the side as to not hurt her but for her to be aware of who controlled this situation. "You may not like the punishment. No impact. I promise." He released her after kissing the side of her face. Then he pressed his hand on her nether lips. "Keep this shaved. I want it clean and smooth."

Philippa's breath caught as he touched her.

"Do you have a gown for dinner?"

She simply nodded.

"I would love to stay here all day with you, but I have obligations today and another rehearsal." He took out his phone. "Give me your number."

"Oh, *now* you want my direct number? What happened to 'Call security and they can get a hold of me'?" She crossed her arms over her chest.

"I don't think you want to relay to security what I want you to tell me."

Philippa spouted out her phone number while Robert typed it into his phone. Then he turned the screen to her to show the listing as *My Filly*.

"I'm going to text you directions on what I want you to do for the rest of the day." He opened the front door. "I want you to send me visual proof that you completed each item. Is that understood?"

She nodded. "Yes." Philippa moved closer to him. "Why could the other woman call you *Master* but I have to call you *Sir*?"

"Easy. I haven't mastered you yet. I need to figure out what makes you tick. Until then, you will continue to call me *Sir*. Slither calls me *Master* because I have played with her before in a club setting."

"Slither? She goes by the name Slither?" Philly shook her head. Then she covered her mouth. "Oh my God. I have to give Helene her dress back and it's ruined."

Robert held out his hand. "Give it to me."

She ran back to the location where Robert ripped it off her body. It remained in a pool on the floor at the base of the stairs. She picked it up and shook it out.

The back zipper had been broken and the seam in the middle of the bodice now had a rip down the middle.

"Helene is going to kill me. She said Lucian bought that dress special for her for some date night." Philippa chewed on her lower lip as she looked at the mess.

Robert accepted the garment. He peered into the inner lining at the tag. "Ah, I know this designer. I can have this fixed or replaced. If Helene asks for it, tell her that I'm taking care of it."

"Won't that open it up for more questions? She'll ask why you would be taking care of her dress that she let me borrow." Philippa leaned against the doorframe.

"It'll be okay. I think Helene has more pressing items to worry about right now." He headed to his car but stopped by the two words.

"Choke me."

Robert kept his back to her but remained still.

"Did you hear me? I want you to—"

Philippa stopped speaking when Robert stormed back to her.

"That's not funny." His face remained serious. "Why would you say something like that?"

"Because it's what I want. I kept trying to direct you there, but you haven't gone for it." She crossed her arms over her chest, and then crept one hand up to her neck. "It's a strange fantasy. I know." She stared at him. "But I wouldn't say this to someone I didn't trust, someone I didn't know. And you're kinky like me. I thought you wouldn't mind."

Robert took a few steps back from her, widening the gap between them.

"You're judging me." Philippa held the door.

"I'm not. I can't. I mean, I can't judge you." He looked back at his car. "You need to think about what it is you really want."

Robert would have to do the same.

Chapter Fourteen

Robert couldn't remember the last time he had been to Master Jude's home. Right after the infamous video chat with Philippa and right before leaving for military training, Robert spent an intensive two weeks with Master Jude. Each return visit home during breaks, he devoted his free time in learning a new skill. Once Robert got out of the service, he practically moved in with the man to sharpen his skills, whether it be in Shibari, whipping, flogging or caning.

As he stood on the porch of his mentor's home, attempting to dodge heavy raindrops, Robert thought about his decision to return here. What more could he learn? Why did it matter?

His mind immediately went to Philippa. Robert pounded on the front door again. After peering off to the side, he spotted an elderly woman ambling down to the end of her driveway to get her newspaper. Robert kept his back to her to obscure his identity. Why would a royal prince be caught in this part of town, especially without his security detail?

Before he could wonder about his life choices, the door opened. Slither stood on the other side, completely naked and with her head down. So that the elderly woman next door didn't see Slither's nude body, Robert rushed into the home, being careful to cover Slither by holding open his coat.

He closed the door behind himself but didn't remove his coat or gloves. Slither turned on the ball of her foot and padded to the kitchen instead of going to the dungeon area where Jude normally did his training.

Probably as instructed, Slither didn't speak. Her brown hair hung like a curtain over her face until she arrived in the kitchen where Jude stirred something bubbling in a large, silver pot on the stove. The blue flame underneath licked the base of the pot. Slither lifted her head and kept her stare on Jude.

"Thank you for having me, especially on such short notice." Robert gave his mentor a respectful nod.

Jude looked like he mumbled something as he fished items from the pot. Eggs. With a slotted spoon, he retrieved several eggs from the pot and deposited them into a bowl filled with water and ice.

He regarded Robert. "Your girl." He sniffed before shaking his head. "She's not ready."

Robert didn't bother removing his coat or gloves. By the topic and tone from his mentor, it didn't look like this would be a long session. "So you've told me." He nodded. "I misread her."

Jude turned off the heat before staring at Robert. "You two didn't talk about this before the scene?"

Robert threw his shoulders back to show some authority. "We talked about her serving me, but not about the discipline." He held his hand up. "My mistake."

"Damn right."

Jude's harsh criticism cut Robert to his core.

Jude continued. "What I liked about you, Robert, and why I took you on as a student is because, despite your age, you came across as responsible. You didn't come with pretenses, and you for sure could have." He leaned his back against the farmhouse sink underneath the large window that faced his garden. "It's apparent that I didn't teach you enough. You have the technique down." He glanced at Slither. "My girl hasn't been able to sit down properly since yesterday, isn't that right?"

Slither smiled but still did not speak.

"The one you had couldn't tell the difference between abuse and safe discipline. I'm surprised that under your direction, she followed through and held Slither's hands."

Robert held up his hand. "I didn't ask her to do that."

Jude blinked. "You mean to tell me that she got down on her knees, held a strange woman's hands who was being flogged, and allowed that woman to use her finger as a pacifier on her own?"

Robert hadn't thought about it that way. He nodded in response.

Jude snickered. "Hell, maybe she is ready. She had good instincts."

"That and some unusual kinks."

"Such as?"

Robert swallowed. "Choking. It's why I'm here." He took a step closer to Jude.

"Ah, that's what I figured about her. She's not an impact player. You won't get her to cream herself with a whip or paddle. But tell her you'll tie her up or constrict her, she's all yours." Jude picked up a dishtowel to wipe his hands. "Is that why you're here? You want to learn about—"

"Breath play." Robert shrugged. "See if it's something I would like to do."

"For her."

"On her."

Jude nodded and looked over at the bowl of eggs. "Breath play can be edgy. A person is trusting you not to hurt them or worse, kill them." He reached into the bowl, removed an egg and, without warning, tossed it to Robert.

Instead of reaching for it to catch it, Robert dodged it and watched the white oval fall to his feet and crack, spilling its gelatinous contents on the floor. Hell, Jude hadn't boiled all the eggs.

"What the hell are you doing?" Robert looked at the mess at his feet.

Jude pointed down. "Teaching you the number one thing about breath play." He retrieved another egg and threw it.

This time, Robert did attempt to catch it. It bounced out of his gloved hands before falling to the floor next to the raw egg. This one, though, had been boiled. The shell cracked, but the contents remained intact.

"Will you continue to assault me with eggs during this lesson?" Robert glanced down before regarding his mentor. "And will you tell me what the important lesson is?"

Jude tossed another egg. This time, Robert did manage to catch it, but didn't catch the next egg that Jude threw that burst at his feet.

"Shit." Robert backed up. "Just tell me the lesson, man."

"You don't get it?" Jude kept tossing eggs. "I let you watch me get what you thought were hardboiled eggs from this pot." He threw more and more eggs.

Robert caught some, but others crashed to the floor.

"You had an assumption that the eggs would be too hot to manage or maybe you thought that if you missed catching one, it would be okay since it was hardboiled and wouldn't make a mess. You thought the eggs would be solid inside. Tough. Am I right?" Jude moved closer to Robert, still tossing eggs at him.

Robert couldn't juggle to save his life, but he did his best. "Yes. Maybe. What does that have to do with—"

"Your girl."

"Woman." Robert meant no disrespect to his mentor, but he didn't see Philippa as a girl. He couldn't have her be referred that way.

"You probably see her as tough, no nonsense." He glanced at Slither. "Probably tougher than her, right?"

Robert gazed at the woman he disciplined last night. Although he didn't say it, in his head, he did think that Philippa could withstand more than Slither.

Jude stood in front of Robert, standing in the mess of broken eggs and cracked shells at Robert's feet. "The most important lesson is listening." He pointed to his ear. "What does she really want? She's telling you she wants breath play." He turned to Slither and wrapped his meaty hand around her slender neck. "I can teach you that. That's the easy part."

Slither gasped a little and balled her hands into fists.

Jude pointed down. "What you have to do is realize that no matter how tough you think your, um, woman is, she's still fragile." He pointed down to the floor. "Make a mistake, and you could break her."

Robert dropped his gaze to the floor at the mess made by not being observant and careful.

Jude cradled his bear-paw of hand underneath Robert's. "If you're careful, you can still protect her and give her what she wants." He plucked one egg from his hand, shook it, and then peeled the shell from it. "Girl, clean this up." He looked at Robert. "Get comfortable. We have some training to do."

After Slither cleaned the mess from the floor, she obediently stood in her assigned spot. Jude approached her and encouraged Robert to stand with him.

"I like training with eggs because the concept is the same." Jude placed his hand around Slither's neck again. "You must be careful. You can squeeze but never too hard."

Slither stood stock still until she emitted a small gasp. Then Robert watched Jude's hand relax. She took deep breaths.

"Good girl." Jude glanced at Robert. "Your turn."

Robert, who hadn't taken off his coat or gloves, approached her. He raised his hand, but before he could touch her, Jude stopped him with a hand on his arm.

"You're new at this. You really need to touch her. Flesh to flesh." He looked at his hand. "Remove the glove."

Robert didn't question his mentor. He pulled off the glove and held it in his other hand before he placed his hand on Slither's neck without pressure.

Her pulse down the side of her neck drummed against his thumb.

"You're not squeezing, right?"

Robert shook his head. "No."

"Good. Just feel her. Listen to her breath." He patted Robert on his shoulder. "Close your eyes."

With anyone else, Robert would question this request. With Jude, he obliged.

"Experience my girl without sight. Listen to her breathing pattern."

Robert concentrated on her and heard Slither's breathing increase. Fear? Excitement? He couldn't be sure without looking at her. He brushed his thumb up the side of her neck, which, from the way her breathing slowed, seemed to calm her.

"What else do you notice?" By the sound of Jude's voice, he moved to the other side of Robert.

"She's excited." Robert continued stroking her delicate neck. "Her pulse is accelerated." He took a deep breath. "I smell her." Her scent didn't match Philippa's sweet one, but he recognized the musky aroma. "She's sweating."

"Good. You're noticing a lot."

Robert felt a hand over his and he flinched at first.

"Keep your eyes closed." Jude put his hand on Robert's shoulder.

"Now, squeeze her slightly."

With direct guidance from Jude, Robert complied and stopped when Jude no longer compressed his hand. Robert's throat felt dry as he held Slither's neck.

"This edge play can either break your partner, your relationship, or you." Jude kept his hand on top of Robert's. "She's trusting you that you won't hurt her, but you'll give her what she wants. She asked for this, right?"

Robert nodded.

"There are easier ways to take her breath away." Jude snickered. "Kiss her hard enough, it'll make her breathless."

Robert hadn't thought of that. Since Philippa specifically said she wanted to be choked, he didn't think that would satisfy her, not completely.

"Cinch her waist. Corset. Rope. That will give her the same sensation." His mentor moved in closer to Robert and Slither. "As someone new to this, I would suggest you fake her breathlessness."

Robert opened his eyes and turned his head. "What do you mean by that?"

"Relax your hand first." Jude tapped Robert's hand that he had around Slither's neck.

When he did, she took a deep breath.

"Remember how much you squeezed her neck. Do a hair easier with your sub."

Robert started to remove his hand when Jude encouraged him to continue holding her.

"By faking it, you do what I had suggested. Squeeze her neck slightly and kiss her at the same time. Or put a corset on her and—"

"Kiss her?"

Jude chuckled. "I was going to say put your hand back on her neck. I'm guessing you have a different relationship with her than I do with Slither."

Maybe instead of learning this technique, Robert should figure out what Philippa meant to him. She had certainly gotten into his head.

"As your friend, I wouldn't suggest you indulge in this."

That statement caused Robert to blink. Jude had taught Robert everything from caning to flogging to needle play. If Jude didn't like breath play, Robert knew it had to be a little dangerous.

"I suspect you have other reasons for wanting to do this." He patted Robert's shoulder. "Come to me two days a week for two months and you might have the basics down."

Robert shook his head. "I don't have that kind of time." He released his hold on Slither. "I have my event and then I'm going out of town."

"With her?"

Robert nodded.

Jude sighed. "I'll show you the basics, the fake version that should satisfy her."

Even Slither smiled at that idea.

"Looks like your friend has a fan." Jude patted Slither on her naked backside. "Take lots of notes. If she gets hurt, I'll come after you myself."

Robert had no plans to hurt Philippa physically. He would have to figure out a way not to get his heart or hers involved. Easier said than done.

* * * * *

Robert stared at his reflection in the mirror in the main ballroom at Baldington. Wearing his former military dress uniform made him feel like his old self, the one who controlled a troop of soldiers, all who assumed he would skate by on his name and royal association. Robert didn't fear combat. Why had what Philippa said had him running for the hills? Why couldn't he control her just as easily?

In the few times he had been with her, he had suspected she wanted more. Choking? Breath control. He had never been with a woman who liked that. Could he even do that? Robert looked down at his hands. The training done by Master Jude helped him. He didn't know if it would be enough.

He didn't even notice the ballroom filling up or Lucian coming up behind him until his brother slapped him on the back.

Robert jumped. "Hey. What's up?"

Lucian took a step back as he regarded Robert. "I should be asking you that. You look deep in thought, my man. What's the deal?" He nodded at something behind Robert. "Thinking about Princess Tight-Ass?"

Robert turned. Princess Elena waltzed into the room wearing a green and gold gown that clung to her thin frame. She topped the look with a diamond tiara. The event had nothing to do with her, and yet she dressed like she should be the focus. Then his attention got pulled by a shining light.

Philippa glided into the room next to Helene. To Robert, he could only see Philippa in that gorgeous yellow dress. Besides a simple set of small hoop earrings, she let the garment and her glowing skin do the talking for her.

"Let me ask you a question." Robert held Lucian's arm.

"You're asking me for advice? This should be good. Shoot." He grabbed a flute of champagne from a passing waiter.

"In all your time of playing, have you ever been asked to do something you didn't feel comfortable doing?" Robert kept his attention directed on Philippa.

Lucian shrugged. "Not really. I'm pretty open to almost anything." Then he leaned down. "Except bodily fluids. One woman wanted me to relieve myself in all ways on her." He shook his head. "I wasn't down for that, and no, it wasn't Helene."

"I didn't ask." Nor did Robert want to know.

"Princess Tight-Ass is a freak?"

Robert didn't confirm nor deny. He kept looking at Philippa, who stood close enough to Elena that Lucian would have thought Robert stared at the princess.

"You know the rules better than I do." Lucian bumped his elbow next to Robert's arm. "Everything is safe, sane, and consensual. You two talk first before anything happens. You know her triggers, but you have to be honest with yours."

That second part of Lucian's statement worried him.

"If you do all that, Little Brother, everything will turn out great." Lucian wrapped his arm around Robert's shoulders. "You really do look concerned. You're the King of Pain."

Robert shrugged out of Lucian's hold. "I am not. Like you said. Safe, sane, and consensual."

"Or you could be a prick."

Robert glared at Lucian. "Excuse me?"

"You know. Personal responsibility, informed consensual kink. P.R.I.C.K. I cannot be the one who teaches you this." Lucian laughed and it raised Robert's internal temperature.

"From one prick to another, I have another question." Robert moved in closer to his brother.

"This is just the gift that keeps on giving. Spill it." Lucian finished off his champagne and set the glass on a nearby table.

"As far as play, I'm well versed in impact."

Lucian snickered. "You think I called you the King of Pain because I didn't know that? I've seen you play. I've watched you bring a woman to her knees in a puddle of tears and have her begging for more. You're ruthless, but kind." Lucian must have noticed Robert about to refute his statement. "Even through blood, sweat, and tears, I've seen you do hour-long aftercare."

Robert had learned years ago that if anyone submitted to him, he needed to treat their submission and willingness to play as a gift. With that gift, he had to be grateful and thankful for it.

"Why are you asking? Someone you played with called your style shit or something?" Lucian snickered.

"In a way, yes."

Lucian's jovial mood changed. "Really?"

"I wanted to start playing with someone new." Robert glanced up at Philippa. "To show off my style, I had her watch me play with Slither."

Lucian blinked and took a couple of steps back. "Whoa. Slither is a bit hardcore. She will push herself before she screams *red*. You had a newbie watch you play with her?"

Lucian had been right. Robert should have shown off his skills with someone equally new in the Lifestyle and to play.

"I flogged her and paddled her. My sub freaked." Robert spoke between gritted teeth. "If I can't play with her like I like, like I know I can, what else can I do?"

"You're fucking joking, right?" Lucian regarded Robert. "You know everything we do is about sensation. There are so many things you could do that wouldn't involve you using impact." He held up his hand and started ticking off items on each finger. "Interrogation, tickling, humiliation."

Robert shook his head. "She nor I want to do that."

"Okay. Glad you two at least talked about that." Lucian chuckled. "Last time I checked, you were still the best at Shibari."

"What about breath play?" Robert brushed his hand over the front of his uniform jacket.

His brother remained silent as he stared at him for a moment. "She wanted that or did you propose it to her?"

"She did. Choking." Robert cleared his throat. "She wants me to choke her." He shook his head. "I've never done that."

"Not even during sex?"

Robert cocked his head. "Hell no. Not really my thing."

"Sounds like it's hers." He put his hand on Robert's shoulder. "Sounds like you need to go back to school, my friend." When Robert didn't respond, Lucian continued. "See Slither's Master, the one who trained you. He could tell you how to do that safely so that she gets something and you feel comfortable." Lucian looked back into the group milling about the room. "Elena is a freak. Wow. Would have never pegged her as a wild one. Talk about you getting lucky. You get your princess and your submissive. What are the odds?"

That would have been great if Elena wanted that, or if Robert had the same level of attraction to her as he did with Philippa. He couldn't stop staring at the goddess in the yellow dress before him. He couldn't admit to his brother that he had already seen Master Jude for help. Now Robert had to get beyond his own issues with the act to try it.

"Thanks for the advice." Robert tried moving away from his brother.

Lucian held Robert's arm. "Wait. Seriously though, if you like her and this is something the two of you have discussed beforehand, it should all be good. What we do should be fun."

Robert brought his attention to his brother. "But you have to be careful."

"Of course. Now think about what could happen if you combine the two. Skill with fun." Lucian splayed his fingers by his head to simulate his mind being blown.

Lucian had it so easy. He got to be with a woman who shared his same kink and didn't think about furthering the royal line. As soon as Robert thought he knew Philippa, she threw him a curveball.

Robert's father went to him. "I'm about to open the ceremony." He put his hand on Robert's shoulder. "Are you ready?"

Robert smiled. "Yes, sir."

King Clive went to the podium, the same one Lucian had been when he renounced his place in line. Now Robert's father would be announcing him as next in line. Would the citizens there take him seriously?

"Please take your seats." Clive waited until all attendees sat down.

Robert sat up front, which gave him a great view of the guests. When he found Philippa in the audience, he couldn't stop staring at her. In turn, she didn't break her attention from him. She almost dared him to look away. He only did when Clive called him up to the podium to give his speech.

A loud applause sounded as Robert approached his father and gave him a hug before standing at the podium.

"Thank you for the reception." Robert stood up straight. "My family comes from a long line of great and noble people. Warriors, fighters, leaders. That tradition will continue with me when it comes time for me to take over here at Baldington." He glanced at his father. "Fortunately, that will be a long time away."

Modest applause occurred after his statement.

"I do not take this responsibility lightly." As Robert spoke, he realized his words meant more than him being the next in line as the king. "The citizens here and our country are putting a lot of faith in my hands." He glanced down at his large hands. Could he put them around Philippa's delicate throat? Robert looked up. "Rest assured. I will always make the best decision and will look out for the reputation of our country. As I ask that the great citizens accept me as their next king, I would also ask that they take a leap of faith. Some may need to push themselves out of their comfort zones and accept the unexpected." He directed that remark to Philippa, who looked like she gritted her teeth. "Although I was not meant to be in this role, I know what skills I bring to the table. I will be a good leader, who should be obeyed and followed."

Attendees clapped with enthusiasm, some standing on their feet. Above their heads, he saw Philippa standing and starting to walk out of the room. He had to stop her.

"Excuse me, Father." He walked briskly from the room.

"The ceremony isn't over yet."

Robert didn't stop. He couldn't. He had to catch Philippa.

When he walked by Elena, she held her hand out to him. He smiled at her but kept going, careful not to run, but hurried enough to be able to reach Philippa.

Robert spotted her going down a hallway, probably headed to the back of the palace out of sight of the paparazzi. "Philippa, wait."

She slowed her trek but didn't stop. "Why? I don't think you're really interested. You want what you want, and the hell with what anyone else wants or needs."

He caught up to her and held her shoulders. "Would I come after you if I wasn't interested?" He positioned her in a darkened corner by a painting of his great-great-great grandmother, or so he had been told.

"You tell me to be open and honest with you. I am, and you freak out." She tried crossing her arms, but he kept a tight grip on her forearms.

"What you admitted is not something I normally hear. You can't be surprised by my reaction." Even in the darkened nook, Robert attempted to gain some eye contact with Philippa.

"Then you spend most of your time staring at that woman." She glared at him as though daring him to contradict her statement.

"Who do you think I was looking at in the ballroom?"

She pointed toward the room. "That tall, thin woman in that green dress." She fluffed her yellow dress up. "You said you wanted me to wear this and then you don't even give me the time of day. You invited me and you don't even speak to me. You give that speech, where you basically say it's your way or the highway. You don't want me."

Robert had so many answers to her assumptions, but one question plagued him. "Are you jealous?"

Philippa blinked. "Are you serious? I'm telling you how I feel and you want to pit me against a stranger like we're back in high school. I don't know her. I thought I knew you." She snickered. "You know what? Don't worry about it. As a matter of fact, don't worry about our arrangement." She tried getting away from him again.

"Stop doing that. When you get scared of an emotion or you don't get your way, stop running. You did that before, and it cost us five years. Don't do it again." Robert did notice Philippa's eyes widen at his statement.

"Oh, so us not being together was my fault?" She tried pushing him back.

"Yes."

"Yeah, it's a shame you don't have your own jet where you could come to Virginia to visit me." She snapped her fingers. "That's right. You do. And you had my number or could have easily gotten it from Helene. If you wanted me that badly, you would have made it happen. Stop trying to put the blame on me. You keep me at arm's length and expect more."

Robert thought about Philippa's statement. She had been right. He could have gone after her, but he hadn't been used to pursuing women. They came after him. He had kept her and others away from him, choosing to control situations that way.

"We both made mistakes. I'm not going to make another." Robert loosened his hold on her.

"What does that mean? You don't want to do anything with me now?" Philippa's voice softened.

"I'm not a quitter. I'd like to think I'm a problem solver. One step at a time." He let her arms go. "Are you ready for our trip to Virginia?"

"You still want to go with me?"

He nodded. Then he moved in close to her where his body pressed against hers. "Are you wearing panties?" He heard her breath catch.

"No. I'm not." She put her hands to his chest but not to push him away. "What do you want from me?"

"You still want to play. You still listened to me." He kissed the side of her face and went to her ear. "We have something here. We can't let this go without seeing it through."

"What are you saying?" She panted.

"I've been thinking about you. I think I figured something out about you." He brought his hands down to lift her dress. "I think you like the idea of getting caught. The night you masturbated for me, you were worried that your brother would come home."

Philippa lowered her hands to work on his pants. "Yeah? Interesting theory. You think it'll work?"

"One way to find out."

She unzipped his pants.

"Condom in my pocket."

Philippa laughed. "You think of everything."

He reached in his side pocket to pull out the wrapper. Robert ripped it open with his teeth and manage to roll it on his cock that Philippa freed from behind his zipper. In one smooth move, he slipped inside her.

"Oh, God." She gripped his shoulders. "Are we really doing this?"

Robert pumped into her slow and easy at first. "Damn right." Then he kissed her.

"This is your event."

He smiled. "What a way to celebrate me, right?"

Philippa wrapped her long legs around him. "So good. So good." She kissed the side of his face to his ear. "You might be right."

He held her up by cupping her ass and squeezed it after each pump. "Never done anything like this before."

She released a dirty laugh. "I'm a bad influence?"

He laughed. "The worst."

She pressed her lips against his before moving over to his ear. "How do you do it? How do you get me to be so mad at you one minute and then have me wanting to rip your clothes off the next?"

Robert continued thrusting in her. "Same." He shook his head. "Not mad with you. Confused." He pressed his forehead against hers. "Want you so badly." He gripped her ass cheeks. "Tight. Good. I don't like when we're separated."

"Me either." She held his shoulders. "Will you do it?" She leaned back against the wall. "Will you—" Her eyes widened. "Oh, shit!" She released her legs from around him and flailed them while he continued holding her.

"What?"

She pounded his shoulders and pointed behind him. Robert turned in time to see a very stunned Edith Throckmorton looking like a statue Medusa had frozen into stone.

"Shit!" Robert slipped out of Philippa and turned to the mature woman. "Mrs. Throckmorton, it's not what you think."

Philippa moved in next to him and lowered her voice. "Your dick is out."

Robert looked down and turned his back on the woman. "Fuck."

"Yes, what Prince Robert is trying to say is that, we were just talking."

Robert zipped up and brought his attention back to the palace employee when he noticed something about Philippa. "Your tit is out."

In their haste, Robert must have pulled down her dress.

"Oh my God." Philippa turned around to straighten herself out. "Your father is going to fire me for sure now."

"No, he won't." Robert heard a loud thump behind him and Philippa. When they turned around, he saw Mrs. Throckmorton in a heap on the floor.

Chapter Fifteen

Great. Philly could now call herself a closeted freak *and* a murderer.

"I killed someone." She sat in Robert's father's office with Robert while a couple of palace security guards stood watch outside the door.

"You didn't kill anyone." Robert paced in the expansive office and kept his arms crossed over his chest and his face forward.

"Edith caught us having sex and she had a heart attack." Philly recalled the sound of the elderly woman collapsing to the carpeted floor after she watched Philly and Robert go at it like horny rabbits. "I killed her." She glanced up at Robert. "*We* killed her."

"Stop saying that, especially with the guards outside the door." He strolled back toward her. "The last I heard, Mrs. Throckmorton was still alive when the medics took her to the hospital."

Philly exhaled. "Thank God for you."

Robert crouched down in front of her.

"If you hadn't performed CPR, she may not have made it." Every time Philly thought she had the prince pegged, he showed another layer to himself.

Robert patted her hands that she had resting on her knee. "Thank you for getting security to contact medical support." He exhaled. "Let's hope between my life-saving efforts, your quick response, and Baldington's NDA, Edith will keep this matter under wraps."

The office door burst open and King Clive strolled inside, which made Robert and Philly stand at attention.

"Son, I'm so sorry this happened during your special occasion." Clive pulled Robert into a hug.

"No worries, Father." Robert patted him on his back. "Just glad we were there at the right time."

Clive released his son and held out his hand to Philly. "Thank you for your efforts as well."

Philly felt her lips curl up into a shaky smile. "Not a problem. Glad to help."

"Mrs. Throckmorton suffered a mild heart attack." Clive brushed his hand over his hair. "They were able to help her thanks to you two. She will be in the hospital for a couple of days."

"Wow. Considering this was all our fault, I'm glad she didn't die." Philly saw Robert's jaw flinch.

She couldn't help but be honest. It didn't matter if that bothered Robert. Philly had to live with herself.

Clive worried his brows as he split his attention between her and his son. "What do you mean by that?"

Philly exhaled. "Robert and I were—"

Robert cut her off. "Edith caught us—"

"Were you two bickering again?" Clive shook his head.

"We were interacting with each other." Robert looked over at Philly with a pleading look in his eyes.

"You two will need to stop arguing, at least for the sake of your brother and his fiancée." Clive sighed and gripped Philly's shoulders as he regarded her seriously. "Unfortunately, young lady, that means you will have to plan the rest of the wedding on your own for now until I can secure additional help for you."

Philly felt her heart racing. She wanted to do this wedding on her own in the first place. Then when the idea of integrating Lesilitho's traditions in with the wedding, she felt a bit of a relief that she had been paired with the old woman. Now Philly started to feel that sense of doubt that used to plague her for most of her life.

"Philippa will be fine doing the wedding."

She gazed up at Robert.

"I'll assist her with the planning, which will include an out-of-town trip."

Philly tightened her hands into fists and felt her insides turning into molten lava as she listened to Robert.

"That's very nice, Robert, but I'm sure you'll be busy with your obligations." Clive headed to the office door. "As the next in line, you will have to start meeting with dignitaries and heads of state and other influential people around the world. Your personal assistant will debrief you on your upcoming schedule."

Robert gave a slight bow. "Yes, sir."

"By the way, you two don't have to stay holed up in my office. Edith will be fine. There are guests still in the dining area." Clive left the office and kept the door open as though signaling Robert and Philly to leave the room.

Philly still had more to say. "I don't need your help."

"And I don't need you telling my father all the sordid details of what prompted an elderly woman's heart attack." Robert held her hand, but not in an aggressive manner. "And if you didn't need my help, why did you look so nervous?"

"I didn't. You saw something that wasn't there." She started to leave, but he stopped her.

"I'm starting to see the real you." He smiled. "And I think you're bringing out the real me."

She cocked her head. "What is that supposed to mean?"

Robert squeezed her hand. "Let me make a couple of calls. I want us leaving sooner rather than later."

* * * * *

Robert had never been this impulsive. Between the risky sex, the near-fatal encounter, and his father's demand, he decided to do what he did best. He would be taking control of his life and this situation.

With everything that had happened, Robert had no designs on waiting, especially when he felt Philippa pulling away from him again. No, he needed to confine her in an area and ask her some tough questions.

When he arrived at Moonwalk Manor to retrieve her, he had expected to find Philippa in her standard sleep attire of black tights, a long-sleeved T-shirt and a scarf around her head. Instead, she had on what she wore the first day she arrived to Lesilitho, which Robert didn't like.

Although he loved seeing her in skin-tight jeans and those over-the-knee boots, he would have rather have her in a dress or skirt. As usual, Philippa would make him work for her.

"Are you ready?" Robert stood in the doorway of Moonwalk with the driver behind him. Robert carried his carryon bag with him.

"I can't believe you were serious." She shook her head. "I packed." She nodded to the side. "My bags are there."

Robert instructed the driver to take them to the car.

"Where will we stay?" She put her hand to her head.

Robert held her shoulders. "Don't worry. I have everything taken care of for the two of us. We will be fine and secured."

When he said the word *secured*, Philippa's shoulders relaxed.

He turned to make sure they didn't have an audience listening to their conversation. "Did you grab the condoms?" He wouldn't beat around the bush about this.

Philippa dropped her gaze. "Why? Trying is futile."

"That's not what I asked." He leaned down to her. "If I thought you would respond to it, I would spank you." He felt her shiver, but he recognized that the reaction stemmed from a negative response and not a positive one. "Answer me."

She shook her head. "I left them on the drawer by the bed."

"I'll get them and some other items. You go to the car and wait for me." He kissed her temple as he raced up the stairs to the main bedroom first.

When Robert opened the drawer next to the bed, he found three strips of condoms. He grabbed all of them and put them in his bag. He didn't see her vibrator, an item he knew she kept in that drawer. Maybe Philippa packed it and wanted to still try achieving an orgasm on her own.

Robert went to the room where he kept his toys. He closed the door behind himself to ensure his privacy. He knew what he wanted. He opened a bottom drawer and looked at the variety of ropes in various colors and types. He picked up a bundle of white parachute rope. He wouldn't get any of the colored ones. He didn't need the colors transferring to her skin and possibly getting asked questions about the stains.

He stuffed the rope into the bag and then snagged some nipple clamps. Robert went to bed with Philippa on his mind despite the nearly tragic consequences of getting caught. If his assessment of her and what she responded to hit the mark, he might be able to crack the code.

He ran back down the stairs in time to see the driver at the doorway.

"The plane is ready for you, sir." The driver stood on the front step, dutifully waiting for Robert.

"Good. Let's go."

* * * * *

"I can't believe I'm doing this." Philly had her arms folded as she sat on the jet with the man who had done the best he could to get her to come. "And with you. I thought you were mad at me."

Robert undid his seatbelt now that the plane had leveled. "Not mad. Surprised. You are for sure the most honest person I have ever met. I like that about you. It does surprise me when you choose to share your, um, honesty."

"If you say what's on your mind, you never leave people wondering what you think and you take everything off your plate." She brushed her hands off like invisible dust existed on them. "I've found living my life that way frees me up to concentrate on what's important."

"Like achieving an orgasm."

Philly felt her face and chest flash hot like someone set her head on fire. "That's a desire, not a need. I need to work. I don't need to have a great sex life."

Robert regarded her for a moment. "You don't believe that. It's the first time I doubted you. I think I have figured out how to get you to respond."

"I don't need your help." To illustrate that point, Philly crossed her arms over her chest and settled back into the most comfortable seat she had ever occupied. "Besides, the last time we tried, we almost killed someone."

"But we didn't." He cocked a smile at the corner of his mouth.

She remembered how luxurious the ride to Lesilitho had been when Lucian and Helene had allowed her to use the plane to get there. Being back in it now with a guest made the trip even more decadent.

A flight attendant came up to the two of them. "May I get you two something to drink or eat?"

Robert stood. "Are there refreshments in the sleeping quarters in the back?"

"Yes, sir, as requested." The young woman gave a slight nod.

He guided the employee away from Philly and whispered something in her ear. Knowing Robert, he probably gave her specific directions on how he wanted his tea. The idea of that had Philly's clitoris throbbing. How did Robert make preparing his tea out to be something so erotic?

Philly imagined herself naked and presenting his drink. Something so simple yet intimate.

The flight attendant looked over at Philly before nodding her head to Robert and returning to the front of the plane.

He held out his hand to Philly. "Come. We are going to retire to the room."

Philly hesitated to take his hand, but finally did. Robert guided her to the back of the plane and opened a door, which led to a large room that resembled an apartment bedroom except for the small airplane windows that lined both sides of the room. A bright, blue sky colored each window view.

"What did you tell her?" Philly stood in the middle of the room.

Robert smiled as he strolled around her. "I told her that I plan to fuck you raw and that she should come into the room in about thirty minutes."

While he stood behind her, she asked, "To join us?" Her heart slowed thinking Robert would want someone else besides her to satisfy him.

He leaned close to her head and whispered in her ear, "To watch."

Robert sauntered to the front of her and held the hem of his sweater.

"What do you think you're doing?" Philly watched Robert remove his sweater and lay it across a chair that had been bolted down next to the bed.

"Getting undressed. You need to do the same." He started undoing his cuffs.

Philly jutted her thumb over her shoulder. "But the flight attendants—"

"Will come in here in thirty minutes." He removed his shirt, revealing his bare chest. "You want them to get a good show, right?"

Philly felt herself wanting to drool at the sight. "Uh, yes, I mean, no. What are you doing to me? Is this part of the scene?"

Instead of answering her direct question, he said, "Take off your clothes."

"Why?"

Robert unfastened his belt and worked on his pants. "I want to talk to you."

"Why naked?" She shrugged.

"I want to see your body." He smiled as he toed out of his shoes and padded over naked to her. "I seem to be more honest when I'm naked." His cock swung majestically back and forth. "You need help?"

As much as she wanted Robert to remove her clothes, at this point, she didn't think it would make a difference. "I can talk with my clothes on."

He glared at her. "Perhaps I wasn't making myself clear. How's my hair?"

Philly felt her knees go weak. "You can't do this to me."

Robert put his hand to the waistband of her jeans and pulled her forward. "What's going on with you? Sometimes you seemed ready to play and other times you don't."

"I'm afraid of losing myself in all this." She tried to take a step back from him, but Robert had a tight hold of her. "Like with your father, the king. He said I would have to plan the wedding on my own and you immediately said you would help me."

"You took offense to that?"

She nodded. "You don't trust that I can do this job."

Robert shook his head as he pulled her shirt from her jeans. "Just the opposite. I believe in you. I believe that anything you put your mind to that you can do it." He pulled her shirt off and wagged his finger in her face. "I saw you questioning yourself for a moment." He rested his hands on her shoulders before easing them back behind her to unclasp her bra. "I'm on your side."

"What changed?" She allowed him to undress her while she listened to him.

Robert worked on her jeans. "You successfully got me to appreciate another side of BDSM play after I had convinced myself that I no longer wanted to be a part of the lifestyle. I think about you when I'm not with you. I think about other ways to play with you than what I'm accustomed. I'm adapting. You are more persuasive than you know." He eased her jeans and panties down to her knees where here boots stopped the trek. Robert eased her back onto the bed. "You are also very strong." He unzipped her boots and removed them. "I keep telling you that when you're afraid of something to not run away. I need to do the same thing." He removed her footwear, jeans, panties and socks so that he had her naked as well. "Tell me. When we were in the hallway, were you close?"

She knew what he meant. "A little. I felt it. I don't know if you had kept going if I would have…" Philly stopped talking as soon as she saw Robert pull out rope from his black carryon bag.

Chapter Sixteen

Philly's heart pounded hard as she stared at the bundle in Robert's hand.

"You are the only woman I have worked this hard for in my life." Robert approached her. "I think about you constantly. I'm finding that helping you is helping me."

"How?" For any other person, the sight of a person with rope in their hands would cause some fear and discomfort. Philly became intrigued and moved to the edge of the bed to get closer to him.

"I have been accused of being a bit self-centered and not as observant about what's going on around me." He touched his temple. "I thought back again to our video conversation. I have every bit of it committed to memory." He climbed on the bed behind her. "One aspect was the idea of you possibly getting caught. But there was another part that I think you liked. I remembered the shoes you wore." He threw the tail end of the rope to the floor in front of her. "The shoes laced up your legs. Between that and your request for some light choking, I think I figured out what will get you to cross over." He let the soft rope dangle between her breasts and legs. "I think you would respond well to being tied up. What do you think?"

Philly felt the rope brushing against her sensitive skin between her breasts. The tickling feeling had her writhing, which brushed her backside against his slowly hardening cock. As much as she wanted to revolt to this plan, she stiffened her body, not out of fear. She wanted to prepare herself to be bound.

"I'm ready." Philly pressed her hands on the mattress on either side of her body.

Her breathing remained steady, even as he wrapped the rope

around her waist. She closed her eyes and leaned her head back. She felt the top of her head connecting to his chin.

Robert said nothing as he continued wrapping her so slowly and intricately, she felt like the most exquisite Christmas gift. After tightening the rope around her waist, he brought it up between her tits in a V shape before he moved from behind her and placed her on her back on the bed. At that moment, Philly opened her eyes and connected her gaze to his.

Robert didn't break his stare from her. She didn't believe he even blinked as he continued working on her, wrapping the rope around her wrists as he straddled her body.

"I'm on birth control." Philly's voice came out so low that she croaked her initial words.

Robert didn't respond.

She wrapped her free legs around his body. "I'm clean. I got tested a few months ago."

He sped up his motions and had both her wrists tied together before he tied them the headboard that also had to be bolted to the floor. Then he turned to glance at the door. "How do you feel? Are you hurting?"

The rope dug deliciously into her sides and the sensitive skin around her arms. She curved her hips up to brush against him. Instead of answering his question, she said, "I'm ready." She hoped he knew what she meant.

From the glint in his eyes, Philly knew he understood her sentiment. Robert lowered his head and smothered her with a kiss that started off so tender before it became commanding and passionate. He slid his tongue into her mouth, and she eagerly accepted it. She wanted more.

He cupped her breast and massaged it. Robert broke from the kiss long enough to go down to her nipple and suck it hard.

Philly cried out and wondered if the flight attendants heard her over the plane's engine. He moved his mouth over to her unattended breast and licked it. While he did that, he grabbed the rope that he had by the breast he had suckled and moved it over her sensitive nipple, brushing it back and forth, causing her body to jerk each time.

"Yes." She arched her back and pulled on her restraints, forgetting the fact that he had her tied down except for her legs.

Robert sat up on his knees and pushed her legs apart. He glanced over at the door and chuckled.

How long had they been in the room? Philly had gotten so lost in the sensation of Robert tying her that she forgot about the time. Would an attendant come into their room soon?

Before she could ask him, Robert aimed the tip of his cock at her core and rubbed it up and down her slick nether lips before he eased himself inside.

"How does it feel?" His thrusts came slow, but deep.

Robert pulled himself back before sliding back in her, always deeper than the time before. The ropes around Philly's waist restricted her breathing. She could only take short, shallow breaths.

"Talk to me." He put his hand next to her cheek while he slid his other hand under her ass and squeezed it.

She shook her head. "Can't." She smiled. "Saving. Breath."

Robert's face went serious. "You can't breathe? Are these too tight?" He touched the ropes around her waist.

"Perfect." She nodded. She curved her hips up. "Perfect." Her stomach tightened. "Yes, Sir." She turned her head and brushed her face against her arm.

"My Filly." He kissed the side of her face and then moved his hand and wrapped his hand around her neck.

Robert didn't squeeze it. Not at first. Then Philly felt the slight pressure. In turn, she tightened her legs around his body and undulated her hips. Philly felt her vaginal walls constricting around his shaft.

"The day after my celebration dinner, I saw a friend of mine." Robert growled in her ear. "He taught me how to do this." He held her neck and tightened his grip ever so slightly. "You like it?"

Philly nodded. She could still breathe, yet she liked his control.

"The attendant will be in the room at any moment." Robert growled in her ear.

"I don't give a shit." She pulled on the ropes that kept her wrists bound. "Don't stop. Don't stop. Don't…"

Philly felt what she had been needing for years. She gasped, which seemed to prompt Robert to tighten his grip on her neck. Her stomach tightened at the same time her body shook.

Robert thrust in her harder and harder.

"Yes. Yes." She nodded and held her breath as she felt a wave of pleasure wash over her body.

"Breathe. Breathe, damn it." He loosened his hold around her neck.

At that moment, Philly released a long, low wail. She felt her body shaking uncontrollably.

"Yes. Yes. Good." Robert pumped into her faster and faster until he came deep in her.

Philly felt his hot semen bathing her insides. When he came down from his euphoric high, he let go of her neck.

Philly tried catching her breath as she stared up at the ceiling. All at once, what had happened to her hit her and her eyes started stinging.

Don't you fucking do it, girl. Don't you dare cry.

She made sure she positioned her face away from Robert's view. "Hey, are you okay?"

With his simple question, the floodgates opened, and Philly did something she hadn't done since her dog died during her freshman year at college. She cried.

Robert started to pull out of her when Philly clamped her legs around him again.

"No. No." She shook her head. "Don't leave. Stay right here, please. Just stay."

"I won't leave." He held her chin and brought her face around so that she had to look at him. "You came."

Robert didn't ask. He must have felt it when it happened to her.

Philly nodded. "You did it."

She didn't elaborate, but Robert gave her a slight smile like he understood.

"You're my first." He let the same hand that he had around her neck coast down the side of her body. "I've never done breath play before."

She smiled. "Is that what you all call choking? Breath play?"

"That's what I have to call it." He adjusted his body, but he kept himself inside and on top of her. "He trained me by having me hold an egg." He held up his hand to her face. "I had to squeeze it without crushing it."

"How many did you break?"

Robert chuckled. "I had enough for the three of us to have a three-egg omelet. But I continued trying until I got it right." His face became serious. "Then I tried it on a live subject. Slither can take a lot, but she's honest. Reminds me of you."

Philly didn't know how she felt about Robert testing his skills on another woman, the same woman he disciplined at the house. Her logical mind argued that if he wanted her, he could have had her.

"Between him and Slither, I became a quick study to get the technique down. I didn't hurt you, did I?"

She shook her head.

"Was it the idea of being caught that pushed you over the edge?" He glanced at the door again.

Philly shook her head. "I don't care about someone seeing us have sex." She caressed the rope by her hands. "No, it was this. All of this. The rope, how you have me tied, the weight of your body, your hand around my neck. I loved it all." She thought about all that and felt the smile disappearing from her face. "Does that make me strange?"

Robert chuckled. "If it does, then I have issues, too."

"Thank you for not giving up on me." She stretched as much as she could while being tied and with Robert still inside her.

"Thank you for believing me." His smile widened. "I lied about the attendant. I whispered to her that you needed some rest and to not disturb us unless the plane is about to land or if there is an emergency. I ordered her to go to the front section of the cabin so that she would not hear us."

Philly laughed, and the feeling opened her chest and release the last bit of fear she had been holding onto for years.

"Now that I know you're into being confined, I'm going to have some fun with you." He ran his fingertips down the side of her body.

An announcement came over the speakers in the room that the plane would be landing in Virginia in about an hour.

"Do we have time for another round?" Philly cocked her head.

Robert shook his. "We need to shower and get dressed. When we get to the safe house, we can resume our activities. But there's something you need to do."

At this point, Philly would do anything for him. The man managed to figure out her kink. Who knew it would be ropes?

"Anything."

"Tell me about this musical act for Lucian and Helene's wedding." He slid out of her. "Despite all this, if I don't approve, they won't be a part of the ceremony."

Damn. Old Robert reared his ugly head again.

* * * * *

Robert didn't remember feeling this giddy about anything since he wanted a horse as a small child. Once he and Philippa arrived at the safe house in Virginia Beach, they had to wait in the chauffeured car a bit longer for the house to be fully checked out before he could go inside.

"We'll take your bags to your room, sir." A guard said as he stood stock straight next to Robert. "You will be in the main room." He glanced at Philippa. "The young lady will be in the guest room down the hall."

Robert stared at Philippa. He wanted so much at that moment to scream for her items to be placed in his room. He desired to go to bed with her and wake up next to her…with her being bound by his ropes, of course.

Instead, he nodded. "Very good." He saw Philippa's shoulders slump down.

She turned her back on him as she glanced around the room.

"The security staff will be housed in the guest house next door." The guard jutted a thumb over his shoulder to point in the direction of the supplemental accommodations.

Robert thought about that place and how perfect it would have been to use it to play with Philippa, particularly since he knew how vocal she could be during play and sex. He replayed in his head the way she moaned when she came, and he immediately got hard. Robert clasped his hands together and placed them over his genital area to cover it.

"Will you please have our items unpacked for us?" Robert held Philippa's elbow while keeping his back to the staff. "We need to work out some details for when we go out. Are we all secure at the venue?"

The older guard nodded. "Yes, sir. We've checked out the location and have spoken directly to the owner and staff. You and Ms. Powell will not be disturbed. After the show, you will be allowed to speak to the musical act in a private section of the establishment."

"What about our entrance?" The more Robert thought about business, the more his cock deflated, despite still holding onto Philippa's arm. "We cannot go through the main entrance or sit with the other attendees."

The guard paused and almost looked like he cursed himself in his head that he hadn't thought about that aspect of their trip. "I'll make sure to arrange for that to happen as well. If you'll excuse me, I have some calls to make."

"Good. We'll be in the office." Robert guided Philippa to an office on the main floor.

After walking inside, he closed and locked the door behind them. Now that he knew exhibitionism didn't rate as one of Philippa's kinks, he didn't feel the need to cater to that fantasy.

"Nice house." Philippa wandered around the room and gazed up at the tall bookcases. "Is this like Moonwalk Manor? Does it stay empty unless you all come here?"

"Depends on the season and circumstance." Robert brushed his hand over the cherrywood desk that sat by a large bay window. He thought about the last time the home had been occupied. Against his nature and better judgment, he glanced up at Philippa. "Lucian made a mistake recently that almost caused a dangerous situation for my country. At the time, he was the next in line as king. He and Father had to be separated." He pointed down. "He was brought here. Father and I stayed in Baldington." He sat on the corner of the desk. "The threat of riots, violence, and damage to the palace were real and constant."

Philippa covered her mouth. "Oh my God. I had no idea. Am I safe there?"

The question had Robert bolting to his feet. "Of course. Lesilitho is a secure country with good people. One incident shouldn't label us in a negative way. You couldn't find a more idyllic place to..." He stopped talking when he noticed Philippa smiling as she stared at him. "What?"

"You." She strolled in front of him. "You are very protective of your country. Your face lights up when you speak about it."

As soon as she had mentioned the way he passionately talked about Lesilitho, he felt his heart pounding in his chest. He placed his hand over his heart. "I do love my country." He felt his back stiffen. "Even when my country doesn't always love me back."

"I think you're wrong about that. I think people in Lesilitho love and respect you." She approached him. "Did you want me here with you for a reason?" She glanced back at the door. "With the door locked?"

Robert stared into her eyes for a beat before looking on top of the desk for items he needed for her. At the other corner of the desk, he found a leather-bound notepad and an ink pen encased in black and gold. "Get the paper and pen." He pointed to the items as he took a seat behind the desk.

Philippa retrieved both and started to sit on a chair across from him.

"No." He shook his head. "Come here."

She sauntered towards him. "So, we're playing? You didn't ask me the question."

Robert glanced up at her. "How's my hair?" Then he pointed to the floor.

Philippa lowered herself to her knees without breaking eye contact with him. "Perfect as usual. It is day fifteen of my submission. I am learning to be yours."

"Good." He exhaled when she obediently complied with his commands. "Write down this list of what I want you to do. For each one you complete, you will be rewarded."

"How?" Her wide eyes had him sunk.

He held her chin. "Don't worry. You will like it." He brushed his thumb over her bottom lip.

"Will you like it, too?" She must have taken his gesture of admiring her full lips as a message to do more. Philippa licked his thumb before nipping the tip with her teeth.

"I like anything we do together." He meant that. Robert found himself looking for her during the day. "Now if you don't complete all the tasks, you will be punished." She started to open her mouth to ask a follow-up question when he stopped her. "Just like the reward, you will have to wait and see for the punishment." He pointed down. "Open it up. Start with *one*."

"Yes, Sir." She did as he instructed.

"One. While here, you will wear dresses or skirts and no panties." That should be an easy directive.

"Uh-oh." Philippa chewed on her lower lip.

"Is there a problem?"

"I packed mostly jeans and leggings. With Virginia weather, I didn't want to freeze."

"Disappointing considering we talked about this before we left. You have two options. You can go home and retrieve other items since you live in Virginia Beach. Or on the days you wear pants, go without a bra." Either way, Robert felt like he couldn't lose.

"Okay. No bra it is." Philippa scribbled something down on the paper.

Robert furrowed his eyebrows. "You do live in Virginia Beach, right?"

She nodded but kept her gaze down on the paper.

"Is there a reason you don't want to go back home? Did you leave your place a mess?" When she didn't answer, he continued. "I welcomed you into a dwelling meant for me and my future wife. You picked the lock and discovered another part of me. And you can't let me in to see your place?"

"It's not a castle." She shrugged.

"I didn't expect it would be." He chuckled to lighten the mood, but her face remained stoic.

She took a deep breath and held the pen over the paper. "You had other tasks you wanted me to do?"

Robert felt that wall coming up again. "I do. Two, I want you to bring me tea in the afternoon at two. Not five minutes before or after. That would also constitute a punishment."

"Should I be naked for that task?" Philippa completely turned over to her business side. She no longer seemed fun or playful.

"Yes. Three, you will not masturbate while here." He heard her grumbling. "Is there a problem?"

She took a moment before she responded. "You got me to come

on the plane. I don't want to lose that feeling." She got up on here haunches and moved in closer to him. "I figured if I kept myself primed and ready for you, I might achieve an orgasm much easier." She placed here hand on his knee. "You can watch."

As much as he would have loved to see that show, he shook his head. "No playing with yourself. I won't repeat myself again. Understood?"

Her shoulders slumped. "Yes, Sir."

"Four, you will go to bed—"

"With you?"

"—when I tell you."

"Oh." She continued writing.

"You will get up by seven each morning to make my breakfast. Each morning will be something different. I will tell you what I want the night before." He leaned forward. "Eggs Benedict and wheat toast tomorrow." He winked at her.

"Yes, Sir."

He noticed her breathing started to accelerate.

"What else? There's more, right?" Her nipples hardened under her top.

"There's always more. Five, each day, I will bind you in some way."

Philippa released a moan she probably didn't think Robert heard, but he did.

"You like being tied?"

She nodded. "But I love this more." She swept her hand over the paper. "The list. I like that you want me to do things for you."

"You may not like these last few items." He sat up taller. "Six, I want you to take me to your home while we're here."

Her eyes widened, but he wasn't done.

"Seven, I want final say on the musical act we see."

Philippa's eyes narrowed to slits.

"Eight, your safe word is *pumpkin*. You can use it at any time to stop playing. Any questions?"

She glared at him as she rose to her feet. "Pumpkin."

Chapter Seventeen

Philly placed the pad of paper and pen on the desk and started to back away toward the door. Robert had pushed her out of her comfort zone a lot while they have been together. Although she loved the list and the regimented nature of completing each item, she knew deep down she couldn't do all of them.

"Don't you move." Robert held his hand up to her.

Surprisingly, his directive halted her in her spot.

"You forgot the list." He pointed at it, which forced her to drop her gaze to it like she didn't recall it. "And you forgot who's running things here now."

"I'm tired, and I want to—"

He motioned for her to move closer to him. "Come here."

Philly shook her head. "I said the word. Pumpkin. I want to stop. I can't. I—"

"Philippa, come to me." He held out his arms this time in a welcoming manner.

Philly tried hard to stand strong. She wouldn't crumble into his arms like some scared little girl. She strolled to him and kept her arms crossed over her chest. "I didn't want to come back home, not this soon."

Robert rested his outstretched hands onto his thighs as he regarded her. "Why?"

She took a deep breath. "I know how I am. I want…" She hesitated in blurting her truth. She had never been one to hold back. Philly wouldn't start now. "I want what you have."

Robert blinked. "Ah, a royal title. The palace. The money."

Philly stood in between his knees as she glared down at him.

"The family." She had to force herself to relax her jaw to talk to him. "I told you how free and unstructured my parents were. I grew up not having a curfew or rules. They didn't care who I dated or what time I came home each night. When I would come home from school, there would be no one there to greet me or even watch me. I had the key to our home to let myself in since I was in kindergarten." She shook her head even harder. "That's not right. For years, I've been reaching out to my parents to sit down and have a meal with them. Dinner, lunch, breakfast. Hell, I'll even do a brunch. Mom will flat-out tell me no, always because she has something better to do." Philly recognized right away that she got her honesty trait from her mother, but nothing else. "Dad is the opposite. He'll readily agree and either not show up or call right before we're supposed to meet and cancel on me." She placed her hand on her chest in hopes of stopping her heart from breaking. "I want to bring you to my home and not because I've been inside your homes. I want to be fully transparent to you." She reached down for one of his hands and placed it over her heart. "I really want you to know me like I've gotten to know you. I haven't lied to you. If I call my parents to have us meet somewhere, I don't want their responses to cause me to lie to you."

This time, Robert shook his head. "You wouldn't. If you arranged to have us meet for dinner and they bail, you can tell me that."

"Yes, but you'll look at me like—"

"Like you are so lucky to spend more quality time with me." He smiled.

The joke hadn't been lost on her. As much as she didn't want to, Philly chuckled a little. "This is the reason I wanted to come back home alone." When she noticed his eyebrows furrowing, she continued with her explanation. "I see you back home and you love your country. You show it off with such pride. Despite their quirks, you do love your family. Your father makes you all sit down for family meals, which I love. I don't have that. I have nothing."

Robert held her hands. "Not true. You have heart. It's what my father has. It's what he uses to raise us and get us together. Despite how you were raised, you came out beautifully." He kissed the backs of her hands. "You're disciplined, hardworking, stubborn, and—"

"Stop." She squeezed his hands and had to press her legs together to ease her throbbing clit. "If you keep going, I'm going to want to do things to you in this office that will get your staff talking."

Robert stood. He placed one of her hands over his cock. "Not everyone on my staff talks."

Philly rubbed her hand up and down the front of his pants and felt his penis growing harder and harder with each pass. "I don't know. This one is saying a lot to me right now." She gazed up at him. "I don't want to disappoint you." She meant that for a number of reasons, from seeing her humble home and possibly her parents to the possibility of not achieving another orgasm. The more she thought about it, the more worried she became.

"The only way you can do that is if you aren't authentic. After what you've just confessed to me, I have no fear of that." He gave her a sweet peck on her lips before kissing over her cheek to her ear.

"That's nice, but what if I can't come again? What if on the plane was a fluke?" She squirmed in her spot as he nibbled on her ear.

"What's number one?"

"What?" She braced one hand behind her on the desk.

"The list. What's the first item on it?"

Thank God for her perfect memory. "Skirts or dresses with no panties. If in pants, no bra." After the incredible sex on the plane, Philly had changed into her jeans, a long-sleeved shirt, and booties.

Without being directed to do so, Philly released Robert's hand and pushed back from him. She pulled off her shirt, reached behind herself, unclasped her bra and let it slide down her arms to the floor.

Robert walked slowly toward her. "I want to see your home."

She opened her mouth to protest, but he stopped her, not with words. Robert removed his sweater and tossed it aside before removing the shirt underneath to reveal his bare chest.

"Yes, Sir." Her mouth watered as she watched him undoing his belt.

"Call your parents." He stood in front of her hand placed his hand on her waist. "You want to. If they show up, great. If not, it's on them. You have to keep trying."

"I didn't tell you my other fear." Which suddenly went out of her head as soon as he started undoing her jeans. "Um, what if I do invite them and they only show because of who I'm with? My parents love the sensation. I'm not using you as bait to get their attention."

He pulled her pants and panties down in one motion. "Now you're going to have to stop talking or I'm going to blow. I think you're the first woman who had no interest in using me for my status." He kissed her.

Philly closed her eyes and sank into the feeling of his full but firm lips against hers. When she parted her lips slightly, he took the opportunity to slide his tongue inside. He commanded her mouth, just like his hands mastered her body.

Robert broke from the kiss long enough to undo his belt and pull it through his belt loops. He turned her around with her back facing him and wrapped the belt around her waist. From the way the belt dug into her flesh, she could tell he didn't put the metal stem through any of the belt holes.

He pulled on the belt like a leash, bringing her back to him.

"Hands on the desk."

She obliged. She obeyed. She wanted him.

Robert pulled on the belt, tightening it around her stomach. Philly's breath caught, but she enjoyed the confined feeling. Then he snaked his hand between her thighs to her core. His long digits danced against her nether lips.

"Ah, you are wet for me."

She nodded. "Yes. Yes." Philly rubbed her backside against the front of his pants. "Inside. Please." Her heart pounded so hard and her clit throbbed so much, she knew she could achieve an orgasm if he fucked her.

Damn, did she want to be fucked. The fact that Robert had gotten her to come on the plane opened her eyes to a new possibility.

Robert brushed his thumb over her extended clitoris. With each pass, her body jerked and came to life. He teased her by brushing the tips of his fingers over her hole. Philly heard her wetness coating his digits. He pulled on the belt more, tightening his hold.

"Yes." Philly nodded. "Don't let me go."

Robert pinched her clit in between his index and middle fingers and slid his hand back and forth over her. "My Filly."

It didn't take long for Philly's legs to start trembling. "Want to touch my nipples."

"I'll allow it." He sounded like a judge. He nibbled on her earlobe, causing her to cry out in ecstasy.

"Can't. Can't move my arms." She locked her elbows in order to stay upright. If she hadn't, she would collapse on the desk.

"That's a shame." He kissed her collarbone. "I have to hold onto the belt. And then there's what this hand is doing."

He plunged two fingers inside her and held it there. The sudden but welcomed intrusion along with feeling the belt around her and his chest pressed against her back, Philly released a scream.

She didn't care if anyone heard her. From the way Robert continued sliding his fingers in and out of her, he didn't mind her being vocal either.

Robert took his time thrusting in her.

"You feel good." Philly continued grinding her ass against him.

He sped up his motions and tightened the belt even more, which she didn't think would be possible. Her breath hitched and came out ragged.

Unable to talk, she simply nodded. She felt her inner walls tightening around his fingers with each pass. As though she had asked him to, Robert increased his speed and pressed his body against her harder.

Philly's legs shook so much that a couple of times she did crumple. Robert's tight hold of the belt around her kept her upright.

"Shit." She shifted her feet as much as she could with her pants and panties around her ankles. "Can't believe it. Can't…"

Philly pounded her fist on the desk and screamed as she came even harder than earlier. Even as she started to come down from the orgasmic high, Robert kept up the piston motion until Philly turned her head to kiss the side of his face, the only part of him she could reach.

He slowed down until he finally stopped but kept his fingers inside her channel. "You're getting better at this."

She laughed. "You are discovering new ways to get me off. I've never had a guy finger me into an orgasm. How did you do that?"

Robert slipped his fingers out of her and released the belt. "I had to bind you some way. I think the belt worked."

When she had enough strength, Philly managed to turn around in enough time to catch Robert licking her juices from his fingers. "You are the sexiest man I have ever been with." She reached for his pants. "Your turn."

He held her wrist with his free hand. "Not this time."

"But I want to." She shuffled up to him. "I want you in my mouth."

Robert growled. "As much as I would love that, My Filly, you have an assignment."

With her head still in a fog, the only thing she could think he meant would be taking a shower.

When she didn't answer, he filled in the blanks. "Call your parents. Arrange for us to see your home. The concert is tomorrow night?"

She nodded. Philly did remember that.

"Good. We can go to your place and eat dinner there."

"You want me to cook?" Philly pulled up her panties and jeans.

"Only if you want to. I know you enjoy it. If not, we can have a staff member pick something up from one of your favorite restaurants. I let you eat cuisine from my country. You can do the same here." He bent over and picked up her shirt and bra.

Robert stared at her black, lacy bra for a moment before he simply handed Philly her shirt. He stuffed her bra in his pocket. "Do you need assistance getting to your room?" He rendered her mute while he reached around her to undo his belt and remove it.

She slipped her shirt over her head. It felt good to feel the soft fabric brushing against her still hard nipples. "If I say yes, would you walk me to my room so we can finish what we started here?"

Robert smiled. "Again, as tempting as that sounds, I am going to hold off."

"Are you sure? I mean, you know how I started. Two in a row, that's pretty big. Don't you want to strike while the iron is hot?"

He put on his shirt but opted not to wear his sweater. "As tempting as that is, I will refrain for now." He ripped off the paper with her directives on it and walked toward her. "Don't forget this." He handed it to her before he guided her to the office door and unlocked it.

Before he opened it, he pressed her back against it and kissed her hard enough for her to want to stay in that room and beg to fuck him.

"Get your rest. Tonight will be special."

"Then I had better go since it looks like I have some homework to do." She held up the paper and waved it at him.

Robert gave her another kiss before he opened the door and escorted her to the open and opulent-looking staircase. Philly noticed a guard standing at the base of the stairs. He flashed a smirk before turning away. Guess he heard what Philly and Robert had done in the office.

Philly didn't care now like she didn't when Robert had made her scream. If Robert changed his mind and decided to join her in her room now, she would scream again.

The man knew how to curl her toes. As she ascended the stairs, she felt both a physical and emotional separation from Robert. Now she started to get permanent thoughts, relationship thoughts. As long as she remembered that at the end of all this, she would come back home to Virginia Beach. Robert – *Prince* Robert – would remain in Lesilitho. Damn, could he make her body sing.

The décor to her new room looked different than Moonwalk Manor. The pale gray walls and cream-colored bed linens along with the tan-and-rust colored rug under the king-sized bed reminded her of home, her home specifically. She attempted to keep only light colors in her home to make it palatable for her and inviting to others. She placed the list on the bed.

"Nice." Philly sat on a light-brown plush chair next to the bed to remove her shoes and socks.

Before Philly did anything else, she needed to shower. She had no problem leaving Robert's smell on her. Philly savored the phantom sensation of feeling him behind her, pressing his body against her back.

Philly wanted to rest comfortably in clean sheets. Besides, maybe if she cleaned her body, she would go to bed with pure thoughts and not the same fantasies of Robert that had been plaguing her since she had arrived to Lesilitho. Who was she kidding? She had been thinking about Robert since she first met him as a teenager. Thankfully, he lived up to her expectations. In some ways, he did.

Despite finding out his fetish, exploring this life together, enjoying sex, and opening herself up to someone besides her family and close friends, Philly felt Robert had a wall up around his true emotions. Maybe showing him more of herself will allow him to open up more. Maybe pushing herself to make this call to her parents will give her some closure.

After a very hot shower that steamed up the bathroom and seared her skin so much that it still felt warm, she wrapped a towel around her body and sauntered back to the bedroom. Although she didn't like the idea of strangers touching her personal items, Philly felt a wave of relief that Robert's staff had unpacked her luggage and put away her items.

Philly sat on the bed and picked up her phone. Before she dialed her mother's cell phone number, she noticed she had missed a text message.

Sleep well. Sleep naked. No touching yourself. Robert

Philly smiled as she texted him back.

All clean. Making my calls then going to sleep not thinking of you. It'll make it easier not to touch myself. Your Filly

Philly called her mother first. This would be a quick call, but not an easy one.

The phone rang three times. Just when she started to hang up, it clicked.

"Philly? What's going on? I thought you were out of town?" Her mother's voice sounded lighter than normal.

Philly didn't think she had ever heard her mother sound so...unfettered. The idea of that angered her. She fisted her hand.

"I'm still working, but I needed to come back home for the client. I won't be here for very long." She exhaled. "While I'm in town, I was hoping to be able to see you tonight for dinner." When Philly heard her mother hesitate, she gave her another option. "Or maybe breakfast in the morning or even lunch. I have plans for tomorrow night." Even for her parents, she would push them aside to spend time with Robert.

"Ooh, baby."

Philly braced herself for the letdown. She brought her legs up on the bed and tucked them under her backside. "I know. It's last minute. I just thought it would be nice for us to see each other as a family."

Her mother snickered. "That's nice, but you know your father and I aren't really together anymore."

"Still married?" With her parents' unconventional marriage, she had to ask.

"Sure, but that's just a formality. We need to get together to split up officially since I want to remarry."

The news of that felt like a punch in Philly's gut. "Mom, you're wanting to get married again and you haven't said anything to me? Who is this guy? I haven't even met him."

"Her."

The silence over the phone seemed to have lasted for decades instead of a few seconds.

"Hello?"

"Yeah, Mom, I'm still here. So, you're telling me you're a lesbian now, too?"

She huffed. "No, I'm not a lesbian. I'm bisexual, if you must know."

Philly felt like the top of her head would explode. "If I need to know? Of course, I would need that information. You're wanting to marry another woman, and this is the first I'm hearing of it."

"You're my kid. I don't need to give you the details of my sex life."

Philly shook her head like her mother could see her. "And this is part of the reason I wanted for us to get together. I don't feel like we know each other."

"Come on, honey. That's not fair. You want me to ask you about your personal life?"

"Yes! You're my mother. You should care about what's going on with me and the people I've associated with." Philly felt the separation she had experienced with her parents most of her life. "I'm not a plant. I'm not a cat. You can't just water me or set out food and let me go. I need you and Dad. I can't believe you."

"Are you saying you're going to talk about your sex life in detail?" The lightness left her mother's voice. That same bitterness Philly remembered returned.

Philly thought about Robert. Would she tell her mother that she enjoyed submitting to him and his stringent expectations? No. As her friend, she had no problem introducing him to her family.

"I'm not talking about that. I'm talking about keeping us included in our lives. I'm planning the wedding of my friend Helene. I don't know if you remember me hanging out with her when I was a teenager." If Philly wanted this to work, she had to lead her mother along this way.

"Oh, is that the girl who would take you away all summer? I liked her. Hilary, right?"

Philly sighed. "Helene." The implication that her mother liked Helene because she took away a distraction for her parents didn't escape her attention. "Yes, I would go to Europe during the summers to stay with her and her parents. I have a friend from there with me. It would be great if you all meet."

"Baby, I would like to see you, but—"

"Don't do this, Mom. All my life, I have always felt like an afterthought with you and Dad. I remember hearing you tell people how much you trusted me so you didn't have to give me so many rules. Me and the boys pretty much raised ourselves. Why can't you ever make time for me?"

"Look, you have always been pretty self-sufficient. You never really needed me, your father or your brothers. It's great that you want to reconnect now. But we're all adults. Our lives are going in different directions. We'll get together soon."

"Thanksgiving?"

The silence answered her question.

"I'll be with Sarah's family."

Now Philly knew the woman's name.

Her mother continued. "That's the other reason I can't meet you. I live in Georgia now."

Philly wanted to scream. "No one told me you moved. *You* didn't tell me." She had so many follow-up questions and comments about her mother's new situation, but she knew there wouldn't be any use beating this dead horse. "I love you, Mom. I always will. I hope we see each other before the year is out."

"Of course, I want that."

Philly exhaled.

"But if we don't, we'll be okay." Her mother disconnected the call.

Not a word about loving Philly or definitive plans on meeting in the future. While she still had fire in her belly, she dialed her father.

Unlike her mother, he answered the call on the first ring. "Hey, Philly. How are you doing?"

"I could be better. I talked to Mom." She pulled on a piece of string on the comforter under her. "Did you know she's with a woman? Sarah. She wants to marry her."

Her father sniffed. "Yeah. I've met her. She seems really nice. She pretty much does whatever your mother says. Plus, I think she wants to remarry before I do." He laughed.

Philly didn't. "Are you with someone, too?"

"Oh, no. I'm still single."

"But married."

He laughed. "Yes, technically still married to your mother. We're going to rectify that. We just need—"

"Time. I know. I heard." Philly got comfortable. "Look, I'm in town. I have some time tonight. Would you like to meet me and a friend for dinner? My treat, of course."

"Um, is your mother and Sarah going to be there? Is she in town?"

"You knew she lived in another state, too? I just found out when I called her." Philly leaned back on the pillows.

"Yes, I knew. Sorry you had to find out this way. I thought she would have told you."

"To answer your question, no, she's not going to be there. Too busy. Too far away." Philly wanted to add that her mother was too absorbed in her own life to care. "Are you still in Virginia?"

"Yes, still in Virginia Beach. Not in the same house. With you and your brothers gone, I downsized. I live in a condo by the Chesapeake Bay Bridge. The views are amazing."

Thank God Philly had been seated while hearing this information. She couldn't believe her family home had been sold. Maybe she didn't want to have dinner with her father. She didn't need to hear any more jarring news about her family.

"Send me the information on the dinner. I'll try to make it. If I can't—"

"I know. You'll call." She wished she could predict lottery numbers like this. "I'll talk to you later, Dad."

"Love you, Philly."

Philly disconnected the call and tossed her phone to the side. Why couldn't she have a traditional upbringing with normal parents? Robert may not like everything Lucian does, but at least Robert can depend on him.

At that thought, Philly blinked. She reached for her phone and sat up taller. The next call she made went to her oldest brother, Lorenzo.

"Philly, how's my favorite sister?" Lorenzo laughed at his tired joke he had been making for as long as she could remember.

"I'm your only sister." Philly smiled anyway. "Hey, what are you and the guys doing tonight?" She chewed on her lower lip as she awaited his answer.

"Why? I thought you were out of town."

"Now you sound like Mom and Dad." She extended her legs out in front of her.

"Did you talk to them?" Lorenzo's voice went up like he seemed surprised.

"I called them first. I'm here in town for work. I would love to see you and everyone else tonight for dinner. What do you think?" She heard a ding on her phone before she felt the vibration. She didn't want to pull the phone away from her ear until she heard her oldest brother's answer.

"It's game night tonight. You up for the challenge?" He laughed.

"I can take it. Would you mind if I bring a guest? He's the brother of the groom. He's helping me with—"

"Uh, huh." Lorenzo released a chuckle that Philly remembered from her childhood that meant her brother knew something she either didn't realize or didn't want anyone else to know.

"What?"

"Oh, nothing. I would love for you to bring your *friend* with you." His laughed lowered. "It should be entertaining."

"See you around seven. Love you."

"Love you, Philly." He disconnected the call.

As soon as the conversation ended, she looked at her phone display.

Show me.

Philly knew what Robert meant. She pulled back the comforter first and slipped underneath. Instead of sending a picture by text, she opened a video call. She didn't think Robert would answer when it got to the third ring. Then the screen blinked before his image appeared.

"You don't trust that I won't keep the picture?" He cocked a smile at the side of his mouth.

"I'm selfish. I wanted to see your face and hear your voice." She reached back and grabbed her to-do list. "No sleeping with your toys. I'll have to sleep with this list." She stroked the paper.

"Show me." He licked his lips.

"Oh, don't do that. I'll wrap the towel around my waist and come down the hall to you." Philly positioned herself on her side with her head on her pillow before she lowered the covers to expose her bare breasts.

She watched his gaze through the phone go down and then see him give an approving nod.

"More." He wagged his finger as though controlling her movements.

Philly obliged, lowering the heavy comforter to show off the rest of her body.

"Very, very nice."

She noticed Robert's bare chest. "Are you naked, too?"

He smiled fully. "You must go to sleep, My Filly. What is number two?"

Philly moaned and writhed. "Tea at two." She smiled at first at the idea of having an obligation during this trip. Then the smile slipped. Her demeanor changed.

"What's wrong? Did you forget the tea?"

"We have plans tonight. We're going somewhere for dinner. I won't have to cook, but you'll like it." She tried smiling to put on a brave face.

"Sounds nice. What else?" Robert could see through her façade.

"I talked to my parents." She shook her head. "Just like I said. Mom isn't even here in Virginia. She wants to remarry to a woman. First time hearing that she's bi. And Dad—"

Philly's phone screen suddenly went blank. Great. Robert wanted her to serve him, but he must not have wanted to hear about her problems. She threw her phone on the nightstand next to the bed at the same time her bedroom door opened.

Robert strolled in wearing a white robe with his initial embroidered on the left side.

"Robert." Philly sat up.

He didn't say a word as he removed his robe, which exposed his nude body. Then he slipped in bed behind her and held her around her waist. "I'm here for you."

Philly's instinct to pull away and assert herself disappeared as soon as Robert enveloped her in his strong arms. "Aren't you afraid the guards will see you, see us together?"

Robert squeezed her tighter. "I think we ruined that pretense earlier."

"I need to get some sleep. You have your tea and we have plans tonight."

He stroked her head. "Sleep."

"I don't want to be disciplined."

"Sleep."

"Don't leave me alone. Please." Philly didn't think she could with Robert behind her. The security he offered her she had to remember would only be temporary. His arms did feel good. The real test would be to get him to meet her brothers and the rest of her family. Just not her parents.

Chapter Eighteen

Robert didn't know when it happened, but he realized when he heard the pain lacing Philippa's voice and saw the disappointment in her face, he had fallen for her. He knew he couldn't stay away from her. He had that same protective feeling when he had heard about the possible intruder on the Moonwalk Manor property on her first night.

Falling for Philippa didn't figure into Robert's plans. As he thought about his life, particularly after Lucian's announcement months ago, he had specific targets in mind. He would have his announcement event. Other than Mrs. Throckmorton's cardiac incident, that went off without too many complications. Then he thought about what he had done that night with Philippa. Damn, she had become a sweet addiction, a nice distraction.

Before rushing back to her room during their call, Robert had gotten a call from Lucian.

"Where the hell are you?" Lucian had always been unflappable.

Robert remembered hearing the frustration in his voice. "I'm in Virginia Beach at the safe house with Philippa."

"Why? She's more than capable of negotiating the deal with this musical group. I don't want you trying to micromanage this aspect of *our* wedding." Lucian made sure to emphasize the word *our* in his tirade.

"What is this call really about? It's the morning here. It has to be the middle of the night."

"Exactly. I should be worried about playing with my fiancée. Instead, I'm covering for you at the charity ball that you were supposed to do. Did you forget that when you shirked your duties to go across the world to browbeat our friend, and by our, I mean mine and Helene's? You have been nothing but antagonistic to her, and now you're foregoing your responsibilities. What is going on with you?" The longer Lucian talked, the more his voice rose.

Robert never thought he would shake his usually irresponsible brother. He had to bite the inside of his cheek to keep from laughing at him. "Thank you for filling in for me at the event. I did forget that I had made a commitment."

"Along with others. Your personal assistant said he tried debriefing you when you decided to go with Philly, but you ignored him and insisted you would be going. Is that true?" Now Lucian sounded like their father.

Robert had never been chastised by their father, but he had heard Clive tearing into Lucian several times. Robert didn't necessarily like being yelled at by his older brother. He remembered feeling his stomach tighten as he talked to Lucian.

"With Mrs. Throckmorton recovering, there was a need to ensure the Lesilitho culture remained infused into your wedding." Yes, that sounded plausible.

"Bullshit. I've told you that I don't give a shit about adding our traditions. I want to marry the woman I love. You're the only one who doesn't seem to understand that." Lucian snorted and sounded like a bull. "You've only been gone a day and you have Princess Elena asking for you. Did you forget about her when you went on this trip?" Lucian paused for a moment. "Jesus Christ. I can't believe this."

Robert sat up in his bed. "What?"

"You're fucking Philly, aren't you?"

Robert felt the hairs on the back of his head stiffen. Had his brother seen the text message he had sent to Philippa only moments before asking to see her naked?

"Answer me." Lucian's voice deepened. "After I specifically asked you not to do anything with her since she was working on our wedding, you take a trip with her. Why?" He snickered. "Now it makes sense."

Robert sat up taller. "I'll never confirm nor deny your claim."

"And by saying that, you just confirmed what I was thinking. God damn you, Robert. You're a piece of work." Lucian released another curse. "All that advice you were asking me about topping a sub, was that for Philly? Are you disciplining her, too? You are a fucking asshole."

"Don't you get high and mighty on me. If I remember correctly, I asked you to do the same thing with Helene a few months ago. How does it feel to be ignored?" Robert leaned back against the pillows on the headboard.

"The big difference is that I loved Helene. Whatever you're doing with Philly is not going to end well. And I know you're doing this just to fuck with me after everything I have put you through."

Robert shook his head as though Lucian could see him. "I don't do that. I don't use people."

Lucian laughed loud enough that Robert would have heard it without being on the phone. "Your whole vibe is that you do use people. You are the king of impact play, so that's all you do. You play with other Dominants' slaves and submissives so you don't have to worry about aftercare. You don't want to own anyone, so you'll never have a submissive. If you show Philly your Dominant side and not just keep it to sex, you will scare her away and ruin my fucking wedding."

Robert balled his free hand into a fist. If Lucian had said that to his face, he would have punched him. "You don't know that. We were friends before."

"Friends? You barely talked to her when she used to visit Helene, and you have made it your mission to have her fired from this job. I'm not sure what's going on with you. I don't know if you hate me or if you're getting something out of your system before seriously pursuing Elena, but I don't like it. Just know you're not the only one who can do whatever the fuck you want." Lucian ended the call and didn't answer his phone when Robert tried calling him back.

Robert hadn't expected Lucian to figure out so quickly that he had been involved with Philippa. He also didn't think he would care what his brother or anyone thought of them being together, or whatever he chose to call what they did.

As he lay in bed, Robert thought of how he could untangle his life from hers. Maybe Lucian had been right. He had ignored his duties, something he couldn't do in his new role. For now, he would enjoy this moment. The way Philippa tried pushing him away when he first got in bed with her, he knew whatever they had would be short-lived. That brought him out of his slumber.

Robert fluttered his eyes open as he reached over for Philippa. When he found the bed next to him empty, he opened his eyes wide and sat up. At that moment, he saw something he didn't expect to see. Philippa, completely naked, sat on her knees by the bed with a cup and saucer in her hands.

He moved closer to the side of the bed near Philippa. "You didn't make the tea like that, did you?"

She smiled. "No, Sir."

He glanced at the clock hung on the wall by the bathroom door. "It's ten after. Have you been like that since two?"

"Yes, Sir." Philippa stared at him in his eyes.

"You're not lying to me to avoid punishment, are you?" He cocked his head while he tried not to smile.

She shook her head. "I wouldn't lie."

Robert believed her when she said she wouldn't lie. Period. "I told you that you didn't have to worry about the tea today. I wouldn't have punished you. What's unfortunate is that you are doing the punishment I would have inflicted on you. I would have made you sit like that and hold my tea until I tell you to stop. That could be ten minutes. It could be ten hours." He picked up the cup and took a sip. "It is delicious." He removed the cup and saucer from her hands. "Come back to bed."

Philippa stood and slipped into bed with him. Robert held his arm up to welcome her inside. When she hesitated, he sat up.

"What are we doing?" She crossed her arms, covering her magnificent breasts.

"We're doing what we originally said we would do. We're enjoying each other's company. We're playing. We're keeping it light." If he repeated that in his head, he could trick his head from wanting this woman.

"Does keeping it light mean protecting me?" She cocked her head. "Before you answer, just know that I never expected to serve you." She straightened herself up. "I also didn't expect to like it. But I'm not some foolish schoolgirl. I know when this is all done, you'll go your way and I'll go mine." She jutted her chin out to look defiant, and then she softened, lowering it while still looking in his eyes. "Right?"

Robert had managed to keep his feelings under wraps. With Philippa, he had to be honest. She deserved that. "I do like you. A lot. I like the fact that you stretched me in my BDSM play. I've learned more about myself as much as I have learned about you." He took a deep breath. "But you are right. When the wedding is over and the job is done, you will go back to the States. I will remain in Lesilitho.

It's better if we keep in mind that what we're doing will end." His heart slowed, but he had to look strong.

Philippa slipped down in the bed and positioned herself on her side with her back to him. "I'm so confused about all of this. I've never been so unsure about anything. I mean, have you said anything to anyone about us?"

Robert wrapped his arm around her. "As a matter of fact, Lucian called me earlier." He chuckled. "For once, I disappointed him."

"How's that?" She rested her hand on top of his arm.

"By taking this trip with you, I missed out on some in-person engagements that he had to do for me. Although I dislike not meeting my obligations, I can't deny that I find it fitting that Lucian had to cover for me for a change. For years, I've had to cover for him when he partied too much and was hungover, or he simply didn't want to do the event."

"Wow. And here I thought you were a goody two-shoes. I'm with a rebel." Philippa laughed. "For now."

With her statement, it reminded him again that in a few weeks, she would be walking away from him, and he would be left with his obligation and…Elena.

"What else did Lucian say?" Philippa patted Robert's arm.

"He figured out that I didn't simply come here to keep an eye on you. He was not happy. He thinks that you will not do your best job because you'll be distracted by whatever it is he believes we're doing."

That bit of news bolted her straight up to a seated position. "He doesn't think I'll do a good job?"

Robert smiled, thinking Philippa had to be joking. When he saw her stoic expression, he sat up with her. "I never confirmed what it is that we're doing."

"Which screams that we're doing something." She rubbed her forehead. "This is what I didn't want. I didn't want to get involved with a client for this reason. This is my livelihood. What will future clients think?"

"Hey, it's okay. Lucian will not say anything." He tried holding Philippa's hand, but she shrugged away from him.

"What if he tells your father?"

Robert hadn't thought of that. "I don't think Lucian will report back to Father about what he suspects we're doing."

"How can you be so sure?"

"Lucian does love and respect you. He's a little angry with me right now. If he does get vindictive and tells Father, I will defend you." He took a deep breath. "Tell me what we're doing tonight. You mentioned yesterday that your parents flaked on you."

"Going to my oldest brother's house. He's an amazing cook, way better than me. His wife is great in the kitchen, too. They're meant to be together." Philippa smiled. "I can always count on my brothers. They raised me more than my actual parents."

"And have you told them anything about me, about us?"

She shook her head. "Not really. I told my brother I would be bringing someone with me tonight."

"Really? Should be interesting."

"Be prepared to eat a lot, play a lot of games, be a personal jungle gym for my rowdy nieces and nephews, and defend yourself against my overprotective brothers."

Robert slid his hands up his arms like he was pushing up imaginary sleeves. "Bring it on." He pushed the comforter off his body. "Speaking of bringing it, we need to get dressed."

Philippa rolled onto her stomach and stared at him. "Why? Don't you want to finish your tea?"

"Cold." He shook his head. "I need for you to show me your place. You need to pack some dresses and skirts. And then we'll see your family."

"No time for anything else?" Philippa got up on her hands and knees, displaying her naked ass to him.

Robert put his hand on her firm ass cheek and gave her a gentle squeeze "As much as I want to do more with you, we have a plan." He patted her backside. "Come on. Let's get dressed."

Philippa sighed and it ended with a groan. "Fine."

* * * * *

After freshening up and getting dressed in leggings and a light sweater, Philly bounded downstairs. At the bottom, she saw Robert talking to his driver. Once she got close to them, she heard their conversation.

"The family jet is tied up right now. You may not be able to leave the day after tomorrow. It may be a couple of days afterward." The guard stood with his feet shoulder-width apart like he needed to brace for bad news.

Robert started to answer until he spotted Philly. "That will be fine."

"You sure you don't have to get back sooner?" Philly understood Robert's love of his country and the palace.

He smiled at her. "Positive."

"But I'll need to get back to continue planning the wedding." Even though she enjoyed this time with Robert, she did have work to do. She hadn't forgotten that.

"You are still working for Lucian and Helene. You're scouting this group for them." He held his hand out. "Ready?"

Philly glanced down at his hand before accepting it. "Sure."

"Good." He looked at the driver. "Get the car ready."

"Yes, sir." The driver nodded before turning on his heel to the front of the home.

Robert turned to her. "You look wonderful."

"Thank you." She leaned close to him. "No bra."

He stood directly in front of her, keeping his back to the door like he needed to block her. Robert palmed her breast over her sweater.

Philly's legs turned into gelatin and she had to hold his arm to keep upright.

"Nice." He bowed his head next to hers. "I can't wait to get you alone in your place. I have a surprise for you."

Now she couldn't wait to get him to her condo. The sun greeted them when they walked outside to the sleek, black car. Philly gave her address to the driver. As soon as she and Robert sat in the back seat, the driver drove toward her condo.

"You're a first." Philly crossed her legs. She noticed right away that Robert stared at them before he responded.

"I know you don't mean—"

She cut him off before he could say anything embarrassing in front of the driver. "You're the first man I've invited to my place."

Robert stared at her like a confused puppy. "Are you kidding?"

She shook her head. "I date. But when I go out, I meet them at the location. At the end of the date, he goes his way. That mainly has to do with my, well, you know."

He gave her a slight nod to let her know he understood. Then he placed a hand on his chest. "I feel honored. I know that if you didn't want me at your place, I wouldn't be there."

She smiled. "You're right about that." Then she placed her hand on top of his. "I trust you." She squeezed his hand. "I also know that you live far away, and I don't have to worry about you popping over and asking me to do your laundry."

That made him laugh. "Is that what American men do?"

"I'm kidding. Not all of them. Just the ones I seem to attract." She glanced at him. "Except you."

Robert slid closer to her. "I don't know. I have my own demands."

Philly didn't notice her breathing increase until Robert whispered in her ear for her to relax. How could she when her mind filled with ideas of what he would be doing to her in her place?

Thirty minutes later, the driver parked in front of Philly's floor-unit condominium. The all-white building shone brightly against the clear blue sky.

Philly reached for the door when Robert stopped her.

"The driver will open the door for us." Robert must have noticed Philly's fighting stance. He stopped her rant. "It's not pompous. It's a safety measure. He scans the area before letting us get out." He held her chin. "I can't let you get hurt."

Philly's cynical, tough heart wouldn't let her respond in her normal way. She folded into him, holding his hand until the driver opened the door. Robert stepped out first and guided her out after him. He followed her to her front door where takeout menus littered her porch area. So much for Old Mrs. Wilson watching out for her home while Philly worked.

Philly gathered the papers before unlocking her door. Her modest place still looked the same. She always kept her place clean. She made sure to keep her condo organized.

"Here's my home." She held her hands up and twirled around her living room.

Robert scanned her living room and kitchen, which all flowed together. Then he crept up to a row of pictures on her bookcase. "My God. That's us."

Philly crinkled her eyebrows as she approached him. In the sea of pictures she had throughout her house, she didn't remember having one that contained him. Her breath caught when she spotted what Robert had in the brief time he had been in her home. Philly had framed a picture of her, Helene, Lucian and Robert as teenagers on her very first trip to Lesilitho.

Each of them smiled so hard that Philly's face hurt from looking at them. She barely remembered keeping this picture and displaying it in her home. Looking at it now and the man next to her, she wanted to pat herself on the back.

Robert looked at her. "I kept the video. You kept this picture." He sighed. "It's a shame I had to delete it." He strolled away from her. "Now to create new memories."

"You don't want to get the tour?" Philly might not live in a palatial estate with more rooms than the high school she had attended, but she liked her home, the one she paid for with her own money.

With his back to her, Robert reached into his front pocket. "I'll get the tour." He turned around. "And I'll enjoy every part of it." In his hand, he held something that looked like two rubber-tipped clips connected with a long, silver chain. "You may not enjoy it as much. I need you to strip down. Now."

Chapter Nineteen

Robert had been holding onto the nipple clamps for a while, waiting for the moment he would use them on Philippa. "How's my hair?"

Philippa shifted in her spot. "Now?" She glanced down at her watch. "We have to be at my brother's in a couple of hours."

"A lot can happen in two hours." He removed his jacket. "Strip." He let one end of the clamp dangle from the chain and swing back and forth. "Tell me."

After toeing out of her footwear first, she said the prepared line. "It is day twenty of my submission. I am learning to be yours."

Philippa pulled her pants down but not her black lace thong. When she removed her top, Robert saw what he had felt earlier. Her naked breasts looked full and round. Her hard nipples poked out as though inviting him to play with them, touch them, torture them.

He stalked toward her. "Panties."

"Is this considered discipline?" She tugged on the side of her panties to pull them down her legs before stepping out of them.

"Depends on how you react." He stood directly in front of her.

Riding in the car with her didn't allow him to fully take in her scent. Her signature musky aroma became amplified in her condominium. The grounded, womanly smell swirled around him until he had to touch her.

Robert put his hand on her waist and lowered his head to capture one nipple in his mouth. Despite it being hard as a pebble, rolling over his tongue as he teased her, he wanted her nipple harder. Plus, he wanted to taste her.

Philippa moaned. She raked her fingers through his hair. Robert's heart raced as he moved his hand up from her waist to her unattended tit. He massaged it while he continued suckling her until he eventually moved his head back so that he flicked her nipple with the tip of his tongue. While Philippa had her head leaned back, Robert affixed one clamp to her now shiny and distended nipple.

Philippa sucked air between her teeth and reared up on her toes.

Robert stood up straight. "Breathe. Breathe through it. You're tougher than this. Remember that."

She didn't speak as she nodded her head in agreement and gripped the collar of his shirt.

Robert peered behind her. He saw three doors down a short hallway. "Bedroom."

Philippa took a couple of measured, long breaths before holding his hand and leading him to the last door down the hall. He held onto the other end of the nipple clamp like a leash.

Despite it being five at night, the room seemed bright. The soft white walls with the light-colored comforter and whitewashed matching furniture helped with the illuminated space.

Philippa started to crawl onto the bed, but will a pull of the chain, he stopped her. She winced when he tugged her.

"Keep standing." Robert sat on her queen-size bed and drew her close to him, positioning her between his knees.

Before she could say anything, he affixed his mouth on her other breast, sucking and licking it like he had done with the other one. When he got it to the hardness that he wanted, he clipped the other nipple clamp to it.

Like before, Philippa moaned and raised herself up on her tiptoes. "Oh, God."

"You know the safe word." Robert rested his hands on her hips. When she didn't respond, he pressed her. "Do you remember the word?"

After a beat, she nodded. "Yes. Pumpkin." Then she shook her head. "Not using it." She gripped his shoulders. "I can take it." Her breath came out in pants.

"Slow down." He placed his hand on the center of her chest. "Breathe in slowly."

Philippa continued panting until her pressed his hand harder to her chest and brushing his fingers over the top of her ass cheek.

"Inhale and hold it."

After a while, she complied.

"Good. Exhale."

She followed his orders.

"Better?"

Philippa nodded. "Getting there."

Robert watched the silver chain swinging in a U between her tits. He hooked his finger around it and tugged it slightly. Even the smallest of movements had her drawing up on her toes.

"Please." Philippa moved her hand to the back of his neck and drew him closer.

He held her wrist and pulled it away from him. "What are you asking?"

She connected her fiery gaze to his. "Need to feel your skin."

Robert couldn't deny that he wanted the same thing. He had to control this moment. "You need to get on your knees and—"

"Yes, Sir." Philippa dropped down to her knees, nearly pulling his hand down with her since he still held onto the chain.

She reached for the zipper of his jeans.

Robert held her hands. "No. I didn't ask you to do that."

"I'm anticipating your needs." She smiled at him and winked.

Damn if she didn't have him wrapped around her little finger.

"Stop or you will be punished." He lowered his voice.

"I've endured this." She peered down at the clamps. "I can do anything. Now let me satisfy you." She continued fiddling with his zipper until he bolted up to his feet and swung his leg over her head.

"Bend over and put your chest on the mattress. I'll be right back." He went out to the living room and picked up his jacket.

Robert had more than just clamps in his pocket. He removed an anal plug from the inside pocket. When he returned to the bedroom, he found Philippa positioned properly but with her head turned to the side so that she could watch him return.

Philippa had a confused expressed as she looked at the pink, cylindrical item in his hand.

"Reach back and spread your ass cheeks."

* * * * *

Philly swallowed hard before she did what Robert had asked. She reached back, gripped her cheeks and spread them.

She had never done anal sex or any kind of backdoor activities before. If Robert planned on disciplining her for disobeying him, did this mean that inserting this upside-down ice cream cone would hurt her?

She felt Robert going down to his knees behind her.

"How are your nips?" He rested his hand on the small of her back.

Philly had forgotten about the clamps while worrying about what he would be doing to her. "Fine. Um, what's that?"

Robert didn't answer her immediately. "Spread your legs apart."

Philly eased her knees apart over her carpeted floor. As soon as she did, she felt his fingers brushing her nether lips and clit.

"Oh, shit." She buried her face in the mattress.

On instinct, she curved her back to raise her ass up higher.

"Good. You are wet. Very." Robert slid his fingers back and forth over her clit.

Philly mewled and writhed until she didn't even notice that, although the rubbing continued, Robert had switched implements, from using his fingers to that toy he had brought. She recognized the change when she felt the walls of the toy brushing her inner thighs.

Robert continued rubbing the tip over her until she felt it moving away and soon felt it at her asshole. She flinched and tucked her ass under her.

"Relax." Robert patted her lower back. "Breathe."

"Yes, Sir."

As soon as she said that line, he inserted the tip inside her and held it there. Philly experienced a twinge of pain that spread like lines of broken glass. Neither of them spoke while he had it inside her.

When she managed to regulate her breathing, Robert pushed more of it inside. Philly groaned and curled her toes under her feet.

Robert rubbed her backside before pushing the toy in flush. Philly cried out and rubbed her face against her comforter. She received some comfort from connecting with the soft material.

"Stay like that until I deem you have been disciplined long enough."

"Yes, Sir." Philly thought Robert would leave her alone in her bedroom. Then she heard rustling behind her. When she heard the sound of a zipper being pulled down, she immediately thought Robert had planned to fuck her from behind.

He surprised her by sitting on the bed completely naked and positioning himself on his side, facing her.

Bastard.

Philly turned away from him and accepted her punishment. She wanted to be angry at this treatment. He had her nipples pinched and her asshole stretched, and she would be damned if she would complain. If anything, she started to enjoy this treatment, mainly because it meant someone paid attention to her. She mattered.

She struggled to keep her breathing steady. It felt like she had been in that position for hours.

"Up."

The sound of Robert's voice forced her to open her eyes. She peered at him before she raised her upper body, which she quickly stopped midway when she felt the plug inside her.

Robert got out of bed and padded behind her to remove the plug. Doing that allowed her to sit up taller, but she remained on her knees. She heard him going into her attached bathroom before returning to her. Before attending to her, he pulled back the comforter.

To her surprise, Robert lifted Philly in his arms and placed her on the mattress.

He got in next to her. "This will not feel good. Keep looking at me." He nodded as he removed the first clamp.

True to his word, as soon as he removed it, it felt like a million and one needles pricked her nipple all at once.

Philly arched her back off the bed. "Ow, ow, ow. Oh, you didn't lie about that."

Robert cupped her breast and massaged it. He did her a favor by licking her sensitive nipple to ease her discomfort. He did the same when he removed the second clamp. He tossed the clamps on the nightstand. After what he put her through, Robert switched to the gentleman she had remembered, and he covered her body with the comforter.

He enveloped her in his arm and press her back against his chest.

"How do you feel?"

To assert herself, Philly answered immediately. "I'm fine. Never better."

"You have nothing to prove to me."

She snickered. "Yes, I do. I need to prove I can take your punishments. I did."

He smoothed his hand over her head. "That's not what I'm looking for when I dominate you. I want to know that you trust me. You've shown me that several times over."

"Why do what you just did to me?"

"Because you wanted it. You have a safe word to stop it. You didn't." He moved in closer to her. "This arrangement is more of a partnership than you think. You have more control than you know." He kissed the back of her neck. "Do you need something to eat or drink?"

"Why are you asking? You want me to cook for you?" She started to move, but he tightened his hold.

"I just disciplined you. I'm taking care of you. Let someone watch out for you."

Robert smiled when he said that, and Philly perceived that he envisioned her as being weak.

"No." She tried pushing his hand off her body. "I don't need anyone."

He clamped down on her wrist. "Don't do that. Stop pushing people away."

"Stop trying to make me soft, make me feel things."

At that statement, Robert rolled her onto her back and got on top of her. This time, he did laugh, right in her face. "You have gotten involved in the wrong lifestyle if you don't think you're meant to feel something. That's the whole idea." He ran the back of his fingers over her cheek and down her neck to her arm. "Sensations. Sometimes soft." He kissed her lips and the tip of her nose. Then he gripped her hip. "Sometimes hard. In the end, you are cared for by the one inflicting the sensations to let you know you're not alone and that they care."

She snickered. "Now you care about me?"

Robert didn't speak. He stared at her like she had invaded not only his country, but also his soul. Philly didn't know when it happened, but he captured her lips in his in a smothering kiss. His hunger for her came through so strong, it left her breathless.

Maybe describing his reaction as hungry didn't fit in this situation. Maybe he needed to feel something as well. Maybe he needed a deeper level of sensation.

Philly felt his hand go between their bodies. Knowing what he wanted, she accommodated him by spreading her legs. His hard cock rested against her inner thigh until he aimed himself at her core and plunged in deep.

"Oh, God." She gripped his shoulders and squeezed her eyes shut.

"Look at me." He held her chin and remained motionless until she opened her eyes. When he regained eye contact, Robert pulled back and slammed into her hard. "I need you."

She nodded.

He did it again. And again. And again. Harder each time.

"I. Need. You." He stared at her with wide eyes that looked wild yet vulnerable.

"I love the way your feel." She kissed his arm and shoulder. "I need you, too." She held his hand and brought it up to her neck. "I trust you."

Robert swiped his thumb over the hollow of her neck before he gave her a slight squeeze.

"Yes." She arched her back. "Say it." She didn't know what she wanted him to say, but she needed to hear something.

"You're mine."

That broke her. Between his grip on her throat, his amazing dick, and his statement, Philly came hard and fast.

"I didn't tell you that you could come." Robert squeezed her neck a little tighter.

Damn, for a man who wanted to control her orgasms, he sure did give her mixed signals.

"You didn't say that I couldn't—"

He pressed his lips against hers again before nipping her bottom lip, releasing her throat, pulling out of her and turning her over on her stomach.

After what Robert had put her through with his discipline tactics, Philly wondered what he would do to her now. When she felt him spreading her ass cheeks apart, she got her answers.

He put the tip of his cock at her asshole, that still felt sore from the previous treatment. "Tell me to stop if you don't want this."

"You mean my safe word?"

Robert didn't answer. He slid the tip inside first, which made Philly fist the pillow that rested under her face.

The more he eased himself inside, the more he cursed. "If you want me to stop—"

"Don't stop." She shook her head and even raised her ass up higher to get him to quicken his thrust. "All the way."

He obliged her, delving deep in her until his pelvis rested against her backside. At that position with his body on top of hers, she felt him breathing heavily. His warm breath blew over the side of her face. The feeling prompted her to sway her hips ever so slightly back and forth.

Robert managed to get her to let go of the pillow in order to intertwine his fingers with hers and hold her hands down while he undulated inside her. She wrapped her feet around his calves as her body moved in easy rhythm with his.

Philly raised her upper body to connect her back to his chest more. "Good." She meant that in every way possible.

She enjoyed the sex with Robert. She liked playing with him. She even didn't mind their arguments. In her mind, and now, slowly her heart, she could see herself falling for this man.

Damn it. How could she break her own rule on this first important job? Rookie mistake.

Philly didn't know how Robert could tell she no longer connected to him emotionally in this moment, but he increased his rhythm and even said, "Stay with me. So tight." He kissed the side of her face. "Almost there."

Hearing that tightened her stomach. "Can I come?"

She felt Robert nodding his head before he grunted and increased his speed.

"Please." He tightened his grip on her hands.

What control Robert had over her. Philly, who never thought she would ever have anal sex, let alone come from it, felt her clitoris throb and every part of her body constrict as she came harder than the first time. Wow, considering her issues with climaxing, she found herself amazed by her multiple orgasms.

Robert plunged into her hard and deep and held himself there as she felt his hot jism bathe her insides. A thin layer of sweat separated their bodies.

"You have got to be the sexy woman I have ever been with in my entire life."

She could hear the joy and surprise in his voice. "You're only saying that because you're inside of me."

"Not true. I thought that even when we were teenagers, even before the call."

She wanted to ask why he didn't act on his feelings then.

He must have read her mind. "I should have done something back then. You used to call me intense."

She chuckled. "You still are."

"I know. I didn't think you would find that attractive. Then that call." He groaned again. "I should have done something."

Philly reached behind her and held the back of his head. "Don't beat yourself up. This is a two-way street here. I could have participated, too." She exhaled. "Now we're here."

He released her hand and brought it up to his face, probably to look at his watch. "As much as I want to stay here just like this, we need to shower and go to your family's."

This time, Philly cursed. "I can call them and say I'm sick."

"You think they would believe that?"

She laughed. "No. Worse yet, they would bring the party over here, and we definitely do not want that." She released his legs. "Be prepared to be grilled."

Robert laughed loud enough that Philly knew Old Lady Wilson next door probably heard him if she didn't already hear their other noises. "I'm sure you're exaggerating. It can't be that bad, right?"

Chapter Twenty

Robert seriously underestimated Philippa's warning. They arrived at a large two-story house in an idyllic and serene neighborhood only to be met at the door by three men and a couple of women and children all crowding the doorway.

Philippa rolled her eyes and crossed her arms over her chest. "Really?"

After their afternoon antics, Philippa had started to put in a skirt, but Robert knew she would maintain their agreement and not wear panties. He insisted she wear pants again. When she crossed her arms, he imagined her naked breasts underneath. Like a good submissive, she wore no bra. Thankfully, she wore a heavy yet loose sweater where her gloriously tortured nipples couldn't be noticed.

"What?" A tall African-American man stood in the center of the mass and volleyed his attention between the two of them. "It's been a while since we've seen you."

"A couple of weeks." Philippa snickered.

"And you come over with a…friend." He glanced at Robert.

Not willing to be talked about without asserting himself, Robert threw his shoulders back and extended his hand. "Robert. Pleased to meet you."

"Robert, this is my oldest brother, Lorenzo Powell." Philippa waved her hand between Robert and Lorenzo.

After a beat, Lorenzo shook Robert's hand. They matched firm handshakes. Robert saw Lorenzo's eyes light up at Robert's strength.

"So, are you like Prince or something? You only go by one name?" Lorenzo snickered.

"Let's stop talking out here and go inside." Philippa started toward the still full doorway.

"That's a nice Uber ride. Is the driver going to just sit out there?" A woman standing next to Lorenzo pointed to the sleek, black ride.

"He's my driver. He'll be fine." Robert started to follow Philippa, but he stopped when he heard a collective gasp from the group.

"Your driver?" the group asked at the same time.

Lorenzo waved at the driver. "Tell that man to come in here. We have plenty of food."

Robert peered back and saw his driver/security guard looking confused as he stepped out of the vehicle. "He normally doesn't do that."

"He will today. That's crazy." Lorenzo stepped out from the doorway. "Hey, partner, come on in." He waved him up. "I don't know who you are, man, but you already have me curious."

Philippa shook her head. "Go inside, everyone. I'll do intros in there." She looked back at Robert. "Are you cool with him coming in?"

Robert smiled at her concern. "It's not standard, but when in Rome…"

He felt a tug on his sleeve, and he turned to see a small girl with bright pink clips all over her hair.

"You talk funny." She covered her mouth and giggled.

"You are very observant." Robert crouched down to get eye level with her. "I'm from a small European country called Lesilitho. Ever heard of it?"

She shook her head. "I'm learning colors in school." She held up her tiny hand and splayed her fingers. "I'm five."

"Ah." He took out his phone and brought up a map view. "See. We're right here."

"I wouldn't let her hold your phone. You probably won't get it back." A woman stood behind the girl and laughed. "I'm Cordi. I'm married to Torrence over there." She pointed to another man who stood next to Lorenzo. "This is our daughter, Francesca, but we all call her Frannie."

Robert stood. "Cordi, nice to meet you. That's an unusual name." He shook her hand.

"It's actually Cordelia, but I've always hated that name. And my middle name is worse. Ethel." She grimaced. "Family name or something."

"I think Cordelia is a lovely name." He peered down at the child before crouching down to her again. "Wonderful to meet you, Francesca."

She furrowed her full eyebrows. "You didn't call me Frannie."

"That's his thing." Philippa stood next to Robert. "He's about the only one who calls me Philippa."

The men in the room laughed.

"Dude, no one calls her that." The one Cordelia pointed out as her husband put his hand to his stomach as he laughed. "Philly works as her name because she can be a little 'hood."

Robert must have looked confused.

"Means that I'm unpolished or rough around the edges." Philippa smirked.

The door behind them closed, and Robert saw his equally confused looking driving standing in the home that seemed to go one for miles. The open-floor plan allowed Robert to not only see the full and bright living room, dining room and kitchen, the wall of glass sliding doors beside the kitchen let him see into the backyard. The luscious green grass and vibrant flowers reminded Robert of the grounds at Moonwalk Manor. No wonder Philippa loved the landscaping so much.

"Okay, so you've met Lorenzo." Philippa pulled Torrence forward. "This is my second-oldest brother, Torrence Powell."

Torrence shook Robert's hand. "Good to meet you."

Robert nodded. "Likewise. You have a lovely family."

"This isn't all of them." Philippa peered around. "Where's the baby?"

Cordelia put her finger to her lips. "Shh, sleeping upstairs." She pulled her phone from her back pocket, tapped on the screen and flipped it around to show Robert and Philippa.

The color video image of a baby sleeping in a crib populated the screen.

"This is little Jackson." As though the baby slept right next to her, Cordelia suddenly lowered her voice to a whisper. "He's a handful." She peered up. "Just like his daddy."

"I resemble that remark." Torrence winked.

"Robert, this is my brother, Neil."

A young man approached Robert and put out his hand. "Very nice to meet you."

"Same here." Robert shook his hand. Just like with the other two brothers, he found his grip to be just as firm.

"Over here is my wife, Brittany." Lorenzo held his arm up and waited for a woman to come underneath it so he could hold her.

She held her hand out to him. "Very nice to meet you. I wish I could say that I've heard a lot about you." She peered over at Philippa.

"You could still say that. When I used to go to Europe for the summers with Helene, we stayed with his family. It's his brother who's getting married. I'm planning their wedding." Philippa cocked her head. "I talked about them all the time when I got back. I've shown you pictures."

"Girl, Lorenzo and I were still in our honeymoon phase back then. If you talked about anything other than your brother, I wasn't hearing it."

A small ripple of laughter sounded in the room.

Lorenzo pointed toward another room off the kitchen. "I have two boys and a girl. They're in there playing some video games. When we eat, I'll introduce them to you."

"Speaking of eating, let's have at it. I'm starving." Philippa headed toward the dining room, but Lorenzo stopped her.

"Aren't you going to introduce the driver?" Lorenzo pointed at the man.

The driver looked at Robert before approaching Lorenzo. "Mortimer." He extended his hand. "This is a bit unusual for me. I normally—"

"Stay in the car." Lorenzo cut off the man, who stood about the same height as Robert. "Interesting. Yeah, let's all sit down to eat."

The front door slammed again, and a woman waltzed inside. "I'm here. Did I miss the excitement?"

"Not sure what excitement you mean." Cordelia patted Francesca's head.

"Philly's new friend." She sauntered toward Robert. When she saw him, her bottom jaw unhinged, and she put her hand to her chest. "Thug life is down with the swirl? Really?"

"Stop it." Philippa shook her head. "Robert, this is—"

"Girl, don't say my government name." She held her hand up to him. "Call me Juicy."

Robert held her hand. "What is your real name?"

"Julissa." Philippa supplied it faster than Juicy could object.

"Damn you." She rolled her eyes. "Everybody calls me Juicy." She peered over at Mortimer. "And you are?" She held her hand up to him.

"Mortimer. Mortimer Protrovich. I'm a driver and guard." He scanned the group. "You may have seen me earlier today checking out your house and neighborhood."

"Okay, will someone please tell me who you really are? The fancy car, the driver, the accent." Torrence looked Robert up and down. "The clothes. What gives?"

Robert took a deep breath. "I guess Philippa left some things out when talking about me and my family. I'm Prince Robert of Baldington Palace. I am the son of King Clive. My family has been in Lesilitho for centuries. We're not a ruling monarchy, though. Think of us like the English monarchy. Respected, but with no real authority."

The silence in the room unnerved Robert. He scanned a sea of people with their mouths dropped open.

"You're serious?" Julissa broke the silence first. "You're a real-life prince?"

Robert nodded. "Yes. I thought Philippa—"

"You could be the next Meghan?" Julissa squealed and held Philippa's hand.

"Stop. He's a friend. I'm working for his family. We're here to do a job." Philippa held up her hands to silence the group, who all started doing searches on their phones. "You cannot talk about him, our trip or anything about this. Please. For security sake, it could be bad for him and me, and well, you also. Think about how they treated the family of Meghan Markle."

"They're famous." Julissa shrugged.

"No, they're harassed and judged and followed." Philippa glanced down at Francesca. "I wouldn't want that for any of you, especially the kids. Now can we eat?"

"Yes, and would you mind if I sit next to you?" Julissa looked at Mortimer and smiled. "I've always had a thing for a working-class man." She winked at him.

Robert's normally unflappable driver looked like he blushed.

"Let's sit down." Cordelia led them all to the dining room area where they set up a couple of card tables for the kids.

Robert had never seen so much food for one family, and he had been to lavish banquets at the palace and with other royal families. Philippa hadn't lied. Her brother, Lorenzo, made fried fish, steak, shrimp, something called pulled pork barbeque and a plethora of side dishes, including one he learned to love thanks to Ginny. Collard greens.

Robert put his hand to his stomach and leaned back. "I don't think I have ever eaten that much food in my life."

"All good?" Lorenzo let his fork hover over the remaining food on his plate.

"Absolutely delicious." Robert smiled. "Thank you."

"Don't thank him just yet." Cordelia stood and collected his empty plate. "My husband is a whiz with desserts, too."

If Robert had a white flag or handkerchief, he would have waved it in surrender. "I couldn't possibly fit anything else in my stomach right now."

"Are you sure? There's peach cobbler, banana pudding, sweet potato pie, and cherry pie." Lorenzo jutted his thumb over his shoulder toward the kitchen.

"You made all this food after I called you today?" Philippa shook her head.

"You know we always have family night here with everyone. Oh, yeah. You're always so busy." He smirked before shoveling more food into his mouth.

"It takes a lot to open and run your own business. I don't have a lot of free time." Philippa stood and carried her plate into the kitchen. "Plus, I have a demanding client." She winked at Robert.

"What is your relationship with my sister like?" Neil flashed Robert a suspicious glare.

Robert looked at Philippa before answering. "We've known each other since we were teenagers. We lost touch after she went to college. One thing you can say about Philippa. She's very focused and driven. She's pretty amazing."

He got lost in thinking about Philippa until he noticed Cordelia nudging Philippa with her elbow. Robert sat up taller and made it a point to look away from her.

"I thought we were going to be playing some games tonight." Julissa looked at Mortimer. "Ever heard of spades?"

Robert's normally stoic guard smiled. "No, I don't believe I have."

"You have a sexy accent. You could read the dictionary and it would get me we—"

"Juicy!" Brittany popped Julissa on her arm.

"What? There's a reason my nickname is Juicy." She winked at Mortimer. "Morty, you want me to teach you how to play?"

"Morty?" Mortimer furrowed his eyebrows. "I've never had anyone call me a nickname before. I like it."

"Lorenzo, I don't think you should teach Robert and Mortimer that game. It'll take too long, and we're not staying." Philippa leaned against the counter.

Mortimer stood. "Oh, if we're leaving soon, I'll need to check out the car."

Julissa stood up with him. "I'll come with you. I want to hear more about your country and your work."

"Really?" He held his arm up for her. "You might be terribly bored to hear those details."

"If I do, I'll find something to entertain myself." Julissa glanced back at the group. "Play without me."

"As usual." Torrence chuckled. "Prince Robert."

Robert held up his hand. "No. Just Robert is fine." With this group, he felt comfortable to drop the pretenses.

"Tell us what it's like to grow up in a castle."

Robert saw Cordelia and Philippa return to the table with small plates of food. Philippa placed one of the plates in front of him with a decadent-looking dessert piled on top. She mouthed the words, "I'm sorry" before she placed the other plate in front of Neil.

"It was nice. I've never known anything else, so I can't compare it to growing up any other way." Robert took a sip of the best, if not the sweetest, iced tea he had ever tasted. "My brother and I attended private school. Because of who we are, we rarely did anything social like school dances or what you would call a prom. I joined the military."

That statement caused Torrence to sit up. "Really? I'm a military man myself. Navy."

"I flew fighter jets." Robert pointed to himself.

"I didn't know that." Philippa sat next to him. "I knew you were in the military."

Robert nodded. "I did four years before coming back home."

"I bet your mother was worried about you while you were gone." Cordelia sat next to Lorenzo.

Robert picked up his fork and stared at the peaches swimming in gelatinous goo and covered in broken crust before he answered. "My mother died shortly after my birth." He heard her and Brittany gasp.

"I'm so sorry. I saw your father was single. I didn't know she

died. I thought he divorced her." Cordelia leaned against Lorenzo.
"You know, like Charles did Diana."

Amazing how death drew people together.

"I've met his father." Philippa placed her hand on top of
Robert's. "He's a great man and a caring parent. Nothing like ours."

"Oh, come on, Philly. Not this again." Torrence leaned back in
his chair and covered his eyes. "And not in front of company."

"Why didn't anyone tell me about Mom? When did she move to
Georgia?"

Cordelia silently removed the other empty plates from the table
and took them to the kitchen.

"That happened right after Christmas last year." Lorenzo took a
bite of his dessert.

Looked like he got the cherry pie.

"Dad said he was going to come here tonight, but as you can see,
he's not here. Didn't even call like he normally does." Philippa
crossed her arms over her chest. "It would have been nice for us to
grow up normally, not with parents who were too busy partying to
watch their kids."

"Don't be dramatic." Torrence shook his head. "We were fine.
We had a roof over our heads and food in our stomachs. So, they
weren't around as much as you would like. We all still turned out
okay. None of us are on drugs. None of us have ever been arrested.
We're all good." He pointed to Philippa. "You need to let it go."

"Yeah, you would think with you being adopted that you would
be okay with the situation." Brittany shrugged.

Robert blinked at her comment. Philippa had never mentioned
being adopted before. Judging by her shocked expression, he
established that she hadn't been aware of this news.

Philippa broke her shocked expression with a smile and laugh.

"Very funny, Britt."

Brittany looked at her husband. "Shit." She turned her head toward Torrence. "I thought she knew."

Philippa bolted to her feet. "Wait. This isn't a joke?"

She must have noticed the same thing Robert did. Everyone kept their gazes down to their plates and away from her glare.

"Kids, go in the room and play your game." Cordelia got up and ushered the children to the other room.

"I'll help you." Brittany stood and walked with Cordelia. When she passed Philippa, she put her hand to her shoulder.

Philippa shrugged away from the well-intentioned touch. When the room emptied with the exception of her brothers and Robert, Philippa delved further into this conversation.

"Is this true? Am I adopted?" Philippa looked at each of her brothers. When no one spoke right away, she slammed her hand on the table. "Answer me!"

"Yes." Lorenzo stood. "I thought Mom and Dad would have told you by now."

"Forget them. What about you all? You're the ones who essentially raised me. Why didn't any of you say anything to me?" She glared at Torrence. "Your fucking wife knew before I did."

Robert tried arresting her hand in his. He didn't want Philippa to lose herself while attempting to get information. She stood and moved away from him.

"Take it easy, Philly." Neil held up his hands.

"I can't. I just found out that my life has been one lie that everyone knew about but me. Thanks."

Lorenzo stood. "It's not like that, Philly. Yes, you should have been told, but that doesn't take away the fact that you're my baby sister. We'll always look out for you because you're family. That's what family does."

"No, family tells each other the truth. Now I get why Mom and Dad treated me the way they do." She looked at Robert. "I'm going. Stay if you want."

He managed to snag her hand before she could make her escape. "Stay and talk to your family. This is important to you. You are not going to get what you need by leaving."

"It's apparent I won't get what I need by staying, either."

Philippa managed to wriggle out of his grasp and storm out of the home to the car.

Robert turned to Lorenzo. "Thank you for the hospitality. You have a lovely home." He shook his hand. "Please tell your wife good-bye from me. I'm sure Philippa would say the same." He shook Torrence and Neil's hands before following Philippa to the car.

Julissa rushed by Robert. "Nice meeting you." She waved to him as she headed to the house.

His driver rushed around to his side to open the back door. Robert slipped in the back seat where Philippa resided, staring out the window.

Robert didn't say anything to her, even after the car took off toward the safe house. He reached for Philippa.

She resisted him. "I'm fine. I'll be okay."

"I know." He enveloped her in his arms. "I need you to comfort me. I'm still full from dinner."

After a beat, she leaned into him. "Fine. If you need me to rub your belly, I will." She exhaled. "I'm not going to talk about it."

He held her tighter. "Rub my stomach. If it comes up, it comes up."

"And when you say, if it comes up, do you mean…"

"Cute. Good to see you still have your sense of humor." He

rubbed his hand up and down her arm.

"I used to think I got that from my father."

Robert kissed the top of her head. "There's a bright side. This is a clean slate."

He didn't know how else to spin this for her, or that he even should. Maybe he should consider this as his clean slate, a chance to not get too involved. Then she rubbed his stomach.

Damn.

Chapter Twenty-One

Philly tried ignoring the incessant knocking on her bedroom door. Her mind and heart wanted her to wallow in bed and let the news she heard last night fester in her head. Her inner strength wouldn't allow her to stop moving to think about the fact that she grew up not knowing her true story.

After the third knock, Philly gave herself one last look in the mirror before opening the door. To her surprise, Mortimer stood on the other side. Of course, Robert wouldn't have been there to retrieve her. He probably already thought she didn't rate as high as him and his family without having any royal blood. Now that he heard of her adoption status, he probably wanted to keep clear of her.

"Good morning, Miss Philippa." He bowed his head.

"Please. Call me Philly." She picked up her purse.

"Yes, ma'am. Prince Robert would like for you to join him in the dining room for breakfast."

She walked up to him. "I'm not hungry. I would like for you to take me back to my place."

"You need to pick up more items?" He worried his eyebrows.

"No. I'll stay there for the rest of this trip so that you and Prince Robert don't have to keep hosting me." She walked by him.

"Um, Miss Philippa. Philly. Ma'am." He followed her downstairs. "I will be happy to take you anywhere, including back to your brother's home."

Philly smirked as she glanced back at Mortimer. She knew he would want to see Juicy again. She noticed their chemistry right away. For his sake, she hoped he got her number.

"You're kind. I'm here for work." She got to the main floor but stood by the steps. "I got distracted. I'm focused now. I'll see the show tonight and immediately fly back to Lesilitho."

"Ma'am, Philly, the family jet will not be available until tomorrow."

Philly remembered that fact, another reason she wanted to leave right away. She didn't want the uncomfortable feeling of flying back with Robert and the conversation she didn't want to discuss.

"I know. That's why I'm—"

"Mortimer." Robert didn't raise his voice from the dining room. His big, booming voice carried to where they stood.

Mortimer stared at Philly while he answered. "Yes, sir."

"I hear you talking. I'm assuming it's not with yourself."

"No, sir. I'm with Miss Philly, um, Philippa. Miss Philippa."

She rolled her eyes when he called her the name she didn't want to hear, especially now when it didn't relate to her father anymore.

"Come inside and bring Philippa with you."

"Yes, sir." Mortimer tried taking her elbow to guide her to the dining room.

"Oh, no. I can see him on my own." Philly waved Mortimer away as she went to the dining room.

Robert sat at the head of the long, ten-person dining room table. He had a place setting in front of him and one on the right side of him, probably meant for her.

"Good morning." Robert looked beyond Philly to Mortimer. "Will you please excuse us?"

"Yes, sir." He bowed his head and walked out of the dining room, leaving Philly alone with Robert.

"Like I was telling Mortimer, my plan is to go back to my place and stay there for the rest of my trip. Then I'll go to the show tonight and leave right afterward to go back to Lesilitho." She cocked her hip as she talked to him. "I know your family's plane won't be available until tomorrow. You can fly back on your own."

Robert held up his hand. "How's my hair?"

Philly shook her head. "What?"

He peered down at his plate. "I believe I was supposed to have Eggs Benedict this morning."

Shit. She had said she would make him breakfast. Things had changed.

"I'm not staying." Philly shrugged.

Robert scooted his chair back and stood. "I'll take my tea in my room." He walked by her. He must have felt her not moving. Without turning around, he said, "Come now."

Damn him.

Fine. This would be her good-bye to him. She poured tea into a white China cup and carried it on a saucer. Instinct kicked in and she held it flat on her palms.

Damn him.

By the time she reached Robert's bedroom, she found him standing by the door, waiting for her. When she stepped inside, he closed the door behind her.

"I know you." He walked by her and sat in an oversized leather chair next to the bed.

Philly snickered. "That's a neat trick since I don't even know myself."

"I asked you a question." Robert leaned back in the chair. "How's my hair?"

Philly set the tea on a nightstand between him and the bed. "I can't do this. I can't."

Robert regarded her for a moment. "Answer. Me."

"Why? I can't keep doing this. You don't want to continue with me."

"Do not speak for me." He rubbed his hands over his jeans. "You received some pretty jarring news last night. I get it."

"No, you don't."

Robert sat up taller. "You don't think I get the fact that your role in your family has changed? I've gone from being the Queen Killer to future king, and the Lesilitho residents don't see me in a different way." He reached forward and held her hand. "You found out from your family that you're adopted. Does that change you? Yes. Did it change how they treated you? No. They love you. I—" Robert stopped himself.

Philly's heart started to race.

"I can see you wanting to retreat. You did it before after our first call. I'm not going to have you do that again. I care about you too much to have you not realize your worth. You're smart. You're resourceful. You're stubborn. You're generous." He ran his hand over his head.

"I'm scared." Philly hated sharing her vulnerabilities with him.

"I know." He nodded. "Answer me."

She stared at him. "Your hair looks great." She took a deep breath before spouting her statement. "It is day twenty-one of my submission. I am learning to be yours."

"I know you want to be anchored. Allow me to be your North Star. Let me ground you." He glanced at the tea.

"What does that mean?"

"Punishment. You will get on your knees in here and hold my tea until I tell you to stop."

Philly shook her head.

"Why?"

"I need to keep moving. If I stand still, I'll get in my head. I don't want that." She pulled her hand out of his grip.

Robert stood up and went to bed. Did he really want to have sex now? The act would get her from thinking about her current situation, but she wouldn't really be into fucking. She couldn't get wet if she tried.

He removed one of the pillows and plopped it on the floor. Then he pointed to it. "Kneel."

"Please don't make me do this." She shook her head. "I don't think I'm strong enough to do this. I'd rather do the nipple clamps and the anal plug again than to kneel in silence."

He held both her hands and stared into her eyes. "You need this. I need this for you. You must settle into thinking about your situation to figure it out. Running away will not solve your problems. But you know that."

Bottom line, she knew Robert had a point. Philly stepped out of her booties and curled her toes in her socks before she lowered herself to her knees on the cloud-like pillow. Then she picked up the cup and saucer and placed it on her hands.

"Very good." He patted the top of her head before kissing her forehead. "I'll be right back."

A few minutes later, Robert returned and sat in the chair facing her. He had a plate of food in his hands. Great. Now that Philly could smell it, her stomach growled.

"When I woke up and found that you hadn't made breakfast, I had the staff make the breakfast I had requested." Robert cut into the egg that sat on top of an English muffin and covered with a creamy, pale yellow sauce. "It probably doesn't taste as good as what you would have made." He held up the piece to his mouth, but then stopped and looked at her. He brought the food to her mouth. "Tell me."

Philly blinked as she looked at the food on the fork. She opened her mouth and allowed him to feed her. The breakfast tasted good, but Robert spoke the truth. She could have made a better breakfast.

"Thank you." She chewed on the savory morsel. "And I'm sorry."

"Why the apology?" He took a bite of the breakfast.

"I promised to make you breakfast. After tasting that, I should have." She swallowed.

Robert laughed. "Hence the punishment." He picked up his tea and took a sip before he offered some to Philly. "When breakfast is done, I will go downstairs. I will retrieve you when I feel you have been punished long enough. This is what I want you to do. I want you to think about what you heard last night. Really think about how the words affected you. After you do that, I want you to look at the cup and saucer and ask yourself why you're holding them."

Philly snickered. "That's the easy part. You asked me to hold them."

Robert didn't confirm her assessment, which already had her thinking.

"After you answer the question on why you're holding these, I want you to think about Lorenzo and what he means to you. Think about your best memory about him. Then think about why you're holding the cup." He glanced at the items in her hands. "Think about Torrence. Recall only the best memories of him. And then think about why you're holding the cup."

"Why do you have me going back to the cup? I don't understand." Philly had more questions than that, like why it mattered that she thought about her brothers?

Robert continued. "Think about Neil, and then—"

"The cup. I still don't understand why—"

"Then I want you to think about your namesake, your father."

Philly went silent. Her shaking started again.

"Philippa, think about only good memories of your father. Did he teach you how to drive? Did you decorate the family Christmas tree together? Did he carry you on your first date? Only think about good memories where he supported you. Go back to the cup."

Philly didn't realize she had been holding her breath until Robert gave her the instructions to think about her holding the cup. Then she exhaled. She finally understood the need for her to focus on the mundane task of her holding this cup. In a way, it would palate cleanser for her mind.

"Finally, I want you to think about your mother, only good memories." Robert's voice sounded soothing, like he tried to lull her into these thoughts. He cupped her hands that held the cup and saucer. "Think about the cup. When you've gotten to your mother, start over with what you heard last night, the cup, each other your brothers, the cup, your father, the cup, and your mother. Keep your mind in that loop until I stop the punishment."

"What if I have to call my safe word? You won't be able to hear me." Her hands started to tremble slightly, jiggling the cup on the saucer. "What if I can't take it?"

Robert held her wrists, probably to help still her hands. "What if you can?" He brushed his thumbs over her arms. "You have learned to rely on your brothers until you started to rely on yourself. I'm hoping that having time alone will get you to do a full assessment of your situation. The good and the bad. Punishment should correct behavior. You should change." Like he did with Francesca last night, he crouched down in front of her. "If you call your safe word, I will hear you. If you still want to go back to Lesilitho after the show tonight, I will have Mortimer to take you to the airport. I hope you'll decide to stay, not just for me, but because you want to remain here…with me." He gave her a sweet kiss and walked out of the room.

Philly didn't hear him closing this door this time, but with her back to it, she couldn't be sure. She held onto the cup and put her full concentration on the lip of it. Between she and Robert, they drank the tea inside.

"Okay, you can do this." Philly took a deep breath and did what Robert had instructed her to do first. She thought about what she had heard last night.

Her sister-in-law, Torrence's wife, knew about Philly's adoption. Philly had been adopted. The blood that went through her veins didn't match her family's. As the only daughter, Philly always felt alone. Now she really felt like she alone existed on a faraway island without any support.

Instead of feeling sorry for herself, anger simmered below her surface. Molten heat ignited in the pit of her gut and rose up to her chest and up to the top of her head. She couldn't believe no one in her family told her the truth, especially her brothers.

When her fury got too much for her to take, Philly brought her attention back to the white cup and saucer. She studied the embossed flower design around the bottom. She even concentrated on her lipstick stain around the lip of the cup. She and Robert shared this drink. The idea of that alone let her realize how much she had grown to trust him, something she didn't think would be possible, despite their history.

Philly took her focus off the cup to look at the wall in front of her and think about Lorenzo. Her brother, ten years her senior, came off as a father figure than an older brother. She could rely on him. Knowing that he knew and said nothing hurt more than perhaps the idea of her parents not telling her.

Then Philly thought she unfairly placed so much blame on Lorenzo. As her oldest brother, he had the obligation to love her and maybe protect her from bad dates, which he did time and time again while she dated in high school. He had even taught her how to hunt and fish. He opened his home for every holiday, and he and Cordi became like parents to her. They loved her. Knowing Lorenzo, he probably didn't say anything to her thinking that their parents would have said something to her by now. She couldn't blame him. If anything, she needed to thank him for protecting her.

Philly shook her head and refocused on the cup. This time, she brought her gaze down to the matching saucer. The slight circular dip in the center of the saucer allowed the cup to fit in it perfectly. When she didn't shake, it nestled in it securely.

Her breathing slowed and her heartbeat steadied. Philly brought her gaze back up to the wall. This time she thought about Torrence, her steady middle brother. Like Lorenzo, Torrence could never keep a secret. Between the two, she would have expected Torrence to tell her something. Through her reasoning, she understood why Lorenzo hadn't said anything to her. She knew Torrence. Even if he thought that someone would have told her already, Torrence would have said something to check in on Philly. He cared about her.

Philly dropped her gaze back to the cup and saucer. She looked at both as a unit, noticed how well they fit together. She thought about her and Robert. Just moments before, she wanted to leave him, forget about this arrangement. In his own way, Robert protected her. By getting her to not give up, he made her stronger.

She brought up her gaze to the wall and thought about her third brother, Neil. Philly had a close relationship with him merely by age. Eleven months separated them, so for one month, they shared the same age.

Neil could always make her laugh. He kept every event light, especially around the holidays. When he came out to her and the family, she nor her brothers judged him. Why was she judging him now for not sharing this information? Maybe he didn't feel like he had the right to share her adoption status, especially if he thought it would hurt her.

When Philly dropped her gaze to the cup and saucer again, she found that she needed to direct her attention to something else. At that point, she appreciated Robert's directive to think about why she held the cup between thinking about her family members.

As she thought about the next person she needed to focus on, Philly's body shook. The image of her father filled her thoughts. He should have been her protector. Instead, he and her mother did their own thing, leaving Philly and her brothers to fend for themselves.

Then she thought about the idea that she had been named after him. Why had he done that with her and not his sons? Why hadn't he or her mother said anything? Why did she always feel in the dark with them?

Out of nowhere but frustration, Philly screamed. The sound seemed to come from the souls of her feet to the top of her head. She curled her fingers around the lip of the saucer just to grip something, not to steady it. Her body curled forward.

"Liar! You lied to me!" Philly hated the tears that streamed down her face because she had no sadness over the situation. She hated being lied to, and this lie topped them all.

She took a deep breath and sat up straight.

Think of the good. Think of the good.

Philly had to admit her brothers had been right. Her parents had them in a nice middle-class home in a good neighborhood and, except for emotional support, they didn't want for much of anything. If her parents chose to adopt after having three children, maybe they thought they had some love to give. Maybe they wanted to try to correct past mistakes.

For the first time, Philly looked forward to looking at the cup and saucer to clear her head. The next task to think about her mother would be harder than her father. Philly struggled to raise her gaze up to the wall to think about her mother.

"You can do this." Philly took a deep breath before bringing her gaze up to the wall.

Her mind went to her mother. The slow-simmering anger she had for her father came more immediate with her mother. Philly screamed and cried and hated herself for crying at all for a woman who had essentially exorcized herself from Philly's life. Why? Had Philly been that bad of a daughter that would force her mother to not tell her about her adoption or her relationship status or even her move?

Philly couldn't wipe her face with her hands occupied. She gazed down at the cup faster than she did with the other members of her family. She finally realized why she held this cup and saucer. She didn't have to think about anything else but holding these items. She needed something to focus on other than her business or her sexual proclivities or her family situation. She needed this. She needed Robert.

Robert tortured himself by sitting outside of his bedroom, listening to Philippa. At the moment he had heard her scream, he surprised himself by remaining seated. In his mind, her release had been no different than the cries and screams of the submissives and play bottoms he had disciplined in his past. The difference here had been the method in which he got Philippa to achieve her release.

He knew he had to let her go through this on her own. She hadn't called her safe word. Philippa had to know that she controlled the moment. Every ounce in his body wanted to rush to her side and hold her, provide her aftercare. Not yet. Philippa had to sit in this a bit longer.

Robert heard stomping coming up the stairs. Mortimer looked harried as he rushed to him.

"Is everything okay, sir?" He stopped in front of him but tried peering into the bedroom.

"Philippa is going through a hard time right now." Robert glanced down at his watch. "Why don't you go out for a bit. Check to see if Julissa is available."

Mortimer started to smile, but he managed to wrangle his emotions. "Yes, sir." He rushed down the stairs and nearly bolted out the door.

By the time Mortimer left, Philippa had stopped screaming.

Robert resumed his seat outside of the room and tried hard to keep seated until he felt she had been disciplined long enough. He heard her crying in between the screams.

"Let her go through it." Robert turned his head. "Come on, sweetheart. Remember to breathe."

His knee bounced as he waited for her wails to die down. When it did, Robert decided to give her at least another hour on her own. That gave him time to think, the thing he had asked her to do this entire time.

This new technique of disciplining tested his patience. The old him would have strung her up on a St. Andrew's cross and flogged her until she broke. He understood that kind of discipline. Since he had never pushed a submissive this way, he had no idea how Philippa would react after he ended it.

Before Philippa came down from her room, Robert contemplated ending their arrangement. He wondered if their kind of relationship would trigger her negatively. Would she see his family dynamic as one she wished she had?

Hell, Robert never thought that his family would be one that could be envied. He also never thought that he would be interested in a woman who had pushed him so far outside of his comfort zone. At the end of all this, did he want her to leave? Did he want this to end?

After an hour since the second scream, Robert stood and slowly sauntered to the bedroom. The afternoon sun attempted to peek through the heavy curtains that he had drawn. He went to the curtains first and pulled the open before he approached Philippa.

With the room bathed in sunlight, Robert saw everything clearly. Philippa remained on her knees but seated on her haunches. She had her hands at the same level of her breasts with the cup and saucer balanced on them.

Robert removed the dish from her hands and placed it on the nightstand. At that time, he noticed Philippa kept her stare straight ahead as if in a trance. She barely acknowledged him. Even after removing the cup and saucer, Philippa kept her hands up in the same position.

When he looked at her face, he noticed the dried tear streaks over her cheeks. She put herself through the depths of her emotions.

Robert held her hands, which snapped her out of her trance.

"I didn't use my safe word." She shook her head.

He helped her to her feet. "Punishment is over." He held her shoulders and looked her in her eyes. "Come." He led her to the bed and eased her down onto her side, knowing her knees must be killing her. "Are you hungry? Thirsty?"

She shook her head. "Hold me. Please."

Robert didn't question her request. Before getting in bed with her, he removed his shoes and removed a plush blanket from a chest at the foot of the bed. He covered her body with the blanket and slipped into bed behind her.

"Thank you." Philippa held his hand and kissed his fingers after bringing them to her face.

"Aftercare is standard." Robert moved his body in closer to hers.

She shook her head. "The discipline made me think about my family, more than I ever had. I was so angry."

"I heard the scream, but no safe word." He kissed the back of her neck.

"I need to talk to my family. Before this discipline, I was ready to shut them out. I have to stop doing that. No one is perfect. I can't get answers if I don't talk to them." Her voice trembled as she talked.

Robert wouldn't stop her chatter. She needed to purge.

"I failed."

Robert lifted his head. "What do you mean?"

"I thought about my family like you wanted, but I also thought about you. I thought about what you mean to me." She pushed back against him. "I never thought I would be into this lifestyle. I'm glad that you introduced me to it and are so patient with me."

The guilt Robert felt wracked his body. He wanted to run from her. When she had proposed leaving after the show, he had almost let her. Then he heard her strength, the same strength that drew him to her in the first place. When she had come into the dining room and he looked at her, he couldn't deny his heart.

"What did you think about when you thought of me?" Robert squeezed her hand.

"How I wouldn't be here without you, and by *here* I mean in the mental space where I'm comfortable being me, the sensual side of me. You've broken down barriers I've spent years bricking up around myself, around my heart." She chuckled a little. "I want you so bad right now, but not sexually. I want you to keep doing this, keep holding me. You make me feel safe."

Robert smiled. "That is a sign of a successful Dom/submissive relationship."

Did that mean he wanted her permanently in his life? He could see it.

"Are you hungry? You want me to make you lunch?" Philippa started to stand.

Robert held her tighter. "Rest. Sleep if you need to. I'll be here for you. We'll get ready for the show tonight."

"Yes. I can't wait."

"Don't forget. If I don't like the musical act, I will reject it."

Philippa remained quiet for a moment before she finally spoke. "I understand. But you'll agree. You'll do the right thing for your brother."

Chapter Twenty-Two

Philly didn't know when she had fallen asleep in Robert's arms. She remembered waking up with him asleep next to her. What a wonderful feeling. She could get used to this, which scared her.

She slipped out of bed and tiptoed back to her bedroom to get her purse. She removed her phone and called Lorenzo first.

"Hey, Philly." He sounded deflated, like he had disappointed her.

After her discipline, her reflection, and some sleep, she had a better understanding of her brother's stance.

"Hey, Lorenzo." She took a deep breath. "Let me start by saying I love you."

She heard him exhaling through the phone.

"That's good. I love you, too." His voice sounded a bit lighter.

"I realized that it was unfair of me to be so angry with you, Torrence and Neil."

"They're here with me."

Philly felt relieved about that. "Put me on speaker so I can talk to all of you."

"Okay, hold on."

She heard Lorenzo saying something, but it sounded muffled.

"You're on speaker. We're all here." Lorenzo raised his voice.

"Hey, Philly," Torrence and Neil said at the same time.

"How are you doing?" Neil's comforting tone oozed through the phone.

She smiled. "Better. I had some time to think. Like I told Lorenzo, I want you two to know I love you."

"Aww, she's a kinder, gentler Philly." Torrence laughed.

"Yeah, something like that." She smiled. "I'm sorry for snapping at you all last night after I heard the news. Despite what I had heard and how shocking that was, you didn't deserve that."

"No, you had every right to be angry." Lorenzo's deep voice made him sound like a demanding dad.

"I did, but not to you guys. You three have always had my back. It wasn't your responsibility to tell me that news. I should have heard this from Mom and Dad, which will be my next call." That would be a harder conversation.

"You are awfully calm about this." Suspicion filled Neil's voice. "I had expected that the next time I talked to you that you would be a raging lunatic."

She took a deep breath. "The old me would have been that way."

"And now?" Torrence asked.

"I was able to establish that you all have done nothing but look out for me. After some deep reflection, I realized that I need to give people a chance and stop leaping to conclusions." The more she talked, the calmer she felt.

"Wow. This is a different Philly. Are you taking some meditative yoga class or something?" Neil chuckled.

She smiled to herself for a while before she looked at the doorway and saw Robert standing there. "Robert helped me get a clearer picture of the situation."

"Really?" Lorenzo sniffed. "Seems like Robert is a nice guy."

"He is a good man." She winked at Robert. "He cares about family. He knows how important you are to me."

"You all should come back over tonight for dinner. We have plenty of leftovers. He barely touched his dessert. And there are the games." Lorenzo sounded excited as he spoke.

"I have to work tonight." Philly watched Robert saunter into the room.

"You're going to a concert. That driver came over today to see Juicy. You all might be going back with her in that guy's luggage." Neil laughed.

"The concert is a part of my work." She glanced at her watch. "I'll talk to you all later. Love you." Philly disconnected the call and looked at Robert. "Hi."

"Hello." He leaned over and kissed her. "I woke up and found you gone."

She waved her phone. "I wanted to call my family now that I'm calmer and have a bit more focus."

"Good idea." He gave her another quick peck. "I'm going to take a shower and change for tonight."

"Okay, I'll call my parents. Don't wait for me." Philly waited for Robert to leave the room before she called her father first. She figured he would be the easier conversation to have than one with her mother.

"Hi, baby. I'm sorry I missed dinner last night." Phillip chuckled. "Time slipped by me."

"I wasn't happy about not seeing you or hearing from you." She sat up taller. "But it was nothing to me hearing that I'm adopted."

Silence met her. The fact that her father didn't immediately deny the story confirmed what she had been told.

"Dad?"

"Um, yeah. I'm still here." He cleared his throat. "How did you find out?"

The old Philly would have popped off on her father that that would be his first question. She had to control this conversation. "Family told me. Why didn't you or Mom tell me this? All these years, I thought I was a blood relative."

"Wait. You are."

Philly blinked. "What are you talking about? Am I adopted or not?"

"You are, but you're still blood." Phillip sighed. "You remember your Aunt Delta, my youngest sister?"

Philly remembered seeing her father's sister at a couple of Christmas gatherings at their house, but soon her visits tapered until she passed away right before Philly started coming to Lesilitho for the summer. "Yes, I remember."

"She's your mother."

Philly placed her hand over her heart.

Her father continued. "She was sixteen when she was pregnant with you. As the oldest, I was already married and had an established household, although your mother and I were still trying to figure out the parenting thing."

Philly wanted to chime in that he had failed at figuring out how to be a great parent, but she had bigger fish to fry. "Go on."

"Your grandparents wanted her to have an abortion. Believe it or not, despite her lapse in judgment, she was a very smart girl. She got accepted into two ivy league schools. I didn't want her to have any regrets. I let her move in with me while she finished high school. Over the summer, she had the baby, you. Before college started, she gave up her rights to you and let me and your mother formally adopt you. There was no way I could let you go to some stranger's family." He sniffed. "I may not have done the best job, but I tried. I really did. We did."

"And you named me after you?" Philly rubbed the back of her neck.

"No. Actually, that was your mother's idea. I mean your real mother. Your biological mother, Delta. She wanted to honor me for looking out for her and for taking you in." He chuckled. "If it were up to me, I would have named you Isabella."

Philly shook her head. Robert would have probably appreciated that name. "Why didn't you tell me?"

"We had always planned on it, but since you were technically a blood relative, we didn't think we needed to rush to tell you. Regardless of who birthed you, you are our family." Phillip groaned. "Before you ask, Delta never said who your father is. She wasn't a party girl. I think she got tied up with a man she shouldn't have, and she wanted to protect him. Does it matter to you?"

With what she had heard and what she had figured out, she had her answer. "No, it doesn't. But it still would have been great to hear this from you and Mom, and it would have been even better to have learned about this years ago and not when I'm in my twenties. I would have also loved to talk to my mother, my real mother, before she passed."

"Understood. Timing is not my forte."

"And you have to be more present with me."

"I try, but to be honest, since you were little, you have always pushed us away. I think your first word was *no*. Your mother and I found it difficult to get close to you. You couldn't wait to go to Europe to hang out with your friends each summer. You jumped at the chance to go away to college. You moved out before the ink was dry on your high school diploma. Honestly, honey, I didn't think you wanted a relationship with us."

Wow. Philly had a history of pushing people away, including her parents. "I'm sorry, Dad. I'm learning to be more open and accepting."

"No apologies necessary. We live and learn." He chuckled. "I love you, dear."

"I love you, too, Dad. I really do." She rubbed her hand against her leg. "Thanks for saving me."

"I'd do it again."

Hearing that made her smile even harder. "Thanks. I'm going to try to call Mom."

He sighed hard. "Be easy on her. She endured a lot. At the time we adopted you, we were having issues in our marriage. Bringing in another baby didn't help us, especially since we already had a baby."

Philly hadn't thought about that aspect. "I'll be understanding. I love you, Dad."

"Love you, too, Philly."

Philly had to stand and walk around a bit before she called her mother. She heard the shower running and remembered she had a great man naked.

She called her mother and only got her voicemail message. "Hi, Mom. We need to talk. I know about…" She thought about mentioning her adoption, but she remembered to broach the topic gingerly. "Call me when you get my message. Love you."

Philly stripped out of her clothing and slipped on a robe in order to go to Robert's room. She closed the door to his room, removed her robe, and stepped into his bathroom.

Through the steam-covered door, she saw Robert under the stream of water going over his fit body. Philly admired the man who could command her without force, figured her out without demeaning her, appreciated her strength without feeling emasculated. Yet, he still asserted himself while not being obnoxious about it. At least not too obnoxious.

Philly knew there would be nothing she could do to get him to agree with her. This act had to be spectacular. After everything Robert had done for her, he deserved a reward.

She opened the shower door and stepped inside. Robert didn't flinch. At first, she thought perhaps he didn't hear her come into the space. Maybe he didn't hear her opening the glass shower door or feel the rush of cool air being introduced into the steamy space. When she wrapped her arms around his waist, he patted her hands.

"I was hoping you would be joining me." Robert ducked his head under the hot, rushing water, letting his normally stiff and stylized hair cover his forehead and eyes.

Without a word, Philly brought one hand down his stomach to his dangling cock. At that moment, she felt his back stiffen. Robert braced his hands against the wall directly under the showerhead while she made slow, easy strokes up and down the length of him. When she kissed the center of his back between his shoulder blades, he emitted a low moan and shifted in his spot ever so slightly.

Philly continued, tightening her grip the longer she progressed and pulsing her fist at the tip.

"Yes." He nodded.

She smiled when she felt him undulating his hips in concert with her manipulations. Philly eased her other hand down to cup and massage his balls.

His breathing came out hard and ragged. Little tremors attacked his body like he anticipated something wonderful, but still wanted to hold off for as long as possible.

Philly stroked him faster. She pressed her face against his strong back, savored his salty skin.

Robert groaned. "My Filly." He pounded his fist against the wall right before his body jerked hard twice.

She felt his shaft pulsate in her hand before it started to become soft. "How did you like that royal treatment?" She chuckled.

Robert turned around after she released him. He framed her face in his large hands and smothered her in a deep, soul-stirring kiss.

"You are so good to me. So good for me."

In between kisses, she managed to reply, "You're not so bad yourself."

He looked her in her eyes for a moment without speaking, almost like he wanted to reveal something to her.

"What?" She searched his eyes and his expression for an answer.

"I wish we didn't have to go out tonight." He gave her another quick kiss. "But I'm glad we have an extra day."

"Me, too. I have yet to show off my city to you. You've been so selfless taking care of me and my needs today." She turned her head to kiss the palm of his hand. "It's time for me to take care of you."

He smiled at her. "And that, my dear, is what being in a BDSM relationship is all about. It's about trust and a mutual exchange of power." He licked her bottom lip as he pressed his body against hers. "The things I want to do to you tonight." He gave her another kiss. "Later."

"Tease." She pushed his body off hers.

"Says the woman, who gave me a better hand-job than me." He laughed as he brought his hands down to her waist and positioned her body under the spray of the shower.

"What? No royal masturbator?" Philly laughed.

"Not officially. There was always a room attendant willing to do anything for me and my brother. I didn't take advantage of that perk. Can't say the same for Lucian." He kissed her shoulder. "I need to stop. We have to shower and get out of here. If I keep touching you and kissing you, we'll never leave this bathroom."

"You say that like it's a bad thing."

"It is when there's an agenda. You are working." He leaned down next to her head. "I'm deciding if what Lucian and Helene want will work."

"You can do that. Just remember it's their wedding and this is what will make them happy." She slathered soap over her arms and upper body.

"Just so long as you remember that what Lucian does will also be a reflection on me. If he fails, I fail." Robert placed his hand on Philly's shoulder. "I can't have that. I can't fail."

Damn. Here Philly thought this decision would be a lot easier than this. Her head told her to only think about Lucian and Helene, her real clients. Her heart – that damn fickle beast – pulled for Robert.

After their shower, Philly dried herself and quickly ran back to her room to get dressed. With more clothes from her condo, she selected a dress that Robert seemed to like when she packed more clothes for this trip.

An hour later, she met Robert downstairs. He looked casually sharp in his jeans, pullover sweater, and leather shoes. He ass looked so good in his loose-fitting jeans.

Damn, did they have to leave this place?

"Arrangements have been made to get you and Miss Powell in securely." Mortimer stood close to the duo. "Are you ready?"

Robert held Philly's hand before answering. "Yes, we are."

She squeezed his hand as they walked to the car. He helped her in first before he got in behind her.

"You look beautiful this evening." He smiled at her.

"Thank you." She watched his gaze go down and hover around her crotch area.

"Do you want to see?" She started to uncross her legs.

He held up his hand. "No. If I look, I'll want to touch. If I touch, we're not leaving the car."

"Okay, how about this? We stay for half the show until they take a break. Then I'll talk to them and then we can go. Deal?" She held her hand out to him.

He shook her hand. "I promise I'll listen."

Good. Philly's next step would be to get him to agree with her.

Chapter Twenty-Three

Robert had to hand it to Mortimer. He managed to get them to this club in what looked like a busy downtown area of Virginia Beach, and had Robert and Philippa ushered inside a back door without any problems.

The owner of the club met them and led them to a darkened VIP area on the second level. To further obscure their identities, the owner pulled a sheer curtain that would allow Robert and Philippa to see and hear the action below, but not allow anyone to see them. Neat trick.

If Robert felt so inclined, he would have used that opportunity to take Philippa in the special room. The space came off a bit vintage, with red velvet chairs and carpeting. Gold trim decorated the curtain and a couple of the pillows. The place carried a sultry scent, like sandalwood and leather.

"This is nice." Robert glanced around the room.

"This area is new, less than ten-years old. Revitalization." Philippa shrugged. "Anything to make a buck."

The waitress brought them their drinks by the time the band got on a small stage to play for the intimate crowd at small tables that littered around the floor.

"Good evening, everyone." The female lead singer waved both of her tattooed arms while her black rockabilly dress swung around her waist. "We're the Slick Mouths ready to rock you."

Robert shook his head. "The Slick Mouths? Is this the group?"

Philippa nodded.

"No."

"What?" She turned her head sharply to glare at him.

"There is no way I can justify a musical act called the Slick Mouths for a royal wedding." Why did Philippa bother to traipse across the world to see this group? She should have known better. Robert wouldn't approve this. He doubted his father would approve, either.

Philippa raised her hand. "Just wait. Hear them out."

The group sang a song Robert hadn't heard of before about a topic he knew all too well. He leaned over to Philippa. "Are they singing about BDSM?"

Philippa smiled and nodded. "It's a Rihanna song. Ever heard of her?"

Robert shook his head. "We're a little behind on popular music in our country." Plus, unlike his brother, he didn't keep up with pop culture.

Philippa pulled out her phone. After tapping the screen a few times, she turned it around to him to look. The woman he showed him on the screen looked stunning with hypnotic green eyes.

"She sang the song originally. It was upbeat with an edge. They changed the feeling into something more approachable." Philippa swayed back and forth until the music got her to stand and dance around.

Robert didn't dance, but he loved watching Philippa move her body. She swayed dangerously close to him, nearly sitting on his lap, which would have been a mistake. He wouldn't have been able to control himself had she done that.

Fortunately, the waitress returned with their meals.

"Thank God. I'm starving." Philippa sat back in her seat to enjoy her food.

Robert kept a close eye on her and a well-tuned ear on the group. As much as he hated to admit it, they sounded great. That didn't mean he would vote for them to perform in Lesilitho. Despite how they sounded, Philippa hadn't convinced him to take a chance.

When the waitress came back to check on them, Robert noticed Philippa slipping her a note.

"What did you give her?" He took a sip of his water. He needed a clear head for this evening.

"Song suggestions." Philippa gazed down at the stage area and watched the young waitress hand the lead singer her note.

"Looks like we have a couple of requests." The singer laughed and nodded. "Done and done." She turned to her bandmates and conferred with them on the songs.

Robert didn't recognize the first song they played. He turned to Philippa. "What song is this?"

"'I Only Have Eyes For You' by the Flamingos. It's one of Lucian's songs he wants played at the reception." She brought out her phone and started recording them. "They're great. Helene would love this." At the end of the song, Philippa applauded before she tapped over her phone's screen. "I need to send this to Helene."

Robert loved seeing the joy in Philippa's face. She truly did love making her clients happy. Her reaction had nothing to do with besting him.

The band ended the song, and even Robert had to applaud their efforts. The next song they played also sounded foreign to him. Where did Helene and Lucian hear these songs?

"Is this another one of your requests?"

Philippa nodded. "It's called, 'Baby, Obey Me.'" She wiggled her eyebrows at him, which made Robert laugh. "Helene wants to have this song for Lucian."

At the end of that song, Robert had to admit, he had become a fan.

"What do you think?" Philippa lowered her phone.

"Nice." He shrugged to seem disinterested. "We still need to talk to them and try and convince them to come halfway around the world to play for people they've never met while keeping all this a secret. I'm not convinced they'll keep this arrangement confidential."

Philippa beamed. "That's the easy part. Mention true love and people will do anything."

Robert stared at the woman with stars in her eyes.

"Why are you looking at me like that?" She crossed her legs toward him.

"You. You've changed. When you returned to the palace, you were jaded and standoffish. Now you've become a romantic." He placed his hand to the back of her neck and brushed the base of her head with his thumb.

"Is that a nice way of saying I've become soft?" She screwed up her lips in mock anger.

He shook his head. "You've become what I thought would happen anyway." He leaned in close to her. "You've become aware."

"You're right about that." Philippa gazed behind them and stood, which made him break his hold on her.

To keep up the connection, she held his hand and coaxed him to stand with her. Behind them sat a long, oversized couch, almost like a daybed. Robert sat down first and pulled Philippa down with him.

She removed her shoes and curled up next to him. As Robert wrapped his arm around her, he envisioned a life where he could have this existence always.

Although Robert couldn't see the band now from where they sat, he could hear them. He started to get used to their sound.

"We're going to take a break," Robert heard the lead singer say in her microphone. "Get something to eat. Definitely drink. I swear we sound better the more you drink."

The crowd downstairs laughed.

"We'll be back in ten. We're the Slick Mouths."

"Let's go down now to talk to them." Robert gave her a couple of taps on her arm.

Instead of standing, she snuggled against him more. "Can't we wait until they finish for the night? This feels like a date. It's been a while since I've had a proper date."

He stood. "That's not the deal." He held his hand out to her. "We agreed to listen to half of their show and talk to them during their break."

She sighed as she took his hand. "Fine." When she stood, she got on her tiptoes to get by his ear. "I don't want to get punished."

"Don't be cheeky. I won't punish you in the same way as I did the last time. You may not like it." He settled the check with the waitress before wrapping his arm around her shoulders and heading downstairs.

"Safe, sane, and consensual." She leaned against him. "I trust you."

"Good."

"I need you to trust me." She broke from his hold to stand in front of him to stop his trek. "Give this group a chance, okay?"

"I know you want to give Lucian and Helene what they want. I don't see this act as being appropriate enough for their wedding."

Philippa managed to get him to stop talking by putting her hand to his chest. "Keep that part in mind. It's their wedding. This is what they want."

The owner of the club led them down a narrow hallway to a room at the end. After knocking, the owner opened the door and ushered them into the room.

"I thought we were doing the meet-and-greet at the end of the night." A tall, thin man stretched out on a blue couch next to the door.

"Different request." He turned to Robert. "This is Prin—"

"Hi, I'm Robert." He held his hand out to each member, but he didn't see the lead singer. "And this is my friend, um, Philly." He gave her a wink.

Philippa smiled as she shook each band members' hands. "Nice to meet you." She peered around. "Where's your lead?"

Robert heard the not so subtle sound of a toilet flushing, a bit of water rushing, and a door opening.

"Whew. Been wanting to do that since I hit the stage." The singer entered the room, but she stopped in her spot when she saw Robert and Philippa. "Oh, shit. Who are you two?"

"We didn't mean to barge in." Robert held out his hand. "Robert. My friend Philly."

"Hi." Philippa held her hand. "You are an incredible singer." She looked around. "And you all are a great band. My friends—" Philippa turned to Robert. "—his brother found you all on YouTube. They would like for you to play at their wedding reception."

The guitarist snickered. "We're not wedding singers." He glanced over at the guitarist. "I knew they weren't record execs."

"You tried." Robert turned to the door. "Thank you for your time."

"No, wait." Philippa stepped up closer to the singer. "This is not some ordinary wedding."

"Philly." Robert tried to keep his composure.

"You see, the man getting married is a—"

"We should go." Robert reached for Philippa's hand.

"Prince."

The room went quiet.

"Wait. William and Harry are married." The singer sat at a vanity.

"Different country. They want you all to play at their reception, and they're willing to fly you out, put you up in a hotel, and pay you for your time." Philippa smiled. "And don't forget the exposure you'll get, which may get you that record deal."

Again, the room went quiet.

The drummer spoke first. "I don't know. Sounds like a lot of headaches with no big payoff."

"Are you kidding? This could be huge for us. We would be playing for royals." The guitarist looked at Robert. "You're the brother. So, you're a…"

"Prince. Yes." The group in the room stared at him as thought studying him. "But I can see you're not interested."

"No, they're not interested because they don't know the full story." Philippa stood in the center of the room. "His brother and my friend have known each other since they were little kids. They have a bond that is deeper than any friendship. When you see them, you can feel how much they love each other. For a man who has everything, they're asking for so little. All they want is their favorite songs sung by this great band for one night." She held up her index finger. "The only thing we ask, whether you do it or not, is that you keep this a secret. We don't want the word to get out about who they plan to use for their wedding." She exhaled. "What do you say?"

The singer looked pensive before she approached Philippa and Robert. "I'm in." She looked around to the other members of the group. "You coming with me?"

After a pause, the drummer chimed in first. "Wouldn't be the worst gig we've ever done. I'm in."

The guitarist sighed. "Sure. Could get our names out there."

"Speaking of names, your band's name." Robert winced.

"Yes, we named it after my mother. Well, not exactly her. Growing up, she would always tell me I had a slick mouth. I liked to talk and when I got older and thought I knew everything, I also started talking back, hence the slick mouth. My mama got me to shut up one time." She held up her index finger.

"How's that?" Philippa asked.

"She told me she had breast cancer. It was pretty aggressive. She died six months after her diagnosis. I named the band Slick Mouths to honor her. It doesn't make any sense to anyone else, but I get it."

Robert didn't expect to care about these people or their story. He put his hand out to her. "Welcome aboard to the craziest show on earth."

She shook his hand. "Thanks."

"Give us your contact information and we can have contracts drawn up for you." Philippa turned to all business in a millisecond. "Again, we ask that you not say anything to anyone about this arrangement. We'll give you details on the wedding date, travel plans, rehearsal, and other items."

The singer wrote down the band's information. "Who's the groom?"

"Prince Lucian." Robert put his hand at the small of Philippa's back.

"Ah, Lucifer's Den. I've heard about him." The singer smiled and nodded. "That's surprising." She glanced at Robert. "You look more like the marrying kind."

Robert smiled at her comment but Philippa's sly smile as she read the group's written information had his stomach doing flips. After saying their good-byes to the group, Robert called Mortimer to take them back to the safe house.

"I appreciate the fact that you didn't shut down the group."
Philippa crossed her legs. "I thought when you asked about their
name, you were going to reject them."

"I started to tell them we weren't interested. When she talked
about her mother, I had a change of heart." He patted her knee.

"Are you going to ask me?" She raised her eyebrows.

Robert knew what she meant, but he didn't want to say anything
in front of the driver, even though the question had no sexual
overtones. "We'll have another conversation when we get to the
house."

That car ride back to the house seemed like it took longer than
normal. They manage to hit every traffic light until they finally pulled
into the driveway. When they got into the house, Robert held
Philippa's hand.

"There's a part of the lifestyle that I haven't shared with you."
Robert led her to his room and closed the door behind them.

"Oh, yeah? What's that?" She sauntered to his bed and sat on it.

Robert removed his jacket and strolled to a tall dresser. "When a
Dominant finds the person he or she would like to play with
consistently, they give them a symbol that signifies a permanent
arrangement."

"You mean like an engagement ring?" Philippa had an expectant
look in her eyes.

"Something like that." He removed a dark green, long velvet box.
"I've known you for a long time. Our relationship has taken a great
progression to a place I never thought we would get to and with a
woman I didn't think would go there with me." He cracked open the
box. "I would like to collar you, My Filly. I want you to be mine, all
mine. Would you wear my collar?"

Chapter Twenty-Four

Philly peered down at the piece of jewelry Robert had presented to her. She couldn't break her stare. The sparkly adornment looked like real diamonds and emeralds linked together in a choker design.

She wrapped one arm around her body and rubbed her neck with her free hand. "What is this?" Philly never stopped staring at the necklace.

Robert removed it from the box and placed the box back on the dresser. "This is a piece from Baldington Palace. To be more specific, it belonged to my mother."

Philly jerked her head up and felt her eyes go so wide that her forehead and cheeks pulled. "You want to use your deceased mother's jewelry for me to show I'm your submissive?"

Robert screwed up his lips like he wanted to suppress a smile. "Yes and no. My mother didn't wear everything she owned. Most of it was given to her. This was a gift from an African county after my birth. It's beautiful, but from what I heard from my father, my mother always wondered if it was made from blood diamonds."

Philly clutched her throat even more.

Robert shook his head. "It wasn't. But my mother never wore it before her passing. Therefore, it was gifted to me." He dangled it front of her eyes. "I would like you to wear it. Be mine."

She reached forward to brush it against the back of her hand to check its validity. Before connecting, she jerked her hand back. "What will this mean for us?" She peered up at him. "We've always talked about keeping this light, meaning after Lucian and Helene's wedding is done, I'm going back home. How will that work?"

He moved closer to her. "Be mine. Wear my collar."

She shook her head. "You're making this sound so simple, so easy. I feel like this is a big deal."

He circled her. "You don't like playing with me?"

"I didn't say that." She saw him bring his hands in front of her face from behind her with the necklace in his hands.

Her heart pounded as she watched this heavy symbol cross in front of her eyes. She leaned back and connected with Robert's chest.

"Do you want to keep playing with me?" He rested the necklace against her bare chest until he drew it up so slowly that the sliding tickled her skin and caused her to shiver.

Her reaction made him move closer to her, bracing his thighs against her backside. He smelled heavenly, rich, like a clean scent. She closed her eyes and drifted into a world where all of this made sense, a woman who grew up tougher than she wanted to be, being resourceful, and having heart, to falling for a royal prince who had a way of controlling her in the way she liked, a way she craved.

"Wear it. Tell me if you like the way this feels."

Philly opened her eyes when she heard him clasping it around her neck. She gasped and touched it, running her fingertips over the bumpy links between the smooth jewels. Her breathing increased, especially when Robert pressed his lips against the back of her neck right above where her new collar sat.

She felt him easing the front flap of her wrap dress open and slid his fingers between her thighs over her nether lips.

"Oh." She reached behind her head to hold him.

Robert wrapped his arm around her waist before he eased his hand up to her breast. She felt his chest moving up and down like he laughed.

"Wearing no panties was a direct order whenever you wear a dress. I can't believe you also went out without a bra." He kissed her neck, dragging his lips up to her ear where he nibbled on her earlobe while he massaged her breast over her dress.

Philly pushed her ass back against his crotch when she felt him getting hard. "Are we going to play?" She imagined him using nipple clamps on her again. She would even be open – for lack of a better term – to a bit of anal play.

Robert removed his hands from her body to hold her waist and turn her around to face him. "I want you." His gaze dropped to the choker and he smiled harder. "You."

She started to pull off his sweater, but he held her wrists to still her. Robert untied the strap to her dress and allowed it flap open, exposing her naked body. He did something that no man had ever done to her before. Robert cherished her.

He framed her face with his hands and brushed his thumbs over her cheeks before lowering his hands to her neck. At that location, he ran his fingers over the necklace, from back to front, the whole time, staring Philly in her eyes.

When he got to her shoulders, he slipped the dress down her arms, rendering her completely naked, save her shoes. As he moved his hands down her body, down her sides, over her hips and to her thighs and calves, he lowered himself to his knees in front of her. Her body felt bathed in his touch. He removed her shoes and even rubbed her feet.

Robert helped her down onto his bed. Still in his kneeling position, he parted her thighs.

Philly's stomach tightened as she watched him. He lifted one of her feet and kissed the tips of each of her toes. With each connection of his lips to her toes, she felt an immediate flash of heat that intensified with each kiss.

Robert kissed her ankle before dragging his tongue and lips up her leg to her inner thigh, close to her juicy core. Philly chewed on her lower lip, waiting, anticipating for this man to use his mouth in that delicious way she liked.

Robert glanced up at her before he placed her one foot down and captured her other foot and gave it the same treatment.

Tease.

This time when he got to her vagina, he blew his breath over her protruding clit. Instinctively, she started to close her legs together, but Robert, with his large, strong hands, pushed them apart.

Robert lowered his head and gave her one long, slow lick from her pussy opening to her clit. Unable to stay upright, Philly fell back on the bed and enjoyed Robert's skilled tongue and mouth.

He laved her lovingly. Slow. Robert gave her every impression that pleasing her had been his only mission. When he dipped his tongue inside her, Philly jackknifed from the bed and groaned.

Robert continued licking her until Philly felt her stomach tightening. She gripped the bed covering around her body. To stave off the orgasm she felt building inside her, she curved her toes and pushed them down into the rug-covered floor.

"Robert." Philly felt her body shaking beyond her control. "Robert."

She wanted to say more than that. She wanted to scream that she wanted to come. She wanted to give her body that release. Her mind went to the submissive side of herself. Filly. Would he allow her to climax?

Philly reached up and touched the necklace. Her collar. "Robert!"

She couldn't stop herself. Philly arched her back from the bed and brought her legs together around his head.

Once her body settled, Robert gave her two kisses before pulling back from her. "Breathe."

Philly peered up at Robert. "I came." She licked her lips. "I came." She said it like a confession instead of pride or excitement. She shook her head. "Don't."

Robert didn't say anything as he stood and undressed in front of her. He did it so slowly, so methodically, it came off as her own lap dance, a striptease just for her. As soon as he stepped out of his underwear, Philly moved to the edge of the bed and held the base of his cock.

Philly didn't want to please him with her mouth to avoid a potential punishment. She wanted to satisfy him as much as he had satisfied her.

Philly found herself craving his essence, that salty, liquid that gave her life. Robert placed his hand to the back of her head. She felt him thrusting himself in and out of her mouth. When she hummed, he growled.

She cradled his sac and massaged it while she stroked his base and sucked his tip. Philly could have done this for hours if he wanted. To her surprise, she found herself wanting to please him, to serve him, even outside of their play relationship.

The moment she felt his body start to tremble, Robert pulled back from her.

Philly licked her lips. "It's okay. I want to." She reached for him again.

Robert held her shoulders and eased her back on the bed while he came down with her, covering her body with his. He positioned his body in between her thighs.

"You look so good." Robert peered down at her and nodded.

When he kissed her, Philly tasted her juices still lingering on his lips. She immediately recalled how his used that skillful mouth on her to make her come.

He reached down between their bodies and held himself. Philly wriggled as soon as she felt him teasing her by rubbing the tip of himself up and down her slick slit. As soon as he eased his tip inside her, Philly gripped his shoulders.

His thrusts came slow but deliberate, determined.

"So deep." She leaned her head back. "So good." Philly brought her head back to look him in his eyes. "Yes."

Robert slipped his hand under her ass and squeezed it while continuing his thrusts. He cradled the back of her neck with his other hand. Philly felt his thumb rubbing the necklace he had affixed to her.

"Beautiful." Robert hovered his mouth over Philly's, barely touching her lips on purpose.

When Philly moved her head up to kiss him fully, he moved his head back. He kept her off balance, which allowed her to concentrate fully on their connected bodies. His breath easily entered her mouth. She accepted it as though she needed his oxygen to survive.

Robert increased his speed.

Philly wrapped her legs around him. That familiar tightening in her stomach happened again, which surprised her. Although Robert had his hand close to her neck, he didn't have it around her throat, choking her like she liked. She didn't have on a corset or anything binding her. Robert hadn't held her arms down. The only thing that changed had to be the necklace.

Philly released Robert's shoulder to touch the jeweled piece. It hadn't been tight enough for it to restrict her breathing. The idea that Robert wanted her, physically and emotionally, pumped her heart. She didn't have to be His Filly. They didn't have to talk about planning the wedding. She didn't even need any tricks to achieve an orgasm. Robert understood her. He had been patient with her. He cared for her.

She removed her hand from her neck and let go of his shoulder to frame his face and make him look at her. "I love you." Philly had never been a woman to confess her feelings in a romantic relationship. Everything about this moment felt right. "I love you."

Robert parted his lips, but she put her hand to his mouth.

"Don't." Philly shook his head. She put her hand over his heart. "Don't say it because I did."

Robert increased his speed. "Mine." Sweat covered his body. "Come with me." He nodded.

"Yes!" Philly gripped Robert's shoulders.

Her body constricted in every way. She locked her arms around him. She managed to hook her ankles to bind his body. Philly even felt her slick inner walls close in around Robert's cock. She didn't want to let him go. She hoped when his sex euphoria wore off, he would feel the same way about her.

* * * * *

Robert lay on his side, staring at the gorgeous woman next to him, the one who had said the three-word phrase he had no idea he ever wanted to hear. As soon as Philippa declared that she loved him, he wanted to push the words from his mind, chalk her utterance to her orgasm, which she managed to achieve without him having to do anything but satisfy her.

He didn't know what to do with her statement. Did he love her? Yes. Philippa managed to do the impossible with him. Robert had worked the hardest with her more than with any other woman he had tried courting. With Philippa, he had no plans on dating her let alone disciplining her. She managed to get him to break all his rules and preconceived notions. If he could only get his country's inhabitants to see him as more than a queen killer, he would be in Heaven.

Robert nuzzled in closer behind Philippa, thankful for the extra day they had together, even if it meant being in America and not his home country. He snaked his arm under her body and brought it up around her enough to cup her breast.

Philippa moaned and eased back against him. Damn, it felt amazing to be needed, particularly from this woman, who had made it known she needed no one and wanted nothing from him or anyone else. She didn't ask for respect. She earned it. She hadn't coveted his attention. She got it by being herself. No matter how much he wanted to deny it, he couldn't. Robert loved Philippa.

Loving her, though, would complicate his life. He had too many obligations to let Philippa enter his life. For now, he would have her. A temporary arrangement. Why did his heart slow down at the thought of letting Philippa go in a couple of months? He kissed the back of her head. He would have to make these next few weeks count.

Robert swept her upper leg over his. Philippa uttered his favorite sound he had ever heard in his life. She said his name in a moan.

"Robert." She rubbed her ass against him.

"Philippa." He enjoyed saying her name, her full name. "Philippa Ruthlynn Powell."

She groaned. "You know my full name?" She kept her eyes closed as she spoke.

Robert nodded. "Required for the flight."

She moaned. "Don't know your full name."

He slid the tip of his hard cock into her slick folds. Robert stopped breathing when her breath caught. She gripped his hand that held her tit.

"Allow me to introduce myself." Robert eased his hand between her legs and slid her clit between his index and middle fingers. "I am Prince." He thrust into her hard. "Robert." He pumped again. "Sterling." He ground in her again. "Frederick."

"Oh my God. More names. Please keep going." She kissed his arm.

"Last one." He slid his fingers back and forth over her clitoris. "Thomas of Baldington." He stopped moving.

"No. More." Philippa tried undulating herself on him, but he removed his hand from her clit to hold her hip still.

"You want more? Tell me my full name." He heard her giggling.

"Prince Robert Sterling Frederick Thomas of Baldington." She pulled away from him.

Instead of holding onto her, Robert let her go to see what she would do. Philippa pushed Robert onto his back and got on top of him. She held the base of his cock before impaling herself.

She rested her hands on his chest. "Prince Robert Sterling Frederick Thomas of Baldington." Philippa undulated her body. "Prince Robert Sterling Frederick Thomas of Baldington."

"Don't stop." He reached up and pinched her nipples.

Philippa cried out. The necklace, her collar, glittered against her dark skin. God, she looked beautiful.

Robert raised his hips. Philippa screamed and her body tensed.

"Again. Say it again." He rolled her nipples between his fingers.

"Prince Robert." She stopped but her body didn't. She kept gyrating on him, faster and faster. "Prince." She moved like a woman possessed. "My king. You're my king."

Robert blinked and sat up. He wrapped his arms around her waist and sat at the edge of the bed. Philippa kissed him and moved her lips to the side of his face.

He stood and carried her to the dresser. This woman deserved every bit of his attention. Robert slammed into her hard and fast.

"I want you to come." Robert gripped her hips and pulled her in close. "Do it for me."

She nodded and wrapped her legs around him. Philippa cried out as she gripped his shoulders. Robert didn't allow her to come down when he continued pumping inside her until he finally came.

He rested his forehead against hers while he tried catching his breath.

"I go from not being able to come to climaxing on demand." She kissed him. "I don't know how you did it."

"I didn't." He patted her hips. "You are a self-made woman. I learned that first-hand." He laughed. "You made me slow down and listen to you and your needs." He tilted his head. "Not everything is about me."

Philippa covered her mouth in mock horror. "What a shocker."

That made Robert laugh out loud. "We have a bit of extra time, but we will fly home tonight. Late tonight."

She shifted on the dresser with him still inside her. "Does that mean we can stay in all day and play?" She leaned forward and licked his nipple. "I thought I saw a candle around here."

As much as it pained him, Robert held Philippa's shoulders and pulled her back from him. "As wonderful as that sounds, I think I have a better idea."

She screwed up her lips. "What could be better?"

"I showed you my hometown. I want you to do the same. Show me around Virginia Beach, your Virginia Beach."

Philippa blinked. "Really?"

He nodded. "Tell me what makes this place special."

"I can do that. But first –" She peered down "– you have to pull out."

Robert scooped her up under her backside and carried her to the bathroom. "I will. I'll do it in the shower."

"You are dirty." She wrapped her arms around his shoulders. "I have to watch out for you."

She had no idea. Robert would never do anything to hurt her. Honesty would be his salvation. Not only did he have to be honest with Philippa, he would have to be honest with himself. He put a collar on her. Did he really want her to be his full-time submissive or did he want more? When he packed that necklace, he knew he would have a hard decision to make. When Philippa questioned him and nearly turned him down, he asserted himself to put the collar on her, not allowing her to refuse.

After their shower, Philippa went to her room to get dressed. She came back to his room just as he finished getting dressed.

"You can take this off now." Philippa, now in jeans and an oversized sweater, turned her back on Robert to have him remove the choker, her collar.

Robert rested his hand on her shoulders. "Keep it on."

Philippa peered back at him. "But we're not playing."

"And we weren't last night, either. I want you to wear it." When she opened her mouth, he continued. "It looks good on you. Natural."

She sighed. "Just here in Virginia. When we get back to Lesilitho, I take it off and we talk about us." She waved her hand between the two of them. "Not now. Let's enjoy our last day here."

Robert took Philippa's hand and led her downstairs to get something to eat before Mortimer took them around Virginia Beach. Philippa had the driver take them down to the Oceanfront area, where Philippa had them walking on the boardwalk and going into tacky souvenir shops for "Virginia Is For Lovers" T-shirts and mugs.

Robert didn't know which part he enjoyed more, going to these different locations or watching Philippa as she took them to each special spot. She reminded him of the giddy teenager he had met years ago. She had that same enthusiasm and bright-eyed wonder. Her infectious energy allowed him to have fun in this excursion.

Philippa had them stop at a soul food restaurant close to her condo for dinner. Thanks to Ginny, Robert had gotten used to this cuisine. It tasted great when he ate with Philippa. She made him forget about labels and protocols.

By the time they had packed up at the house and got on the plane, Robert had decided he had had the best day with Philippa. Despite the great day, he needed to talk about Philippa's love declaration. He hadn't said it back, and she didn't demand that he do so, which would have been a different response with any other woman he would have dated.

When the plane leveled off and Philippa snuggled up next to him in the open seating area on the plane, he didn't want to ruin the moment. Decisions would have to be made once they landed. Philippa would decide if she wanted to continue to wear his collar. He would need to figure out what he wanted from her. He needed more time. Perhaps he could convince Lucian to push out his wedding plans for a few more months, maybe even a year.

After they landed, Mortimer loaded their luggage in their waiting car.

"You can drop us both off at Moonwalk Manor." With all the toys there, Robert had plans of playing with Philippa.

"I'm afraid I must take you to the palace." Mortimer opened the door for Robert and Philippa.

"Why is that?" Robert stood outside of the car and held onto the door.

"The king needs to speak to you." Mortimer turned to Philippa.

"And you as well, Miss Powell."

Philippa looked at Robert. "Do you know what this is about?"

He shook his head. "We'll find out." He helped her into the car. "At least take Philippa's bags back to Moonwalk Manor."

"Yes, sir. I'll deliver her belongings after taking you to Baldington." He gave a slight nod as he drove to the palace.

Robert took that moment to check his phone. He hadn't received any calls from his father or even the public relations staff. No urgent text messages had been sent, either. As he looked over at Philippa, he wondered why his father would demand to see her as well. Did Clive know about what they had done while in Virginia Beach? He glanced down at the necklace she wore. Maybe his father had a problem with him taking this expensive piece out of the country.

Robert brought his gaze up from Philippa's neck to notice her looking at him.

"Maybe you should take this off now before we get to the palace." She turned her back to him in the back seat.

"No. Not yet." He patted her shoulder. "We'll see my father and then we can go back to Moonwalk and talk."

The car pulled up to the front of the palace. Robert waited until Mortimer opened the door for them. After Robert exited the car, he held his hand out for Philippa. She accepted it; however, when they walked up to the palace, Robert released her hand. Whatever his father had to say, he didn't need to add Robert's attraction to Philippa into the conversation.

An attendant directed Robert and Philippa to go to the dining room. He led Philippa to the room, but he stopped at the opening to the room when he spotted Clive at the head of the table with Lucian and Helene seated on one side of the table facing the doorway and Helene's parents sitting next to her.

"This is looking rather serious." Robert smiled to defuse the tension in the room.

Except for Lucian and Helene, no one else smiled.

"Son, have a seat." Clive looked at Philippa. "You, too, my dear."

Robert held a chair out for Philippa and eased the chair under the table for her before sitting in the seat next to her and closest to his father. "What's going on? This feels like an intervention."

Clive took a beat before speaking. "During your trip to the States, you were told that you would need to extend your stay another day. Do you know why that was?"

Robert shrugged. "Something about the plane. Was that not the case? Did something happen?"

Clive glanced at Lucian and Helene. "Yes, something did happen." He cleared his throat. "Lucian, care to let your brother and your wedding planner in on your current events?"

Lucian chuckled. "You make it sound like what I did was a bad thing." He looked at Helene with the same adoration he had seen him give her before. Then he held her hand and winked at her before bringing his attention to Robert. "We used the jet to make a special trip."

Robert rolled his eyes. "Fine. This is about me missing some speaking engagements while Philippa and I were in Virginia. I get it. I let you down. For once, it was nice to have Lucian step up to do these events instead of just me."

Clive shook his head. "That's not it. I know you two were there to acquire talent for Lucian's wedding. It may have been for naught."

Robert felt his eyebrows rut together. "What? Are you two breaking up?" He saw Lucian still give Helene a look like she held the key to his happiness.

"No, little brother. Just the opposite." Lucian held up his left hand, showing off a silvery band on his left-hand ring finger. "Helene and I took an impromptu trip to Vegas." He laughed. "We're married!"

Chapter Twenty-Five

Fuck, fuck, fuck!

Philly tried keeping her expression neutral while the worst news she could have heard rattled around in her head. Her high-profile clients, the ones who could have put her business on the map, had ruined her chances by eloping. No wonder Helene's parents looked so despondent.

"Is this a fucking joke?" Robert had less of an understanding than Philly.

"Son." Clive held up his hand.

"No. This cannot be happening. This wedding was supposed to be the event of the year for Lesilitho." Robert looked at Philly. "And what about Philippa? She had a job to do."

"The king had an idea about that." Ginny nodded toward Clive.

"Word is starting to spread. Someone took a picture of them getting married and posted it on social media. This isn't a secret." Clive sat up taller.

Yet because Philly had been so consumed with Robert and work, she never checked the news or looked at her phone to even know something like this had happened.

"Philly, I know this may not be ideal, but I would like for you to help plan a party to announce their, um, sudden nuptials. Officially, the palace is happy about this. That said, we will have a real wedding in a couple of months as planned." Clive pushed his chair back.

"Yes, I'll be happy to help in any way that I can." Philly smiled, but on the inside, she screamed. "I'm happy you all would still like to use my services."

Clive nodded. "Thank you for your willingness to stay on despite this change." He stood. "If you'll excuse me, I have some calls to make."

"I'll go with you, sir." Quincy stood.

"Cooking calms my nerves." Ginny stood, hesitated before patting her daughter on the shoulder. Then she rushed from the room.

Helene glanced down. "Mom's not really pleased about us getting married without them."

"Then why did you do it?" Philly didn't mean for her question to come out so bluntly, but she had to know how these two could have risked so much. She touched the necklace she wore.

"There were lots of reasons, but one that made sense." Helene stared at Lucian. "We loved each other, and we didn't want to wait."

"I guess the hell with everyone else, huh?" Robert snickered. He glared at Helene. "You denied your parents the pleasure of seeing you get married."

"Hey, don't get on her." Lucian held up his hand.

"And you just thumbed your nose to our country. What do you think the people of Lesilitho will think? Not only did you marry an American, but you married her in her country, not ours." Robert pushed himself back from the table and bolted to his feet. "You selfish son-of-a-bitch."

Lucian stood. "Me selfish? Your whole reason for caring about my wedding was how it would make you look. You didn't care about us." He waved his hand between himself and Helene. "If you cared anything about me, about us, you would be congratulating us instead of admonishing us for being in love."

Philly wanted to still be angry, but she couldn't. She and Robert had acted just as impulsively with their trip. They didn't get married. Again, she brushed her fingers over her choker.

Robert came around the table to face off against Lucian. "We can put out a statement that the wedding in Las Vegas wasn't real. That way we can still have the real wedding instead of this quickie party."

Lucian shook his head. "That's not going to happen. You may not like the choices I've made throughout my life, but I've told the truth."

"Oh, now you want to be righteous."

Philly could feel Robert's anger seething.

"Jesus Christ, man. Come down from your high horse." Lucian patted Robert's shoulder and started to walk by him.

Robert must have taken the gesture as something dismissive. He shoved Lucian back using both hands on his chest.

"Robert." Philly stepped closer to him.

He didn't regard her. He kept his piercing stare on Lucian. "We need to talk. Now."

Robert didn't want to lose his cool in front of Philippa. His stomach turned from the fact that she saw him shoving his brother. He could keep his cool, but this incident knocked him on his ass.

"Will you excuse us, please?" Lucian wrapped his arm around Helene's waist, pulled her close, and kissed her.

Helene placed her left hand on Lucian's chest as she leaned into the sensual expression. Robert noticed the ring. He coupled the antique ring he had given her with a diamond-encrusted band. When she broke from the kiss, Helene and Philippa walked out of the room.

Robert wasted no time in getting his point across, that included giving a swift right hook to Lucian's jaw. Lucian stumbled and nearly fell to his knees.

Lucian straightened himself while holding his red jaw. "What the hell is wrong with you?"

Robert shook his head. "You don't get it, do you?"

"No. *You* don't." Lucian pointed to him. "Let me tell you something since we're being transparent here. The Internet service at the palace, I'm the reason it stopped working."

Robert scratched his head. "What? And why are you bringing this up now? We're talking about you and your marriage."

Lucian crossed his arms over his chest. "I can't believe you're marrying that gorilla."

Robert cocked his head. "What?"

"You couldn't pick someone better than that?"

"You're talking in riddles." Robert didn't have time to play with him.

"As soon as I announced my engagement to Helene, these were some of the comments people posted on the palace's social media account. They were all aimed at Helene, and they were nasty and disgusting. I never realized how cruel people could be until that moment." He strolled away from him and stood by a window. "At first, I asked our social media team to disable the comments. That helped a little, but it didn't stop people from posting comments on news stories or YouTube videos. When the death threats started coming in, I had our IT department disable the web services here. I didn't want Helene seeing any of that." He braced his hands on the sill.

Robert strolled over to the window next to his brother. "Why didn't you tell anyone?"

"I didn't want to panic anyone. I wanted to handle this on my own."

Robert chuckled. "We are brothers. Both of us trying to do things on our own. When will we learn to ask for assistance?"

"We're both hard heads." Lucian smirked until he became somber again. "Seriously, though, when the death threats started, I decided that I would do everything in my power to protect her. Marrying her would get her even more protection. I get to officially move her into my home. Plus, if something happens to me while I'm protecting her, she would get my benefits."

Robert put some distance between him and Lucian. "Damn. There's a lot to unpack here." Then he closed the distance between him and his brother again. "You know you can't control what people say or do."

Lucian kept his stare on the scenery outside.

When his brother didn't talk, Robert continued. "Marrying Helene for that reason is admirable, but I'm surprised your initial reaction was out of fear. As a Dom, I would have thought you would have been stronger, fought against succumbing to outside pressures and influences."

Lucian turned his head to give his brother his full attention. "You find that you'll do whatever you can for love, you know, like collaring a woman out of fear of losing her."

Robert crossed his arms over his chest. "Are you referring to me? I haven't—"

"That was a nice choker Philly was wearing." He turned his full body toward Lucian. "You want to talk about what happened during your trip?"

"We booked the musical act you wanted."

Lucian held Robert's arm and moved in closer to him. "Sounds great. And I know if you collared her, you did it with the intention of this relationship going further. I know you wouldn't have done it to secure her allegiance to you."

Robert let his words roll around in his head. Had he reacted out of fear of losing Philippa? No. His feelings had been deeper than that.

"The party is happening in a couple of days." Lucian put his hand on Robert's shoulder. "In that time, you're going to have to figure out how you really feel about Philly."

"Why is that? You're still having your large wedding." Robert wanted more time, but he'll at least have that time.

"Two words for you." Lucian held up two fingers. "Princess Elena."

Shit. Robert had almost forgotten about her. He would have to be honest with her...after he established his own truth. What the hell did he want? Lucian managed to buck tradition and follow his own path. If anything, what Lucian had done had been a Dominant move. He ignored expectations to follow his instincts.

"Oh, and one other thing." Lucian released Robert.

"Yes. What's that?"

Before Robert could react, Lucian balled his hand into a fist and punched Robert in his gut, doubling him over and almost had him dropping to his knees. No way would he give his older brother that satisfaction.

Lucian bent over to get by Robert's ear. "Now we're even."

* * * * *

Philly didn't realize she had become absorbed in her own thoughts until she felt Helene's hand on her arm.

"Earth to Philly." Helene smiled. "That's the second time you've spaced out on me. You can't be this wrapped up in planning my party and wedding."

Philly flashed a cordial smile. "I have a lot of things on my mind, like how we're going to pull off this party."

"That's actually the easy part. The party will be a small affair, very intimate with only family and a couple of close friends, not a big event like the wedding." Helene patted Philly's hand. "I'm guessing you have your mind on something else." She cocked her head. "That's a new piece I haven't seen before." She gestured to her own neck and then pointed to Philly.

Philly knew she should have had Robert remove the necklace before they came back home. She should have known Helene could tell she wore the piece for a different reason.

"It's beautiful." Helene nodded. "Any special meaning to it?"

Before Philly answered, Helene clasped her hands together and placed them on the table in front of her. The sleeves of her shirt pulled up, showing off an impressive tennis bracelet around her right wrist. Helene winked at Philly when she made eye contact with her friend.

Philly touched the choker before peering over her shoulder. They sat in an office, but it always seemed like palace personnel milled about the place. "Robert asked." She didn't elaborate for fear of revealing too much.

"And?" Helene sat up taller.

"I didn't say no...or yes." She brushed her fingertips over it. "I'm trying it out."

That answer got Helene to tilt her head like she didn't understand Philly's response. "Is this something you want to do or not?" She placed her hand to her chest. "For me, it's not something I wanted to try out like take an exercise class. I discovered more about myself through the Lifestyle than I ever did in college or through working. You haven't felt that way? Or maybe I'm assuming you two have played. Lucian and Robert are so different. I can see him being very strict with the protocol. He probably has you reading books about it first and quizzing you on it afterward, right?" She chuckled.

Philly found no humor in talking about the subject or discussing

Robert's methods. In a subject that should have brought Philly closer Helene, Philly felt isolated. "How were you so sure that this was what you wanted, that it went beyond, um, foreplay?"

Helene looked pensive before a smile spread over her face. "When I wanted the play even if it didn't result in sex, which a lot of times, it does not. I knew when I saw what it did for him as much as it does for me. The feeling I got serving became like a drug, the best kind."

"I've never heard of a good kind of drug." Philly snickered.

"There are drugs that can be abused and can irreparably damage your body or kill you. I know what Lucian does is safe. I know he loves me and would never harm me." She unclasped her hands to rub her hand up her arm. "At the end of a hard session, I look forward to the aftercare. It is the best feeling in the world." Helene leaned forward. "He's so protective over me. He thinks I don't know he had the technical department disable the Internet services here."

Philly blinked. "Why would he do that?"

Her mind immediately recalled Lucian's lascivious past behavior. Had he been cheating on Helene and wanted to hide it from her?

Helene sighed. "Not everyone is happy about us being together. What's funny is that Americans are more supportive of us as a couple than Europeans, especially those here in Lesilitho. The comments have been particularly nasty about me. I know he's trying to hide that from me, which is nice, but not very realistic. I'm tough. I can take it." She covered Philly's hand. "If you and Robert pursue a relationship, whatever kind you like, you have to be prepared to withstand the slings and arrows from people who have no say so in your life."

Philly brought her hand down from the necklace. "Like I said, we're just keeping it light. It's not a big deal."

Then she remembered that she blurted that she loved him. Philly did. Robert made her feel needed, desired, yet strong. He didn't look to break her down when she asserted herself. He capitalized on her strength to make their play interesting, challenging. Rewarding.

Philly exhaled as she thought of Robert. She should have been concerned that he didn't say he loved her when she had said it, even though he wanted to collar her.

Wanted to? He had collared her.

"I know you must be tired from your trip back home." Helene brought out her tablet. "Let's make some decisions about the party to get that going."

"Is your mom helping?" Philly pulled out her phone to take notes. When Mortimer told her and Robert that they had to come to Baldington directly from their flight home, she hadn't been prepared to work.

"She will although right now she's not very happy with me." Helene smirked. "I'm her only child and I got married without her being there. Hopefully, between the party and the wedding happening later, she'll forgive me." She sat back and crossed her legs. "Regardless, this is my life. I can't live it for anyone else but me, and now my husband. At the end of the day, that's all that matters to me."

Philly smiled and it made her think even more about her decisions. The choker now felt like it constricted her neck and weighed a ton. After talking to Helene, she understood the gravity of being in this lifestyle. She also got a glimpse of what it would mean to love Robert, more than him being her Dominant.

After their planning session, Mortimer drove Philly back to Moonwalk Manor. Thankfully, the Baldington staff unpacked her belongings and put them away without getting her permission. Exhaustion hit her harder than she had expected, especially when she saw the freshly made bed waiting for her.

Philly stripped out of her clothes, took the fastest shower she had ever taken, and threw on an oversized T-shirt over her nude body. She gave herself one last look in the mirror before going to bed, and caught the choker glittering under the lights.

"Shit." How the hell had Philly gotten so used to wearing this expensive piece of jewelry with a heavy meaning after one day? A part of her felt like a fraud, like she hadn't earned the right to wear it. It still unnerved her each time they played. Maybe she should have felt that way.

As she started to slide into the bed for a well-earned nap before dinner, a knock sounded on her door.

"Damn." Philly thought about ignoring it, but with everything going on with Lucian and Helene, she didn't want to take a chance on missing out on more big news.

She covered her nearly naked body with a heavy robe and padded down the stairs to the door. "Who is it?"

"Robert."

Her body stiffened. Not that she had been avoiding him, but she hadn't expected to encounter him now. Her body betrayed her by reacting to him. Her nipples hardened right away as though ready to be tortured again. Her pussy dripped with her essence. Would he be able to smell her?

She opened the door. Robert looked good albeit tired. Dark circles ringed his eyes.

"May I come in?" He stood in the doorway in anticipation.

The power had her wondering what would happen if she said *no*. "It's your house." She stood off to the side.

Robert strolled in and closed the door behind himself. "How are you feeling?"

Philly crossed her arms before sitting on the couch. "So many emotions. Shocked. Overwhelmed. Unprepared."

"Are you talking about the news about Lucian and Helene or do you mean us?" He waved his hand between the two of them.

She had meant the party and wedding plans, but as she thought about it, she could have meant her and Robert and their situation. "There is a lot going on right now. Helene and I have the party under control. At least the wedding is still happening."

Robert had been standing. At that comment, he sat down next to her. To say I'm not happy about what has occurred would be an understatement." He held her hand. "Their decision could have ruined your business and could have appeared negatively on me."

She pulled her hand from his grasp. "But it's their lives. They have the right to live it the way their want." Helene's words made sense, especially now with Robert.

"In a way, you are right. They do have a right to live their lives, but they also have to acknowledge that their lives belong to the public. Everyone here owns a piece of them, which brings me to why I'm here." Robert moved closer to her.

Philly's heart raced. As tired as she was, if he wanted to play or fuck or both, she would have done it. She found her body ached for him.

Robert brushed his large thumbs over her neck. Philly thought he wanted to hold her throat in his hands, give her some relief. He slipped his hands behind her head and undid the clasp on the choker, evident from the sound she heard when he undid it and the way one end of it dangled under her shirt and brushed against her chest.

"I'm removing this for now."

"Because you don't want to play with me anymore?" She watched him slipping the item in his pocket.

"I want you to want it." He patted his pocket. "I'll hold onto this until the party. That'll give you a couple of days to make your decision."

Philly's heart raced for a different reason. "I won't see you for two days?"

"Not in the intimate way. No playing. No sex." Robert's face remained still and almost somber.

"Why? We said that we would keep this light." She scooted closer to him.

"Let's face it. We are no longer keeping anything light. The time apart will give us both the opportunity to decide what it is we want because I don't see me being satisfied with a temporary arrangement. If you want more, I have an idea." He reached into his pants pocket and pulled out a piece of paper. "I know you're fond of lists, assignments."

Her stomach tightened in a good way. This man knew what drove her crazy. She had to practically sit on her hands to keep from ripping the paper from his grasp.

"I have a list of assignments for you to do over the next couple of days. Some mundane. Some kinky. Some risqué." He held up the paper. "If you enjoy these tasks and feel you are ready to be My Filly, you have to tell me that you want the collar. I need to hear it from you. If you don't like this arrangement, we can agree to stop this altogether."

"What?" Her knee bounced out of nervousness. "If I say I don't want to be your submissive, we can no longer play and we'll stop having sex? Is that what you're saying?"

Without missing a beat, Robert said, "Yes. I think the longer we merge the two sides, the more confused we're getting. You need to focus on your task at hand. I have my duties." He held up the paper.

"Do you agree?"

Philly split her gaze between the paper and the prince. She took the paper from his hand. "I'll do it."

"Good." Robert smiled.

"But not for me."

His smile disappeared.

"You've changed since we've come back here. I liked you better in Virginia Beach. You seemed more open, freer. You played more. And the sex we had after the Slick Mouths show was the best I have ever had." She held up the paper. "I know that man is still there. I want him to come back. If I do this list, I'm hoping he'll return."

Robert dropped his gaze for a moment and stood. "I'm the same man. Keep that in mind in your decision."

"Are you saying you've made a decision about me? If you have, you need to share that. Right now, I feel completely exposed." Philly's gut twisted at how vulnerable she made herself by expressing her feelings to a man who kept his emotions close to the vest.

Robert leaned down and gave Philly a quick kiss. In his close position, he said, "You are very important to me." He stood as though that statement would have appeased her.

"I need more than that." Philly stood and remained close to Robert. "I guess we both will have to make some decisions."

Robert said nothing as he walked out of the home. Philly closed and locked the door. She leaned her back against it while she glanced over the list. As much as she didn't want to, the list made her heart pound and her stomach flip.

1. *You will not touch yourself unless given permission from me.*
2. *Every morning, you will get out of bed by seven, you will kneel next to the bed, face Baldington Palace and say, "Thank you for*

allowing me to serve."
3. *You will text me when you wake up and include a picture of a body part of your choice.*
4. *You will text me when you go to bed and include a video of you telling me good night.*
5. *Continue to wear dresses and skirts with no panties or pants and no bra under your blouse.*
6. *When you behave, you will be rewarded at my discretion.*
7. *When you misbehave, you will be punished. Punishment will include no interaction with me until I decide you have been punished long enough.*
8. *Never forget – I appreciate you. I need you. I want you.*

How could a man who managed to say all the right things to get her knees to turn to pudding keep his feelings so under wraps?

Chapter Twenty-Six

Robert glanced at his phone as he stood in the corner of the palace's ballroom to study Philippa's picture again. She had been faithful with her assignments these last couple of days. He found himself waking up early in anticipation of her picture. The one he studied now came that morning. He would have viewed her video that Philippa had sent last night, but he didn't want the audio being heard by anyone around him, and he definitely wanted to hear her voice.

He had meant for the time away from each other to give her clarity regarding the two of them. When Philippa said she loved him during sex, did she really mean it? Did she really want to submit to him?

Robert didn't know how she would answer. He knew how he felt. After only a couple of days away, he didn't just miss Philippa. He found he ached for her. He had to stop denying the truth. As much as he tried to fight it, Robert knew in his heart that he loved Philippa. She fit in his life.

"I know you're not thrilled about my marriage, but you can at least mingle." Lucian slapped Robert on his back.

Robert cleared his phone's screen and shoved his phone in his pocket. "Very funny. This event isn't about me. This is all about you and Helene."

"I appreciate your understanding. Your happiness concerns me, too. What's going on with you and your special lady?" Lucian wiggled his eyebrows at him.

Robert scanned the ballroom area, searching for her. He hoped to God she would be in a dress. He would know that she would be without panties. "I haven't actually seen Philippa yet. I can't wait to see her."

Lucian cocked his head. "Interesting. I was referring to Princess Elena. She's here. I didn't invite her, and I doubt my lovely wife did. I assumed you did."

Robert hadn't. He had tried calling her since coming back home to meet her and tell her that he didn't see a future with her. As much as he didn't want to make tonight about him, Robert would have to take his focus off the main couple to deal with his own personal issues.

"Are you men behaving yourselves?" King Clive sidled up next to Robert.

"Yes, sir." Robert nodded.

"Yes, healing up nicely." Lucian rubbed the eye that Robert had punched a couple of days before. "I see my wife is talking to that nice African princess."

Clive peered over before Robert did. Robert did notice Helene talking to a woman in a colorful gown.

"Excuse me. Duty calls." Lucian walked toward Helene.

"Son, I know this whole process has been trying on you." Clive put his hand on Robert's shoulder. "I love both of you. I must say, you have always been my reliable one, the one who will do the right thing, who will never disappoint me. I want you to know that I appreciate you and all you do. I love you and Lucian." He pulled him into a hug. "I'm a lucky man."

Robert patted his father's back and glanced over at Elena. Could he do the right thing and still be happy? His answer came when Philippa glided into the ballroom.

In her floor-sweeping gown in silver and the richest red lip he had ever seen on her or any woman, she looked more elegant than he had ever seen her.

"Will you excuse me, Father? I need to speak to someone." Robert broke from the hug and nodded over.

"Ah, Elena." Clive beamed. "She seems very nice."

Robert couldn't lie to his father. "Actually, I need to talk to Philippa."

Clive glanced around. "Is something wrong with the party?"

Robert shook his head. "No." He trotted away from him before more questions could be asked that he didn't think he could answer.

Before he reached Philippa, Elena stepped into his path. "Prince Robert." She gave him a slight head bow.

"Princess Elena." He leaned his head down. "Why are you here? You were not invited."

Her smile trembled. "You called me several times. I thought—"

"It was to tell you that…" He stopped himself. He couldn't have this conversation now, not in front of Lucian and Helene's other guests. "After this event, we need to talk."

She nodded. "I'll be here for you."

"Excuse me." He sauntered to Philippa, who had her back to him.

He got to see the low dip in the back of her dress. Robert would have to punish her for wearing something this inappropriate to a royal event.

The women Philippa talked to became silent when Robert stepped up behind Philippa. Their eyes became wide and they each gave a slight nod. Philippa turned and made eye contact with Robert.

Damn, she looked gorgeous. He had to harness every bit of strength to avoid kissing her.

"Prince Robert." Philippa smiled. "You look very nice this evening."

"Thank you. May we talk in private, please?" He kept his hands clasped behind his body and nodded toward the main hallway.

"Of course." She excused herself from the group of women and headed out of the ballroom. "Where?"

"The corner. Our corner." Robert had hoped she would know which one he meant.

Philippa stepped up her pace and raced toward the darkened area of the main hall where they had incredible sex that had almost killed a spectator.

As though reading his thoughts, Philippa asked, "How is Edith?"

Robert stood in front of Philippa as soon as she positioned herself in the corner. "Last I heard, she was resting comfortably at home. That's probably the best place for her." He placed his hand on the wall above her shoulder. "You have behaved admirably these last couple of days." He cocked his head. "I'm assuming you didn't play with yourself."

"That one was difficult. I think about you and I wanted to reach for my vibrator. I haven't had a response like that in a while." Philippa writhed against the wall. "I've missed you. If these last couple of days have taught me anything it's that I need to be honest with myself." She took a deep breath. "I'm ready. I want to serve you." She smiled hard. "I want to wear your collar and do it proudly." She moved closer to him, pressing her breasts against his chest. "I want to worship you, your cock, everything about you. You push my body and me in ways I didn't think were possible. I've said it before, and I'll say it again. I love you, Robert. I'm ready to make this work."

Robert wanted to scream in happiness. He wanted to pick this beautiful woman up in his arms and twirled her around the room. Damn him, he wanted to fuck her right there and then, marking her as his in every way.

"Aren't you going to say anything?" Philippa leaned back against the wall.

"Yes. Your dress is inappropriate for this event." He leaned down next to her face. "Are you ready to be punished?" He felt her nodding next to his head. "It'll require me tying you down and pouring a lot of wax on your body."

"Shit." She held his free hand. "Let's go."

Robert laughed. "No. We must stay. It's a celebration for Lucian and Helene. You are the event planner." He kissed the back of her hand. "I'm holding you up from your responsibilities, so I will say this now. I love you, too, Philippa."

She smiled wide enough to show off her beautiful white teeth.

"These last two days have been torture." He pulled his phone from his pocket. "Your pictures and videos weren't enough. I miss the smell of your skin, hearing you moan, tasting you, talking to you for hours. I want you." He pulled the necklace from his pocket after stowing his phone again. "After this event, I will come to Moonwalk and formally collar you."

"Yes." She placed her hands on his chest.

"We can make this work. You can stay there at Moonwalk even after my brother gets married. I can stay at Baldington." He watched her smile soften.

"Why would you continue to stay there? We could be together." She rubbed his chest.

Damn, that felt good. "I think it would appear odd to have the three of us together."

"Three?"

"I'll marry Elena to secure the legacy of our family. The marriage would only be for show." He put his hand to her hip. "What I have with you is real. You will have my heart."

"I'll be in Moonwalk Manor as your, what, sidepiece? Plaything? Whore?"

Everything in Robert's body turned to stone. "I wouldn't think of you that way."

She spat out a mocking laugh. "Are you kidding me? In the same breath that you tell me you love me, you say that you want to marry someone else, and that supposed to make me happy. Is that what you think?"

"I thought you understood. There's a structure to being in a royal."

She removed her hands from his body and stepped away from him. "What you don't seem to understand is that you have yet to learn how to dominate your own life." She pointed toward the main ballroom. "Your brother gets it. He went with his heart." She dropped her gaze for a moment. "Keep your choker. I can't believe you thought this is what I would see as love. If you'll excuse me, I need to finish doing my job. You enjoy your life with Elsa."

"Elena."

"I don't care."

No way could he let this woman go. He had to have her in his life. Robert caught up to her and pulled him close to him. Before she could protest, he pressed a long kiss on her soft lips. He felt Philippa attempt to push him back until he felt her hands soften on his arms. Her grunts turned to moans, that sound that always revved up his heart. He attempted to turn her back to their corner, but she managed to break free of him again.

"I need to clean up now." She wiped around her mouth and then pointed at him. "You need to do the same. You look like you've been kissing a whore."

She stomped by him to go to the bathroom.

Damn.

"Son-of-a-bitch." Philly slammed her purse on the counter by the sink before peering at her reflection.

Robert had said he loved her, and then crushed her by offering her a deal where she would be the woman on the side. The hell she would be his Camilla, waiting for him like some dutiful lapdog. Did he honestly think she would be happy with that deal? Did Philly think that she could fit in this family?

Helene had a leg up on her. She lived in the palace for years. She worked for the family. She understood protocols. Despite being American, Lucian fell in love and married her. Philly had hoped for that fairy tale. Now what would she do? Maybe she could plan this wedding remotely. If she had to stay, it wouldn't be at Moonwalk Manor.

The door to the bathroom opened. A pale, blonde strolled in wearing a light blush chiffon dress that washed her complexion out completely. Philly recognized her as Princess Elena.

Philly pulled her lipstick from her purse to replace what had been kissed off by Robert. To her amazement, Elena stood next to her to adjust her own makeup.

"What a beautiful affair."

Philly knew she meant the party, but her mind thought about the moments she'd had with Robert, capping it off in Virginia Beach. Maybe she needed to get him back there.

No. If he couldn't be his authentic self here in Lesilitho then it didn't matter if she brought him back home. She couldn't trust him. The woman who had won his respect, apparently, stood next to her.

"Are you responsible for this party?" Elena's accent, height, and thin frame gave her a model-like vibe, very aloof.

This was what Robert wanted? He could have it. That didn't mean it didn't hurt.

"Yes. The family used me." Philly swallowed and reframed her statement. "I'm the wedding planner. The family asked that I also help them with this party. I'm glad it's going well considering how we put this together last-minute."

"Yes, it's lovely. The décor, the music, the ambiance." Elena touched Philly's arm.

Philly wanted to pull away from her. She had to keep a cooler head.

"Can you keep a secret?" Elena lowered her voice.

This woman had no idea. "Sure."

"I think Prince Robert is going to ask me to marry him. Since you've done so much for the family, it would be great if we could use your services for our wedding, too."

Philly wanted to pull every hair off this woman's body. She smiled. "I'll have to check my schedule." Hopefully, this woman didn't understand industry speak for *no*.

"We would pay you handsomely. And if you could also plan our honeymoon, that would be amazing."

The air in the bathroom space became thick and unbearable. Philly snatched her purse from the county. "We can certainly discuss this later. We're missing a great party."

She went to the door and pulled it open with a jerk and found another jerk standing on the other side. Robert started to approach her when Elena emerged from the bathroom behind her.

"Elena? What are you—"

Philly held her hand up to the woman. "Elena—"

Elena cut off Philly. "*Princess* Elena."

Philly snickered. "Of course." She glared at Robert. "Princess

Elena and I were talking."

Robert's face remained somber.

Philly continued. "She wants to hire me to plan the wedding between the two of you."

Elena giggled. "That's if you ask."

Philly dug into her small, silvery purse. "Speak it into existence." She pulled out one of her business cards. "Here's my contact information. Whenever you're ready to start planning, let me know." She handed it to Elena.

"What about your schedule?" Elena stared at the card before placing it in her purse.

"Just cleared up." Philly pointed to Robert's face. "You have some lipstick on your face. But on the plus side, your hair looks great." She turned on her heel and walked away with her head held high.

Philly would do this party, mingle with other guests and secure real business. She should have kept her head in the game. Her heart paid the price for her unprofessionalism. After the party, she would have to pack up and go. No way could she continue to stay in Lesilitho so close to Robert.

Chapter Twenty-Seven

Robert felt like a zombie for the last few hours when everything turned on its head. He managed to control everything in his life, but he didn't expect Philippa to flip out over his offer. He loved her. He admitted it. Shouldn't that have been enough?

It hadn't. As soon as the party ended, Philippa returned to Moonwalk, packed her belongings, and had Mortimer take her to the airport. She refused to even use the royal jet.

Robert sat alone in the dining room before breakfast. He went from feeling so in control to out of control in a matter of seconds.

"My wife is not happy." Lucian strolled into the room.

"What did you do?" Robert kept his gaze down to the table as he spoke.

"Not me this time. Believe it or not, I'm finally not the screw up here." Lucian sat down next to his brother. "What happened with Philly?"

Robert didn't feel like talking about her. He sat back in his chair. "Did you ask her?"

"We did. She said she preferred to work remotely. Then she kept referencing a negative element here. She didn't say your name, but it was implied." Lucian groaned. "This is why I told you not to play with her and for sure not to fuck her."

Robert pushed back from the table and jumped to his feet. "I don't need to hear this right now."

"Yes, you do." Lucian stood and grabbed his arm. "The making of a good Dominant is the ability to listen and adapt. You need to listen to me."

Robert shrugged out of Lucian's grip but remained in his spot.

"I can tell you love Philly."

Robert started to refute his claim, but Lucian stopped him.

"Don't deny it. I've never seen you act this way about anyone you've ever played with, or even anyone you dated. You look like shit, man." He patted Robert's chest.

"Thanks." Robert started to walk away.

"Just being honest. And if you were honest with yourself, you would go after that woman."

"Me go after her? I'm the Dominant here." He poked out his chest.

"Not much of a Dom without someone submitting to you."

The air deflated in his chest.

Lucian moved closer to him when the staff began setting up the table for breakfast. "What happened between the two of you?"

"I made her an offer. She could stay in Moonwalk."

"Yeah?" Lucian shrugged.

"She could submit to me. I would collar her."

Lucian cocked his head. "She was good with that?"

Robert nodded. He remembered how her eyes lit up when he made the offer.

"What scared her off then?"

"I told her that I would marry someone else but we could continue playing."

The silence that existed between Lucian and Robert gave the room a heaviness Robert had never experienced.

"You are a prick." Lucian shoved Robert.

"Are you kidding me? All the times you have been careless with women, playing with their emotions. I'm the one who was honest, and I get burned." Couldn't anyone see this from his end. "I need to give this country another suitable queen. It doesn't matter how I feel."

"Jesus, is that what you think? You need to let that Queen Killer label go. You didn't kill Mother. Despite this severe lack in judgment, you're not a bad man. If you truly love this woman, you have to go after her before it's too late." Lucian looked at something behind Robert. "And your first step is to be honest with everyone."

Robert turned and saw Princess Elena standing in the dining room. Damn, he had forgotten that he had invited her over for breakfast to talk. He should have set her straight a while back.

No. This wasn't her fault. Robert buckled under the assumed pressure to marry a certain way because of his new station. He had to make this right.

"Will you excuse us?" Robert patted Lucian's shoulder.

"Certainly. Do the right thing."

Robert headed over to Elena. She looked fragile, like a porcelain doll. His words would probably crack her. It would be better than living a lie.

"Good morning." He gave her a polite kiss on the cheek. "Please, have a seat." He guided her to another room beside the dining room to have a private conversation. "I've been meaning to talk to you for a while."

"I know." Elena sat across from him. "I have to be honest. I avoided your calls sometimes." She dropped her gaze. "I had a feeling you would say something I didn't want to hear."

"That's no reason to not respond." Robert had to give it up to Philippa. She spoke her mind and gave him no doubt about what she thought.

"You're right. And I know you want to tell me something important now, but I need to say something to you first. Please." She reached over and held his hand. "It's okay."

Robert blinked. "Excuse me? What's okay?"

She took a deep breath and attempted a smile. "If you want to keep, um, her, that woman. If you want to still see her even after we, um, marry, it's okay. I ask for your discretion. I'm fine with it."

Robert pulled his hand from under hers. He now understood what Philippa felt like when he had made the offer to her. Even with her tiny hand, it felt like Elena had punched him in his gut harder than Lucian had.

If Philippa felt that way, Robert would spend the rest of his life making it up to her.

"At the party when we were outside the bathroom, I noticed the color of the lipstick around your mouth."

Robert touched his face as though he still had the offending stain on it.

"I watched you look at her throughout the night." Elena moved to the edge of her chair. "I can be the queen you need for Lesilitho. We can be a family."

"Even if I didn't love you?" Robert started to feel hollow inside, a foreign feeling since he never felt that way with Philippa.

"You could learn to love me, right?" She smiled like she tried to convince herself of this story.

"I thought I could do this, but I can't." Robert shook his head. "You and I deserve the kind of love that doesn't need assistance or an explanation. I think you're a lovely woman, Elena. You and I know a relationship between us will not work."

Elena sniffed like she wanted to cry. No tears appeared. "Why?"

"I don't love you. I love someone else."

"Her?"

Robert stood, uninterested in explaining his choices to her. "You're more than welcome to stay here for breakfast. I need to go."

He had a lot of ground to cover and not a lot of time.

"I will not stay where I'm not wanted." She stood and started to go by Robert but stopped. "And it's Princess Elena."

Robert could have asserted himself that way, but he didn't care what she thought. The woman he loved had run from him. He needed to get her back.

Clive strolled to the dining room area, missing Elena as she exited the front door.

"Good morning, Robert." Clive turned when the front door closed. "Was someone here? Is it Philly?"

"No, that was Elena leaving." Robert nodded toward the door.

"Leaving? She didn't want to stay for breakfast?" Clive turned toward the door.

"No. We established something. I came to a critical conclusion." Robert held his father's shoulders. "I can't marry her in order to maintain our royal lineage."

Clive furrowed his eyebrows. "Do you think that that's what I would want for you? You think I want you to marry out of duty?"

"You said I was the one who always did the right thing?"

"You are. That means being honest. You're not one to use people." Clive wrapped his arm around Robert's shoulders. "Don't start now." He sighed. "Do you have feelings for Philly?"

"I love her, Father."

Clive smiled.

"I know she's not a royal."

Clive shook his head. "And that doesn't matter. You know between your mother and me, she had a stronger royal blood line. You can't control your heart. You love who you love. I would only be disappointed in you if you married someone out of some warped sense of duty. You don't owe me or this country your happiness."

Robert nodded.

"I would like Philly to continue to work with Lucian and Helene for their wedding." Clive took a step back from Robert. "Do I need to arrange for the family jet to—"

"Yes, sir." Robert started down the hallway toward his room. "I'll be home in a few days."

Clive waved his hand. "Take your time. I think the major items for the wedding have been decided on already. I don't know what happened between the two of you for her to tear out of here. Whatever it was, work it out. I hope she comes back with you."

Robert could only hope. He couldn't strongarm this situation. As a Dom, as a man, he needed to listen to his woman. His woman.

* * * * *

"This is a surprise."

Philly continued standing on the front step of her mother's cottage home in Georgia. "We need to talk, and I didn't want to do it by phone."

Mary Powell patted the colorful headscarf that held back her trumpet of an Afro. "Come on in."

Philly purposefully left her luggage back at the hotel when she drove down to Georgia to visit her mother. She'd stopped in to see Lorenzo when she returned home from Lesilitho.

"What happened? Why are you here?" Lorenzo had asked her. "Where's your friend?"

"Back where he needs to be." Philly remembered feeling defiant. "He saw us in a way that didn't honor me."

"And you fixed it by leaving?"

Philly groaned. "I don't need to hear this from you. I didn't expect my own brother to side with someone else."

Her body had refused to call Robert a stranger. Even in their kinkiest antics, nothing felt strange with him…except when he offered to keep her as his plaything.

"You may not see it this way, but I'm actually on your side. You have always been headstrong, which made you great when we played football as kids. But we're not kids anymore, and you're not playing a game." He wagged his finger at her. "I saw the way you looked at him and how he looked at you. The big brother in me wanted to tell him to not look at my baby sister like that. But I couldn't say anything when you were doing your own visual groping of the man."

Philly had popped her brother's arm. "Don't call it that."

"Whatever you two have, it's was obvious. You have a nasty habit of running away from folks who piss you off."

Philly grunted. "I do not."

"I believe the kids call it *cancel culture*. I'm not saying this because he's royalty. I don't think you should dismiss him because of a disagreement." Lorenzo pulled out a piece of paper and scribbled something on it before he handed it to her. "Dad told me you two talked. Time for you to talk to Mom, but I think you need to do more than talk on the phone."

Philly remembered staring at the address. "I don't have time."

"You have nothing but time. You walked away from your job."

"Will you stop—"

"Telling you the truth? No." He knocked his knuckle against her forehead. "Stop being stubborn. While you're home, go see Mom. You probably won't figure everything out with her in a visit, but it's a great start. Then you need to get with Prince Rob and clear up that misunderstanding."

"Robert. Don't call him Rob. He doesn't like that." She shook her head.

"You're defending him. That's always a good sign." He pushed her away from his kitchen island where they talked. "Now get going. You want me to take you to the airport?"

"I'll drive."

And Philly did. She dropped her luggage off at her condo, pared down her clothing and toiletry needs to one suitcase, and hit the road to see her mother without announcing her visit. Mary would either embrace her or turn her away. Either way, Philly would get her confirmation that her cancel-culture mentality protected her instead of being a hindrance.

"Want something to drink?" Mary padded in her bare feet to her open kitchen with all white cabinets.

"Sure. Water is fine." In case her mother kicked her out after five minutes, she didn't need to drive back to her hotel with alcohol in her system. She sat at the breakfast bar. "I talked to Dad."

Mary cleared her throat before she sat across from Philly. "You probably think I'm the worst mother ever, like I didn't love you."

Philly wanted to respond right away like she had always done, assert herself to be right. She sat back and listened to her mother to allow her to tell her story.

"You don't understand. Your father and I had problems. We got married so young and had children too quick. We didn't know ourselves before we involved other people, and by other people I mean you kids." Mary leaned her head down. "When we had Neil, I told your father that we needed to stop having children until we fixed what was wrong." She gazed up. "Then you came." She shook her head. "Whenever I looked at you, I saw you as the thing putting a wedge between me and my husband. He didn't listen to me. It didn't help that you seemed to know I wasn't your real mother. Your first word was *no*."

"Dad said I said the same thing to him, too." Philly shook her head. "I didn't have a problem with you, Mom. Maybe I felt the tension between you and Dad. I can understand why you would feel a certain way."

Mary's eyes glossed over and became red. "Not against a baby. I should have told you a long time ago that you were adopted, especially before your real mother passed away. I should have done a lot of things. If I could have a do-over, I would have had a different relationship with you."

Philly stood and went over to the woman who she recognized as being a cold, unfeeling mother and now saw her as a lost woman with some unresolved pain. Philly hugged her mother. When Mary embraced her, Philly found that she needed to have this contact, this acceptance as much as her mother.

"Despite my lack of involvement, I know that you have grown up to be an amazing woman. You have always been so sure of yourself and honest." Mary pulled back from her and framed Philly's face. "You are going to have a successful business."

"Thanks."

Her mother held Philly's hands. "What's wrong?"

"I wish I could get my personal life on track like my career." Her mother didn't have to know that Philly left her assignment to work it from another part of the world.

Mary pulled up a chair next to her and encouraged Philly to take a seat. "I know you are smart enough and strong enough to power through whatever issues you may have."

Philly shook her head. "Maybe that's the problem. I'm tired of always having to be strong and put up with crap because I can."

"I get it." Mary nodded. "Sometimes you want to be taken care of."

Philly glanced at her mother and wondered if she knew about her arrangement with Robert. Did Mary know Philly called a man *sir* and bowed for him? Could Philly be honest with herself and admit that she missed that? She missed reporting the number of days she served him.

"Even to be taken care of, you still have to say what you want."

Damn, now her mother sounded like Robert.

"Sarah should be home soon. Will you stay for dinner?" Mary patted Philly's hand. "I really would like my daughter to meet the woman I love."

Philly smiled. "I would love that, Mom."

Despite hating to admit that Lorenzo had been right about Philly seeing their mother, Philly had enjoyed the trip. She didn't get reacquainted with her mother. Philly made a friend.

She took her time driving back to Virginia. Why rush? She had nothing there.

Philly had to stop thinking like that. She would have to get a game plan together to resume her work for Helene and Lucian. The trip back home gave her a second wind. She needed to keep focused on her job. That didn't mean she needed to forget about her intimate life. If anything, Robert gave her a taste for the Lifestyle. She would do some research and see if she can find a local club. She could play and not be attached. Too bad she couldn't convince her heart.

Philly pulled up to her condo at nearly midnight. The cool night air greeted her as she got out of her car and retrieved her luggage from her trunk.

"Hello."

Philly froze at the sound of the voice. She recognized it and didn't want to, not right now. After taking a deep breath, she turned around. Her breath still caught when she saw Robert standing a few feet from her.

Chapter Twenty-Eight

Robert stared at this gorgeous woman, who looked exhausted based on the dark circles under her eyes and her dour expression.

"What are you doing here?" Philippa pulled her suitcase up to her door.

"I've missed you." He stopped a few feet from her when she unlocked and opened her front door. "May I come in so that we can talk?"

She dragged her luggage inside and stood in the doorway. "I want to say no. I don't care how long it took for you to get here. You hurt me."

"I know." He nodded.

"No, you don't. You don't know how I felt when you made me that offer."

"No, actually, I do. After you left, I saw Princess Elena."

Philippa groaned. "Good night and good-bye, Robert." She started to close the door, but he stopped it with his hand.

"Please listen."

She opened the door. "Go."

"Elena came to the palace for breakfast and we talked. I told her I didn't want to be with her. She said that if I wanted you while being married to her, she would be fine with that." He saw Philippa gasp before shaking her head. "When she mentioned that, I knew exactly how you felt." He huffed. "May I please come in?"

Philippa didn't say anything as she moved to the side. Robert took that small window of opportunity to come into her home. She closed the door and locked it behind herself.

"Is Mortimer here?" Philippa went to the living room and sat in an oversized chair.

Robert sat across from her on the couch. "He waited with me in the parking lot. I barely kept him as my driver. When you left, he asked if he could change his assignment." He rubbed his hand across the back of his neck. "You've made an impression on him. You've made an impression on me, too."

Philippa stood. "You want something to drink? I need something."

"No. Listen to me."

She padded to the kitchen. "I have wine. Maybe I should mix something. I think I have some juice."

Robert removed his jacket and followed her to the kitchen. "When Elena said she was okay with me having you as some sort of dirty, little secret, I understood your pain. I will do whatever I can to take that hurt and doubt away from you."

"Ah, Moscato. I'll have some of that." She acted as though she didn't hear him as she took a bottle out from her refrigerator to pour a glass for herself. "You want some?"

"I love you." Robert had his own agenda.

Philippa tried bringing the glass of wine up to her lips, but her hand trembled. "Damn it."

"I know I have a horrible way of showing you how much I love you. In my desire to do what I thought was right for my family versus what I wanted in my heart, I hurt the one person who has made me both grow and be the happiest version of myself. Nothing with you came easy. You brought me out of my shell. I play differently. I dominate differently. I love differently. I want you to give me another chance." Robert reached for Philippa's hand, but she moved away from him and headed back to the living room without her wine. "Please."

"No." She wrapped her arms around her body and sat down again. "I can't do this again with you. You have no idea how horrible I felt that the man I loved was too ashamed of me to be with me in public, to have a real relationship. I can't do that again."

Robert crouched down in front of her. "You wouldn't. I would rather give up my title, my country, my family than to make you feel like you don't matter to me. You're everything to me." The more he spoke, the more his heart opened. "I missed the way you questioned everything I did. I missed your need for lists. I missed the way your moaned." He captured one of her hands and placed it over his heart. "You have this. Even if you send me away right now, you will always have this. Philippa, I love you."

She remained quiet for a moment, before a small smile peeked out. "If you really loved me, you would call me Philly."

Robert exhaled. "Philippa is your real name and I love it as much as I love you." He reached in his pocket and removed a small black velvet box.

Philly sat up taller and didn't take her stare from the box.

"Philippa, please allow me the rest of your life to make you happy."

"H-h-how would you do that?" She brought her stare up to him.

Robert opened the box, showing off a white and black diamond ring. "By making you my wife…and my submissive. I want you as my Philippa and My Filly."

Philly placed her hand at her neck as though the choker still hung from it. "You tested me at every turn. When I came to the palace, you tried to fire me. You made me work with a woman who didn't respect me or my skills. You put me on a three-strike penalty system." She took a deep breath. On the exhale, she said, "Then you listened to me. You watched me. You figured out how to make me have an orgasm, over and over and over again. You made me crave order and discipline. I never thought I would respond to a lifestyle like this. But I like it. I love it. I love you." A tear rolled from her eye.

The only time he had seen Philippa get emotional had been when she achieved an orgasm for the first time.

He wiped the tear away with his thumb. "You haven't answered my question."

She didn't look at the ring. She kept her stare on him. "My work. It's in Lesilitho now, but I could be anywhere doing anything."

"I respect that. As my wife, you will be asked not to work in order to come with me to in-person engagements and speeches." He smiled. "As my father reminded me, we are a modern royal family and not tied to our standard traditions. I will learn to compromise. I don't want to take away your identity. That's not what the D/s lifestyle is about."

"Where would we live?"

Robert held Philippa's left hand but made no advances to slip the ring on her finger. "We would have Moonwalk. We could have a home here in Virginia Beach." He glanced around. "Not your condo. We would need a more private home with better security."

"What would my last name be?"

Robert laughed. "Are you saying yes?"

Philippa smiled and nodded. "Yes, Prince Robert Sterling Frederick Thomas of Baldington. I will marry you. I will submit to you. I love you."

Robert slipped the ring on her finger and pulled her in to kiss her. He slipped his tongue in her mouth and she sucked on his hungrily.

Philippa started to pull off his shirt. "Is Mortimer outside?"

Robert nodded. "In case you kicked me out."

"Tell him he can go. I'm sure he wants to see Juicy." She smiled.

Robert removed his phone from his pocket and sent a text to him. He stood and picked up Philippa to carry her to her bedroom. When he set her down, she worked on his pants as he removed her top.

"You're in a bra and you're wearing pants." He reached behind her to unclasp it.

"Punish me." She pushed down her pants and planted her hands on her dresser as she bent over.

Robert held the base of his cock before he aimed himself at her core and slide himself hard inside. Philippa moaned and pounded her fist on the dresser.

"I've missed you so much." Robert cupped one of her breasts and pinched her nipple. "I love you."

"Love you." She nodded. "Missed you." She pushed back against him. "Don't hurt me again. Please."

He shook his head. "Won't. Promise." He gritted his teeth.

She rotated her hips to match his thrusting. When he gripped her hair and pulled her head to the side, she cried out in ecstasy. For her response, he rewarded her with a kiss on her neck.

He held onto her hip when he felt her body responding to him. "I feel you. Closing in. Ready?"

Philippa moaned before she released a slight scream. He felt her inner walls tightening around him. He continued thrusting until her body settled. Robert held her arms as he pounded into her hard and fast until he came, shooting his cum into her hot channel.

"So good." Philippa turned her head to the side and rested it on the top of the dresser.

"Damn good." He kissed the side of her face while trying to catch his breath. "I just have one question for you."

Philippa craned her head back as much as she can to look at him. "I've said yes to marrying you and being your submissive. What else is there?"

He smiled. "How's my hair?"

Philippa laughed. "Messy. Very messy."

This woman completed Robert in every way. He would treat her like a queen. To make her happy, he would be her king in every way.

"Can we start over? Clean slate?" Philippa tried catching her breath as she spoke.

Robert shook his head. "We must continue."

"It is day thirty-five of my submission. I am learning to be yours."

"That, my dear, is the best thing I have heard in a long time."

Epilogue

"What a turn of events." The same Lesilitho journalist who had interviewed Lucian and Helene now sat with Robert and Philippa to interview them. "Less than two months ago, I was talking to your brother and now sister-in-law, the Duke and Duchess of Essexville, about their marriage. Now that they have married again just a week ago, you and Philippa Powell are preparing to wed, too."

Robert looked at Philippa, who seemed to glow as she smiled at him. "Life is funny. Had I really thought about it, I would have figured out a long time ago that she would be the woman in my life. She's known me for a long time, and she keeps me honest."

"He's pretty amazing." Philippa started to cross her legs and must have remembered her royal lessons. She crossed her ankles instead.

"This is pretty out of the ordinary for you. An American marrying a royal." The journalist gave her a suspicious glare.

"I wasn't looking for a relationship or even love when I came to work for the family. As a matter of fact, right after this interview, I have to verify some details for my new clients. My business has been improved greatly since the Duke and Duchess's wedding."

"Marrying Prince Rob would be lucrative for you, huh?" The reporter sniffed and it came out like a snort.

"If you don't want this interview to end right now, you need to apologize to my fiancée for your baseless assumption, and you need to apologize to me for calling me an incorrect name. I am Prince Robert, the future king of Baldington Palace here in Lesilitho. We will not be disrespected." Robert leaned forward, careless of the cameras in his face.

The journalist lifted his hand and dropped his gaze. "I apologize,

Prince Robert and Ms. Powell. I meant no disrespect."

Robert held Philippa's hand. "My future wife is an accomplished woman. She started her business on her own. She didn't need me to acquire clients. She's intelligent, generous, kind, and resourceful." He squeezed her hand. "I'm lucky to have her."

Philippa gazed at him with the widest smile. "I'm equally lucky to have him. He gives me the freedom I need while giving me the safety and security that anyone would want in a successful relationship."

"Prince Robert, I'm sure you've heard the concerns from the citizens of Lesilitho about you and your brother marrying—"

"What?" Robert sat up taller.

The journalist cleared his throat. "Americans."

Robert settled back into the couch. "Lucian and I have been very fortunate to find women who love us unconditionally. I cannot speak for my brother, but I offer no apologies for who I have selected to be in my life." He stared at Philippa. "She is my world. I love her."

She sighed. "I love him. He is a protector and honest. He allows me to be me. I can't wait to spend the rest of my life with him."

Robert leaned forward and gave her a kiss. Forget royal protocol.

"Aren't you afraid that the citizens here will see you as turning your back on them?"

Robert glared at him. "I can no longer live my life trying to please other people. By making myself happy and this woman here, I will be a better person. I'm following my brother's lead with him and his wife deciding to not televise their wedding." He kissed the back of Philippa's hand. "If you don't mind, we need to attend to other matters."

"Certainly. Thank you for your time." The journalist rocked a couple of times to propel himself out of the chair.

"You're welcome."

"Will I be invited to your wedding?" He stood and laughed, which contained a combination of a snort.

"No. Our lives aren't meant to become a spectacle." Robert extended his hand. "My staff will show you out."

Robert continued holding Philippa's hand as he led her to the front of the house where their car waited for them. Mortimer opened the door for them before he got in the driver's side and drove them to Moonwalk Manor.

Philippa exhaled when they both settled in the back seat. "May I?"

Robert cocked his head. "May you what?" He had to bite his cheek to keep from smiling.

"May I take out the vibrating egg now?" She closed her hands into fists and rubbed them over her thighs.

"You know the rules. Tell me."

Philippa smiled. "One. Do a great interview."

"You did. Very proud of you." He kissed her cheek.

"Two. Dress appropriately." Her knee bounced.

"You look wonderful." Robert rested his hand on her thigh. "I could barely hear the latex dress under your dress." He brushed his thumb over her knee. "Did it feel good to wear it?"

Philippa nodded. "Better than a corset." She ran her hand over her midsection. "Three. Act appropriately."

"Did I see you almost cross your legs during the interview?" He reached his hand under her dress and pressed his hand against the seat of her panties.

The soaked fabric transferred her essence on the pads of his fingers. Philippa moaned and closed her legs around his hand.

"Yes, you did." She leaned over to his ear. "Master Robert."

"That's a shame."

The car pulled up to the front of the house.

When Mortimer got out of the car to open the back door, Robert said, "You'll get an anal plug."

"Yes, Master Robert. Thank you." She kissed him and the back of his hand when Mortimer opened the door.

"Thank you, my beautiful Filly." He placed his hand at the small of her back.

"I do have to make some calls."

Robert opened the door for her. "You can make the calls. Later." He locked the door, remembering what he had done to Lucian and Helene not too long ago. "Get naked, go upstairs and assume the position."

She smiled. "May I pick the plug size?"

"Yes, you can, My Filly."

Philippa went upstairs to their playroom and stripped out of her dress, latex, undergarments, including the vibrating egg, and shoes. Then she knelt on the floor in the center of the room.

Robert removed his jacket and shirt before grabbing a bundle of rope and kneeling behind her. He wrapped the rope around her body while she leaned against him with her eyes closed. When he looped the rope over her head to a hoist system and lifted her from the ground, she emitted a moan. He bound her so that her upper body and one leg had been supported by the rope. He tied her arms behind her body. He allowed one leg to dangle.

Robert sat on the floor and reclined back to admire his work before he would insert the anal plug.

"I'm ready." Philippa opened her eyes and stared at him.

"Sex?" He shook his head. "You're supposed to be punished, which is why I left one leg free. If you continue, I will bring you down and put you in the quiet room. Do you want that?"

She shook her head. "No, Master." Philippa remained quiet for a moment before breaking. "I'm ready for the flogger." She licked her lips. "I trust you. I'm ready."

Robert smiled. "My Filly."

The End

About the Author

Best-selling author of interracial BDSM erotic romance, Bridget Midway has been published since 2005 with various small press and electronic publishers. The multi-award winning and award-nominated author has found her niche with readers with her scintillating interracial BDSM erotic romance including the 2008 EPPIE Award finalist, Love My Way, and 2010 Romance Slam Jam Steamy Novel of the Year finalist, Corporate Needs. With more than 26 published short stories, novellas, and novels under her belt, she shows no signs of stopping. For more information on Bridget Midway, go to her website at http://www.bridgetmidway.com/